GLENN MULLER

RUGGAGE

RUGGAGE

First Edition

Copyright 2022 Glenn Muller

Uncorked Ink Press

PRINT ISBN 978-1-7772673-3-9

Licence Notes

This book is licenced for your personal enjoyment only. Except for brief passages embodied in reviews or other non-commercial uses, this book may not be reproduced in any form without the prior written consent of the author. If you would like to share this book with another person, please purchase them a copy. Thank you for respecting the hard work of the author.

Disclaimer

This is a work of fiction. All names, characters, places, and incidents are either the product of the author's imagination or are used fictitiously, and any resemblance to actual persons, living or dead, businesses, companies, events, or locales is entirely coincidental.

I do not much wish well to discoveries, for I am always afraid they will end in conquest and robbery.

Samuel Johnson

CHAPTER 1

Traffic at five minutes to six on a Tuesday morning was as light as it got in Burlington on a weekday. Taking advantage, a transport truck with hazard lights flashing slowed to a stop and blocked the lane. As it rocked slightly on its suspension, the passenger hopped down from the cab and waved his arms to halt the approaching vehicles. He smiled apologetically at the blonde woman behind the wheel of the lead car, then walked back to make sure the rear of the lengthy trailer angled correctly into the driveway.

Yet another cloudless day in the first August of the New Millennium, the warm breeze off Lake Ontario was a precursor of the late-summer heat to come. The young man's sky-blue t-shirt, hanging loosely outside of his jeans, was already dark along the spine. His Blue Jays cap, worn with the brim to the back, covered light-brown hair that curled softly over his ears. The blonde woman thought he was kinda cute and smiled brightly when he waved her through.

Threading the rig slowly past the FOR SALE sign, and between wrought-iron gates, the driver carefully backed down the long driveway. The young man stayed visible in his mirror and signaled 'stop' when the trailer's back bumper was about ten paces from the middle door of the three-car garage. A hiss of air brakes, a final stutter from the diesel engine, then all was quiet. The driver dropped down to the concrete and both men surveyed their surroundings. The silence gave way to the gentle rustling of leaves, and various birdsong intermingled with the sound of wavelets lapping on the rocky beach behind the house.

Out front, a generous lawn bordered by tall shrubs for privacy ran the length of the driveway. The two-storey house was of a Mediterranean design with light ocher plaster on the outer walls and curved clay tiles on the roof. The window frames all had an arched top, as did the main entrance, which was flanked by hanging baskets of flowers. Hard to tell at a glance when the house had been built, or rebuilt, but it was all tastefully done and style-appropriate for one of the most expensive housing sectors in the city.

The young guy knelt to retie his boot lace. "What d'yer think she's worth, Marsh?" he said, looking up at the driver.

Marshall Stober gave a little squint. "Three mil, give or take."

"And what do you think the stuff inside is worth?"

Now Stober smiled and said, "Let's go find out."

Donning fresh pairs of black leather gloves, the snug kind that ballplayers and golfers wear, they unlatched and swung open the back doors of the trailer. An aluminum ramp was rolled out from beneath the box, and the end lowered to the ground. From where they stood, the empty box looked cavernous. It was time to get to work.

"Where's the code, Devon?" Stober lifted the flap of the garage door keypad.

"Right here." Devon Millcroft pulled a scrap of paper from his pocket. "Let's hope it works." He punched in the numbers and hit the ENTER key. The door began to roll up. Millcroft pumped his fist.

"What'd I tell ya. Worth every penny."

Stober stepped past him into the garage. "I'll concede that when we're driving out of here."

In the furthest space was a late-model Land Rover, a machine capable of chasing sherpas up the Himalayas, yet probably hadn't seen so much as a gravel driveway. The rest of the interior was empty save for a wheeled, chest-high Snap-On toolbox beside a workbench, and a trio of high-end mountain bikes. These were quickly rolled into the trailer, then Millcroft returned with a crowbar. He inserted the tapered end between the inner door and jamb. There was a satisfying *crack* as the frame splintered and the door swung open.

They had chosen wisely. Hard not to on this road. They walked into an expansive kitchen equipped with top-of-the-line stainless-steel appliances. Next to a six-burner gas stove, a pair of stacked ovens were set into the wall. There was an enormous refrigerator-freezer, a vast island with a wine cooler, and granite countertops everywhere.

"Where you want to start, Marsh?"

"Something we need to do first. It's upstairs."

Stober led the way up a wide, white-carpeted, curving staircase to the second floor. A front-facing room had been furnished as an office. There was an oil painting on the wall, a misty lake scene with a red canoe tied to a dock. He gave a little tug on one side of the frame. It broke a magnetic contact and the painting swung on a hinge to reveal a recessed safe. The little door also had a digital lock. When the garage keypad combination didn't work, Millcroft hacked away at the surrounding drywall with the crowbar.

"It's bolted to a wall spar," he said, peering into the jagged hole. "I'll get some tools."

Stober had unplugged the computer equipment. "Take this printer with you. No sense wasting a trip."

After they removed the safe, the pair spent the next ninety-minutes packing the trailer with anything from the above-ground rooms that wasn't actually fixed in place. Televisions, sound systems, and small appliances. Beds, bureaus, and the contents of wardrobes. Drawers of silverware were pulled from their cabinets and carried out along with the chesterfields, coffee tables, artwork, plants, and pottery. If it could be picked up, they carted it off. Taking a smoke break, Stober gauged there was just enough room left in the trailer for a small desk, or maybe an upright piano.

"Right." He pinched out the cigarette and was careful to put the butt in the trailer. "Let's finish up and get out of here."

Devon led the way down to the basement, another expansive space. Set up for entertaining it had a pool table, a well-stocked wet bar, and a sectional sofa that could probably seat eight.

"Too bad we don't have room for that billiards set," said Millcroft. "Bring a good buck."

"Yeah, well, we don't. I'll get some boxes for those bottles," Stober said, and went back upstairs.

Millcroft didn't really mind. Professional-grade slate tables were heavy and a bugger to move. He began to walk past it, toward the bar, then he stopped.

Over by the sofa was a rolled-up rug. Millcroft could only see the underside, but he'd seen the underside of enough rolled up rugs to know it was of the Persian style, if not the genuine article. He figured Stober had bundled it up earlier, but wondered why he'd left it. It was only seven feet long, easy for one guy to shoulder. Then he noticed the uneven shape. He gave it a shove with his foot. It moved a little, then settled back in place.

"What'cher lookin' at?" Stober was back with a couple of boxes.

"Somethin's funny here, Marsh. Give me a hand."

They knelt and pushed at the lumpy roll. It only had to flop over once for Millcroft to look anxiously at his partner.

"You sure we want to do this?"

Stober put his knee on the exposed edge and gave the rug another shove. This time when it flopped over, an arm appeared. With an intake of breath, both men rose from their crouch and stepped back.

The limb was slender and the hand relatively small, though not a child's. Probably a woman.

"Oh, fuck," said Millcroft quietly. "Now what are we supposed to do?"

Stober stared for a moment more. Then he turned and picked up the boxes he'd brought down.

"Empty the bar," he said, handing one to Millcroft. "Leave the rug."

CHAPTER 2

Fenn was two minutes out from his first pickup of the day when his cellphone rang. Not quite nine, and the driving school itself not yet open, the possible callers could be Dieter and Carole Lundsen, the owners of Burlington's DriveCheck franchise, or Asha Fabiani, the school's booking clerk. Since Fenn had kissed Asha goodbye only twenty minutes ago, he figured that both caller and message could wait until he got to where he was going.

He rechecked the client sheet for the address and slowed the car as the street numbers on Lakeshore Road ran into the low four-thousands. His destination had a FOR SALE sign at the curb and stone plinths flanking the entrance to the gated driveway. He signaled, pulled in, and let the Toyota coast toward the house.

It was a nice piece of property. Out of his price range, as was most of the housing market until he and Asha could save enough for a down-payment. For now, though, they were happy with their basement apartment. The rent was reasonable and their landlady, a former student of Fenn's, was a real gem. The cellphone rang again as Fenn braked to a stop facing the three-car garage.

"Y'ello."

"Hi Chas. Are you at Mandy Rolland's house, yet?"

Fenn could tell by Asha's tone that Mandy wasn't about to come bouncing out her front door.

"I think so." He read back the address. "Has she canceled?"

"Um, no. She must have called last night and left a message on the machine. She wants you to pick her up at her grandma's."

"Alright. Where's grandma's house?"

"It's a townhouse at Appleton Estates. Forty-seven McIntosh Lane."

Asha heard Fenn's sigh. "I know. Want me to tell your ten o'clock you might be late?"

Fenn scheduled his lessons to minimize the distance between them, and Appleton Estates was across town. Extra travel always had a cost that was hard to recoup.

"Leave it with me. We'll call Sam Parsons if I'm still running behind."

"A good start to your morning, huh?"

"It is what it is," he said. "Hopefully it gets gooder. I'd better go."

"Oh, hey."

"What?"

"If you're passing a pet shop, could you get a bag of kibble for Mogg? She's just about out."

"Already?"

"She's a big cat."

"She's a fat cat."

"Nah, that's all fur."

"Uh-huh."

Mandy Rolland was a self-confident seventeen-year-old who'd spent most of the summer as a camp counsellor, was about to start grade twelve in September, and wanted to be a psychologist. Fenn rarely asked for personal information: he'd pulled her age from her learner's permit, and the rest she'd told him as they cruised along quiet side streets in upper Burlington. New students were either excited or nervous, and while some would scarcely speak, others would tell their entire life story.

"We're selling our house and the agent said it would be easier to keep the place tidy for showings if we weren't there. So, I've been staying with my granny. Mom and dad are in Toronto for some film festival thing. They should be back this morning."

Their session nearly over, Fenn's cellphone rang again and interrupted his explanation of a safe following distance. He tried not to take calls while teaching, feeling it disrespected the client, but the number displayed was that of the office. Sensing that today would be one of those days, he answered.

"What's up?"

"Do you still have Mandy Rolland in the car?" It was Carole Lundsen.

"Well, good morning, Carole. How are you?"

"I'm fine. Is Mandy with you?"

"Yep. She's just driving us back to grandma's house." He glanced over at Mandy, who took her eyes off the road to give him a quick grin.

"Change of drop-off. She needs to go to her own house. Do you have the address?"

"Even better. I've got someone who lives there."

"Oh, of course. Well, could you tell her there's been an incident. Her parents are there, but so are the police."

"Just a sec." Fenn pointed through the windshield. "Turn right at the next street, Mandy."

"Where are you now, Chas?" Carole sounded like she was on speakerphone.

"Uptown. About ten minutes from Mandy's place. Better call Sam Parsons and tell him I'll be a bit late."

"Okay. And, Chas,"

"Yes."

"Just drop her off. Don't get involved."

"Now, why would you say that?"

"Oh, gee. Let me think."

Had Fenn not been to Mandy's house already, he would have spotted it by the policeman standing at the end of the driveway. Even though he'd prepared her with what he knew, which was next to nothing except that

7

her parents would be there, she almost hit the gas instead of the brake when they were motioned to stop.

"Put your window down," he told Mandy, then said to the cop. "She lives here."

Waved through, they didn't get far before having to park the car on the grass strip bordering the concrete. There were two squad cars, an unmarked Buick with a whip antenna, a Jaguar, an Audi coupe, a van, and an ambulance.

"Pull up your parking brake, Mandy," prompted Fenn. It was all he got to say before she threw off the seatbelt, flung open the door, and ran down to the house.

Fenn shut the engine off. He'd had the foresight to book a tentative next appointment while they were driving down, so he put his binder in the back seat and followed the girl up the steps to the front door. This was an unusual situation, and he wanted to make sure the teen had the support she needed from an adult she was familiar with.

A tall woman wearing white coveralls and disposable shoe covers intercepted her at the door.

"You must be Mandy." The woman's smile was friendly and there was warmth in her eyes. "I'm Koki. Your parents are inside, but we'd like everyone to stay on the main floor for now. Okay?"

Mandy nodded, and Koki let her past.

"I'm Chas Fenn, her driving instructor. I just want to make sure Mandy's looked after before I leave."

"Alright. Main floor only and don't touch anything."

"I'll only be a minute," promised Fenn. The coveralls, not the clipped British accent, told Fenn that Koki Motungi was a forensics expert. Not exactly the profession one wanted padding about a home. Fenn stepped inside and glanced around. The place appeared to have been completely cleared of its contents. Hardly surprising since it was for sale, yet someone was upset about it.

"Beth, they even took the safe. Pulled it right out of the wall." This was from one of the two men coming down a curved staircase. The speaker was somewhere in his mid-forties, short dark hair starting to gray. He wore a pastel green golf shirt, tan slacks, and canvas boat shoes. The other man wore a lightweight charcoal suit and was familiar to Fenn. It was Detective Inspector Evan Lareault from the Halton Police Service major crimes section, or whatever Lareault's department was called.

The inspector was making a note and before he looked up, Fenn stepped into the kitchen where a group of people had congregated. He spotted Mandy. She was standing with her arms around the waist of a woman that Fenn assumed was her mother. Facial features and tanned skin tones were similar, though where Mandy's hair was dark and shoulder length, her mother's was blonde in a stylish shag cut. Mandy's figure also hadn't filled out to her mater's proportions, which were accentuated by a stretchy tank top and hip-hugging designer jeans. Fashionable sandals with raised cork soles completed the look.

Both females were a head shorter than the man they were talking to. Someone else Fenn recognized. Sergeant Frank Bloomfield. The large policeman sensed his presence and glanced over his shoulder.

His questioning look prompted Fenn to say, "I'm just making sure Mandy found her parents."

"O-kay," said Bloomfield slowly. "Since you're here, how about you wait across the hall in the living room. I'd like a word."

Fenn complied, fully expecting that Bloomfield's word would likely be, 'why the hell are you in another of my cases?'

He passed Lareault in the arched doorway. The inspector raised an eyebrow but said nothing.

The rooms were so empty they echoed. Since there was no place in the living room to sit, Fenn stood and examined the walls where small brass hangers denoted where pictures had been. If he looked carefully, he could see the paint was slightly darker where the frames had prevented sun fade.

From snippets of conversation in the kitchen, he gathered that the furniture removal had not been authorized. In fact, Mandy's father, the chap in the golf shirt and slacks, became indignant at the suggestion that his household goods had been repossessed.

The main floor wasn't entirely open-concept yet the entrance to each room was wide. From where he stood, Fenn had a good view of the kitchen, foyer, connecting hallway, and the stairways that went up to the second floor and down to the basement.

The basement seemed to be where all the forensics techs were going.

Fenn checked his watch. Carole would have rescheduled Sam Parsons by now. If Sergeant Bloomfield kept him waiting much longer, he'd also have to rebook his eleven o'clock.

The sound of footsteps on tile, undamped by rugs or drapes or the fabric of furniture, signified movement from the kitchen. Inspector Lareault led the way to the basement followed by the Rolland family. Sergeant Bloomfield detoured to the living room.

Fenn gave him a friendly smile but kept his hands in his pockets.

Bloomfield flipped to a fresh page in his notebook.

"Charleton Fenn," he said as he wrote. He looked up. "Did you do it?"

"Do what?"

"Do you know who did it?"

"Did what?"

"Why are you here, Chas?"

"Mandy, the daughter. I'm teaching her to drive."

"Right, I remember. You were a driving instructor."

"Still am."

Bloomfield gave a flat smile. "Anything you can tell us?"

"Always check your mirror when you brake."

Bloomfield's flat smile curved up a little. "So, you brought Mandy here this morning. Where'd you pick her up?"

Fenn told the big cop what little he knew. If Bloomfield decided not to reciprocate, he might get more details the next time he took Mandy out.

"It was her first lesson. I picked her up at her grandmother's house."

"What time was that?"

"About ten past nine. I take it someone burglarized the Rollands."

Bloomfield looked up from his pad to glance around the empty room.

"Not much gets past you."

"Is there a body in the basement?"

That drew a hard stare from the sergeant. "Are you a journalist now, too?"

"C'mon, Sergeant. Perhaps we can help each other."

"Mr. Fenn, you can do us both a favour by telling me everything you know then minding your own business. Now, got anything else?"

"Only that I was here before I went to grandma's house. A couple minutes before nine. The place was deserted."

"Did you notice any doors or windows open?"

Fenn shook his head, and Bloomfield made a note. "That everything?"

"That's it, unless there's something you'd like to share with me. Probably take a tractor-trailer to empty this place. I'm on the road, driving around town, all day. I could keep an eye out."

"If we need your help, we'll put out a media release."

"Okay. But don't blame me when the headline reads 'Bloomfield Baffled By Burlington Break-In'". Fenn checked his watch again and headed for the door. "I really do have to go, but you've got my number."

CHAPTER 3

Dennis Collier rose from his crouch and nodded to the men standing beside the pool table. A body bag had been laid out and by the time the coroner had stripped off his nitrile gloves, the paramedics were ready to pull up the zipper. One of them wheeled a collapsible gurney over.

Collier put up a hand. "Leave her there for a minute, lads. The Inspector wants to bring the homeowners down for a look."

It was only due to the clean state of the corpse that the coroner hadn't objected to Lareault's request. His first impression was the young woman, perhaps in her mid-twenties, had suffered a single killing blow to the back of the head. Otherwise, she was 'presentable'. Clothed in summer attire: baggy t-shirt with a faded McMaster University logo, cut-off-jeans shorts, and a grubby pair of Nike running shoes, her tanned skin suggested plenty of outdoor activity. The rug she'd been rolled up in had a Persian pattern. It was wider than the body had been long, and longer than it was wide.

All that, in itself, was not unusual. Bodies had been bundled in broadloom since time immemorial. A body with two skulls, however, was a first for any of the team. Collier and Motungi had carefully unrolled the carpet, taking several photographs as each detail was revealed. It was as the rug lay flat and the corpse completely exposed that the second skull, devoid of skin, flesh, or contents, was discovered tucked between the victim's knees.

Ancient-looking and missing the lower jaw, Collier could tell it had belonged to an adult male. The attached upper teeth, worn down and the same tea-stain colour as the skull, were in surprisingly good condition. Their lack of decay, usually caused by sugar which was unavailable until the seventeenth century, led him to estimate an age of at least three-hundred years. Motungi took several more photographs and placed the artifact in a sealable chain of custody envelope. While she used a HEPA-filtered hand-vac to collect any minute particles left on the tiled floor, Collier wondered what connection an ancient skull had with a twenty-first century corpse.

He made a mental note to check the victim's fingertips, something he'd do anyway though, in this case, he'd look for rough skin and short, possibly broken, nails with dirt beneath. There had been no wallet or purse, pockets had been empty, not even a necklace pendant with initials for identification. If it could be determined she was an archaeologist, it would be a place to start.

The possibility that one of the Rolland family knew the victim was why the Detective Inspector had them coming down the stairs. Seeing that Koki Motungi was still vacuuming, Lareault stopped on the bottom step.

Lareault raised a hand to halt the procession. "Just give her a minute, folks." To Collier he said, "Can we show them the artifact?"

Collier brought the evidence bag over and passed it to him. "It's not fragile, but please handle it gently."

"Is that a skull?" Mandy Rolland leaned forward to look over her mother's shoulder.

Mr. Rolland held out his hands. "May I?"

Lareault handed him the bag. "Have you seen this before?"

Julian Rolland slowly shook his head. He turned it over to look inside the cavity. "What's it doing here?"

"Let me see it, Dad."

"It came in the rug with the victim. What about you, Mandy? Not part of a school project?"

"I wish." The teen showed none of the distaste currently on her mother's face.

"Give it back to him, Mandy. I'd rather not touch it." Beth Rolland had spotted the body bag and clearly wanted to get the next bit over as soon as possible.

Koki Motungi, now finished, had moved to a corner of the room to seal the vacuum's sample pouch.

"Okay, folks," said Collier. "If you can walk carefully in my footsteps to just over here." He led them to the wet bar where they could look at the unrolled carpet.

"Was this always here in the basement?"

"No," said Mrs. Rolland. "That's not ours."

"Looks like a nice one," said Lareault. "Have any of you seen it before?"

Mandy and her dad shook their head. Beth went down on her haunches for a closer look. "It's not that nice."

With a thumb and forefinger, she rolled back a corner to look at the underside.

"Machine-made. Probably polyester. Wouldn't waste my money on this." She stood back up.

"Beth's family sells antiques," said Julian Rolland.

"Oh? Ever had any skulls come through the shop?" Lareault handed the evidence bag back to Collier who returned it to the pool table.

"My father once bought and sold a pair of shrunken heads," said Beth.

"I guess there's a market for everything," he replied diplomatically. "Dennis, perhaps we could look at the victim now."

Collier knelt beside the cadaver and slowly undid a zipper that ran in an L-shape to reveal a clear vinyl window. The face of the corpse was visible, yet the layer of plastic gave it a wax figure appearance. The Rollands inched closer and bent forward. Mandy now had an arm round her father's waist.

Beth Rolland peered down for maybe three seconds, then turned away. Her husband and daughter had an almost scientific detachment to their posture. Collier looked up at them.

"Anyone you know?"

"No," they said together and straightened up.

"How about you, Mrs. Rolland," said Lareault.

She shook her head. Her summer tan seemed to be a shade lighter. "Why is this person in our house? Our whole life has just been stolen and we're left with a dead body. What sort of sicko does that?"

Julian Rolland tried to take his wife's hand, but she folded her arms and turned away. He looked at Lareault. "Are we done here? We'd like to go upstairs."

Lareault indicated the coroner could zip up the viewing flap. "Sorry to put you through that, folks. Thankfully, it's nobody close to you. Let's convene in the kitchen."

Collier gave them a head start, then motioned that the paramedics could remove the corpse. When he and Motungi were alone, he said, "What do you think?"

They began to roll up the rug. Koki had a bag large enough to seal it in, but Collier would let one of her team help with that. Union rules.

"The only reaction I would call genuine was that of the daughter. Not saying the parents were lying, but they've had a lifetime to work on their poker face."

"What did you think of the rug appraisal?" The coroner packed up his examination gear.

"She was showing off. Could be a defensive reflex. This has turned her world upside down and she likely felt the need to regain some control."

"Understandable, I suppose."

"So, who discovered the body?"

"The real estate agent. She had a viewing booked and arrived early to open up, and to air the place out a bit. Was surprised to find it empty and called the homeowners to see if they'd arranged movers. Came down here and found the vic. That's when we got the call." Collier looked around to make sure he'd collected everything he'd come in with.

"Where is she now?"

"The agent? Frank Bloomfield took down her particulars and let her leave. She'll go to the station later to sign a formal statement and give a set of fingerprints to compare with what we find here."

"Bet she's bummed." The forensic tech placed the collection pouch containing the floor particulates next to the skull.

"Yeah. Nice commission on properties like this. Did you know that Evan Lareault lives about a mile down the road from here?"

Koki Motungi gave a coy smile. "Actually, yes, I do."

"Oh," said Collier, and quickly snapped his bag closed. "Right."

CHAPTER 4

The diesel clatter of the Freightliner changed tempo as Marshall Stober downshifted and pulled off Barton Street into a nearly empty parking lot. He drove along the side of a large building that had once been a warehouse for a DIY home renovation store. Customers would order from a catalogue and drive their vehicle directly into the warehouse to pick up the product. The owner had hoped that with less overhead for displays and staff, the lower prices would allow him to compete with the big chain stores in town.

He was wrong.

So he cut his losses, leased the property out, and with rent payments deposited monthly to his bank account, barely gave it a second thought.

There was one vehicle, an older model Mercedes sedan, parked next to the office. Stober stopped the rig to let his passenger jump down.

"Tell Benny to open the bay door, Devon."

He waited until Devon Millcroft went through the frosted glass entrance, then put the truck back in gear and rolled slowly toward the rear of the building. He cranked the wheel to aim the rig at a large, segmented metal door and braked to a halt. The dash clock showed it was a few minutes after nine. They'd made good time. Only three hours to empty the house and drive to the depot in the east end of Hamilton.

That was the good part.

The memory of the corpse made him shake his head. Who on Earth leaves a frickin' stiff rolled up in a frickin' rug, in a mansion? That crap might happen in a crack house but, jeez! They were fortunate to have started upstairs and had the trailer pretty well loaded by the time they got to the basement. Then again, to look on the bright side, it might distract the cops. Take the focus off the burglary.

The door rolled up.

Just inside, Millcroft stood beside a balding heavy-set man in black slacks and a white shirt unbuttoned at the collar. He looked like one of those guys who might have played on the offensive line of his high school football team, then, for the next thirty years had given up sports for pasta. He'd been christened Maurice, but since his last name was Goodman, he was known to all as Benny.

Benny held up two fingers and Stober eased off the clutch. The Freightliner rolled forward between red lines on the shiny concrete floor that marked out aisle two. The first aisle already had a trailer, and there was a third aisle currently vacant. The rest of the cavernous space was taken up with rows of industrial shelving. To walk among them was like shopping in a well-stocked consignment store. Many of the items were in nearly new condition, and those that weren't would be priced accordingly. Benny was always ready to make a deal.

Benny was a fence. He was the first to pay cash for stolen goods that would then be passed along until there were enough degrees of separation that their next owners either wouldn't know of the illegality, or wouldn't care. It was a different kind of chain store, one with many links. Guys like Stober and Millcroft supplied the product. Benny then distributed his stock to a variety of consignment shops, auction houses, antique stores, and second-hand or thrift shops who put the items back into the retail market. Most outlets were in Ontario, but occasionally he'd send a truckload to Montreal. The further from the source, the better.

Stober killed the motor and got down from the cab, ready to unhitch the trailer and hook onto the other if it was scheduled to go. He was surprised when Benny stopped him.

"Not so sure I want this load," he said, holding up a pudgy hand. A chunky gold bracelet slid around his wrist. He stood sideways as if prepared to walk away. "The kid just told me about the stiff."

Stober was reaching beneath the trailer for the stabilizer crank. He straightened up. "Hey, it's not like it's in the truck. We didn't even bring the rug."

"The goods don't matter. All the cops will do is jot down what got took and 'keep an eye out' for it." Benny liked to emphasize with finger quotes. "Dead bodies, now. That's a whole other story. They'll have a BOLO on you guys before the day's out. I don't need that kind of heat. Probably best if you just abandon the trailer at the airport."

Stober shot a look of exasperation at Millcroft.

"Relax, Benny. Nobody saw us. There were no security cameras. We wore hats and gloves, so no prints or DNA. We were in and out. Got some really good, high-quality stuff."

Benny had started ambling back to his office.

"At least look at it, Benny. Dev, open up and show him what we got."

Millcroft unlatched the doors, and they lowered the ramp. Benny stopped walking and turned around. For a moment, he stood with hands on hips and gazed at the back of the trailer. Stober and Millcroft were steady guys who never brought him chipboard. Muttering something they couldn't make out, he walked up the incline to the top of the ramp.

"What're ya going to do with that?" He pointed with his shoe at the wall safe they had packed by the door.

"That goes to our connection as payment for the security code," said Millcroft.

"And who's that?"

"Got ourselves some kind of cat-burglar. Gave us the door code in exchange for the safe." Millcroft was proud of his contact, but Benny didn't seem to care. He peered at a long-case clock and a couple of paintings that were easily accessible. What could be seen of the furniture revealed expensive fabrics and actual wood. It was a nice haul. He still grimaced and shook his head.

"The stiff changes everything. Problem with quality stuff is it attracts attention."

"Yeah, but it also sells fast," argued Stober. "Won't stay on the market long enough to get noticed. Send it to Montreal. Different language, different culture. It's almost like a different country, up there."

Millcroft opened a carton and brought out an art déco vase with nude women in relief around it. It looked like frosted glass.

"You like this La-li-que, stuff, don't you, Benny," he said, reading the inscription on the base.

"That's Lalique, La-leek, you cretin. Hand it here before you drop it."

Millcroft grinned at Stober. Though he knew little about expensive crystal, he did know Benny had a weak spot for it. He unwrapped another piece. "Bunch more in here—but if you're not interested."

Benny leaned over to peer into the box. Millcroft closed the flaps.

"C'mon, Benny. Time's wasting. Wha'd'ya say?"

"I'll give you two-hundred for the crystal. The rest, either find someone else or dump it. It's part of a murder investigation, for Crissakes. If it comes back on me, it'll shut me down."

"Who said anything about murder? The stiff could be dead from natural causes." The last thing Stober wanted was to drive the trailer away still full. He'd figured on at least ten or twelve grand for the load.

Benny flipped his hand dismissively. "This ain't frikkin' I-raq. We don't bury our dead in rugs."

Millcroft looked at Stober and shook his head. "Forget him, Marsh. There's other folks who'll take this stuff." He put his hand out for the vase. Benny pretended not to notice.

"Alright. I'll give you three grand for the load, but only 'cause you're my best team, and you've got your own rig." Most of the goods Benny fenced came in the trunk of a car, or the back of stolen vans or cube trucks. Stober owned his truck, and freelanced as an owner/operator making regular runs for legitimate businesses.

"Yeah, an' this rig costs money to run." Stober pointed toward the cab. "I can show you the bills. Three ain't going to cut it. The load's worth at least ten, probably fifteen. How about we do eight?"

Benny grimaced again. "Once you dump it here, the risk is all mine. I'll give you four."

"Risk?" Stober stepped onto the ramp. "Exactly how much risk did *you* take this morning, loading everything up? Screw you. Gimme the vase, we're done."

Unlike Millcroft, he was well aware of what the sculptured crystal could sell for. At auction, a vase alone could draw bids of two or three grand. And they had a box of the stuff. Even here, at the bottom of the food chain, the truckload was worth a hell of a lot more than four large.

"Okay: Five."

"Seven."

"Five and a half."

"Six and a half."

"Five and a half."

"You're a cheap cunt, you know that?"

"Best offer you'll get today. Tell you what, Marshall, I've a load going to Ajax in a few days. I'll give you top dollar to haul it."

Stober looked at Millcroft, who shrugged.

"Go get your measly tens and twenties, Benny."

Still holding the vase Benny walked down the ramp. It flexed slightly under his heavy steps until he turned at the bottom. "Hey young fella," he said to Millcroft. "You got a girlfriend?"

"Yeah, why?"

"You decide to get hitched, come see me. I'll find you a nice ring. On the house."

Millcroft just nodded. A wedding wasn't on his mind right now. Only getting paid half of what he'd expected, was. Still, for three hours' work it wasn't bad.

CHAPTER 5

Fenn met Asha for lunch across the road from the DriveCheck office, at the King's Head Pub. Though nestled in a utilitarian cinderblock plaza, the interior's faux-oak beams, antiqued wood tables, and British beer logos on the draft pump handles gave it a cozy tavern atmosphere.
Fenn ordered his usual battered haddock and chips with gravy. Asha went for the soup and salad special.

"And to drink?" The server, a freckly college-aged girl with CHERISE on her name tag, placed a couple of cardboard coasters on the table. Since they had to return to work, Fenn asked for a large chocolate milk. Asha had an iced tea.

"Carole was hoping you'd come into the office," she said. "She's dying to know what happened at the Rollands' house."

Fenn grinned. "Precisely why I had you meet me here." That made Asha's eyes sparkle with amusement. They'd been employees of Dieter and Carole Lundsen for years. Long enough for both management and staff to be in the 'if I could find someone better I'd get a divorce' phase.

"So, what did happen?"

"Well, this may come as a shock, but even rich folk have their problems. If you've got something of value, somebody always wants a piece, or even the whole thing."

"Don't I know it," said Asha. "Look at all the strife we had with that stash of cash you found."

"Yeah, but that money was tainted from the start. I'd like to think that Mandy's parents had honestly earned their large house, expensive cars, and summer camps in Muskoka." Fenn paused to drink some of his brown milk. "Probably have a chalet up at Blue Mountain, too."

23

"So, they got robbed?"

"Burgled. Totally cleaned out: furniture, artwork, wall safe, the works. Not only that: there was a dead body found in their basement."

Asha put a hand to her mouth. "Do you know who it was?"

"Who cleaned them out, or who the dead person was?"

"Yes. Both, though mainly the body."

"Nope. Sergeant Bloomfield wouldn't tell me."

They both looked up as the server brought their food.

"Enjoy," said Cherise as she moved ketchup and vinegar bottles over from an adjacent table.

"When you talked to Sergeant Bloomfield, was he friendly?"

"If you mean suspicious, then, yeah, we were like old buddies. Inspector Lareault was also there. He saw me but said nothing."

Asha nodded and blew across the soup on her spoon to cool it. Fenn drizzled some malt vinegar onto his fries. The pub had decent food at a decent price. They spent a few minutes eating in silence.

"So how was Mandy?" Asha poked a fork into her salad.

"Nice kid. She'll probably pass her test within the twelve-lesson package."

"She wasn't freaked out about everything at her house?"

"A bit. Perhaps more than a bit, but she seemed to handle it okay. How's your salad?"

"Is good. Want some?" Asha offered a wedge of tomato.

Fenn shook his head and dipped some fries in the gravy. He wasn't a big fan of eating off other people's forks. He watched as Asha speared some spinach leaves. Fenn liked watching Asha do just about anything. Today she'd worn a thin-strapped black halter, white culottes, and white canvas running shoes. The halter came down to her waistband, but when she leaned back, it revealed her navel piercing, a little dangly diamond thing. Like Fenn, she tanned well and this late in the summer, her skin had a lovely coffee tone to it.

She looked up and saw the faint smile on Fenn's lips. "What?"

"Just enjoying the view."

"Well, I'm afraid your viewing time is just about up. Gotta get back."

"Why? We won't be busy until the school year starts."

"True, but you know what Carole's like. I don't want to spoil a lovely lunch by getting sniped at 'cause I was five minutes late."

Fenn caught Cherise's eye and requested the bill. Asha retrieved a compact mirror from her purse and checked for food in her teeth.

"I may not be home for supper, though."

"Poker night with the girls?"

"No. I'm going to the mall with Kim Klaasen and her sister, Elaine. We want to find something to wear for Kim and Tony's wedding."

"Won't Kim be wearing a wedding dress?"

"Well, yeah, but Elaine and I thought we'd try to find a couple of outfits that sort of matched."

"So you're not going for the lavender or periwinkle bridesmaid's dresses?"

"Periwinkle bridesmaid's dresses? What decade are you from?"

"Do you think Tony will wear a tux?"

"How should I know what Tony is wearing. You're his best man. Don't you guys talk?"

"Not about clothes."

"The wedding is less than two weeks away. Just sayin'. Anyway, I've got to go. Gimme a kiss."

Fenn selected a few notes from his wallet, dropped the cash on the table, and wandered out into the heat. Across the road, he saw Asha pull open the door to the DriveCheck office. Parked nearby was a blue Nissan Sentra with a driving school roof sign. Joe Posada's car. Fenn still had time before his next lesson, so he drove over and parked beside the Nissan. He sat with the windows up, engine and a/c running. When Posada came out of the office, Fenn shut off the engine and rolled his window down.

"How's it going, Joe?"

"Howdy, Chas. We all heard you had some excitement this morning."

"I guess Asha brought everyone up to speed."

Posada just nodded, busy re-lighting a cigarette. He sucked in the first lungful, then said, "I'll bet the cops were happy to see you."

"Just as happy as last time," said Fenn. "And the time before that."

"I don't know how these things always happen to you, Chas. The last adventure I had was when Clara Fellino came for a night driving lesson wearing nothing but a trenchcoat. Tried to seduce me in her driveway."

Something about the diminutive instructor made him irresistible to the opposite sex. Fenn grinned. "You let her, of course."

"No way! Her husband's in the armed forces. Those guys have guns." He exhaled smoke as if it would banish the thought.

"Are you busy with lessons these days?"

Posada shrugged. "'Bout average for this time of year. You?"

"Same, though I'm glad we dropped that farm worker's program. I burned a tank of gas each day, out there in the country."

"No profit in that." Posada drew his Marlboro down to the butt and flicked it away. "Ever think of doing something else?"

Fenn leaned back in his seat. "Just between you and me, Joe, Asha and I are thinking about starting our own driving school."

Posada looked over at the office and drummed his fingers on the roof of the car. "Well, if you do, I wouldn't mind coming along."

Fenn nodded. "We're just kicking it around, right now, but you'll be the first to know."

"I'll hold you to that. Anyway, I'd better go. My two o'clock has a test booked."

With only a couple of lessons that afternoon, Fenn was done by three. Since Asha wouldn't be home for supper, he bought a foot-long turkey sandwich and headed up to Kilbride, one of the little villages north of Burlington.

As he drove away from the lake and up onto the escarpment plateau, pastures and horse paddocks gradually replaced the houses. Some fields were fallow while others had crops of corn, hay, sunflowers. The road dipped down through Cedar Springs, a small settlement of homes fronted by connecting ponds, then snaked out of the valley to straighten for a kilometer until it ran past the barn where Fenn and his buddy, Tony Demmers, kept their project cars.

Within the workshop, neither Fenn's 1970 Dodge Challenger nor Tony's 1967 Pontiac GTO were beneath a tarp since summer was the prime time for cruising. The Challenger was more or less complete, having recently been painted a pearl-finish gray. The GTO was also only a few interior panels from a complete rebuild after a crash that had almost killed Tony. Demmers called it *The Black Mariah*, since the original owner, a North Carolinian bootlegger, had given it a flat black paint scheme. The only noticeable change, now, was the re-installation of passenger and rear seats, which had been ditched to make room for moonshine.

There was a picnic table in the shade beside the barn. Fenn took a beer from the fridge and twisted off the cap. He'd just unwrapped his sandwich when a familiar rumble announced the arrival of Tony's pickup truck. Demmers stepped down from the cab and came over to the table. No longer using a cane, he still limped a little.

"Want half a sandwich?" Fenn raised the beer bottle to his lips.

Tony shook his head. "I've got a chicken snack pack in the truck. Kim's gone shopping."

"I know. Asha said you and I should talk about clothes."

"Clothes?"

"You know. For the wedding. Are you wearing a tux?"

"Yeah. I went to TuxMaster last weekend for a fitting. Are you? You don't have to."

"Think I should?"

Tony gave a little shrug. "You know what they say about a sharp-dressed man."

"Good point."

Tony fetched the snack pack from the truck and a beer from the barn. He sat down and opened both. "So, what's new?"

Fenn tried to not smile as he picked up the rest of his sandwich. "Stumbled onto a crime scene this morning."

"Another one? You're getting to be like what's'er name. Fletcher."

"Murder She Wrote."

"Yeah."

"Lareault and Bloomfield were there."

"Bet that went over well."

Fenn waggled his hand. "I had to go there. New student. Her house had been cleaned out, and there was a dead body in the basement."

Tony lowered the chicken thigh he was about to bite.

"Do these things happen to other instructors, or only you?"

"Well, Brenda Woodhill once brought a student back to their house and found it on fire. And one of these days, Posada's going to get shot by a jealous husband."

"So today was no big deal, then." Tony dropped the chicken bone into the box and picked up his bottle of ale.

Fenn crumpled the paper wrapping from his meal. "Yup. Just another day in the life."

A few wispy clouds to the west promised a gorgeous sunset, and the evening would likely stay warm. A perfect night for a cruise. Maybe they'd drive along Lakeshore Road.

CHAPTER 6

Frank Bloomfield tapped on the door to Lareault's office and stepped inside. Opposite, a bank of windows looked down onto the parking lot and the highway beyond. On the wide sill a solitary plant pot, its vegetation having died and dried up, served as a placeholder to discourage further gifts of such sort. To the right of the entrance was a bank of filing cabinets, to the left the inspector's desk.

Lareault didn't need to look up to see the sergeant's bulk in his peripheral vision. He kept two-finger typing on the computer keyboard. On the wall behind him were three picture frames. Two held certificates and the third was an outdoor shot of the inspector in his dress uniform on graduation day. There was another chair in the room, but Bloomfield didn't want to sit.

Lareault hit the ENTER key and sat back.

"Yes, Frank?"

"Catrina Pailin has come in to give a formal statement."

"Who's that again?"

"The Rollands real estate agent. She's in the lobby. I assume you'd like to talk to her."

Lareault rose from his chair. "Yes. Absolutely."

The foyer of the architecturally modern Halton Regional Police Service headquarters was spacious, with a high ceiling and good light. Across from the curved reception desk was a lengthy chrome and leather bench. Its sole occupant was an attractive blonde woman who Lareault guessed was somewhere in her late forties. Well-developed calves and toned upper arms suggested a workout regimen, though indoors rather than out, for her skin was almost albino pale. She wore a gray above-the-knee skirt beneath a mauve frilly shouldered blouse. Her four-inch pumps matched the small purple clutch purse she clutched in her lap. They shook hands and Lareault judged by her abundant jewelry that Catrina Pailin was successful in business.

"Thanks for coming in, Ms. Pailin. I'm Detective Inspector Evan Lareault."

Even with stilettos, she just came up to Lareault's chin. Her brown eyes conveyed concern. "Least I could do. Do you know, yet, who the person in the basement was?"

"We're still working on that. Let's find somewhere that we can talk in private. Would you like a coffee or water?"

"No, thanks."

"According to Sergeant Bloomfield's notes," Lareault said, once they were seated in an interview room, "you arrived at the Rollands house about 9:30 a.m."

"That's right. I had a second showing at ten and wanted to get the place ready."

"A second showing?"

"A return visit by a potential buyer. I was hoping to close the deal today."

Lareault nodded sympathetically. "Was there any sign of activity at the house when you got there?"

"None. From the outside everything looked as it had when I left, the day before."

"And what time did you leave yesterday?"

"I had an evening viewing, so I closed up about eight o'clock."

The inspector kept skimming the sergeant's notes.

"The house has an alarm system, is that correct?"

"It does. There are door and window detectors, and motion sensors inside."

"And you set it before you left last night."

Pailin gave an indulgent smile. "I've been selling premium properties in the area for over twenty years. Locking up is second nature."

While Lareault accepted that, experience had taught him that technology can give a false sense of security.

"Any chance the alarm wasn't working?"

She shrugged. "The system beeped when I set it."

"How many keypads are there?"

The agent thought for a moment. "Four. One inside the front door, and one for each of the garage doors."

"And which one did you use?"

"I always used my key to get in the front door, then disarmed the alarm with the foyer keypad."

"And they are all programmed to the same combination?"

Pailin nodded. "8 7 1 9."

That confirmed Koki Motungi's assertion the burglars had gained access to the house through the garage, since it only needed the keypad combo to open, and then jimmied the kitchen door. The middle car bay entrance had the only keypad where the buttons 8 7 1 9 were clean. Most likely from the thieves using gloves, which would have wiped away any prints left by the owners.

Lareault jotted that down. "So, you let yourself in the front door and disarmed the alarm."

"Yes. Well, not exactly. I punched in the code and the system gave the tone to indicate it was arming—instead of disarming. At the same time, I noticed that the place looked rather bare."

"And what did you think about that?"

"I—I wasn't sure what to think. Sometimes homeowners who are moving store some pieces. Perhaps they'd come over for a few odd pieces and left the alarm off. I also wondered if they'd parked in the garage and were in the house somewhere. You've seen the place. It's pretty big."

Lareault gave her an encouraging smile but stayed silent.

"Once I saw that the living room was empty, I felt that something was wrong. I've always had good communication with the Rollands. They would have mentioned if they'd intended to move *all* their stuff. And I'd have tried to talk them out of it: you can get more for a property with nice furniture in it, and theirs was good quality. I didn't even need to stage the place."

"When did the Rollands list with you?"

"For this property, a little over a month ago. It's priced right, but the market's been kind of slow this year."

"So, this wasn't your first dealing with the family."

"Oh, no. I actually sold them that very house thirteen years ago."

"So now they're moving again. Have they found a new place?"

Catrina Pailin leaned forward and said conspiratorially, "Julian's done quite well for himself. He's in film production. Toronto's the new Hollywood, you know."

Bloomfield chuckled. He'd been sitting quietly beside the inspector. "Arlene and I always try to spot the locations that are passed off as New York or Chicago. There's been some splendid shows filmed in Hamilton, too."

"Exactly," said the agent enthusiastically. "The Rollands' house was once used in a murder mystery episode. It's a perk of being in the industry: you can rent out your home, and write-off any landscaping expense."

"And did you help the Rollands find a new place to live?" Lareault never interrupted a statement or testimony but did like to keep it on track.

"Oh, absolutely. Just the land, though. I helped them to purchase a plot where they can build the home of their dreams."

"Have they started the build?"

Pailin indicated no. "There's been some sort of holdup at the site. The foundation should have been poured a couple of weeks ago."

"And where is this site?"

Pailin looked around the windowless interview room but couldn't find north. She gestured vaguely. "They bought an acre up near the foot of Rattlesnake Point. You know where that is, right?"

The policemen both nodded. They could get there by driving twenty minutes into the countryside.

"So, if construction hasn't even started yet, the Rollands would have no reason to move their furniture," said Lareault.

"Yes, and that's what puzzled me. When I walked further into the house and saw how empty it was, I knew something wasn't right."

"What did you do?"

"I called out to see if any of the family members were there."

"But they weren't."

"No. When I saw the kitchen drawers gone and cupboards left open and empty, I took out my flip phone and dialed Julian's number. While waiting for him to pick up, I went down to the basement."

"Why the basement?"

"I wanted to see what else had been taken. I could have gone upstairs first, I suppose, but I didn't."

That sounded reasonable to Lareault. He looked over at Bloomfield. The sergeant's face remained impassive.

"What did you see when you got to the basement, Ms. Pailin?"

"Well, the pool table was still there. I figured it was too heavy to steal. Then I saw the rug." Her face took on a look of sadness. "At first, I didn't notice the arm sticking out, but then I did."

"And what did you do?" said Lareault softly.

"I, er, that's when Julian answered the phone. I told him something terrible had happened. He and Beth were on their way back from Toronto. We agreed they should come to the house as quickly as possible, and that I would call the police."

"Which you did."

"Yes. Then I went up to the top floor to see if the upstairs looked like the downstairs. The bedrooms and office had also been emptied, as you know. After that, I sat in my car until your lot showed up."

"And what time was that?" Though Lareault knew when Pailin's call had been logged at the precinct, checking timelines always helped to verify testimonies.

"About twenty to ten. The first officers arrived maybe eight minutes later."

Lareault took a photograph from his file, a head shot of the victim, and pushed it across the table.

"Do you recognize this person?"

Pailin looked at the picture for several seconds, then shook her head. Lareault returned it to the folder.

"Who were you going to show the house to this morning?"

"Jonah and Emeline Rossiter. I called them to postpone, though I'll be surprised if they still want it, now. Dead bodies usually toll the death knoll for a sale, if you'll pardon the pun."

Lareault nodded, and Bloomfield said with a smile, "We thrive on puns around here."

"Okay, Ms. Pailin." The inspector rose from his chair. "You've been very helpful. I'll leave it to Sergeant Bloomfield to write up your statement and get you to sign it. After that, the only thing we'll need is a list of the people you showed the house to, if you have one."

The agent gave a little head bob. "Unless they want a callback, I don't take names at open houses. But I've got contact information for those that requested private viewings. Will that do?"

"That would be fine." Lareault shook her hand. "Thank you so much for coming in."

CHAPTER 7

It wasn't often that Superintendent Heatherington sat in on an initial briefing. Probably had some personal connection with the Rollands, Lareault surmised as he angled the whiteboard toward the boardroom table. Wearing the crisp white shirt with black epaulets, black tie, and black slacks of her uniform, Jennifer Heatherington took the chair closest to the door. Her hands were clasped loosely on the table's Formica surface and her expression impassive, but Lareault knew her presence signaled additional pressure on the team to solve this case quickly.

Besides himself and Frank Bloomfield, Heatherington had assigned three others: Roy Flock and Sharin Adabi who were both detectives at the precinct, and Sunil Naipaul, a computer technician who would research digitized files and other online media. Bloomfield, the last to enter, nodded deferentially to the superintendent. He pulled a chair away from the long table and sat down. Lareault finished attaching photographs to the magnetic surface and started the briefing.

"Our unidentified victim is female." He tapped a finger on the five by eight glossy at the top left corner of the board. "Age still to be determined but somewhere in her twenties. She was found rolled in a rug in the basement of a house currently listed as for sale. There was blunt force trauma to the back of her head, though the coroner cautions against assuming that as the cause of death, pending release of a tox report."

"Which should be forthcoming," cut in Heatherington. "I've requested it to be given priority."

Lareault nodded. If the Super was going to crack the whip, it may as well work in their favour.

The head shots below the victim were of the Rollands. "Beth and Julian Rolland are the homeowners. They had been attending some functions prior to the upcoming Toronto International Film Festival. Julian Rolland is in film production. Beth Rolland dabbles in antiques. Mandy, their daughter, was spending time with her grandmother who lives in upper Burlington."

He tapped on the bottom picture. "Catrina Pailin, a real estate agent, found the body at approximately nine-thirty this morning. This, of course, after she discovered the house had been cleaned out. We don't yet have a time of death for our victim, and can only say the burglary took place between nine, last night, and nine this morning."

"Do you think the two incidents are connected?" Somewhere in her early forties, Sharin Adabi had large dark eyes and jet-black hair. She'd transferred over from Brampton on making detective a couple of years ago.

"Be a hell of a coincidence if they're not," retorted Flock. He sat slouched in his chair, an elbow resting on the table. A veteran investigator, he'd been on the force nearly as long as Bloomfield.

"I agree," said Lareault. "Though it conjures up some interesting scenarios when looking for a motive. Is someone sending the homeowners a message? If so, what are they mixed up in? Could this be some sort of vendetta?"

"Oh, yeah," said Flock. "Like that horse-head-in-the-bed scene. Very cinematic, I love it."

The comment got an irritated glance from the Superintendent. Flock pretended not to notice.

"Or perhaps," continued the inspector, "the victim was actually known to the real estate agent. Pailin lures her to the Rollands' house, kills her, and rolls her in a carpet while deciding what to do with the body. Then figures she'll just call it in and pin it on the burglars."

"Then where did Pailin, or whoever, get the rug?" Bloomfield knew Beth Rolland had declared the Persian carpet as below her standard.

"Good question. Does one bring their own broadloom to a murder?" That brought a chuckle from the room. "Regardless, it does suggest the victim had died elsewhere, so finding where the rug came from would be a good start," said Lareault.

"And who's that handsome fellow?" Flock pointed at the picture of the skull that Lareault had put on the right side of the board.

"We may never know, and I doubt his name is pertinent, though the skull's presence might be symbolic. It was found tucked between the young lady's knees."

Flock looked around the room. "Well, I'm not much into symbolism, but that's where I'd like my skull to be found, when I go."

His joke got a mixed reaction. Bloomfield gave a little snort: Lareault pressed his lips to contain a laugh: Heatherington tried a look of reproach: and Adabi changed the subject by asking how the burglars gained entry into the house.

"Our forensic team believe the perps had the alarm system code. They entered through the garage, then forced the access door into the kitchen." Lareault wrote INSIDE JOB? on the whiteboard.

"It could be someone who was given the code but not trusted with a key," suggested Bloomfield.

"A cleaning service, perhaps," said Adabi. "Or maybe landscapers who needed access to the garage."

Lareault jotted both down with his marker. "Okay, Sharin, ask the Rollands who they may have given the code to, and follow up on any names."

"Perhaps the agent gave it out, unintentionally," said Flock. "Got careless hiding the code when opening for a potential buyer."

Lareault nodded. "She's going to send us a list, but we'll keep everything on the table for now. We'll see what falls into place when we get a time of death, and can nail down when the place got burgled."

"Depending on their alarm system, I may be able to help with that last item," offered Sunil Naipaul. "Most keypad setups store a rudimentary log of when codes are entered. We know when Ms. Pailin used the foyer unit. Whenever it was disarmed, between her leaving and coming back, should be when the thieves gained entry."

"How soon can you do that?"

"I'll head over there the minute we're done here. Shouldn't take too long."

"Okay, you do that. Sharin will follow up on any tradespeople that may have had access to the house. Roy, let's have you canvas the neighbourhood: perhaps someone saw something in the wee hours. In the meantime, Frank and I will pay a visit to the morgue and see what Dennis Collier can tell us about the vic." He scanned the room. "Right, I think we can set off, unless the Superintendent has anything to add."

Heatherington shook her head and rose to leave.

"In that case, we'll meet back here tomorrow morning, if the case doesn't get solved before then."

As the room emptied, Lareault gathered his paperwork into a manila folder. Bloomfield waited for him.

"How about I meet you in the parking lot in five minutes, Frank. There's something I want to do first."

The big sergeant gave a casual salute. "See you down there."

Lareault took the stairs up to the next floor and strode along the hall until he got to Superintendent Heatherington's office. He knocked, opened the door, and poked his head inside. Heatherington had a phone receiver in her hand and was in the process of dialing. She looked up and replaced the handset in the cradle.

"Something I can do for you, Evan?"

The inspector stepped the rest of the way into the office. Not much larger than his own, it appeared to have bigger windows. The extra elevation of the third floor also afforded a glimpse of the lake. A cargo ship was headed for the port in Hamilton.

Lareault closed the door and leaned back against it. "May I ask why you are interested in this case?"

"I'm interested in any murder that takes place on my patch."

"And?"

His persistence got a wry smile from the Superintendent.

"And Mrs. Rolland is an old friend. We shared a flat at Uni together."

Lareault could see the connection. Jennifer Heatherington's path to police command hadn't been through dark garbage-strewn alleys or the hallways of crack houses. There'd been no calls to domestics, slapping of cuffs on pimps, or breathalyzers administered to wrinkle-suited workaholics, except maybe as a brief stint as an observer. She'd gone the financial and corporate management route.

"Did you two have the same classes?"

"Somewhat: we both took an economics course. Beth was being groomed by her parents to take over the family business."

"Antiques?"

Heatherington nodded. "Julian was one of their employees. He did pickups and deliveries, part time, while working on a cinematography degree."

"Which I assume he got," said Lareault.

Heatherington waggled a hand. "More or less. Sometimes it's not what you know, but who you know. While on a work term, Julian met a cameraman who hired him as an assistant. He's a pretty smart guy and soon worked his way up the ladder. Now he's on the board of some studio."

"How close are you and Beth these days?"

39

Heatherington held his gaze for a moment before answering. "Close enough that she calls me when a corpse is found in her basement. Not so close that it has any bearing on the case."

"Would you like to take part in the investigation? The Rollands may tell you something they wouldn't tell me."

Heatherington picked up the phone receiver again. "I've assured them my best team has been assigned. But let me know if you get stuck and I'll have a chat."

She started to punch in numbers, which the inspector took as his cue to leave.

Lareault felt the heat slow his steps the moment he left the building to walk across the parking lot. Bloomfield was waiting in the car with the air conditioner running. He'd taken off his jacket, the cuffs of his white shirt turned up on his thick forearms. Lareault got in the passenger side and loosened his tie.

"So, was our superintendent an old lover of Julian, or maybe Beth?"

Lareault smiled. Bloomfield hadn't always been a sergeant. He was a detective when he'd retired, shortly after being shot during a takedown. However, four months of recuperation and rehab, followed by two months of gardening and golf, were all Frank could handle of sitting on the sidelines, and he'd applied to become Lareault's sideman. The HRPS was glad to have him back.

"She roomed with Beth, back when they both had big hair and wore leg-warmers."

"I had big hair once," said Bloomfield.

Lareault gave a sideways glance at the sergeant's bald pate. "Afro?"

"You bet. I looked just like 'Linc' on The Mod Squad."

"I'm sure you did," said Lareault. "And now you're Samuel Jackson when he played Shaft."

"Tha's cool. He's one bad mutha—"

"Don't say it."

Besides a dentist's chair, the morgue was the inspector's least favourite place to be.

"Got any gum, Frank? Spearmint would be good."

"Sorry, Boss. Not even a flavoured toothpick. Dennis might have a scented mask."

Dennis Collier wasn't in a mask, just a white lab coat over his shirt and slacks as he sat at a desk making notes. The place didn't actually smell too bad, for once. Maybe he was getting used to it, Lareault thought. Then again, there was a young woman on a metal table, her complexion pale and waxy, her lips bloodless, and a zipper-like Y scar running between her breasts that hadn't been there when she came in. So, maybe not.

"You doing okay, Evan?"

"Yeah. All good. What have you got for us, Dennis?"

"I can give you the time, and cause, of death. Cause, first." The coroner showed them a close-up photograph of the wound on the back of the victim's skull.

"A rock, softball-size inflicted this. There were grains of shale and sandstone found in the abscess. That, however, is not what killed her. Any guesses?"

Bloomfield looked at the body. "Doesn't look like strangulation, or a broken neck. And I don't think she drowned. Overdose?"

"Your experience speaks for itself, Frank. Toxicology identified cocaine and fentanyl. I'd blame the fentanyl: it's very potent, and pushers and partiers often get it wrong."

"Unless, in this case, somebody got it right," said Lareault.

"True," agreed Collier. "It would be relatively simple to poison someone and blame the victim's drug use, though I don't understand the basement broadloom burial."

"You can leave that part to Frank and me. What else do you have?"

"Stomach contents. The last supper consisted of spaghetti and red wine, and there was a later snack of crackers, cheese and oysters washed down with white wine, probably a Riesling."

Lareault wanted to know how much later.

"Couple hours. I'm putting time of death as being close to midnight."

"Still no identification?"

"I had her prints run through the database. Either she's been a good girl or never got caught because there are no priors. However, I suggest you circulate her picture around the schools offering archaeological courses. She was wearing a McMaster t-shirt, so you might start there. Her hands and knees had minute particles of earth and rock embedded, especially under the fingernails. In fact, some grains matched those in the head wound."

"But if she was already dead, why the blow to the head?" said Bloomfield.

The coroner gave a slow headshake. "All I can tell you is she'd been in the area where the rock came from. Her hands were fairly rough as from working outside with a shovel or trowel. Matching traces of rock dust under her nails. Might also explain why she wasn't wearing any rings."

"Do you think they killed her on a dig somewhere?"

"Only if it was in Persia. Forensics can tell you more about the rug, but I'm thinking the murder, or at least the blow to the head, happened indoors."

"Alright, Dennis," Lareault said, turning to leave. "As usual, we now know more than we did when we walked in."

"Then let me tell you one more thing you didn't know."

"What's that?"

"She was a polydactyl."

"Six fingers or toes?"

"Toes. On her left foot."

Lareault and Bloomfield stepped closer to the table as Collier lifted the sheet covering the feet.

"Well, look at that," said Bloomfield. "Another little piggy."

"Too bad it didn't run away home," said the coroner as he went back to his desk.

CHAPTER 8

So Asha could apprise instructors of changes to their schedule in real time, Dieter Lundsen had mandated the use of cell phones. Viewed by his employees as yet another expense, Fenn's response was to call his fiancée at least once a day for a chat. Having made good time crossing town between students, he had a few minutes to kill, so he hit the number on speed dial and waited.

Three rings.

Four rings.

Asha must have been busy because it was Dieter who answered on the fifth ring.

"DriveCheck Driver Training. How can I help you?"

"Hi Dieter. It's Chas. Is Asha close by?"

"Oh, Chas. Glad you called. I'd like a word."

"Fabulous, I've got all kinds. Big ones, little ones, even popular phrases."

Pause.

"What do you want, Dieter?"

"Well, it's about this thing with Mandy Rolland."

"What thing with Mandy Rolland?"

"I see you have her booked in for this afternoon."

"Careful, Dieter. Don't let Asha catch you with her schedule sheets."

Dieter rose to Fenn's bait. "Your fiancée doesn't own this franchise. I do."

"Yeah, but she hates folks messing up her files."

"I didn't mess up any—." Dieter took a breath. "Look, I just want you to tell me if the young lady offers any information about that, you know, incident at her home."

"Why?"

"Superintendent Heatherington, of the Halton Regional Police Service, is a friend of mine. Since we have a connection to a murder investigation, I feel obligated to help her out."

It was Fenn's turn to pause. The extent of any friendship Dieter Lundsen might have with the superintendent was likely from a chance meeting at a charity function, or a standard thank-you letter for donating to the police department's widows and orphans' fund. Rather than call him on it, Fenn played along. He just wanted to talk to Asha, and the sooner he got Dieter off the line he could.

"I doubt she's going to tell me anything, but if I hear of something useful, I'll let you know."

"That's all I want, Chas. Be sure to phone me right away: anytime."

"Will do. Can you put me through to Asha, now?"

"Sure thing. Hold on."

He was treated to a few seconds of an old hit about a Chevy at a levee, then Asha said, "Hey, dude."

"Hey, there. What do you want?"

"What do I want? You called me. What do you want?"

"Nothin' much."

"So why d'ya call?"

"I like to hear your voice." Fenn wondered if he sounded as good on the phone as she did. Maybe. He always lowered his voice an octave to counter the tinniness of the little speaker.

"Actually, I do have something to tell you," said Asha.

"What's that?"

"Dieter wanted to talk to you."

"Funny. He just did. Asked to be kept in the loop about the Mandy Rolland thing."

"Is it a thing?"

"Apparently it is in Dieter's life."

"No kidding. Today he came in wearing a white linen jacket and slacks, a peach shirt, and loafers with no socks."

"Very Miami Vice. Isn't that a decade or two past his preferred seventies?"

"Well, he still wore orange-tinted John Lennon shades. With his ponytail, it was kind of a Don Johnson meets the Beatles vibe."

"Think I should wear a white linen suit for Kim and Tony's wedding?"

"Totally up to you."

"How about loafers without socks?"

"How about I wear rubber boots to bed?"

Despite having downplayed the incident at Mandy Rolland's house, Fenn had to admit he was just as interested in the case as anyone else. Her bed having been taken with everything else, Mandy's stay at grandma's had been extended. From the townhouse at Appleton Estates, Fenn had her drive to the Tyandaga neighbourhood to practice hill-parking.

As they traversed Upper Middle Road, Fenn asked, "Any news of who burgled your house?"

Mandy shook her head. "My mom knows a big cheese at the police station. She says they've put their best team on the case. Did you get to see the body?"

"I didn't," said Fenn. "Did you?"

"Yeah. I thought it would be gross, but it was just sad. She didn't look much older than me."

"But not anyone you knew." Fenn looked ahead. "Change lanes. We're going to turn left soon."

Mandy signaled, checked her blind spot, and moved over. After a moment, she said, "You know what was weird? The body was rolled up in a rug with an old skull. I got to hold it."

"The body?" Fenn feigned shock.

Mandy laughed. "No, the skull. It was really old and pretty neat. You want me to go left, here?"

"Yeah: and then turn right at the next intersection."

The afternoon traffic was light. Fenn glanced at his instructor's mirror. The car behind didn't seem impatient to pass.

"Are your parents also at your grandmother's?"

"Nope. Still at the house. They're going to buy new stuff for our bedrooms and the kitchen today. We'll need it for the new place, anyway. My aunt has an antique store in Hamilton, so they might borrow some furniture from her."

"That's handy."

"Yeah. Family business. My mom's other sister also has a shop up in Kingston."

Mandy made the turn, and a few minutes later Fenn had her on a street with a good gradient for hill-parking. Uphill: turn the wheels left and reverse slightly. Downhill: turn the wheels to the right. Remember the parking brake. They spent a few minutes on that, then drove over to Brant Street.

As Mandy drove toward the lake, Fenn said, "So, have you found somewhere to move?"

"Sort of. We bought a plot of land from a developer, up near Rattlesnake Point. Do you know where that is?"

Fenn smiled. When he didn't have time to go further afield, the bluff at Rattlesnake Point was a favourite spot for rock-climbing.

"That's a pleasant area. Out in the country, but not too far from Burlington or Toronto."

"Yeah, though we still need to sell our house. And who wants to buy a place that had a dead body in it?"

"I wouldn't fret too much. People die in houses all the time. Even if that person was killed in your basement, and it gets in the paper, within a few weeks it'll be another forgotten news item. While it might take longer, your house will sell if the price is right."

"I hope so. Mom and dad got into a pretty good fight last night."

This was getting into personal territory, so the only prompt Fenn gave her was to make another left turn at Caroline Street. The light was green, but Mandy had to wait for oncoming traffic to clear.

"I was hoping they'd patch things up while in Toronto," Mandy continued as they picked up speed. "My dad's away a lot for work. I think they both get lonely and, well, things happen, you know."

If Mandy suspected one, or both, of her parents seeking comfort beyond the marital bed, Fenn could relate. His grandmother had practically raised him due to an unstable environment at home. Still, he wasn't about to go there.

"Where does he work?"

"Ever heard of Kettle Studios? They make films and TV shows."

"Can't say I have. Is he a director or something?"

"A producer. He brings scripts home and talks a lot on the phone about money."

Fenn checked the dash clock. It was time to head back to granny's house.

"Do you know how to get to your grandmother's place from here?"

Mandy nodded. "Do you care which way I go?"

"Not as long as you keep heading north-east," Fenn said.

They passed a mall on Guelph Line. A small traveling carnival company was setting up some amusements in the parking lot: a modest Ferris wheel, a kiddie roller-coaster, a carousel with fiberglass replicas of wild animals, and a paddock for pony rides.

"Kids get so excited by those little fairs," observed Fenn.

Mandy smiled. "I still have a plastic bead bracelet that I won squirting water at a clown." She turned right onto Harvester Road. "Actually, my dad's company is filming a carnival scene in Hamilton this week."

"Will it be at Gore Park?"

"Yeah. How'd you know?"

"It's a popular spot for festivals. Close to downtown."

"They're doing a night shoot. Carnivals always look best at night with all the coloured lights."

Fenn had to agree. He'd often enjoyed the midway at the annual Canadian National Exhibition in Toronto. While somewhat shabby and sordid in the light of day, the hundreds of neon and incandescent bulbs energized the air with excitement after dark.

"Have you ever been to a shoot?"

"Couple of times. It's pretty interesting, though there's always a lot of waiting around. You've got to be quiet during a take, and be careful where you walk." She giggled. "My mom won't go on set anymore. She once wandered into the middle of a scene that took ages to stage. That was when my dad was still directing. He runs that clip every once in a while for friends, as a sort of joke, but mom still doesn't think it's funny. Should I take Walker's or Appleby Line?"

"Your call. Either one will get us there."

She went past Walker's Line and headed for Appleby.

"If you'd like to watch them film, my dad could put you on the guest list. They often need extras, so you might even get on screen."

"That sounds like fun. Could I bring my fiancée?"

"Don't see why not. I'll talk to pops and let you know."

A few minutes later Mandy signaled, steered into her grandmother's complex, and parked more or less centered in a spot reserved for visitors.

She shut the car off and turned to Fenn with a smile of accomplishment.

"When are we going out next?"

Fenn had his appointment book open. "Well, since we're both waiting for the school year to start, how about the same time in two days?"

"Okay, great! I really enjoy driving. I thought I'd be nervous, but you're an excellent teacher."

Fenn was as self-deprecating as they came but thanked her for the compliment. His day done he drove home and, with time to kill before Asha got off work, washed his Toyota in the driveway. Small car, small job, so after he ditched the dirty water he knocked on his landlady's door.

Muriel Stafford had once been Fenn's student. As sharp of mind and ready for adventure as any senior he'd met, she'd offered the apartment in her basement after Fenn's previous unit got trashed. She came to the door wearing a loose-fitting cotton shirt, and a pair of denim shorts hemmed just above her plump knees.

"Hi Muriel. I've got the hose and bucket out. If you like, I'll wash your car."

"That'd be lovely, Chas. Let me get my keys." She retreated inside but called back, "I've just made lemonade. Will you have some?"

Fenn accepted both the keys and the drink, then raised the garage door. Muriel owned a 1989 Dodge Dynasty that she'd driven more often since Fenn had discovered her lessons were more for companionship than for confidence. Confidence was never an issue. The woman had wrangled army trucks through war-torn France following the D-Day landing.

Fenn started the engine and rolled the mint-green sedan onto the driveway. He opened the hood and leaned on the fender to check for leaks or other problems. The 3-litre V-6 motor had ample power for getting groceries, although, he thought with a smile, if Muriel ever wanted more pep, he and Tony could turn it into a bona fide street racer.

CHAPTER 9

Heatherington didn't attend the next morning's whiteboard briefing, but the Superintendent's desire for a quick result seemed to linger in the room. Or perhaps it was the urgency of the first 48 hours, after which leads cooled off, that sharpened the team's focus.

Lareault began with what he and Bloomfield had learned at the morgue.

"The coroner thinks the victim may have enrolled in an archaeology course. McMaster University has one, so Sharin, why don't you circulate her picture there, and at any other local campus with such a program."

Detective Adabi made a small motion of acknowledgement.

"The vic's head wound was caused by a rock, possibly from the area she was excavating, though it was inflicted post-mortem. It appears she died from an overdose. The tox screen showed traces of cocaine laced with a fatal amount of fentanyl."

"That fentanyl's nasty stuff," said Roy Flock. "Vice has seen a real increase in circulation over the past couple of years, 'specially around Niagara Falls. Do we have a time of death?"

"The coroner figures midnight," replied Lareault. "Nine hours or so before the estate agent discovered her." He turned to the computer tech. "Any luck with the alarm system, Sunil?"

Naipaul tapped a key on his laptop to wake it up. "It's a basic off-the-shelf kit, so doesn't record which keypad was used. However, I managed to download a log file off the hub." He peered at the screen. "The evening before the body was discovered, the system was disarmed at 6:17 p.m. and re-armed at 8:06 p.m. That could have been the agent showing the place.

Anyway, it was next disarmed at 1:42 a.m., then re-armed once more at 1:51 a.m."

"It never took only nine minutes to clean that place out," said Flock.

Naipaul held up a finger. "It was disarmed again at 6:07 a.m., before being armed and disarmed at 9:36 a.m. There were other time stamps, after you guys had attended the scene, of course. By the way, I informed the homeowners they should change the code." He rapid-typed a keystring, and hit ENTER. "I've forwarded the log file to your workstations."

Lareault had jotted the times on the whiteboard as they were read out. He studied the sequence for a moment. "If we assert the burglars disarmed the system at the earlier 6:07 a.m. time, and we know the agent fumbled with it after that, it still leaves the intriguing question of—"

"—what happened between 1:42 and 1:51?" finished Flock.

"Exactly. Now, without jumping to the convenient conclusion, can we come up with other scenarios?"

Adabi poked her cheek lightly with the end of her pen. "Could a power fluctuation do that, Sunil?"

Naipaul shook his head. "The system would have recorded a switch over to back-up power. It didn't."

She tried again. "How about the agent, or one of the Rollands, came back to the house to pick up something they needed immediately, and didn't want to mention?"

"While that's possible," said Flock, "the time slot is a little odd."

"Let's keep that on the table. Though I think that whoever came in did so to drop something off. And the short timeframe fits the assumption the victim was killed elsewhere, and dropped off at the house." said Lareault.

He looked at Bloomfield like a coach assessing an athlete. "Would that be a one person or two-person job, Frank? Could you have carried that body down to the basement and reset the alarm within nine minutes?"

The big sergeant smiled at the question. "It would only take me that long if I stopped for a beer in the kitchen."

"Even if two people shared the load," said Flock, idly tilting his coffee cup, "I'm don't see the burglars as the killers. I mean, why come in at one-something to plant the vic, then come back five hours later to clean the place out? Nor do I think they dumped the corpse when they came at dawn. The way the rug was half unrolled suggests they went to the basement, discovered it, and promptly scarpered."

"I'm with you," said Lareault. "The Rollands are by default the common denominator, since both crimes culminated at their home. It's time we delved into their personal and professional connections, and worked up a financial picture. Discreetly, of course. We don't need any irate calls to the Superintendent about invasion of privacy."

"The real estate agent is also invested in the house in terms of making the sale," noted Adabi, "and seems to know the family well." She tucked back a loose strand of hair and scanned her pad. "As for connections, I enquired about tradespeople. They have landscapers, a cleaning service, and a pool service on contract." She ran a finger down the page. "They had a few rooms repainted back in June. Probably to prepare for the sale. Only the cleaners and the painter were given the alarm code. The cleaning service is a bonded company, and the painter is a set-builder at Kettle Studios where Mr. Rolland works."

"Let's take that a step further, Sharin. Get a list of clients from the cleaning company. See if any had break-ins. And check if the painter has any form."

"Okay, Boss."

"Get anything from the neighbours, Roy?"

Flock rolled his hand on the table so it was palm up. "Not really. A tractor-trailer snorting up a driveway in the middle of the night might attract attention. At six in the morning, not so much. And during rush hour, a moving truck leaving a house that's for sale could go unnoticed.

By the same token, a small van or large car could easily drop off a rug-wrapped corpse in the wee hours."

"So, nobody saw anything," summarized Lareault.

"None of the nearby residents, anyway. But just down the road is a water treatment station. For some reason it kept getting vandalized, graffiti and such, so surveillance cameras were installed. I've got the tapes for the past two days. I'm hoping they show the road. Might give us something."

"Good thought. Few large trucks travel that residential stretch of road. You could also try polling the sidewalk, in front of the house, between six and eight in the morning. Dog walkers and joggers are creatures of habit. A passer-by might remember seeing a trailer in the driveway."

"Sure thing. As long as I don't have to pooper-scoop or sprint after any of them. My running and bending isn't what it used to be."

"You and me, both, mate," agreed Bloomfield. "By the way, I've got Catrina Pailin's list of people who requested showings."

He handed a page to Lareault, who glanced at the four names and said, "You and I can start interviewing these today. Sunil, we'll have you assist Sharin with the cleaner's client tracing. Also, audit the financials of both the Rollands and Catrina Pailin—bank statements, credit cards—something might jump out."

The inspector paused in case anyone had something to add, then ended the meeting. He and Bloomfield surveyed Pailin's list as they walked to the sergeant's car. There were four names and addresses, all within an hour's drive of Burlington. They decided to start with the furthest afield: Howard and Joan Locke who lived in Port Credit, a suburb of Toronto.

The Lockes owned a nice bungalow in a mature neighbourhood. Joan, a wiry woman with gray hair and wire-rimmed glasses, was a retired schoolteacher. Howard, a good head taller than his wife, owned a metal fabricating business located in Mississauga. The scars on his hands attested to the years he'd spent building his business. Now he hoped to sell it and join his wife in retirement.

"I rarely do the tin-cutting, anymore. In fact, I only go in two or three days a week to make sure the guys and the bills are paid. The factory does a lot of custom work, high-spec stuff. We've got some good contracts, but I no longer have the desire for it. I've put in the time. Now Joan and I want to travel while we're still young enough to chase whales and explore castles."

"Our daughter lives in Burlington," added Joan Locke, sensing the policemen really wanted to know why they had booked a viewing with Catrina Pailin. "We thought it would be nice to be closer to our grandkids for babysitting and such."

"Did you put an offer in?" asked Lareault.

"No," replied Howard. "It was more of an exploratory thing to see what our budget would buy. Delightful house, but I think we can get more for less elsewhere in town."

Lareault showed them a head shot of the victim.

"Do you recognize this person?"

Neither of them did, so he thanked them for their time.

When they were back in the car, Bloomfield said, "You know what Arlene wants to do if I retire permanently?"

"What's that?"

"She wants to do one of those river cruises in Europe. You know, travel up the Rhine and visit the old buildings and vineyards. Howard's comment about castles reminded me."

Lareault could relate. He wouldn't mind chasing castles instead of criminals for a change. He'd squandered the opportunity with his ex-wife. There'd always been a case or some other reason. He wondered if he and Koki Motungi would find the time to just enjoy life. Then again, time isn't something one finds, he thought. It was either created within or chiseled out of a daily life.

"Where next, Boss?"

Lareault brought his attention back to the list. Devika Sumra lived in Oakville, halfway between Port Credit and Burlington. He checked his watch. Almost noon.

"Let's see if Ms. Sumra is available." He tapped in the phone number and put the cellphone to his ear.

"Hello. Ms. Sumra? This is Detective Inspector Lareault with the Halton Regional Police Service….Yes, the police service. We're investigating an incident at a house you recently viewed with realtor, Catrina Pailin. Could we come by and ask some questions? It would only take a few minutes." Lareault listened for a moment, then said, "421 Spears Road. Right, we'll be there in twenty minutes."

He ended the call. "She's at work. Weiss Windows and Doors."

"421 Spears Road," confirmed Bloomfield as he put the car in gear.

Devika Sumra was an attractive woman of Indian or Pakistani descent, in her late twenties. Her work attire this day was a short linen jacket and slightly flared pants, both black, over a ruffled white shirt and fashionable sandals. Straight hair, as dark and shiny as coal, fell about her shoulders and framed an oval face.

She greeted them as if they were potential clients.

"Let's talk in my office," she said, and led them through the showroom of window and door displays.

"Thanks for seeing us on your lunch hour," said Lareault.

"That's okay," she replied. "I usually eat at my desk, anyway. What can I do for you?"

"It's about your viewing appointment at the house on Lakeshore Road in Burlington. It was the scene of some criminal activity, so we're looking for help from anyone recently on the premises. Can you tell us when you were there?"

"It was last Friday. We're only open until noon, Friday's, so I went in the afternoon."

"It's quite a large house," said Lareault. "Do you have a family?"

Sumra indicated no, with a slender hand. "I was checking the place out for my uncle and his family. He and my father own an import business. My uncle ships from Mangalore, in India. My father runs the distribution centre in Mississauga. Anyway, my uncle wants to retire and live in Canada."

"Do you think he will buy the house?"

A little head bob. "He said he wanted a water view, then decided he'd rather be closer to my parents, who live just above Toronto, in Vaughan."

She didn't recognize the victim from the picture Lareault showed her, so he gave her his card and thanked her for her time. She walked the two policemen to the door.

"If her family has a thriving business importing goods from India," Lareault said as he dropped his jacket into the back seat of the car, "why would she not work for them, rather than a window and door place?"

Bloomfield put his foot on the brake and turned the ignition key. "She seemed pretty independent, to me. You know how families can be." He put the car in gear, then said, "Fancy some lunch before we do the other two?"

"You know, I've suddenly got a taste for something spicy, and there's a pretty good curry place just down the street."

"Right or left."

"Left."

Devika Sumra watched the dark sedan drive out of the parking lot, then went back to her office and closed the door. She dialed a number from memory and listened to the phone ring. An answering machine kicked in almost immediately. It gave a long beep.

"Thought you should know the police were just here, asking about the Rollands' house. What the hell? How did they get my name? I don't think we should wait on this one. We need to wrap it up. Call me back."

Biting lightly on her top lip, Devika sat back and waited for a return call. When the phone stayed silent, she reached for the thermos containing her lunch. The soup was hot and flavourful: however, after a few sips she again reached for the phone. She dialed another number and a man's voice answered.

"You got me."

"Devon, it's Devika. What the fuck happened? The police are all over this job."

She began to doodle words on a pad while she listened. She'd almost finished writing *corpse* when she realized what she'd heard.

"In a rug? What the fuck?" She thought for a moment. "Alright, I'm going to give you an address. I want you to bring the safe and meet me there."

CHAPTER 10

The expansive view over Lake Ontario drew the eye away from the small size of Lareault's condo kitchen. Koki Motungi sat at the counter, the palm of one hand laying flat on the polished quartz surface and the long fingers of the other caressing the delicate stem of a crystal wineglass. Her gaze alternated between the waves breaking on the granite blocks below, and her host as he first stirred a pot of linguine, then grated Parmesan cheese over a Caesar salad.

"Sure you don't want any help, Evan?"

"Well, I do seem to be completely surrounded by no wine."

"Oh my! A code-three. I'll get right on it." Koki slid off her stool and retrieved a half empty bottle of Pinot Grigio from the refrigerator. She refilled Lareault's glass and leaned over his shoulder. "That's starting to smell really good." She kissed his neck and went back to her perch.

"The clams just need to simmer a couple more minutes, then we can eat." Lareault adjusted the heat under the pans. He handed the salad bowl to his guest who reached back with a slender arm and put it on the table.

Their agreement to not discuss work while off duty had lasted for maybe three dates. It had evolved into waiting until after the first drink, which they'd now had, so Koki said, "Did you have time to read my report?"

Lareault poured some extra virgin olive oil and balsamic vinegar into a small mason jar.

"I always have time for your reports. Let's see, around the house you found fingerprints belonging to the Rollands, Catrina Pailin, and three unidentified people. None from the victim." He added a little salt, pepper, and mustard powder to the jar.

"One set, limited to the freshly painted rooms, you propose belonged to the painter. Samples of the other sets, found sporadically throughout the home, likely were those of the cleaning service." Screwing a lid onto the jar, he shook it vigorously. "How am I doing so far?" He poured the salad dressing into a cruet.

"Apart from the keypad, I didn't bother to mention smudged prints. Those may have been from the burglar's gloves smearing pre-existing marks." She took the cruet and put it beside the salad.

"No, but you did state the gloves weren't the cheap latex kind that leave powder everywhere."

"They weren't complete amateurs."

"Exactly. The key code, transport truck, the timing all took forethought and organization."

Lareault strained the linguine noodles, divided it onto two plates, ladled clam-laden sauce onto each, and sprinkled a little parsley over the top for colour.

"I think we're ready." He carried the steaming dishes to the table.

"Looks mah'velous, dah'ling. Cheers."

They clinked glasses, filled their bowls with salad, and dug in. Of a like mind, neither spoke, preferring to savour the food and let the light-rock station on the radio fill the gap in conversation.

"Best meal I've had today," said Koki, as she dabbed her lips with a napkin.

"High praise, indeed. What was lunch—a hotdog?"

"I wish. All I had time for was a packet of crisps."

"A packet of crisps? Where were you, a pub in London?"

Koki, careful not to spill her wine, laughed. "We called them crisps in Kenya. Must be the British influence. I must remember they are po-tay-toe chips."

"Not to be confused with french fries. Unless you're having fish and chips."

"So you eat crisps with fish?"

"No, fries."

"This is nice wine."

"It is, isn't it."

"So, the bit about the rug."

"Right, yes, the rug. Your report said the rug was quite new. Machine-made from polyester. Not a genuine Persian rug. But since Beth Rolland told us that, why did we need to call you in?"

"Because she couldn't tell you the blood was only from contact with the vic's wound, not from bleeding out. Unless Beth did the deed, in which case she might be able to explain the breadcrumbs and oyster juice."

Koki left the table to get the wine bottle from the fridge. Lareault took the opportunity to admire the fit of her skinny jeans.

"Since Dennis said cause of death was a drug overdose, the head wound could have been from the vic collapsing and bashing her skull on a rock. Or, it was an attempt by someone to cover up the cause of death?"

Lareault was skeptical. "I don't see that. Poisoning is a subtle way to kill. Why try to cover that with something obvious, like a blow to the head?"

"Because drugs, though less obvious, can often be traced back to their source. A rock is a lot more random. Anyone can pick one up from anywhere. Dennis said the rock would have been fairly small, so I doubt that just falling on it would be fatal. And," she held up a finger to prevent Lareault interrupting. "Since there was no evidence of gravel or soil on the underside of the rug, we can also assume they at least rolled her up indoors."

"Okay," said Lareault. "Two things. First, let's say the vic wasn't alone when she started to OD. Why didn't her companion call 9-1-1? And, second, if that same person also supplied the drug, then it'll be involuntary manslaughter at the very minimum. Hitting her with a rock, after the fact, is likely an attempt to disguise the true cause of death. In my books that crosses into homicide territory. What I'd really like to know is where the rug came from. That would at least tell us where she died."

"The label said it was made in Turkey. I'll start tracking down distributors to find out where it was sold. As for where the body got rolled up, I'd say it was inside a building. One with little foot traffic, as there were no obvious wear patterns. The rug had been vacuumed after it was laid down, and before the bread and oysters."

"What about the hairs you found?"

"We found a few brunette strands from the vic, of course. A couple of shortish gray hairs, male, and two longer gray ones that had been coloured blonde. So, an older female."

She half filled their glasses with the rest of the bottle.

"Got any more nectar?"

"Should be another one in the crisper."

Koki smirked and returned to the fridge. "The crisper—why not? You never have veggies in here."

"Wine is made from grapes. Aren't grapes veggies?"

"No, they're fruit."

"Close enough. Want me to open that?"

"Pretty sure I can twist the cap off."

Koki topped them up from the fresh bottle

"After I wrote the report, I tried again to lift prints off the carpet's backing label, and the vic's clothes. Hard at the best of times, and I got nothing definitive to determine gender of either who killed her, or even rolled her up."

When Lareault just nodded pensively and started gathering the plates, she said, "So what's for afters?"

"Afters?"

"You know, something sweet after the main course."

Lareault gave her a crooked smile. "You're something sweet."

She grinned over the rim of her glass. *"The soul of sweet delight can never be defiled'."*

"Never?"

"Not according to the poet, William Blake."

"Mind if I try?"

"I was actually hoping you would."

CHAPTER 11

When Sharin Adabi was in university, the bars were smoky as hell. Sometimes it was from weed, which she didn't mind so much, but fifteen years later she was glad of the ban. She hadn't smoked or been much of a drinker, even in those heady days of newfound freedoms, and was less inclined to now, particularly when working. Wanting to make the others feel at ease, however, she nursed a gin and tonic while Professor Sandra Robbins introduced her to a small gathering of students and members of McMaster's faculty.

They sat around two small tables pushed together, in a trendy little place on Leland Street called The Brown Mouse. The mood was subdued, since all had known the deceased. Once the detective had found her way to the registrar's office at McMaster University, it hadn't taken long to connect with Sandra Robbins, who taught one of the anthropology courses. Robbins had identified the woman in the photograph as Pamela Hovarth, and offered to gather a few people who had known her.

When talking to friends, family, or associates of a murder victim, Adabi always felt awkward in that she could only ask questions, and not answer theirs.

"I'm sorry," she said. "While the investigation is ongoing, we can't release any information."

What she could impart—that they had found the body of their colleague in the basement of a house—had already been reported by the press. However, these were intelligent people who could read between the lines.

The detective had her notepad on the table beside her barely touched drink. "I understand the graduate anthropology course is quite a wide-ranging field. Did Pamela have a particular interest?"

"The upcoming term was to be her last as a graduate student at Mac," said Robbins. "She really liked the archaeological aspects. I'm sure Graham can tell you more about that."

Graham Ford had a ruddy complexion and thinning white hair. The hands wrapped around his pint glass were rough, the knuckles dry and cracked.

"Oh aye," he said. "Not all the kids can handle kneeling in mud, hunched over and scraping away at dirt all day. Pam loved it. She'd be there until it was too dark to see anything. She'd actually found her own little dig this summer. Told me she was going to make it her thesis."

"And where was this?"

"North of Burlington. Do you know where Rattlesnake Point is?"

Adabi nodded.

"Close to there. An ancient settlement of the Wendat Peoples was not far away, at Crawford Lake. There's actually some reconstructed longhouses, now, that are worth a visit. Pam had an idea that the bluff might have been used for hunting. She thought she might find evidence of temporary camps, but she actually uncovered a burial site."

"How interesting."

Ford supped some of his beer. "The really interesting thing was that the remains were those of Europeans, not the local natives. Not totally surprising. Europeans arrived in numbers starting in the sixteen hundreds. Traders, prospectors, clergymen. Pam's appeared to have been Jesuits."

"Missionaries?"

"It was a nice find. A pair laid out, side by side. One was wrapped in the remains of a blanket, the other was found with fragments of a priest's hassock and a silver crucifix."

Adabi didn't need to be a detective to be curious. "What were they doing there? Was it an old churchyard?"

"From what we know of the early Jesuit incursions, we think they were trying to convert the Wendats at Crawford Lake. They were usually ferried in by coureurs-de-bois, who were expanding the fur trade. The priest found in the blanket was missing its thumbs, a suggestion of torture which happened often. Can't say I blame the locals, considering what the church and government institutions would later do.

"Anyway, far as we can tell, there wasn't an actual Jesuit mission in the area. In fact, the Wendat's settlement was burned to the ground around the same time. Back then, the Iroquois often made raids on other tribes. Not a safe time for native or missionary to be wandering around the area, so we don't know if both men died at the same time, or separately from different causes. Either way, somebody had to bury them, and we doubt the pall bearers were indigenous."

The coroner's photo of Pam Hovarth wasn't the only one Adabi had brought.

"What can you tell me about this?" She produced a photo of the skull found with the body.

"That's from one of the skeletons she found," said Robbins. "Did she have it with her?"

Adabi nodded.

"She probably wanted to show a girlfriend." This was from Corey Schumacher, a fellow student. Corey had a boy's haircut, short at the back and parted on one side. She wore faded jeans, black high-top running shoes and a camo-pattern t-shirt. Around her neck was a thin leather thong with a single wooden bead.

"And who would that be?" Adabi hadn't been recording anything, but she had her pen ready.

"Pam and I weren't that close. I just know she preferred chicks to guys."

Adabi looked at the others. "Anyone know who she was involved with?"

None did. They only knew that Pam Hovarth was from Tiverton, and had kept her residence in Hamilton throughout the summer so she could work on the burial site.

"The registrar's office can give you both addresses," said Robbins

"What kind of person was she? Outgoing? Shy? Did she drink, smoke, take drugs?" Adabi focused on the students for those answers. There were two girls and a guy. They glanced at each other but stayed silent.

"Look, she can't get in trouble now, so if you know anything…"

"She wasn't averse to taking a toke," offered Corey. "And I once saw her do some coke at a party."

"Yeah, but it wouldn't have been hers," put in one of the girls. "Who has that kind of money when you're in school? She had a part-time job, though."

"Oh, where?"

"She worked some afternoons and weekends at the Joseph Brant Museum in Burlington. It wouldn't have paid much, though. Mostly volunteers, there."

Adabi wrote that down.

"If her dig was out in the country, I imagine she had a car."

"A Ford Escort, I think," said Corey.

"Do you know the colour?"

"Blue? Sorry."

"Don't worry about it. I'll get that from the Ministry of Transportation."

Graham Ford drained the last of his beer. "Any idea when the funeral will be?"

Adabi gave a sympathetic smile. "As soon as I know I'll get word to Professor Robbins, and she can let you know." She gave her card to each of them. "If you think of anything else that might help us, please call me."

Adabi had parked on the street. As she hit the UNLOCK button on her keyfob, she heard someone behind her say, "Can I tell you something?"

It was Cory Schumacher. Adabi waited for her to catch up. Schumacher glanced behind her, but the rest had gone toward the university.

"I didn't want to mention this in there because it's really none of their business, nor mine, really. We all have to live our own lives, you know, and there was a side of Pam that she sort of kept under wraps."

Adabi motioned they should walk and talk. "I'll keep it as confidential as I can," she said. "What do you know?"

"Pam was rather a loner, but I saw her a few times down at the Nook."

"Nook?"

"Cranny's Nook. It's in Hess Village. Popular with the LBGTQ crowd. Ever been?"

Adabi went for tact over truth. "I'm pretty new to the area."

"It's popular with some lady cops, but maybe not your scene."

"You mentioned in the bar that Pam preferred her own gender. Was there something else?"

"Well, I don't know how Pam looked when you found her, but she cleaned up pretty nice. Her persona at the Nook was what you'd call a lipstick lesbian: nice hair, nice makeup, sexy dress, and flirty."

"Flirty. So she didn't come with anyone in particular?"

"Both times I saw her, she was already there, but I'd say she was cruising. And both times, she left before closing time with someone different."

"Do you know the people she left with?"

Schumacher shook her head. "No, but they were both old, like probably in their forties. If you ask me, I'd say our Pam was a bit of a rent-girl."

CHAPTER 12

The birds had been active since dawn, chirping and flitting around. Birds did that. What Roy Flock couldn't fathom was why people would want to jog before the sun came up. Stationed at the end of the Rollands' driveway with coffee and cigarette in hand, he'd intercepted first a man, then a woman, between five-thirty and six. Hell, it was barely light out.

Both had the gear. The male wore Lycra mid-thigh shorts, a skin-tight matching shirt that showed off his ribs, pecs, and biceps, and the latest design in running shoes.

Flock stood casually in his path with a hand up and said, "Excuse me, sir. Police business."

The man stopped, pushed a button on a rugged-looking wristwatch, and replied brusquely, "What do you want?" He shifted his weight from foot to foot in a subtle protest at the imposition.

"Sorry to interrupt your run. We're looking for anyone who might have seen a large truck at this house two mornings ago."

Hands now on his hips, the man arched his back while he thought about it.

"Today's Thursday, so that'd be Tuesday." He shook his head. "'Fraid I can't help you. I was on my way to Toronto for an early meeting at our head office."

Flock thanked him and turned his attention to a young woman approaching quickly from the other way. Showing excellent form, each foot landing lightly on the balls of her feet, she too had dressed to impress. Instead of Lycra, she had gone with high-cut silk shorts and a pink cotton top. A white baseball cap, with her ponytail through the back strap, kept the hair in place.

Like the guy, she glanced at her watch when stopped but didn't push any buttons.

"Tuesday? I can't say I noticed anything. When I run, I just look ahead and concentrate on my breathing. Sorry."

"Appreciate you stopping. Have a good day." Putting the cigarette back between his lips, Flock watched the silk shorts sway until they crossed the road and went up a side street.

Traffic got more frequent as the sun rose, and he wondered if any of the drivers might have seen something. It would take an organized roadblock to answer that question. A little early in the investigation for Heatherington to budget that sort of manpower.

Getting on for seven-thirty, an elderly gent with a little long-haired dog came by. Both the senior and his pet seemed friendly. Flock said, "Is that a Shih-tzu?"

"Lhasa-Apso. This is Alfie. Say 'hello', Alfie."

Also a senior, Alfie wagged his tail obligingly and sniffed Flock's hand.

The detective ruffled the dog's ears, then straightened up and said, "I'm with the Halton Police Service. We're hoping someone may have seen a truck at this house on Tuesday morning."

The old guy peered down the driveway. "Tuesday? The memory's not so good anymore, but I think I did. I remember saying to Alf they must have sold the place because it looked like they were moving out."

"They? So you saw someone moving furniture?"

"Well, only briefly. Two guys carrying a sofa."

"What did they look like?"

The senior shook his head. "It's not only my memory that's bad. Eyes are not so good, either. Like I said, only caught a glimpse and they were down by the house. Could even have been two women, but I think they were men."

"That's okay, sir. This is good information. Do you know what time you would have seen them?"

"Oh, sure. About same as now. Alfie always gets his breakfast at seven, then we come out for a walk."

Flock checked his watch and made a note. Then he held out his hand. "My name's Roy, by the way. What's yours?"

"Johnson. James Johnson. Would you like my phone number in case you have more questions?"

"That's very kind. Thank you, James."

Flock took down the number, then said, "Can you tell me anything about the truck?"

"It were a big'un. Tractor trailer. White. Black fenders. Squarish front end." He chuckled. "If I'da known, I'd have tried for the plate number."

"Not to worry, James. You and Alfie have really helped me out today."

About an hour after Flock bade farewell to Mr. Johnson, Fenn got pretty much the same information. He had a call from Brenda Woodhill.

"Hey, Chas. Joe Posada said you were looking for the truck that was at your student's house. I think I saw it backing in, though I was really watching the cute guy directing traffic."

In her late fifties, Brenda liked to say she was old enough to know better, but young enough to still do it.

"Since we're low on clients, I've taken to volunteering at a rescue shelter," she said. "I help feed the animals and take the dogs for a walk. It gets me up and gives me some exercise."

"And you drove past Mandy Rolland's house," Fenn prompted.

"Lakeshore Road, right? That Mediterranean-style place on the lake side."

Driving instructors spend all day, most days, driving the same streets. They know the scenery intimately.

"That's the one. What did you see, Brenda?"

"The guy was in his mid-twenties, brown hair, friendly smile. Wore a Blue Jays cap."

"And, the truck?"

Brenda giggled. "Oh, very well. The truck was a Freightliner. Not new, but not old. White with black fenders and some black numbers on the doors."

"Numbers?"

"You know, like when a business registers as a numbered company."

"Good way to stay anonymous," observed Fenn.

"I suppose. And it had a chrome sun visor over the windshield."

"What about the driver?"

"Sorry. Couldn't see him for the glare off the glass."

"So, what time was this?"

"Had to be about six'ish. If I get to the shelter for six-thirty, I can give them an hour before my first lesson of the day."

"You've a kind heart, Brenda. Did Joe tell you there was a body in the basement?"

"Yeah, and I heard on the news the cops are calling it a suspicious death. How's your student handling it?"

"Fairly well. Apparently not anyone she knows."

"Could the cute guy have been the killer?"

"No idea, but I think you need to pass this information on to the police."

Fenn couldn't see Brenda grimace, but he heard it in her voice.

"Can't you tell them, Chas?"

"I could, but they'll probably want you to describe the guy for a sketch artist."

An audible sigh. "Okay, if I have to."

"Tell you what. Dieter wants to suck-up to some police superintendent. I'll tell him what you told me, and he can pass it on. If you have to talk to the cops and want some company, just give me a call."

"Alright. Bye, Chas."

Brenda hung up, and Fenn cradled the handset. He glanced at the kitchen clock. Asha had left for work and should be arriving at the office. He doubted Dieter would even be out of bed, but he had the Lundsen's home number and thought, what the hell.

Three rings and a female voice said, "Hello?"

"Hi Carole. It's Chas. Is Dieter there?"

"He's in the shower, Chas."

Even better.

"Okay, well, could you tell him I've got some details on the Rolland case. I'll be heading out in a few minutes, so he should call me on my cell."

"I'll let him know." It was a control thing with Carole that she had to hang up first. Fenn smiled.

"Want to bet the phone rings within the next minute," he said to Mogg. Sprawled on a mat near the sink, the cat briefly paused licking her long gray fur, then went back to grooming.

The second hand swept past forty, forty-five, fifty seconds.

The phone chimed.

"I win," he said to Mogg, and picked up just before the answering machine kicked in.

"Good morning, Dieter."

"Hi Chas. Carole said you knew something about the Rolland case."

Fenn grinned, envisioning his boss with a damp towel, dripping hair, and water puddled around his feet.

"Uh, yeah. What was it? Oh, Brenda Woodhill saw a truck backing into the Rollands' driveway, and got a pretty good look at one of the alleged burglars."

"And?"

"And what? That's all she saw."

"Well, did she say what the guy looked like?"

"He was cute."

"Cute? That's it?"

"That's Brenda." Fenn stifled a laugh.

"Was the truck cute, too?"

"It was a Freightliner. Black fenders and a chrome sun visor. Black numbers on the doors. If you want to know more, you'll have to talk to Brenda."

"I will. But why did she call you and not me?"

"Mandy's my student. Anyway, do you want to pass this on, or should I call the cop shop?"

"Let me handle this. My good friend, Superintendent Heatherington, will be most interested."

In Dieter's case, it was excitement that made him start to hang up.

"Maybe towel off first," said Fenn.

Dieter put the phone back to his ear. "What was that?"

"I said, 'you're welcome'."

"Oh, right. Thanks, Chas."

CHAPTER 13

For all their flamboyance, the big house, flash cars, and antique chairs, the Rollands had really scrimped on security. More money than brains, thought Devika Sumra as she shrugged on a baggy pair of coveralls. It was an expression of her father's. The wall safe sitting on her workbench, like their DIY alarm system, was a testament to that. The casing, though fire resistant, was simply stainless steel and not hardened alloy. Sumra tapped it lightly with a small pry bar, then pushed it around on the bench to look at the back. About the size of a small microwave oven, the safe had some weight to it. Within the steel frame would be a cheap concrete liner to help fireproof the box and give an impression of robustness.

The back had little more to offer than poorly welded seams and a manufacturer's label. Made in China. No surprise, there. Granted, any strongbox could be broken into. The purpose was to discourage or at least delay the burglar as long as possible, but all this cheap unit had really done was impress the buyer.

Though the workshop had no shortage of tools to hack through the casing, her favourite was the cutting torch. It could slice a hinge off in seconds, and there was something about donning the welder's helmet and heavy leather gloves that made her feel like a dude. A dude with a blowtorch.

She wheeled a cart with oxygen and acetylene tanks over to the bench, and was about to spark the torch when the shop door opened. With the welder's mask still propped on top of her head, she smiled and said, "Couldn't stay away, huh?"

The visitor closed the door. "Looks like I'm just in time. What have we got?"

Sumra put down the torch and removed her helmet. She beckoned.
"The answer to that will cost you."
A husky laugh. "Oh, I do love a woman wearing canvas."
The kiss was long and deep. Devika felt the zipper of the coveralls being pulled down. When it got below her navel, a hand slipped inside and then snuck below the waistband of her slacks. Opening her stance, she gasped softly when first one, then two fingers entered her. She reached up to grasp her partner's head with both hands, but as the climax grew near, the fingers withdrew. She moaned in disappointment.

"Hey, don't stop. That was just getting good."

"Sorry, my love." The fingers stroked their moisture across her lips. "If I go further, we'll end up on the floor, and I've only got ten minutes."

"You're such a fucking tease."

"Here." A small plastic pouch containing a few grams of white powder was dropped on top of the safe. "This should keep you purring until I get back. I won't be long."

Sumra licked her lips and looked at the pouch.

"You'd better be quick. You know what that stuff does to me." She slid a hand inside her coveralls and leaned forward. "I might decide I don't need you."

Her lover laughed. "I'll hurry back."

"Your choice, but if the door's locked don't bother knocking."

The latch clicked. Devika continued to stroke herself, then thought it would be better with a little snort. Or two. The safe was good for one thing, at least. It had a smooth top for forming the powder into lines.

Her wallet had the obligatory credit card but lacked anything she could roll into a tube. She remembered the soft-drink cup she'd tossed in the trash can. It had a straw. Perfect.

The rush drenched her like a champagne shower, and she thrust her hand back into her crotch. This was fucking good stuff. Electrified, she began to shed the coveralls for more freedom when her stomach unexpectedly lurched and bile rose in her throat. The next spasm made her look for the trash can in case she had to puke. Something was wrong.

A sudden lethargy made her grip the workbench for support. The room began to spin, and her legs felt like they would give way. She sank to the floor before she fell to it, and rolled onto her back. Her limbs were now very weak. From where she lay, the welding tanks looked like twin towers.

Oxygen, she thought, now gasping like a fish out of water.

I need air.

The fire crew were stowing their hoses when Bloomfield pulled into the lot. He parked beside an ambulance, and he and Lareault surveyed the scene. The charred smell of the burned-out workshop hung in the humid air, and a shallow ash-laden stream ran toward the gutter. The coroner was already on site, clad in the standard white coveralls with hood and booties. He beckoned from the door of the shop.

"Do you think that if I had a Jaguar, like Dennis, I could beat him to a crime scene, just once?"

"Doubt it," replied Bloomfield. "We're always the last to be called in."

Dennis Collier wasn't normally one to direct foot traffic, but he'd been around long enough to know how Lareault worked.

"Apparently, the fellow over there has some information that might be useful, Frank," he said to Bloomfield, indicating a middle-aged man standing by the entrance to the adjacent unit. "Evan, the body's already in the ambulance, but first I've got something else that might interest you."

Collier led the inspector into the workshop. Mainly a cinderblock construction, the fire had been confined to the interior of the unit and, by the look of things, mainly along one wall where there was a steel workbench, a set of welding tanks, and a welder's helmet.

"That face shield was on the vic," said Collier, by way of explanation. "The first responders got her out but couldn't revive her."

The Fire Marshall, who'd been peering at something on the bench, turned as they approached.

"Hi Evan," he said.

"Hi Paul. That looks like a safe."

Paul Kuchar stepped back a pace to let the inspector get closer. "From what I can tell, and don't hold me to this, the deceased was attempting to slice it open with that cutting torch." He pointed at the brass nozzle on the end of twin hoses running to the welding tanks. "Something happened, and the torch set fire to the shop."

Lareault glanced at Collier, who said, "Our victim apparently didn't have the combination. Didn't the Rollands have their safe stolen this week?"

Lareault took stock of the space. There were assorted fixtures that a plumber might have, plus lengths of pipe: copper, ABS, galvanized steel. Other than that, it had been a tidy space before the fire.

"Let's have a look at the vic, Dennis."

Leaving the Fire Marshal to his own investigation, Lareault and Collier went to the ambulance. The paramedics stood to one side, chatting to a couple of smoke-eaters. The body was on a collapsible gurney, locked into place within the transport.

The coveralls were unzipped to the navel and the blouse unbuttoned. Lareault wondered if the paramedics had used a defibrillator in their attempt at resuscitation. The victim's dark complexion had lost its glow and a white crusty streak ran down her cheek from the corner of her slack jaw. Although the long black hair was now in a ponytail, and the plum lipstick had smeared, the inspector recognized the woman in the welder's garb.

He straightened up and said, "Devika Sumra."

"You know her?"

"We interviewed her yesterday. She viewed the Rollands' house, ostensibly with a view to buying it."

"Looks like she went to cherry-pick instead."

"The Rollands will need to identify the safe, but, yeah, pretty much."

"Was this her workshop?"

"That I don't know, Dennis. She worked for a window installation company."

"Did they do the windows at the Rollands' house?"

"Worth looking into."

Collier nodded and peeled off his nitrile gloves. "The sooner I get her to the morgue, the sooner you'll know what killed her."

"Fair enough. Let me know when you've got something."

Lareault stepped down from the rear of the ambulance and waved his thanks to the medics for their patience. Inside the shop, the Fire Marshall said, "Check this out." He slid his pen into the mouth of a liter can to stand it upright.

"This had turpentine in it. And now it hasn't."

"Arson?"

"Or extreme carelessness. My crew found the deceased lying prone by the bench, the torch-cutter still lit. It would appear that she collapsed and the torch then set fire to nearby boxes and the rest, as they say."

Kuchar pointed to the floor below the soot-blackened can on the workbench. "That scorch mark, however, runs directly to where the torch was found."

"Funny how that happens," said Lareault. "The can gets knocked over and drains down to the floor to where a burning torch just happens to be."

"So, what are we calling it?" This from Sergeant Bloomfield who had just come into the shop.

Lareault looked to the Fire Marshall who nodded.

"Paul's calling it arson, which means we're investigating a cover-up."

"So, murder, then."

"Let's say manslaughter, arson, and indignities to a corpse, at the very least."

"Do we know who the victim was?"

"Devika Sumra."

"No shit."

"Do you think that safe belongs to the Rollands?"

"Tell you in a sec." Bloomfield flipped back a few pages in his notebook. He stepped closer to the workbench and poked at the safe's keypad with his pen.

"Paul, you've got gloves on. Do you mind?"

Kuchar reached over, turned the latch, and pulled open the strongbox door.

They all peered inside, and there was plenty to look at, but they knew better than to handle anything.

"Right, Frank," said the inspector. "Have the talcum squad catalogue and bag everything, then I think we'll go visit the Rollands."

CHAPTER 14

Gore Park, in the heart of Hamilton, was a green expanse of mostly flattened grass. Large enough for fairs and concerts, it was now host to the carnival scene of a film shoot. The array of spotlights that allowed the technicians to do their thing at night had the grounds lit up like a sports stadium. A stationary patrol car, its red and blues silently flashing, partially blocked the access road for a young woman in a reflective vest who screened incomers by checking names on a clipboard.

"Cash, right?" she said.

"That's right," Fenn replied, having been told by Mandy that a 'Cash' extra was one who could be hired as needed once the quota of unionized actors had been filled.

The woman put a checkmark on her list and steered Fenn toward a sign that said FILM SHOOT PARKING.

"Gore is not a very nice name for park," observed Asha. "Was it named after someone?"

"Nope. A gore is a triangular piece of land, just like this park."

"Aren't you full of trivial information."

"A student told me that. Funny what you learn when teaching people to drive."

Fenn followed the direction of another attendant, this one with a green lightstick, and found a spot to park his car. Being a pleasant night, he'd driven the Challenger.

"Speaking of students, will Mandy be here?"

"I don't think so. She said she had something to do tonight, but I forget what."

The previous day, Mandy Rolland had informed Fenn that they could be extras if he wore a white t-shirt and jeans. It apparently didn't matter what Asha wore. The film was set in the fifties, and since few young women still wore poodle skirts or saddle shoes, those items would be provided on set.

"We're here to be extras," he said to the guy with the lightstick.

"Go to that big white tent and ask for Terry."

The large white marquis that sat on the corner of the parking area anchored a row of trailers, beyond which the coloured lights of the midway illuminated the film set. Bright yellows, vibrant purples, fluorescent greens, amid flashes of white, strobed around a Ferris wheel while fairy lights, strung around the tops of booths, twinkled invitingly. Missing, though, was the lively carnival music that always enhanced the excitement in the air. Instead, an amplified voice called for an electrician to attend the west-side sound board.

The tent was a sort of staging area for the actors, most of whom, like Chas and Asha, were extras. Terry was a thin woman in a sleeveless top and loose-fitting cotton slacks. She gave them a once-over through black-rimmed glasses.

"Cash?"

They nodded.

"Fill out one of each form on that table, sign them, and then bring the papers to me."

They did as they were told, and Terry put the forms into a satchel. "Men are on the left side. See Brian," she said to Fenn. "Okay, sweetie. You go to the right and see Marie." She pointed over Asha's shoulder toward an older woman hanging a jacket on a long rack of clothing. "Ask her about a ribbon for your hair. I think a ponytail would be nice."

Fenn figured Brian was the small chap kneeling beside a tall shoe rack. He was handing sneakers to a dumpy-looking fellow. Seeing Fenn standing patiently, he said, "I'll be with you in a minute, Hon."

The sneakers appeared to fit, so Brian turned his attention to Fenn.

"You actually look pretty good—but," he beckoned Fenn to follow. "Do you smoke?"

"No. And I'd rather not."

"That's okay." From a trunk with several compartments, Brian produced a pack of Camels. "This is just a box. May I?" Deftly he rolled the pack into the short sleeve of Fenn's t-shirt. "Give us a flex. See if it falls out."

Fenn complied, and Brian laughed. "Good enough. Just take it easy and don't crush the box. I want it back." He knelt and turned up the bottom of Fenn's pant legs to make cuffs. "I doubt you'll need makeup, but let Scarlett put a little product in your hair—it'll keep her happy."

For sheer brilliance, the lights around the makeup mirrors gave the outside spots a run for their money. Fenn was ushered onto a tall-legged folding chair, and draped in a paper smock. Scarlett had neither red hair nor a ruddy complexion, sporting instead a shaved head and summer tan. She ran her fingers from the back of his neck over to his forehead.

"I'm just going to rub in some pomade, okay, darlin'?"

"Would that be Dapper Dan?"

"Wow, a Coen Brothers fan. I love it. Actually, this stuff is by Fuertes." She held up a small pail. "If you want a cut, later, I could give you a nice hip look."

Figuring he'd end up with a short back and sides, New Millennium style, Fenn simply said thanks when Scarlett released him from the chair.

"Break a leg, Handsome."

Between the makeup area and the carnival midway, a conglomeration of extras milled about. Fenn began to wander toward them when he spotted Asha coming out of the tent. He grinned. She had on bobby socks and saddle shoes, a poodle skirt with a poodle silhouette, and a letterman jacket that looked like it would fit Fenn, which was the whole point. A blue ribbon held her ponytail in place. A quick stop in the makeup chair saw a coat of bright red lipstick applied.

"What do you think?" she said, giving a twirl that made the skirt flair.

"Gee, doll. You's much too pretty for a hayseed like me."

"Oh, you big palooka, I'd kiss ya, but Scarlett might get mad."

"Actually, that's not a bad idea." This from a fellow wearing a canvas vest over a linen long-sleeved shirt. "Plunk a big smooch mark on his cheek. I'll get Scarlett to freshen you up."

To the delight of the assembled extras Asha, on tiptoe, planted a red lip imprint on Fenn's right cheek.

"Don't touch that—what's your name?"

"Chas."

"Looks great, Chas. And your girlfriend?"

"Asha—his fiancée, actually." Asha couldn't resist flashing her ring, as if Fenn had just asked her to go steady.

"Very nice. Okay, get touched up and get back here. We're almost ready to shoot."

Working his way through the assembly, the man walked toward the midway, causing the crowd to follow. He stepped up onto the platform of a carousel, for a little elevation.

"Okay, folks. We've just one night to get this scene in the can before the carnival caters to its real patrons tomorrow. We're on a tight schedule, so here's the plan. First, we want some filler footage we can splice in as needed, so disperse fairly evenly and enjoy the rides, booths, and the food—yes, it's all edible and free. You'll have twenty minutes. Then we'll shoot the dialogue."

He stepped off the carousel. "When you hear the music, that'll be your cue." He raised an arm and twirled a finger. The carnies went to their stations and within two minutes, the fair came to life with the motion of machinery, the calls of buskers, and the bustle of an excited crowd.

"Here's a tip," said the dumpy-looking fellow Fenn had seen in the tent. "Stay off the Ferris Wheel if you want to get on camera."

"Oh?" said Asha. "I love Ferris Wheels."

"Up to you, but once you're on, you probably won't be getting off. Just sayin'."

"Okay, good to know. Thanks."

"You're welcome. Love the skirt, by the way."

Asha giggled. "Have you done many of these?"

"A few. I'm trying to break in. Do you mind if we form a little group? I could be like the third wheel, otherwise I'm wandering around by myself. Not very convincing."

"Sure. You don't mind, Chas?"

"Not as long as we can wander by that pretzel stand."

Vincent turned out to be a pretty funny guy, and he encouraged them to tell each other jokes. "The director wants to see people laughing and energetic," he explained. "The nice thing about having three of us is that we can form a triangle, which means one of us will always be facing the camera. Hey, look at that!"

There was nothing to see but Vincent said, "Asha, grab your boyfriend's arm and pull him to where I just pointed - you're on camera."

Not sure where the camera was, Asha did as instructed while Vincent mimed exasperation, then followed. When he caught up, he said, "That might be our five seconds of fame, but it's better than nothing."

They tried their hand at a few of the games of skill: a ring toss, throwing darts at balloons, knocking coconuts off posts with baseballs. For some reason, the carnies seemed to give Asha more chances than Fenn, and she 'won' a stuffed plush panda. When they figured the twenty minutes was about up, Vincent suggested Fenn stop by the food booth as there'd probably be a wait while the crew set up the dialogue shots.

Perched on the edge of the carousel platform Fenn munched on his pretzel while Vincent ate a foot-long hot dog and Asha dipped into a bag of popcorn.

"Do us a favour, luv," said one of the crew as he walked past. "When you're done, toss the bag on the ground. Can't have a carnival without litter."

"I've got litter, too," said Vincent. "And so does he." He pointed at Fenn's paper-wrapped pretzel, then muttered, "Sexist swine."

"Hang around Asha long enough, and you'll get used to it," laughed Fenn.

"'Scuse me, buddy. Can I bum a smoke?" One of the carnies had approached and pointed at the pack of Camels rolled into Fenn's shirtsleeve.

"Sorry, pal, but it's a prop. Pack's empty."

"Fuckin' land of make-believe. Should you even be eating that?"

"Oh, yeah, the pretzel's real."

"Figures. Mind if I sit? It's been a hard day."

"It's your platform," said Fenn. "Been doing this long?"

"Over thirty years, for my sins. Family business." Whether the thin man in the greasy jeans and stained t-shirt was telling the truth, Fenn couldn't say, but he could tell the man's thirty years had not been easy.

"You must have seen a lot of changes," he said tactfully.

"Some. Rides are safer now, though maybe not as exciting. Nothing like having rickety pine boards splintering under your roller-coaster. Everything is more family-friendly—there's not quite the same thrill. No more burlesque, and the games are mostly honest these days."

"Mostly?" Asha offered her bag of popcorn, which was politely waved away.

"Take that ring toss game where you've got to get the plastic hoop over the prize, and the block it sits on. The carny shows you how easily the ring fits over the block, but then he slips you one that won't. Or the basketball game: the rim is angled so you don't notice it's not actually round. And the basket has a sprung bottom, so if the ball does go in, it gets bounced out."

"Hey, we played both those games," said Asha, playfully flicking a kernel of corn at their new acquaintance.

"The booths here are all kosher, although if you expect the cork-firing rifles to shoot straight, then you deserve to be fleeced."

There was a buzz from the PA system, then a voice said, "Two minutes. Run-through for scene 41."

"Here comes the chief with the king and queen," said Vincent, nodding toward a trio consisting of the canvas-vested production coordinator and a couple dressed in fifties garb.

Asha gave Fenn a nudge. "Hey, wasn't she in that TV show we watched last week?"

"Which one?"

"She was a Viking shield-maiden."

The trio appeared to be heading for their platform, so they vacated the spot.

"Right, folks, you know the drill," said the vest. "We'll have you do again what you did in the last few minutes, but this time without sound. ACTRA members only, now. Go find your mark and I'll move people as necessary."

Vincent gave Fenn a pat on the back. "Well, it was nice hanging with you guys."

Asha looked puzzled. "What's happening?"

"They're going to be doing some close-up shots of the two leads, and don't need so many extras. Since we're extra-extras, our night is done."

Asha smoothed down her poodle skirt. "Do you think we'll be in the final cut?"

Vincent shrugged. "You never know. Anyway, I gotta go. See you around."

87

As they left the midway, Fenn said, "Do you want to watch?"

"Maybe. Let me get changed first."

"Okay, I want to find the potties, anyway. Meet you right here in a few minutes."

Asha entered the costume tent and Fenn went in search of the portolets. There were about a dozen lined up in a blue row. They formed a wall that bordered the transport parking area. Out of interest, he wandered along the parked vehicles, most of which were tractor-trailers. Lit only with ambient light from the set on one side, and streetlights on the other, it appeared to be paved in shades ranging from dim to dark. Windscreens and chrome trim seemed to flicker as the midway strobed.

The alleyway was deserted, apart from a person who walked toward Fenn while talking on a cell phone. The closer she came, the more familiar she looked. Short of stature, raised somewhat by the cork soles of her sandals, straight blond hair in a shag cut, and a large purse hanging from one shoulder.

Rather odd to see her on a film set, after what Mandy had told him, he thought. And to find her in the truck corral, so late at night, was stranger still. The woman walked on past without so much as a glance his way, but by then Fenn had recognized her.

It was Mandy's mother.

CHAPTER 15

Fenn let Beth Rolland get a few paces past him, then he sidestepped between two tractor-trailers and peered around a fender to watch her progress. After a moment, he heard a truck door slam, and a man came to meet her. The newcomer was of average height, with a wiry build. He wore loose-fitting work clothes and a baseball cap. In the dim light it was hard to determine his age, though Fenn gauged he was on the far side of forty.

Taking care to move quietly, Fenn went to the rear of the vehicles, then along behind a couple until he felt he'd be close enough to hear the conversation. Moving up between the next rigs, he found himself within metres of the pair.

"Of course he doesn't know I'm here," the woman was saying. "And he doesn't need to know, so keep your trap shut if you see him."

Chancing a look over the truck's hood, Fenn saw the couple were standing close, but there was tension in their posture.

"Look, I don't have much time. Let's settle up the cash, then we'll deal with the other thing." Beth Rolland held out a hand.

Fenn didn't catch the man's response but caught the gist when Rolland said, "That's ridiculous. How in hell did Benny find out?"

"Doesn't matter. He did. Why the fuck was the body in your basement?"

"Why the fuck did you leave it there?"

The man cast a glance around. Beth Rolland held him in a stare.

"Tell me, what was I supposed to do with a dead chick in a Persian rug?"

"Not leave it in my house!"

They stopped talking when another voice called from the rear of the truck that concealed Fenn. "Hey! Is this your rig?"

A bright beam flashed in his eyes. Fenn made like he was pulling up the zipper on his jeans.

"Just taking a leak, man. I'm part of the shoot."

Fenn's inquisitor wore the uniform of a security guard.

"Really? There's toilets over there, you know."

"They were all occupied and I couldn't wait. Sorry if I alarmed you." Fenn had backed into the main corridor and was in sight of the woman and her companion. The trucker gave a little wave to the guard while Beth Rolland kept her back to them.

"I think I just heard my cue," said Fenn, turning back toward the big white tent. "Have a good night."

He strode away, shoulders hunched, hands in pockets in the best James Dean fashion, and entered the large canvas hall. After glancing back to make sure the guard hadn't followed, he pulled the cigarette pack from his sleeve. Brian was rearranging clothes on a rack.

"Looks like I'm done with this," said Fenn, placing the pack on top of Brian's prop trunk.

Brian gave a mock pout. "Sorry to hear that."

"They only gave me a small part."

Brian gave him an obvious once-over. "Honey, five minutes with me and it'll be a large part."

Fenn gave a genuine laugh. He hadn't been propositioned like that since college. The standard response, back then, had been 'thanks, but you're not my type', though the parties had been great. When the bars closed, a bohemian mix of gay and straight, students and teachers would often migrate to one of the large Victorian homes converted to residences. Fenn's smile at the memory encouraged the costumer.

"At least let me try," said Brian. "What's your type?"

Fenn saw Asha waiting outside the tent. He pointed. "She is."

"Story of my life," said Brian with an exaggerated sigh. "Always the bridesmaid. Run along then. Be happy. Don't worry about—not that rack, are you colour blind?" Brian's attention was now on one of the extras who was attempting to return a jacket.

"I thought you'd fallen in," said Asha when Fenn draped his arm across her shoulders.

"Mandy's mom is here."

"Did Mandy come?"

"I didn't see Mandy, just her mom."

"Did you speak to her?"

"No. I saw her in the truck corral. She met with one of the drivers."

"Okay." Asha wasn't sure where Fenn was going with this.

"They talked about the body that was in the Rollands' basement."

"Not so unusual. If I found a body in my basement, I'd tell some people."

"They were arguing about it."

"Ohhh."

"And Mrs. Rolland wanted money."

"For the body?"

"Shhh!" This was from one of the passing crew members who nodded toward the midway where it seemed a silent pantomime of people enjoying a fairground was being played out.

"Sorry," said Fenn quietly. He led Asha away from the tent. "Beth Rolland mentioned someone called Benny."

"Has Mandy ever mentioned Benny?"

"No, but I could ask her. Funny thing is, Mandy said her mom never came to shoots, anymore."

"And yet, here she is." Asha reached back and idly twirled the ponytail that still had the blue ribbon.

The best acting they did that night was as a couple casually wandering the outskirts of a carnival shoot. However, they saw neither Beth Rolland nor the man she'd been talking to. Their shot at stardom apparently over, they headed for the parking lot. Not one to pass up a good night for cruising, Fenn pushed a Springsteen cassette into the tape deck and aimed the Challenger toward downtown.

The heat absorbed throughout the day now radiated from the asphalt lanes and concrete walls. A hot wind blew through the open windows of the car and brought with it the sound of a city that had shucked its nine-to-five work clothes for jeans and running shoes. There was plenty of activity within the stores that were still open, and a different type of business in the doorways of those that were closed. Chas and Asha were at a red light, watching the impromptu street fair on King Street, when a shiny black Chevelle SS pulled up beside them. Like the Challenger's Hemi, its big-block motor rocked the car with a syncopated beat. The driver looked over with a friendly smile.

"Nice car," called Asha through the open window.

"You too," came the reply.

Side by side, the musclecars rumbled up the road, turning pedestrians' heads as the sound reverberated off the downtown canyon walls. At the next red light, the Chevelle driver called over.

"We're heading to the Tim's at Main and Dundas. There's usually something worth seeing, there. Want to come?"

Worth seeing meant restored or modified cars, but more importantly the invite was a chance to talk shop with other gearheads.

Fenn looked to Asha who nodded and called back, "Lead on, MacDuff!"

The light turned green and both drivers finessed the gas to reach the speed limit with only small chirps from the tires.

Close to a dozen vehicles were parked around the Tim Hortons coffee shop, half of them modified street racers. Asha went inside to buy drinks, and Fenn walked over to check out the cars and chat with the owners. While they discussed compression ratios, carburetors, and transmission kits, Asha handed Fenn an orange juice and wandered over to the small group of wives and girlfriends. A little after midnight, she wandered back.

"I'm getting tired."

He checked his watch. "Wow, it's tomorrow, already. Well, guys, have a great night. We'll catch you later."

As they buckled their seatbelts, he said, "Would you mind if we rolled past Gore Park before we head home?"

"Why?"

"A couple of reasons. I'm curious to know if they're still filming. And, if Mandy's mom was talking to the truck driver that emptied her house, then maybe the truck is there."

Asha, reclining, looked at Fenn. "Why would she arrange to have her own place burgled?"

Fenn shrugged. "Her family does own antique stores. What if it's an insurance scam?"

"How do you think of these things?"

"Devious mind, I guess."

"And you're hoping to see the truck leaving the film set?"

"Does that make sense to you? We know what it looks like."

Asha gazed at the bright interior of the coffee shop. Open twenty-three hours a day, and always customers inside.

"I think the odds are slim but drive past if you like. Just watch for paparazzi rushing out to take my picture."

"Maybe put your sunglasses on."

The carnival lights were still flashing when they got to the park. It appeared like they would be for a while, and no tractor-trailers were leaving the grounds. Fenn tried driving into the truck corral and found the way blocked by a set of portable barriers. Reluctant to go back in on foot, in case the security guard was still on patrol, he turned the car around.

He caught Asha stifling a yawn.

"Thanks for indulging me," he said. "Let's go home."

CHAPTER 16

Stober lay in the bunk of his Freightliner and idly watched the wisps of smoke rise to the upholstered ceiling. It was about all he could see in the dim red light, but at least he could have a Marlboro in peace without losing his night vision. If you weren't driving or sleeping, then you were waiting to be loaded or unloaded, weighed, inspected, or processed. All part of the job, and mostly out of his control like the price of gas, cost of insurance, or taxes. Well, taxes he could sort of control by not declaring all of his income—not his fault the government frowned on profiting from stolen goods.

And then there was Benny.

Cheap cunt.

If that fat fuck undercuts another load, he thought, I'll take my business elsewhere.

Not that Stober had much option. Reliable networks for fenced goods were thin on the ground in this neck of the woods. And Goodman's hub could turn over a truckload of just about anything if there was a buck in it. Only reason Benny had balked about the stiff at the last job was to get the price down. Hadn't bothered him, last year, when a jewelry store got knocked off and the lowlifes shot the owner dead. He'd probably Jew'd those guys to rock bottom, as well.

Of course, that white witch, Beth Rolland, was no better. Recalling that encounter, Stober took a deep drag and exhaled it with force. Nerve of the broad expecting to profit both ways, then having a hissy fit when it didn't work out. Benny might be cutthroat, but Rolland was merciless. Stober sensed she hadn't discussed her grand plan with either husband or daughter. Who would that do to a kid? Have her come home to find all her shit gone. When on the job, he and Devon never thought about that because it was just the job, but, c'mon, your own daughter?

He'd asked her why she hadn't told them it was her house.

'Arm's length,' she'd said. 'Anything goes wrong, the less you know, the less you can tell the cops.'

'So, you fed your code to Devon's contact. Arm's length, again?'

'Something like that.'

Stober wondered if her marriage was getting to be arm's length.

He could see she might not pass a fart for Julian Rolland. They were two self-centered peas in a pod, and Beth was solely into him for the money. In fact, Stober got the sense she didn't like men, in general, though, given the chance, he'd bang her twice on the buffalo-hide sofa she'd fenced a while back. His phone chimed before he got too far into that thought. He struggled to pull it from his jeans pocket.

The display read MG DISTRIBUTING.

He hit the TALK button before the call went to voice mail.

"Just been thinking about you, Benny."

"That's sweet, but put your dick away, I got a run fer'ya. Simple pick up and drop off. Want it?"

"When?"

"Next Saturday night. It'll be here, at the warehouse. Going to Windsor."

From Benny's to Windsor, just across the border from Detroit, would be a six-hour round-trip.

"How much?"

"Twenty-five hunnerd. Straight up."

Straight up. Take it or leave it.

"Flatbed or box?"

"They didn't say. It's a pass-through from the border. I'll check it out when it gets here."

"FOB dock or destination?"

Freight on board dock meant the receiver paid the shipper. With FOB destination, the supplier paid for the shipping.

"It's their load, so they should pay. But I owe 'em a favour so I'll put up the two-and-a-half. Have it for you when you get here."

Stober stubbed the cigarette in the ashtray resting on his belly. Benny was strictly a fence for hard goods that could be sold in any store. He didn't deal in drugs or what he called morally decrepit contraband, though didn't mind acting as a depot, like in the stagecoach days. Anything from the border meant the U.S. of A. The original driver would return home while Stober drove the last leg to the Canadian destination.

"What about that Ajax load?"

"Ajax load?"

"Yeah, Ajax load. You said I'd get top dollar."

"Oh, right. Yeah. It's not ready. Couple more days. It's yours, no worries."

Stober closed his eyes. Benny kept his promises. Usually. You just had to remind him.

"Fine. What time for Windsor?"

"The load should be here by nine. Come on by around eleven'ish. After midnight the cops are busy with drunks. You can make good time. Okay? I gotta go."

"Oh, Ben," He caught Goodman before he hung up. "Who's unloading? Do I need help?"

"Nah. It's their load. You're just a mule in this pony express." Benny chuckled at his joke. "Pick up. Drop off. Twenty-five hunnerd."

Stober's phone went dead before he could reply.

He checked the time. The shoot was supposed to end by five a.m. Pack up the set and clear out before the morning traffic. Still a couple hours to go. Enough time for a snooze. He flicked off the light.

The snooze lasted twenty minutes. The phone's display told him it was Millcroft. He sounded panicked. Out of character for a guy who was usually so laid back.

"Hey, Marsh, we got a problem!"

"Wass'up?"

"Did I wake you? Sorry, man. I've been afraid to call in case my phone was tapped."

"And why would your phone be tapped, Dev?"

"Because of the stiff, dude! And now, Devika's dead. It's all turning to shit, and I don't know what to do!"

Stober swung his feet off the narrow bed and sat up. "Who's this that's dead now? What's going on?"

"Devika. The cat burglar. The chick we gave the safe to. She's dead."

This was the first time Millcroft had divulged his secret contact. Personally, Stober hadn't cared one way or another as long as he could get in, get out, and get away, with a minimum of fuss. Even when he'd found out Millcroft's cat burglar had been fed the door code, her identity still hadn't mattered.

Unless she'd dropped off the stiff.

"Did this Devika leave the stiff in the rug?"

"What? No. I don't think so. Like, why would she?"

"And now she's also dead? Better start at the beginning. Can't help you unless I know the entire story."

"There's no time. If my phone's bugged, I've got two minutes—even less now, before they trace my call."

Stober sighed. He hoped loud enough for his young associate to hear.

"Are you on your cell, Dev?"

"Uh, yeah."

"Nobody is tapping your phone. Stop being paranoid and tell me about this Devika."

There was a pause during which Stober imagined Millcroft peeking through his curtains looking for a SWAT team descending on the apartment where he lived.

"We met in a bar."

"Of course, you did."

"What?"

"Nothing. Keep going."

"We dug each other. Went back to hers and, well, you know. Anyway, I told her I moved furniture and stuff, and she said if I wasn't too anal about legalities, we might be able to work together. I said we sometimes moved stuff without permission, and she said she could bypass alarms. Match made in Heaven, right?"

Stober was about to light a cigarette. He had the filter between his lips and the lighter ready. His thumb moved off the striker wheel.

"I've got something to tell you about that. But first, how'd you know she wasn't undercover? Could've been setting you—us up."

There was silence while Dev processed that. "Nah, by that point she'd already swallowed me whole. Would a cop go that far to bust us?"

Stober flicked the lighter and put the flame to his cigarette. He was just yanking Devon's chain. Besides, if she had been a cop, they'd have been busted before they'd half-filled the trailer.

"Alright, you told this chick about the Lakeshore job. Then what?"

"She told me she was also a safecracker but that sometimes it took too long to open them on site. It would be easier, for her, if someone could just carry the thing off. I said we had the same problem with alarms. There was never enough time."

"So she gets us in, and we get the safe out. Everybody benefits."

"Like I said, Kismet."

Stober tapped his Marlboro over the ashtray and lay back on the bed. The pieces fit, but the shape was weird. That Devon Millcroft, a garden variety housebreaker, would just meet a safecracker at a bar seemed awfully coincidental. Then again, criminals do tend to find each other. He'd met Beth Rolland while moving stock for one of her antique stores. He'd suggested a more profitable though less legal way to gain inventory. She hadn't blanched though didn't want goods with a dubious pedigree coming straight to her stores. As it turned out, they were both familiar with Benny.

"You still there, Marsh?"

"Yeah, I'm just thinking. The white witch didn't tell us we were raiding her own home—"

"That was her home?"

"Yeah. Cold, right?"

"Cold enough to plant a body in it?"

"She says not, but now I'm not so sure."

"So why not just give us the code, instead of getting Devika involved?"

"Arm's length."

"Whose arm?"

"I dunno. Devika's?"

"Who's now dead, as well?" Millcroft had relaxed a little, but his voice now rose a notch.

"Is the SWAT team there yet?"

"No, but I ain't ruling that out. Devika's been killed, and my DNA is all over her place."

"Have you ever been busted, Dev? Fingerprinted? Spent time in Juvie Hall?"

"No."

"How about one of those genealogy DNA tests? Maybe found out your ancestors were on the Mayflower."

"Nah, nobody in my family sailed with Chris Columbus."

Stober let it go. The kid at least had the right continent.

"In that case, the cops won't have your prints or DNA on file. And we always wear hats and gloves on the job. Are you sure she's dead?"

"There was a fire at her workshop where I'd dropped off the safe earlier. I went back last evening to see if she'd opened it. The parking lot was full of EMS—cops, firetrucks, the whole nine yards. I asked a guy what happened, and he said someone had died. He didn't know who, but the fire had been in her unit. Far as I know, she was alone in there." Millcroft's voice had gone quiet.

"Just to be safe, Dev, maybe you should crash at my place for a couple days. I'll be there in a few hours. I just got a couple of runs from Benny. You could come along."

"Alright. Yeah. Thanks, Marsh."

The line went dead, leaving Stober to contemplate the glowing tip of his Marlboro. He took a deep drag, stubbed it out, then rubbed his eyes. What had started out as a walk in the park was turning into an arm's length shit show.

CHAPTER 17

The discovery of Devika Sumra's charred body, and the apparent link she had to the Rolland burglary case, had changed the dynamic of the investigation. To comb through the residue of the late afternoon fire at the workshop had taken the forensic technicians until ten that night. Koki Motungi and Dennis Collier knew Inspector Lareault would appreciate reports by the next morning, so they gathered, tested, analyzed, and sent over their findings with the usual provisos about preliminary results.

Lareault strode into the briefing room a few minutes before seven and dropped the folder with their results on the boardroom table. He got a sunny smile from Detective Sharin Adabi, who had the rosy glow of someone who'd leapt out of bed, gone for a run, showered under a waterfall, and had a peach smoothie for breakfast. Detective Roy Flock, on the other hand, had the appearance of someone who'd slept in the chair he currently had back on its hind legs, and kick-started his day with black coffee and unfiltered cigarettes. Nonetheless, he raised a hand in greeting and gave Lareault a slight smile that belied his enthusiasm for the work.

Moments later, the door opened and was held by Sergeant Bloomfield for Sunil Naipaul. The computer tech had a carrying case in each hand. He placed them on the floor beside the boardroom table and set up a laptop and a portable digital projector. Flock watched him cable them together and plug everything into a nearby wall socket.

The briefing room had now gained a second whiteboard, to which Lareault was attaching glossy photographs from the folder. The wall next to the boards was also white, more-or-less, so it became a screen for the projector. Naipaul adjusted the angle of the image and brought the HRPS logo into focus. Lareault uncapped a marker and wrote on the second board as he spoke.

"Devika Sumra, age twenty-seven, an employee of Weiss Windows and Doors, was interviewed by Frank and myself the day before her death in a burned-out workshop that she leased. Inside was a wall safe matching the one reported stolen by the Rollands. The contents appear to match those listed on Mrs. Rolland's missing contents form—we'll confirm that later today."

"Oh, boy," said Flock, in a been-there-done-that tone.

"Yes, Roy?" said Lareault, though he knew what was coming.

"Sorry, Boss, but I gotta put it out there."

Lareault nodded and glanced at Bloomfield who shrugged.

"So, you and Frank interviewed someone who died a few hours later under suspicious circumstances: who was found to possess stolen goods—goods related to a case you were working on. And, you didn't bring her in."

Flock held up his hands. "Hey, I understand it's early days and all that, but will 'she who must be obeyed'?" He pushed a thumb toward the ceiling. "And once the press gets hold of this, as they always do, well…"

"Let's worry about the superintendent, and the press, later," said Lareault, "and try for a result before the shit actually hits."

He held up reports from the folder. "Hopefully, these will help us."

He scanned the pages to review what he'd read in his office, then said, "Despite the fire, the victim did not die from burns, or even smoke inhalation. Cause of death appears to be a fatal toxic reaction to fentanyl."

Detective Adabi paused her note taking to say, "So, an overdose?"

"Same as the victim at the Rollands' house," observed Naipaul, glancing up from his computer screen.

"Easy to do with that stuff," said Flock.

"At least it works in our favour," said Lareault. He pointed at the whiteboards. "Two similar deaths with a connection to the same case should narrow the suspect field. Let's see who they had in common."

"So you're treating both as homicides?" Adabi said.

"The first death could have been a simple OD," said Bloomfield. "But the victim didn't roll herself in the rug, all the way to Rollands' rec room. And the fire chief thinks the workshop scenario is suspicious."

"Any prints?"

"There were a few, Sharin," Lareault flipped a page. "No matches in the database, unfortunately, though surfaces like doorknobs, and such, appear to have been wiped."

"Absence of evidence can also be considered evidence," said Adabi as if by rote.

"That what they're teaching these days, at the OPC?" Flock was old school and not one for catchphrases.

Adabi let that go. The Ontario Police College was one of the most comprehensive training facilities on the continent. And she'd passed with honours.

Lareault continued. "The coroner agrees with the fire chief that some staging had taken place. He thought it unlikely the vic would have attempted welding, or torch-cutting, with that amount of drug in her system. He also noted the coveralls were unzipped. The helmet was in place, but should have fallen at least partially off the head when the vic collapsed. The fingers were also mis-aligned in the protective leather gauntlets."

He let them mull that over for a moment then said, "The safe contained some jewelry, and a few contracts, but the overall value was significantly less than the Rollands claimed."

"Often is," said Flock.

There was a general nod of agreement and Lareault drew a line down the whiteboard to separate the half with the pictures and his previous text from the unused portion.

"Okay, let's explore some scenarios. See if any have the sticky stuff."

"I'll start," said Bloomfield. "Both victims knew each other and shared the same drug supply." He waited while Lareault jotted that on the board. Then he said, "Or, perhaps both victims shared the same supplier but didn't know each other."

"Was the drug intentionally spiked?" The inspector acknowledged Flock and wrote that down.

"How did Sumra come to have the Rollands' safe?" Adabi then offered an answer to her question. "She could have planned the break-in."

"It's possible," said Bloomfield. "The safe would be the cherry, though only if you knew the contents, otherwise the payout would be a crap-shoot."

"And if she's not the mastermind, then was the safe a payment for the part she played?" said Flock.

As Lareault wrote payment, with a line connecting the picture of the safe to that of Sumra, he said, "So why pay her off with a few trinkets, then kill her? And, why leave the safe for us to find?"

Although he was just there for technical support, Naipaul sat back and said, "The welding fire wouldn't be plausible if she didn't have something to work on."

"Which, again, points to another clumsy cover-up of a homicide." Flock let his chair drop back on all four legs. "All designed to mis-direct our investigations."

"Mis-direct how?" asked Adabi.

"Within twenty-four hours we'll have come up with people who had close relationships with Devika Sumra. It wouldn't take much in the way of circumstantial evidence, or lack of an alibi, to make a case to pin the deed on any number of people."

"Not a very strong case, though. These days, courts are reluctant to convict if there's any degree of reasonable doubt."

"Exactly. It's a simple way to distract the investigation and muddy the waters enough to cast doubt on any further evidence we may come up with. The longer a case goes unsolved, the colder it gets—they teach you that at the newfangled detecting course?"

"I guess the asteroid didn't get all the dinosaurs," she muttered, to Bloomfield's amusement.

"I'm inclined to agree, Roy," said Lareault. "My money is on two murders perpetrated by the same person."

"A fentanyl overdose is essentially poisoning," said Bloomfield, not needing to point out that poisoners were women, more often than not. The team contemplated the photos of Beth Rolland, Mandy Rolland, and Catrina Pailin.

"So, no chance that Devika Sumra could have supplied our first vic with a tainted batch, and succumbed to it herself?" One of the traits that made Adabi a good detective was her ability to play Devil's Advocate.

"That's possible," said Lareault, "but there's just too much going on here for such a simple solution."

"Fair enough, but if the murderer is going for subterfuge, then using fentanyl might be another mis-direct. Don't be so quick to blame the sista's—could be a bro." Adabi's little head bob in emphasis made Bloomfield smile.

"Point taken," said Lareault. "Though I think we agree that solving the Rolland break-in is likely the key to solving these deaths."

"I think that's our cue, Sunil," said Flock.

Naipaul nodded and woke up the projector which had timed out.

"I was able to get the video recording from the Lakeshore water plant. Sunil has isolated the frames I'd hoped for. Go ahead, Sunil."

The HRPS logo disappeared from the wall screen and was replaced with a monochrome image of Lakeshore Road from the perspective of a camera, beneath the eaves of a building, looking down a crushed gravel driveway. The image stirred to life and cars streamed by on the road. A cyclist pedaled past, then in the far lane a tractor-trailer sailed through the frame.

CHAPTER 18

Traveling a mere fifty kilometers an hour, the tractor-trailer still covered nearly fourteen metres each second. It stayed within the camera's field of view for less than two of them. It had entered from the right, a half-second after a bus appeared from stage left. The timing was such that the black fenders on the white truck were easily seen but, with the bus in the near lane and filling the screen, only the tail end of the trailer was seen exiting the frame.

"That's the truck," said Flock emphatically. He had Naipaul replay the clip. "My witness described a white truck with black fenders, and check the timestamp." He pointed to the corner of the picture where white numerals were frozen at 08:38:13 08/29/2000.

"Mandy Rolland's driving instructor was at the house a couple minutes before nine, and the truck had left by then," said Bloomfield. "What time did yours get a visual?"

"Mr. Johnson and his pooch, Alfie, wandered by about seven-twenty, so we're within the time frame, and this is the only truck with black fenders that comes by."

"There's numbers on the driver's door," noted Adabi. "Too bad the bus gets in the way."

"Yeah, Sunil and I have run this backwards, forwards, and frame by frame. The first three numbers are 289. We think the lettering above is the start of OWNER/OPERATOR, which at least tells us the driver probably owns the truck."

"I also isolated the driver," said Naipaul, overlaying a magnification of the truck's side window that showed a man in profile wearing a baseball cap. The definition wasn't great, but they now knew he was Caucasian.

"Numbered companies have seven digits, so only getting the first three doesn't really narrow the field, but it might be worthwhile to poll the trucking companies in the area and see how many hits we get."

"Worth a try, Sunil," said Lareault. "Since you had success with this video, Roy, how'd you like to canvas the local businesses around Sumra's workshop for footage of the parking lot? There didn't seem to be any cameras in the plaza itself, but perhaps across the road."

Flock nodded, and Lareault turned his attention to Detective Adabi. "Sharin also had some success. We have more information on the first vic." He tapped the picture of the deceased woman on the first whiteboard and uncapped his marker.

"Her name is Pamela Hovarth," said Adabi. "Twenty-three years old, she was a student in McMaster University's anthropology course. The skull found in the rug was from one of her digs. The profs seemed to think it was about three-hundred years old. Possibly belonged to a Jesuit missionary."

"Do we know where the dig was?" said Bloomfield.

"We do." For a moment, Adabi looked like the cat that swallowed the goldfish. "It was at the base of the bluff at Rattlesnake Point, which, according to our shared reports, is where the Rollands' new house is to be built."

"Oh, hello," said Flock.

Lareault flipped through his notes. "I believe the realtor said there'd been a delay at the building site. If the area was found to be of archaeological importance, development could be held up indefinitely."

"And those are multi-million dollar lots, if you're looking for motive," said Bloomfield.

"So, the Rollands', their builder, and anyone else who bought property there would be affected," put in Adabi, making sure she stayed in the light of her revelation.

"Just when you think you've narrowed your suspect list," said Flock, once again balanced on the rear legs of his chair.

"Anything else come from the university folks about Ms. Hovarth?"

"Yes, Boss. She was well-liked but not really sociable. Her compatriots thought that she may have a girlfriend. Didn't go to many parties, but wasn't averse to the odd toke, if offered."

"Family members?"

"The university's admissions form names her mother, Bonita Hovarth, as next of kin. She lives in Tiverton. I'll confirm the address and then go up and do the notification—unless someone else wants to go." Adabi looked at the others, but there were no takers. Notifying next of kin about the death of a loved one was never a welcome task.

"Thanks, Sharin. Make sure you take someone from Victim Services along."

"Already got a call in."

"While you're doing that, we'll get a forensics team over to Hovarth's residence. Did she stay on campus?"

"No, she was renting the second floor of a house a few blocks from the university. The street and house number are in my report."

Turning back to the first whiteboard, Lareault wrote PAMELA HOVARTH and RATTLESNAKE POINT beside Hovarth's picture, then an arrow and BUILDER CONFLICT?

"Before we go visit the Rollands, Frank, let's take a drive into the countryside?"

"Should I bring a picnic?"

"How about coffees from Tim's?"

"I'll go fetch the car."

Less the detour for double-doubles and a couple of donuts, the trip to Rattlesnake Point took about twenty minutes. Beneath the deep blue sky, the light-gray shale of the south-facing bluff glared almost white in the morning sun. Given that it was a weekday, there were no climbers but soaring on large black wings with their tips spread like fingers, turkey vultures kittled on the updraft.

Nestled between the base of the bluff and the country road that ran past, plots of land had been cleared and staked out for the new homesteads of *Rattlesnake Bluffs,* as the builder, Klaasen Construction, Inc., was calling it.

Bloomfield turned onto the sideroad that led up to the plateau's conservation area, then, before the road began to rise, he pulled into the driveway of the development's sales office. Next to the building, a billboard proclaimed, 'Country chic within easy reach'. Though no houses had yet been erected, the site's desirability was plain to see. For a moment, the two policemen admired the view.

"Think it's worth the price of admission, Frank?"

"Arlene would love this, but my pension wouldn't come close."

"What if you sold your house?"

"I'd still be a million short."

The sales office was the standard relocatable building built as a scaled-down model-suite. The only thing marring the idyllic facade was a plywood board, instead of a glass panel, in the top half of the front door. A late-model Cadillac was parked by the steps that went up to the little front porch. Bloomfield eased off the brake and rolled in beside it.

The bell that chimed when they entered summoned a young man in an off-the-rack suit. His smile dimmed when they showed their identification.

"Nice of you to finally show up. I called two days ago."

"Sorry for the delay, sir," said Lareault, with the standard response, though he had no idea what the call was about. "We've been really busy. Please tell us what happened."

"Well, it's pretty obvious, isn't it?" The man gestured at the door. "They smashed the glass, opened the door, and stole the rug." He looked down at the floor, which had a tasteful bleached oak version of luxury vinyl plank.

Bloomfield opened his notepad to a fresh page. "And when did this break-in occur?"

The salesman gave a half shrug. "We're only here Thursday through Sunday, for the weekend traffic, so it could've been anytime between Sunday night and Thursday morning."

"Can you describe the rug?"

"It was about eight by ten, tight weave, Persian-style."

"Anything else taken, damaged, or even left behind?"

"No. Sometimes kids break into model suites to party. They'll treat it like a motel room, leave their garbage and such, but this time they just took the rug."

"Do you have a computer here?" asked Lareault.

"Just my laptop, but I take it when I leave."

"But there is an Internet connection."

"Oh, yes. We've a satellite dish out back."

Lareault called Naipaul and had him email over a photo of the rug Pamela Hovarth was found in. He got the sales rep to open the attachment.

"Is this your rug?"

"It looks like it."

"Take your time."

"Yes. Yes, it is. That's the rug that was here."

"Do you have any security cameras on site?"

"No. At this stage we just insure the property for the minimum."

"Okay," said Lareault. He opened his cellphone again. "We're going to have to ask you to leave. This property is now part of a murder investigation."

"Do you mind if I call my boss about this?"

"That is actually a good idea, and tell Jack we want a word."

Although Klaasen's larger than life picture was displayed on billboards at most of the local construction sites, Lareault and Bloomfield knew 'Jackhammer Jack' from a previous case in which the developer's daughter had been kidnapped.

"Mr. Klaasen," said Lareault, when the salesman handed him the phone, "we're having to cordon off your building site. The archaeologist who was excavating here has died under suspicious circumstances. Could you come up to the sales office, or would you prefer to meet at the station?"

Klaasen agreed to be at the bluffs within the hour.

Bloomfield retrieved his portable fingerprint kit from the car.

"Just to eliminate your prints from any others we might find," he said, and had the salesman press down on the ink pad and the two white cards. He and Lareault then waited patiently for the man to wash his hands, pack up his laptop, and leave.

The Cadillac drove away, and Lareault pocketed the keys to the suite. They spent the next few minutes walking the site. Most of it had been cleared by bulldozers though there was a section partitioned by a string perimeter. It had been trenched out by a trowel. This was Pamela Hovarth's excavation of the Jesuit's grave. Lareault and Bloomfield stood beyond the ankle-high line of twine and pondered the significance of the shallow trough.

"Have you ever been to Crawford Lake, Evan?"

"I've heard of it. Somewhere nearby, isn't it?"

"A few minutes' drive north of here. Used to be an important native settlement. Conservationists have recreated a few of the longhouses. Worth a visit."

"That would explain why the Jesuits came this way."

Bloomfield looked across the cleared acreage. "How many homes are going in here, d'ya think?"

Lareault pointed toward the road. "See those orange-tipped stakes? Probably lot markers, and there's six."

"The land, alone, must be worth twelve mil." Bloomfield pushed a rock with the toe of his boot. "We should have forensics take samples from here. They might match the particles Collier found on the vic."

"They might, though it wasn't a rock that killed her. We'll see what Jack has to say, but I'm not convinced it's a motive for murder. The dig had been registered, so killing her wouldn't have stopped the excavation."

"Unless Klaasen thought it hadn't been."

Lareault turned to walk back to the sales office. "Yeah. There is that. And he might have hit her, anyway."

CHAPTER 19

Fenn drained the bottle into Asha's glass and placed it on the counter. He'd already put the plates, pots, and cutlery into the dishwasher. That was the rule: if she cooked, then he washed—or vice versa. Mogg, who had her own routine, wound around his legs, wanting her after-supper treat. Fenn got the pouch from the cupboard and dropped a couple of morsels into her bowl.

"This was a tasty wine," Asha said, giving the goblet a little swirl.

"It's a Pinot Noir from that winery in Beamsville. We have another bottle."

"Okay."

"Okay, what?"

"Okay, open it."

"Thirsty?"

She pressed her lips together to suppress a smile, then said, "Sure, we'll call it 'thirsty'."

Fenn didn't suppress his smile. Asha having a single glass of wine was one thing, but when she wanted more, one thing often led to another. He ran a finger along one of her legs. They were lean, tanned, and extended across an adjacent chair.

"Your wish is my command," he said. "After this, you get two more."

"Only two?"

"Better use them wisely." Fenn uncorked the fresh bottle and topped up their glasses. He was about to sit when the phone rang. The display said KK. Fenn picked up the receiver but handed it to Asha.

"It's Kim."

"Probably wants to talk about the wedding," Asha said as she took the phone.

"Hey, Bella. What's up?"

Fenn sipped his wine and watched Asha as she listened intently. Unexpectedly, her brow creased and she frowned. She held out the phone. "Kim wants to talk to you."

Fenn raised his eyebrows. He and Kim hadn't spoken directly since their one and only date had placed her in the middle of a vendetta against him. He didn't blame her in the least. The fact she was now Asha's BFF, and her fiancé, Tony, was Fenn's closest buddy made things a little awkward, but there wasn't much he could do about it.

"Hi, Kim," he said neutrally, unsure of where the conversation would go.

"You know that student you have, the one who found a body in her basement?" Kim said.

"Mandy Rolland," confirmed Fenn.

"My dad's just been arrested for it." Her voice rose in pitch, though Fenn couldn't be sure if it was from anger or distress. Maybe both.

"Arrested for what? What's the charge?"

"We haven't been told. I just got a call that he's being questioned at the police station about it."

"You do understand it has nothing to do with me, Kim. Mandy is my student, that's all."

He wasn't sure if the sound she made was a sniff or a snort, or even what that meant, but then Kim said, "I know. Tony told me all about it. How you were just dropping her off. Look, I'm just calling to see if you know why they might have arrested my dad. We're desperate for information, but when I call they say either it's a privacy matter, or a police issue. Is there anything you can tell us?"

Fenn leaned back in his chair and stared at the ceiling. He knew Jack Klaasen was a developer, and that the Rollands were having a new home built.

"Does your dad have a project near Rattlesnake Point?"

"Yeah. It's pretty new, though. I don't think they've started building yet."

"It's possible the Rollands are one of his clients. Mandy said they were planning to move up there. Perhaps the police found something that connects your dad to the victim, but if they have, I've no idea what it might be."

Kim was silent for a moment, then said, "Okay, Chas. Thanks. If you do hear anything, will you let me know?"

"Of course. Don't worry. I'm sure they will straighten it out."

More silence, so Fenn said, "Do you want to talk to Asha?"

"No. I'd better go. I've got to call my mom in San Diego."

Kim's parents had divorced, and their relatively amicable relationship depended on the relative distance between them. Simone Klaasen liked to travel, and the legal settlement meant Jack paid for it. The last Fenn heard, she was in Hong Kong. Now, apparently, Simone was enjoying the American west coast vibe. Nice life if you can get it.

He put the handset down and looked at Asha.

"Was Kim's dad arrested?" she said.

Fenn nodded.

"You didn't tell her much."

"What could I say?"

"How about you heard Mrs. Rolland discussing the body with the truck driver at the film set, and demanding money?"

"We don't know enough about that. And if I told Kim, she'd tell the cops, and they'd want to talk to us. Bloomfield has already told me to stay out of his case, so I'd rather not stir that pot until I've got something worth stirring."

"Well, you've got to help her. After the last time, you owe her that much."

Fenn drank some of his wine and looked at his fiancée, who was now sitting schoolmarm straight in her chair. This was not how he expected the evening to go. Asha also raised her glass, but she drank like she was actually thirsty and not to enjoy the bouquet.

"You're right, Ash. We need to step up our game. I'll ask Mandy if she's heard anything else, but perhaps we need to get more proactive."

"Like how?"

"I think we should tail Beth Rolland. See what she's up to."

Asha smiled. "Yeah, like a stakeout. That's a great idea."

"We'll need help. No idea what sort of schedule she has. And you and I can't watch her all the time." He picked up the receiver. "I'm going to call Tony."

Fenn pressed a couple of buttons to speed-dial the number.

Demers picked up after two rings. "Hey Bud," he said, "I guess you heard about Kim's dad."

"Still want to marry her? Could run in the family, whatever it is."

Tony laughed. "In for a penny…still, this could be something serious. Jack's called in his lawyer."

"Do you know who that is?" Fenn, having been involved in a couple of cases recently, was getting familiar with the local legal teams.

"I don't, but you can bet it's someone good."

"No doubt. Listen, we want to help Kim's dad, and think that Beth Rolland isn't such an innocent victim here. We might surveil her for a while: you know, stake out her house, see where she goes, who she meets. Ash and I can't do it alone, though, with work and such."

As usual, there was no hesitation. "Alright, well, I'm still on reduced hours 'till my leg heals so, if you have a schedule started, I could probably fill a time slot or two. I assume this will be a round-the-clock thing."

"Yeah, at least until we establish her routine. I can probably get a couple of instructors from DriveCheck to help us out as well."

"That would be good. Shorter shifts, and we can switch out the cars. When did you want to start this covert operation?"

"Uh," said Fenn, momentarily distracted. Then he laughed. Asha had left the kitchen while he and Tony were talking. She now returned wearing the gray fedora that Fenn sometimes wore in winter, and her wide-lapelled raincoat with the belt cinched and the collar turned up.

"I think Asha's ready to go now, but we'll work something out and call you in the morning."

"Fair enough. You know how to get me."

Fenn put down the phone but had absolutely no luck in suppressing his grin as Asha tipped her hat over her eyes and sipped some wine, leaving freshly applied deep-red lipstick on the rim of her glass.

"Well, you certainly know how to put the Noir into Pinot Noir," he said.

"Then pay attention, padfoot," she said, loosening the belt, "'cause this shill is looking for a hot tip." The coat fell open and Fenn's mind flashed back to an underground garage of a five-star hotel where Asha had been clad only in her Prada heels, and this coat. It was like déjà vu, all over again. Fenn couldn't remember who'd said that, and right now he didn't really care.

CHAPTER 20

Beth Rolland, according to daughter Mandy, was a late-night reader. Meaning she rarely rose before the crack of ten. While that helped the stake-out schedule, it was still a bit loosey-goosey, as Asha called it, with the surveillance team having various commitments and only able to show up on an ad hoc basis. The team, such as it was, consisted of Chas and Asha, Tony and Kim, Joe Posada, Brenda Woodhill, and Muriel Stafford.

Their landlady had been Asha's suggestion. Retired and widowed, Muriel kept herself busy with bridge clubs, gardening clubs, book clubs, and walking clubs, but she was always game for an adventure, as Fenn well knew.

The stretch of Lakeshore Road that ran past the Rollands' house had a wide gravel shoulder between the sidewalk and the asphalt lanes. Lined on both sides with mature trees, they cast a dappled shade that somewhat camouflaged any car parked beneath. Stationed a hundred metres from the Rollands' driveway, Muriel sat in her mint-green Dodge and unwrapped one of her freshly baked raisin scones. Having just relieved Joe Posada, who had a student road test at noon, she expected to hand-off to Fenn in a couple of hours.

A yellow ribbon sat on her dash. The team had decided that should someone have to leave the stake-out before the quarry, they'd tie a ribbon to the branch of a tree. If there was no-one at the site and no ribbon, it would mean the quarry was being tailed by the person on watch. While not a foolproof system, it could save a lot of calling around with updates.

Posada had seen Julian Rolland leave in a Land Rover, just after nine, and head east toward Toronto. Julian wouldn't have to punch a clock, so could afford to wait for the morning rush hour to subside. That would leave the Audi for Beth, so when a taxi pulled into the driveway Muriel paused mid-bite of her scone. Empty, save for the driver, meant this was a pickup. Wrapping the rest of the pastry into a paper napkin, Muriel re-attached her seatbelt and started the car. When the taxi reappeared moments later, it had a young, dark-haired female in the back.

That would be Mandy. False alarm. Muriel shut off the engine and wondered why Mandy's mom hadn't driven her daughter wherever she was going. Conflicting appointments, maybe?

Muriel reached for her scone but kept the seatbelt on, anticipating an imminent departure of Mrs. Rolland.

"Damn, I'm good at this," she said, when minutes later, a champagne-coloured Audi nosed into view.

She swallowed the last morsel, brushed a few crumbs off her chest, and restarted the car. The Audi turned in her direction and accelerated with quiet power. Muriel checked her mirrors and the oncoming traffic, then after waiting for a van and a pickup truck to pass, U-turned and followed the sleek sedan toward downtown Burlington.

The main road of the downtown core was Brant Street. Rolland went past and turned at the next one, Locust Street. She parked in a municipal lot next to a bookstore. Muriel followed, hoping there were coins in her purse for the parking meter. It was a small unattended lot, so she found a spot facing away from the Audi where she could watch it in her rearview mirror. She saw Rolland feed her meter then make her way toward Brant Street. Muriel dropped in enough quarters for an hour's protection from the ticket dicks and walked quickly toward the shops.

Rolland had crossed Brant Street and was heading north. Unless there was a festival, Burlington's downtown was never crowded. The popularity of covered malls had shifted much of the commerce to other segments of the city. This area was now mainly boutiques and personal care establishments: trendy gyms, hair stylists, nail salons. Rolland entered one of the latter called Chic Tips 'n Toes. Thinking it had been a while since she'd had a pedicure, Muriel crossed over and made the bell chime when she entered the shop.

The interior was deep and narrow. It had ten stations, five-a-side, half-filled with patrons. The employees, identified by their white smocks over black slacks, were all Asian. Muriel guessed Vietnamese. Beth Rolland, already seated, was in conversation with a technician. The receptionist nodded enthusiastically when Muriel asked if they could fit her in. Across the aisle Beth Rolland glanced up long enough to return her smile, but it was all the opening Muriel needed to start a conversation.

"Nothing like a little pampering to pick up your spirits," she said brightly.

Another brief smile.

"Lost my best watch this week. A Gucci. It was an anniversary present. I think the clasp broke while I was at the farmer's market. Didn't notice 'til I got home. I went back and looked everywhere. Asked the stallholders if it had been turned in, but what are the odds? I even put up flyers offering a reward. So far, nothing."

Her sigh earned a sympathetic look from Rolland. Their respective technicians kept their attention on their work.

"Ever lost any jewelry, dear?"

Rolland seemed to ponder the question. "Matter of fact, we got burgled this week. Cleaned us out. Ripped the safe right out of the wall."

This got the attention of all in hearing range, but Rolland seemed most interested in Muriel's reaction. Nothing like a little one-up to make one's day.

"Oh, my! That's awful. Makes losing my watch seem so trivial. I see you still have your wedding ring, at least. Heirlooms are so important. Did you lose, like, everything?" Muriel backed that up with a glance at Rolland's diamond tennis bracelet. She also had a large diamond stud in each earlobe, and a chunky gold necklace that had to be worth the down-payment on an Italian sports car.

"Luckily, we were at some prep-parties, getting geared up for the Toronto Film Festival—my husband's a producer—so I'd taken a lot of good pieces with me. Of course, I was still out-blinged by the few A-listers who showed up, mainly those involved in Julian's film, though we all know that their trinkets are usually on loan. However, bit of a shock when we got home."

There were nods of empathy.

"Rather makes you wonder where they sell all that stuff. Being stolen, and all," said Muriel.

"Oh, they probably shift it cheap to a fence named 'Benny'." Rolland's tone was sardonic, but her attention suddenly went back to her nails.

Muriel pursed her lips. Some women just can't keep a secret and it seemed like one had just slipped under the wire. She glanced down at her technician who was now giving her a foot massage. Muriel had never been to this salon but appreciated the way the massage extended to her calves. They hadn't done that at her other place. She might have to start coming here instead. Twenty minutes later, she was admiring the *PumpkinSpice* polish on her toes. Rolland had opted for a classic French manicure and was now getting ready to leave.

Muriel's nails were still wet, and she regretted having worn her sneakers instead of sandals. She'd wanted to be prepared in case Rolland had gone any distance on foot. Now, having a better sense of the woman, she decided that Beth's pedestrian activity was likely the length of Mapleview Mall. Not that Rolland was out of shape. While somewhat short, she had a nice hourglass figure for a mother in her forties. As if anticipating Muriel's haste, the young technician brought over a nail dryer and turned on the fan.

"This polish set very quick. Two, three minute. Okay?"

Rolland could be out of the parking lot in less than two. She was already pulling a credit card from her wallet.

"Before you go," said Muriel, "can you recommend a good hairdresser? I'm new to Burlington." She knew it was a stretch: her white perm was nothing like the blonde shag that so suited Beth Rolland's oval face.

The younger woman's eyes seemed to agree, but she said, "I go to *Kim's Cuts* on Guelph Line." She gave the receptionist her credit card.

"You wouldn't have their phone number, would you?" Muriel looked upward as if she could see her tight curls. "I really need to do something about this mess."

"Oh, um, maybe." Rolland dug into her Louis Vuitton bag and retrieved a cellphone. She scrolled through her contact list until she found the number, then wrote it on one of the nail salon's business cards.

"Thanks." Muriel took the card and quickly slipped on her sneakers. She pulled enough bills from her purse to cover the pedicure and tip and left the shop in time to see Rolland cross Brant Street on her way back to the parking lot.

The Audi made only one other stop, in front of a pharmacy, and Rolland came back out with a small white bag. The receipt stapled to it flapped in the breeze. Probably a prescription. Muriel then followed her home and pulled in behind Fenn's car, which was parked in the stakeout spot. She rolled down her window as he walked back.

"Just got here," he said. "When I didn't see a ribbon, I figured I'd wait a while and see if you came back."

"We went to get our nails done," Muriel said. "I'd show you my toes, but I think I've smudged them. Anyway, madam conveniently managed to keep all her best baubles from the burglars, and she mentioned Benny." She gave Fenn a knowing look.

Fenn and Asha had filled everyone in on what they knew, though exactly how Benny fit into the story had been unknown. Thanks to Muriel, they now knew he was a fence. And that was an important piece of the puzzle.

"Too bad we don't know anything else about him," said Muriel.

"No, we don't," said Fenn. He pushed some gravel around with his shoe, then looked up. "But I might know someone who does."

CHAPTER 21

"Are you fucking nuts? The last time we dealt with Nicolas Wray, we barely got away unscathed. Actually, I did get scathed, and it wasn't fun. And now you want to ask him for a favour!"

It had occurred to Fenn that the best way to solve a crime was to ask a criminal, and they didn't come much better connected than Nicolas Wray. After Muriel had briefed him at the stakeout spot, about Beth Rolland's slip of the tongue, Chas had pondered how to broach the subject with Asha. He'd waited until they were making supper. However, the way she stood with hands on hips, fists balled in her oven mitts, suggested there was no good time to bring up the mobster who'd put both their lives in danger.

"Actually, Sweetie," he said with a sheepish grin. "I was thinking *you* should ask him. He likes you."

Fools rush in, mulled Fenn as the look that flashed in Asha's eyes made him glad that he had the bread knife and she the oven mitts. Not that it would make a damn bit of difference. With her martial arts skills, the knife would be at his throat before he could butter the baguette in his other hand.

Instead, she turned her back and put the casserole dish in the oven. The door was shut with a bit more force than necessary.

"Look at it this way," he persisted. "Kim and Tony are due to get married next week. Her dad can't walk her down the aisle if he's in jail on suspicion of murder."

"Jack's not in jail. They released him a couple of hours after bringing him in for questioning. He wasn't arrested, and wouldn't have been taken to the police station if he hadn't insisted on getting a lawyer."

"When did you find that out?"

"Kim called me just before you got home. Apparently, the murder victim was an archaeologist who'd discovered some bones on Klaasen's new survey by Rattlesnake Point. There's a sales office on site that the cops have cordoned off."

Fenn thought about how Rattlesnake Point was where the Rollands' new home was being built.

"I'm pretty sure that Kim's dad is not a murderer," he said. "But evidence can be manipulated so the wrong person is convicted. Just because Jack is now at home, probably enjoying a glass of Scotch, doesn't mean he won't get arrested on suspicion later."

Still looking pissed off, Asha removed her oven mitts and leaned back against the counter. The last thing she wanted was anything that could interfere with her best friend's nuptials.

"What makes you think we can clear Jack of any suspicion?"

"I just don't think he did it. Jack may not be the most honest businessman: you need to dull your scruples to make it in the building trade, but we're finding too many odd links with Beth Rolland not to consider her our prime suspect."

"And how does Nicolas Wray figure into this?"

Fenn turned to cut the bread to hide a small smile.

"We'd hoped that tailing Rolland would tell us what she was up to. Thanks to Muriel's spa session, and the conversation I overheard at the movie shoot, we can be pretty sure that Beth's involved with a fence called Benny. Problem is, we don't know how to find this Benny, and we could sit on Rolland's ass for weeks before she goes to see him, if she ever does. The closest link we have between the two is the trucker she met at the shoot. And the odds of finding him are even more remote."

Asha nodded. "So, you're thinking it could speed things up if Nicolas Wray told us where to find Benny."

"Got it in one," he said, saluting her with his glass.

Asha looked down at Mogg, who was always nearby when cooking was involved. She slowly shook her head, though it was more an act of resignation than refusal.

"Wray gives absolutely nothing away for free, you know that. Ask something of him and he'll extract two or three times that in return. Plus interest. He's a predator."

"I get it. Still, would it hurt just to ask where we might find Benny? Who knows, maybe Wray doesn't like Benny and would want him out of the way."

"Regardless, he's going to want something in return." Asha stuck her chin out and stroked the bottom of it, like Brando in The Godfather. "Someday, and that day may never come," she said hoarsely, "I will call upon you to do a service for me."

It was a pretty good impression, and Fenn grinned.

"Listen, if he asks too much, we can say forget it. Though I still think we'll get the best deal if *you* ask him."

Asha had caught the attention, and respect, of the mob boss after she'd fought his ninja bodyguard, twice, and bested her. He'd then tried to recruit her, but Asha couldn't see herself in the employ of an underworld scumbag.

"Have you still got his number?" Fenn knew he'd have to keep pushing to get Asha to do this thing.

"I might have. I was going to toss it then thought it's not often you get a calling card from the devil himself." She put her glass on the counter and walked toward the bedroom. "If the timer dings, take the casserole out."

Asha returned before the ding with an embossed business card that proclaimed Nicolas Wray as the managing director of Wharfmine Investments, a West Coast enterprise located in British Columbia. Wray had only recently expanded into Ontario's Niagara Region, which, being close to the border with the United States, was an important hub for illicit goods.

"Let's eat first," she said, putting the card on the counter and donning the mitts. "Otherwise, I might lose my appetite."

The Niagara Falls branch of Wharfmine Investments Inc. was located in a strip mall on Drummond Street, several blocks from the touristy part, and intentionally innocuous with its mirrored glass and discreet signage on the front door. The long black Lincoln parked outside could have belonged to the lawyer situated two units down. Fenn knew it didn't.

A small plaque above the doorbell said PLEASE RING FOR SERVICE. Fenn pressed the button and looked up at the surveillance camera without smiling. Asha stood beside him, one hand on the shoulder strap of her black leather purse. Accustomed to working with tight schedules, they were a few minutes early for their nine a.m. meeting. Her phone call the previous evening had been answered by Wray's fixer, Milo Dsuban. It was he, dressed as sharply as ever in a charcoal three-piece suit and polished black shoes, who now ushered them inside.

"Mr. Wray will be with you, shortly," he said with a cultured Eastern-European accent. Dsuban closed and relocked the front door. He crossed the room and went into a back office without inviting them to sit or partake of the coffee station, where an expensive-looking espresso machine sat quietly steaming beside a tray of fresh pastries.

Knowing how long they waited depended on Wray's desire for control, they stood patiently on the spotless tiled floor and looked around. Within its whitewashed, picture-less walls, the reception area was sparsely furnished. Opposite a black leather sofa stood a white Scandinavian-style boardroom table surrounded by eight matching chairs.

They apparently rated a mere seven minutes, for at 9:05 Wray swept into the room wearing a natty dark blue suit and a starched bright white shirt open at the collar. His head and face glowed pink from the close attention of a barber's blade. Dsuban followed discreetly.

Hands extended, Wray greeted Asha with a jocular, "Ms. Fabiani, how marvelous to see you again!" The smile remained, though the eyes hardened slightly as he shifted his focus. "And I see you have brought Mr. Fenn along. I hope you don't mind if we remain upstanding: something I learned from the Queen of England, who likes to keep her meetings short."

Fenn thought that was an interesting gambit, seeing how everyone else in the room was taller than the Don. Another point of control that said, 'your business, whatever it is, is unimportant to me: and, no matter how big you are, I will stand up to you.' He imagined Napoleon had the same attitude.

The little despot inclined his head toward Asha and raised his eyebrows in enquiry.

"So, um, Mr. Wray," she began, taking the cue. "We're looking for someone called Benny, who may or may not be a fence for stolen goods."

Wray stared at her for a few seconds, as if expecting her to add something, then said, "That's what I like. Straight to the point. No beating about the bush. And look at you two, trying to hook up with a fence. You must tell me more."

Asha looked over at Fenn. He was doing his best to maintain a neutral expression but gave her a slight nod.

"There's been a murder and, while we don't think Benny did it, we need to show that our suspect was up to something that might have given her a motive."

Wray seemed amused. "A murder. Oh, my! So, are you a pair of private snoops now?"

Fenn saw Asha tense up. While she might be intimidated, she would let no one belittle her. "My best friend's father is a suspect. We're just trying to right a wrong. Do you know Benny, Mr. Wray, or not?"

Wray interlaced his fingers down at his waist. "I really wish I had a video of you at Madame Dynes' house, when you grabbed that shield and flew through the window like a warrior princess. That was absolutely priceless, wasn't it, Milo."

Milo smiled in agreement, as right-hand men do, then glanced at his watch.

"Yes, Milo, I know. I'm so glad I don't have your job: too many things to think about." Then, to the couple standing before him, he said, "Maurice Goodman. He's the man you're looking for. Now, while I doubt you'll tell the authorities where you got the information, I'm sure you'll understand it would be unfortunate for all concerned if Benny got wind of this conversation."

All jocularity gone from his voice, Wray's dead-eyed stare conveyed his point.

"Not a problem," said Fenn, speaking for the first time. "We just want to know where he hangs out."

"And I will give you that. But first, you must give me something in return."

Fenn felt Asha stiffen beside him. Her Brando impression of the night before didn't seem quite so funny now. Nonetheless, he looked Wray in the eye and said, "Alright. What do you want?"

CHAPTER 22

Fatima Luiza De Sousa, Pamela Hovarth's Portuguese landlady, still carried the Old World in her speech, dress, and heart, which she clasped when Koki Motungi informed her of her tenant's death. She muttered a quiet prayer, kissed the small gold cross on her necklace, then led Motungi and her assistant up to the second floor where she unlocked the door to Hovarth's flat. To the left was a small living room that had a view of the street. To the right was the bedroom, bathroom, and kitchen, which overlooked the postage stamp backyard.

"Is that your laundry?" Motungi pointed to the sheets drying in the breeze below.

"Yes." Then, fully understanding the question, said, "Pamela always went to the laundromat."

"When was the last time you saw Ms. Hovarth?"

The landlady's brow furrowed. "I heard her walking around up here more than I saw her. I did see her go out about a week ago and, come to think of it, haven't seen or heard her since."

"Did she ever have visitors?"

De Souza shrugged. "If she did, I never saw or heard them, either."

"Well, I'm sorry to bring you this bad news," said Motungi. She motioned they should leave the kitchen as a subtle way to usher the landlady to the door.

"We might be an hour or two up here. I'll let you know when we're done."

She watched their host navigate the narrow stairwell, then closed the door.

"Okay, Trevor," Motungi said, pulling on some nitrile gloves. "If you want to start in the kitchen, I'll take the bathroom."

Like the rest of the apartment, the bathroom was functional but worn. The scatter rugs couldn't hide the decades old linoleum, and a coat of paint would do the whole place wonders. The small space had a bathtub with a showerhead, a single-sink vanity beneath a mirrored medicine cabinet, and a toilet. Motungi pulled on the mirror to check the shelves behind. There were the usual items a single young woman might have: toothpaste and brush, makeup and nail polish remover, acne cream, tampons, nail clippers and file, tweezers. No prescription drugs, though there was a container for birth control pills. Motungi calculated the last one was taken within twenty-four hours of when Hovarth had died.

More interesting was the collection of soaps, shampoos, and conditioners. All in the little bottles that are complimentary in hotel rooms. It was one thing to economize, by bringing the sample-sized bottles home: however, the labels suggested Hovarth had been in most of the major chains.

Her petty thievery hadn't been confined to just soaps. Motungi noticed the mismatched towels were all embossed with the logos of Sheraton, Hyatt, and Holiday Inn. On the back of the door hung a robe from the Royal York, one of Toronto's finest hotels. That would have been charged to the registered occupant of the room. There was no way of checking who that might have been, but Motungi was pretty sure it wasn't Hovarth. Still, she made a mental note to suggest that Lareault's team circulate Hovarth's picture to the local bed renters. Perhaps one would remember her coming in, and who she was with.

The small trash bin yielded nothing of obvious interest, so she pulled out the liner bag, tied it, and put it aside for later. Moving on to the bedroom, she met Trevor coming from the kitchen. He'd been briefed to look for the same type of food as found in Hovarth's stomach contents.

"We'll have to check when garbage collection is around here," he said. "I haven't found any empty wine bottles, oyster tins, or containers of spaghetti sauce. If that was her last meal, I doubt she ate it here."

In the bedroom, Motungi bagged the bedsheets and pillowcases. The dusting for fingerprints and vacuuming for hairs and fibres would also come later. On the bedside table was a box of tissues and a library book. It was *Death du Jour*, a novel by Kathy Reichs about a fictional forensic archaeologist. Hovarth was about halfway through. Motungi could have told her how it ended.

The closet had one set of bi-fold doors that didn't fully close due to all the clothes crammed on the hanger bar. The left side was for casual wear: jeans, blouses, sweaters. The right side was more dressy, with several skirts and dresses, and a couple of pantsuits. Motungi checked the labels. Mid-level designer brands: not high-fashion, though pricey enough to strain the budget of a student archaeologist. Coupled with the pilfered hotel goods, it wasn't a stretch to imagine how Hovarth had afforded the slinky threads.

"Boss?" Trevor peered around the door-jam. "Come and look at this."

Furnished in typical student-resident style, the living room had a threadbare loveseat, oversized seventies-throwback bean bag, a tarnished brass floor lamp with a dented shade, and a Mezo-American clay pot sitting in the alcove of a bricked-up fireplace. There was also a large wooden desk beside an assemble-yourself bookshelf.

The desk hadn't been readily apparent when they'd first entered, having been covered with a bedsheet. When Trevor removed the sheet, he'd found a large hand-drawn map. The map had grid lines within which were other seemingly random rectangles and squares. Rattlesnake Bluffs Excavation: June-August 2000 was printed neatly across the top.

"Our vic sketched out the dig she was working on," said Trevor. He reached down beside the desk and pulled out a cardboard box. Inside were several plastic bags, similar to the evidence bags the forensic techs used. "The numbers on these bags match numbers on various parts of this map."

Some of the bags contained bones which, at first glance, Motungi identified as animal. Others had rusted iron or clay pieces inside.

"Well, I guess it proves she was working at Rattlesnake Point," said Motungi.

"It does," agreed Trevor, "but what caught my eye were the contents of this other box." He tapped a second container with the toe of his shoe.

The other box contained similar bags. Trevor brought out a bag from each.

"Notice anything?"

Motungi read the labels. "This other box has artifacts from another dig," she said, handing back the bags.

"A few other digs, actually. Not so unusual for an archaeologist to have, right? However, the catalogue numbers from the other digs seem to have migrated onto Hovarth's map." Trevor let that hang knowing his boss would come to the same conclusion that he had.

"She wouldn't be the first to salt a site," said Motungi.

They gave each other a grim smile. Forensics was as much about archaeology as it was about blood analysis and time of death estimates. Both techs knew that *salting*, introducing objects onto a site with the intent to deceive, was unethical at the very least. It was akin to dropping a few nuggets of gold in a Yukon creek to incite an investor to buy a thousand acres of barren tundra.

Motungi took out her phone and found the number for Detective Adabi.

"Sharin, who should I talk to at Mac University about the dig Hovarth was on?"

Graham Ford, head of the archaeology department, took a moment to catch his breath at the top of the stairs, then shook hands with the two forensics techs.

"That's what you get for letting the students do all the digging," he said good-naturedly. "Of course, numerous pints of Guinness don't help much, either."

"Well, thank you for responding so quickly," said Motungi. "We'd like your opinion on something we found in the living room."

She brought him over to the desk with the map and stood quietly by while he leaned over and peered at it.

Trevor placed a few of the artifact bags on the desk. Ford looked at the descriptions and catalogue numbers and ran his finger over the map to locate the designated place for each. As he found each one, he checked the information on the bags again. When he'd checked four, of which Trevor had placed two from the dig and two from the older samples, he straightened up with a frown.

"I hate to speak ill of the dead," he said soberly, "but this is so…disappointing." He went to the loveseat and sat down. "If it gets out that one of our students salted a dig, it would absolutely ruin the reputation of our archaeology program."

Motungi could see his shoulders sag as the implication sank in.

"Is there a phone? I need to call the Dean."

"Before you do," she said, "let's just take another look at everything. Trevor, did you match all the items on the map with the bags in the boxes?"

"I didn't go through them all, but I will." He began to pull the bags from the nearest box. As he read off the catalogue numbers, Motungi and Ford matched them to the map. They scored one hundred percent.

"Okay, then," said Ford, relief evident in his voice. "While this looks like a plan to salt the dig, she hadn't yet corrupted the site." He looked at the bags again. "The writing on some of these is definitely in a different hand, not Pam's. I think these other items belong to the Joseph Brant Museum, where she worked. If you can show me that phone, now, the curator is a friend of mine."

CHAPTER 23

The morning whiteboard session over, Lareault told Sergeant Bloomfield he'd be ready to travel in about twenty minutes.

"The Chief called down for a command performance," he said, which meant Superintendent Heatherington wanted to be briefed in her office rather than attend the earlier meeting. To be fair, she'd had to take her daughter to school, and Lareault gave her kudos for putting family first. He stepped into her enclave and stood by the door.

"Have a seat, Evan. I'll be right with you."

Heatherington put her signature on a couple of forms, then placed the papers in a manila folder, which she slid to one side of her desk.

"Okay. So where are we?"

"We're getting a clearer picture of our first victim."

"Pamela Hovarth."

"Correct. It appears that she supplemented her income with some evening work as a rent girl. While we don't know if all her partners were Janes, rather than Johns, we believe most were. She was also planning to ransom the housing development at Rattlesnake Point, the one where your friend Beth Rolland had bought a plot of land. She'd discovered some artifacts on the site and told the developer, Jack Klaasen, that she could hold up construction indefinitely, unless he paid her half a million dollars."

In anticipation, Heatherington displayed a rare grin. "And how did Jackhammer Jack react to that?" She and Klaasen had been to a few of the same functions, mostly charitable dinners, and had a passing acquaintance.

"According to Klaasen, who brought his lawyer in, he told her she'd better present her Ministry 'Stop Work' order before he used his excavator to crush her dig into dust. There may have been a few expletives in there."

"Knowing Jack, as I do, I'd be surprised if there weren't."

"Forensics found samples of Jack's hair in the rug, but that's to be expected and proves only that he was in his sales office at some point."

"There were also a couple of bottle blonde hairs, female, weren't there?"

"At this point, those will only strengthen the case if we're able to get hard evidence on a suspect with matching DNA. The perp could be a bald guy for all we know."

"Or, a bald woman..."

"Oh fuck, I hope not," said Lareault, knowing they both remembered the murderous harpy, Brittany Reis, who'd suffered from alopecia.

"Let's just back up a bit. Did Hovarth have enough archaeological evidence to warrant a stop work order?"

"We found a box of artifacts, pilfered from the Joseph Brant Museum, that she planned to 'discover' in various places on the estate."

Heatherington nodded. "So did Jack trample her dig?"

"No. Hovarth died before either of them acted on their threats."

"So, what's your feeling about Jack as a suspect?"

"There's evidence of trauma to her skull, probably from a rock endemic to the site, but that was post-mortem. She died from a fentanyl overdose and, even if Jack was so inclined, I don't think that's his style."

"I agree. So, do you have a suspect in mind?"

"It's still a bit early to place a bet, but we think Hovarth's death is linked to that of Devika Sumra. Sumra was in possession of the wall safe from the Rollands', and also died from a fentanyl overdose. Only, this time, there was a fire at her workshop that may have been an attempted cover-up. The Fire Chief is calling it arson. Detective Flock sourced some security camera footage of vehicles parked near the workshop. Unfortunately, it was from across the road, so with delivery trucks blocking the view and other passing traffic, he's still trying to distinguish the licence plates."

"Are you any closer to identifying the tractor-trailer used at the Rollands' place?"

"No, but we also have footage of a Caucasian male wearing a ball cap exiting an SUV. He watches the emergency crews for a minute, then quickly leaves. I'd dismiss him as a gawker except he matches the description provided by Roy's witness on Lakeshore Road."

Superintendent Jennifer Heatherington may have taken the bureaucratic route to her desk, but she'd overseen enough investigations to spot a key point.

"Do you need more resources to get those plate numbers? I want to know who that ball cap fellow is."

"I'll let you know on that. Since Sumra had the Rollands' safe, she may well have been in their house. If so, could she have killed Hovarth and left her body there?"

"That would be convenient, but if Sumra spiked Hovarth's coke with fentanyl, would she be dumb enough to snort from the same batch?"

Lareault's assessment of his boss went up a notch. "Then, whatever part Sumra played, it likely got her killed. Someone is tying up loose ends, though how Hovarth figures into the burglary, and why she was murdered, is still unclear."

"What about phone records?"

"Neither victim had a cellphone with them. Both had registered land lines, and Sumra had a phone in her office. Our tech is going through the lists of calls, in and out. Usually good for a lead or two."

Heatherington swiveled her chair slightly and mused out the window for a moment. "I hate to say this because Beth was a friend of mine, but there are too many connections between the Rollands and these cases to be coincidental."

That gave Lareault the opening he'd been waiting for. "I know you and Beth Rolland went to school together. Did she ever show any inclination for same-sex relationships?"

Heatherington pursed her lips, but that didn't stop the edges from creeping up into a small smile. "Well, it was the age for experimentation, wasn't it? I'm sure you've been there."

Lareault hadn't, but he nodded and said, "Just trying to cover every angle. We've got two dead women. Both essentially poisoned. Both with links to the Rollands."

He rose from his chair. "I'm a firm believer in *where there's smoke—* and we've actually had a fire, so…"

Bloomfield slipped his phone into a cup holder when Lareault opened the Crown Vic's passenger door.

"Just took a call from the forensics team at Devika Sumra's townhouse. Apparently, they've found a few things we might find interesting." He put the car into DRIVE while Lareault buckled up. "

"Who were you talking to?"

"Koki Motungi." Bloomfield glanced at his boss as he eased off the brake pedal. Like many of the Halton Region Police Service staff, at least those who had seen the Detective Inspector and the elegant Kenyan CSI together, he suspected their relationship had progressed beyond common workplace etiquette. When you work with professionals trained in reading body language, not much slips by.

Bloomfield held his glance and Lareault's lips formed a barely perceptible smile.

"How long've you been married, Frank?"

"Thirty-nine years, as of last June." Bloomfield was aware of Lareault's recent divorce. Something they hadn't discussed much, though he was glad to see the inspector move forward with his life.

"We're taking it slowly."

"Slowly is fine. Arlene said she'd like to have you both over for dinner sometime."

Lareault opened the folder on his lap and scanned the first page of a report.

"Does anyone else suspect us?"

Bloomfield raised one hand off the wheel.

"You work at a cop shop, Evan. We're a suspicious lot."

Lareault gave a small headshake, but his rueful grin had sprouted tiny wings.

Devika Sumra's home was a three level, two bedroom, one and a half bath townhouse, with a garage, on a cul-de-sac in Mississauga. It was also close to schools, shopping, parks, the freeway, and downtown Toronto. All of which would warrant a hefty mortgage. One that Sumra had closed out a few months ago. In the smallest bedroom, used as an office cum dressing room, Motungi had found a folder with bank statements. She summarized for Lareault.

"Sumra gave a thirty percent down payment, then paid off the mortgage in five years."

Lareault was yet to learn Sumra's salary at Weiss Windows and Doors but knew that should have stretched her finances.

Motungi's coy smile could, with little effort, have been quite seductive. "While it's nice she could live here debt-free," she opened a drawer in a dressing table, "just how many Rolex watches does a girl really need?"

Laid out on a thin foam liner were eight Rolex timepieces: five with wide, manly bands and three with thinner straps for women. With a fluid motion, like that of a game show hostess, Motungi extended her hand toward the vanity.

"And, if you'd like to step this way, gentlemen, we have our collection of fine jewelry."

Opening two multi-level containers, couture versions of fishing tackle boxes, she revealed a treasure trove of necklaces, rings, bracelets, and earrings. Gold, silver, platinum. Diamonds, emeralds, opals, rubies, and sapphires.

"Or," said Motungi, really getting into the role, "perhaps you would prefer the cash. You can choose from shoebox one, shoebox two, or shoebox three."

She slid back a mirrored closet door. Beneath the clothes hanging on the rack were several shoeboxes. Three of them had their lids removed to show they contained bundles of currency.

"Oh, boy," said Bloomfield, his tone suggesting what Lareault was thinking.

This much loot indicated a professional thief and represented several, likely unsolved, burglaries. Sumra may also have been part of a network. The case was expanding by the minute, and would certainly require more manpower. That would be Heatherington's problem, though, not theirs. Solving the two murders was still the present team's main objective.

"Answering machine?" said Lareault. He and Bloomfield had donned nitrile gloves but tried to be hands off until Motungi's team had checked everything out.

"She has a newer digital unit. There were no messages, but..." Motungi led them to the kitchen. "We found these in a cupboard."

In a large plastic evidence bag were three pay-as-you-go cellphones still in their original packaging.

"Burners," said Bloomfield.

"I've got Trevor checking the garbage bins in case she'd already tossed one nearby," said Motungi.

"Good to see you're on top of everything," said Lareault, briefly touching her shoulder.

"Well, you know me." Motungi's sotto voce reply made Bloomfield clear his throat at the obvious innuendo.

"If you'll excuse me, folks," he said, edging between them to get to the door. "I'll just go have a chat with the neighbours."

CHAPTER 24

Fenn drove the Challenger slowly along the pot-holed road. Asha sat silently beside him. With the windows down, the throaty burble of the muscle car's exhaust pipes reassured that if they had to leave quickly, not much could catch them.

"Are you sure you still want to do this?" he said, still hoping she'd say no.

Asha's assessment of Nicolas Wray had been spot on. Ask him for a favour and he'll give you nothing for free. In exchange for the location of Maurice 'Benny' Goodman, Asha had to compete in a fight club he'd organized. A Friday night unsanctioned martial arts competition with loose rules and unlimited betting.

A provincial champion, in her own right, she felt confident even while suspecting the bouts might be rigged. Her only doubt had been when Wray mentioned that she'd be matched up with Yunni, his ninja assassin.

"Nope. No way." She'd been adamant until Wray explained that instead of fighting Yunni, they'd be partners.

"Like a tag team. You'll be up against a couple of good ol' boys, to swing the odds, but it'll be easy peasy—I doubt you two will break a sweat."

"Uh-huh, and how does Yunni feel about this?" The last time Asha had been in the same room with Yunni she'd had to fight for her life.

"If she wants to work for me, she'll do as I say."

Hardly a ringing endorsement of cooperation. It would have to do.

"Show up and Yunni will give you the address to Goodman's warehouse. He's there most days. Again, leave my name out of it."

So here they were. Pulling into yet another empty strip mall the recession had left in Hamilton's commercial sector. The front lot had parking for maybe twenty vehicles, mostly vacant like the units. A driveway along the side led to an area large enough for several tractor trailers, beyond which was a large metal-sided warehouse. There was only one truck. A one ton with an eighteen-foot box that had probably brought in the equipment for evening's activities. The rest of the lot was almost filled with cars, a steady stream of fight fans threading between them to a side door in the warehouse.

Fenn found an open space and backed in.

"If Yunni doesn't give us Benny's address right away, we're out of here. I'm going to leave the car unlocked and the spare key is under the mat if you have to split without me."

Asha gave him a look of trepidation, then just nodded. She was used to Fenn covering every base. She got out and had him put her purse in the trunk. Beneath her lightweight sweatpants and hoodie, she wore a black Lycra top and shorts. Hair in a tight bun. Ready to compete.

It was a humid night. Sky glow reflected off smog trapped by the low cloud cover. It created an amber dome and while looking up, Fenn almost wandered into the path of a motorcycle. Asha pulled him back as it rumbled past. The chopper slowed to a stop as the rider contemplated where to go. Fenn followed his gaze and saw that there were two cadres of bikes, all of which appeared to be Harley-Davidsons. There were maybe thirty in each group, and the rider glided over to the impressive row of chrome parked along the side of the warehouse.

"Let's just go over here, for a sec," said Fenn, and taking Asha's hand ambled toward the bikes near the front of the building.

"Man, these are gorgeous hogs," he said, loud enough to be heard by the leather-vested dude smoking nearby. Likely assigned to keep watch. Still holding hands, they moved close enough for Fenn to identify a club insignia on several. It was that of an outlaw gang that often made the news.

They strolled on toward the other batch of bikes. The rider, having dismounted, had gone to greet the guard for that group. The two guys embraced in a quick man-hug and Fenn noticed the club colours on the back of their vests. It was a rival gang. Equally notorious.

"I hope the fighting stays in the ring," he muttered, and Asha's serious expression became a full frown.

"C'mon," she said, steering him toward the door. "Let's get this over with."

"Fifty bucks each." The bouncer had a shaved head, a neck-collar tattoo, and wore a tight black t-shirt and black slacks.

"I'm on the card," said Asha.

"Other door," he said with a flick of his head, then focused on the bike rider, who was now behind them. "Fifty bucks."

They went further down the side of the warehouse to where light spilled from an opening. A couple of guys stood nearby, sharing a joint.

"Fighters only," said one, trying to hold the smoke in his lungs at the same time. It came out funny, and they both laughed.

"She's on the card," said Fenn.

The guys looked Asha over with interest in their eyes.

"And what about you?"

"Manager," said Fenn, then added. "She's with Yunni."

That seemed to be the magic word. The stoners stepped aside and let them enter. The staging area for fighters was simply a section cordoned off by curtains on movable racks. There were several people milling around, mainly guys in various fighting garb, and some others in t-shirts and jeans. A couple of them were laced into boxing gloves, suggesting the card had a bit of everything. Yunni was stretching-out in a corner. She appeared to have more space around her than anyone else.

They walked over and after Yunni straightened up, Asha said, "Hi."

For a moment, the two women stared at each other, dark eyes unwavering. They were about the same height and build, with Yunni being slightly slimmer. It was the first time Fenn had seen her and he was struck by her Asian beauty. Only a small scar on her cheek marred her flawless olive complexion. A scar that Asha had given her. Fenn suddenly realized that the noise of chatter had reduced significantly. Many had turned to watch the face-off, a common occurrence in fight circles, and this one had particular potential.

Yunni shifted her gaze to take in the room, then with a bright smile offered her hand. "No hard feelings, eh? Let's save it for the ring."

Asha took her hand but didn't return the smile. "Fair enough. Have you got what we came for?"

Yunni turned and reach down into a knapsack. She handed Asha one of Nicolas Wray's business cards. An address was printed on the back. Asha gave it to Fenn.

The chatter had resumed, and Asha looked around. There were a couple of other women dressed to fight. They were sparring without making contact.

"Who are they?" said Asha.

Yunni smirked and began to wrap her silky black hair into a bun like Asha had. "No-one to worry about. Tell your guy to bet against them."

"Okay, what's the format?"

"There's a couple of boxers up first, then the two douche bags will fight those Russian dudes," Yunni pointed out a pair who looked like twins with their angular features and close-cropped blond hair. "Then it's us against a couple of bigger guys. They're not here, yet." She paused to high five a huge, bearded dude in motorcycle leathers.

Asha had to ask. "There seem to be a lot of bikers. Is that normal for these things?"

Yunni grinned. "That's tonight's main event. A grudge match. If you don't get hurt too badly, stick around: it'll be a bloody one."

Asha gave Fenn a meaningful glance. He nodded and said, "Since you two seem to be playing nice, I'm going to look around."

He found a gap in the curtains that led into the main part of the warehouse. It was noisier and smokier. A conflation of tobacco, cannabis, cigars, perfume, cologne, and unwashed bodies assailed Fenn's nostrils. There were perhaps a couple hundred people around the fighting ring in loose groups. Even with the high ceiling, it seemed fairly claustrophobic, and Fenn realized the venue was just a section walled-off from the larger structure.

Along one side, they had set up a bar. It was doing a brisk business. To blend in, Fenn joined the line and bought an overpriced can of Molson Canadian. Sprinkled in the crowd were a few women. Mainly biker chicks in tank tops and denim shorts. The others, in halters, miniskirts, and stilettos, were draped over the arm of their boyfriends, or perhaps pimps. This function wouldn't attract the same clientele as the last soiree of Wray's that Fenn had attended. It didn't even attract Nicolas Wray, nor his fixer Milo Dsuban. Another reason to be concerned.

Fenn walked the perimeter of the space. It was well lit with banks of lights fastened to the steel beams supporting the roof. Thick electrical cables ran from them and down the wall to a junction box by the door, where people continued to file in.

A set of speakers near to the ring suddenly came to life with the opening bars of AC/DC's *Hells Bells*. It was the perfect tune to get the room amped up. By the time the last notes faded out, Fenn could sense the energy level had risen. The Master of Ceremonies, an unshaven guy who looked a bit old for this crowd but might've been a contender in his day, climbed into the ring and was handed a microphone.

"Good evening, ladies and germs," he began. There was laughter and a comment Fenn couldn't make out to which the MC replied, "and fuck you, too," which got more laughs.

The crowd pressed in toward the ring. There were no chairs, only a table for the score and timekeepers, upon which sat a large bell and a heavy mallet to strike it with. A rope perimeter kept the spectators a couple of paces back from the ring, and four bruisers made sure the space wasn't invaded.

"We've got a great card for you tonight." The MC's voice was raspy. "Make sure to get your bets in early with the friendly folks in the red caps."

Fenn now noticed the half-dozen men circulating with clipboards and waist pouches. He briefly considered acting on Yunni's tip, and while confident that she and Asha would likely win, he kept his money in his wallet. The presence of rival biker gangs in such close quarters made the place a tinderbox. Should it ignite, the first people to scarper would be the bookies.

He'd just found a spot along the wall, where his beer wouldn't be jostled, when the crowd let out a roar. The first two combatants, boxers, were entering the ring.

"Okay, folks," said the MC. "Let's get ready toooo…RRRRRUMBLE!"

CHAPTER 25

The boxers were middleweights. Built for speed, both had ropey muscles and lean physiques. With the rule that fighters had to punch or block at least once every five seconds, speed was the theme of the night. Points were awarded for attacking rather than defending, and penalties given for simply dancing around or going into a clinch, a sort of fighting hug that Fenn never understood.

Both pugilists were of average height. One looked to be of Mexican or Peruvian heritage. He bounced side to side on his toes while the other, a very dark-skinned fellow with long arms, came at his opponent flat-footed and rarely backed up, despite taking several hard jabs. They went at it hammer and tongs for the full three rounds. Fenn never found out who won. When he heard the final bell, and the MC's unintelligible announcement, he was on his way to the can, thinking it would be vacant.

Wrong.

The single toilet stall was occupied, which was fine. However, blocking the two urinals was a naked Latina bent forward with her feet well apart and her hands on the side of the stall. Behind her was a biker, pants around his ankles, laying pipe like he was being paid by the foot. The woman grunted with each thrust, head turned sideways so her face wouldn't bash into the wall. She had an elaborate leafy vine tattoo that started at her ankle, wound around her calf and thigh, crossed her hip to encircle her waist, then went up and over her shoulder.

Perhaps her name was Ivy, Fenn thought, involuntarily personalizing while trying to mind his own business.

Ivy's clothes, though not folded, were piled together on the counter. Her shoes had been kicked off under the sink. There were four other guys present, yet it didn't appear to be rape. Two were snorting coke off the laminate top between the sinks. The other two could have been waiting for a turn at the coke, the urinals, or the woman who now had one hand on the butt of the biker. Fenn didn't stick around to find out. It wasn't the first time he'd come across weird shit in a bathroom and gone outside to piss on the wall. Some joints were like that.

He went through the staging area to get outside. Asha was sitting cross-legged in the corner, meditating.

"Where's Yunni?"

"Getting some air."

"Still good to go?"

"Who, me or Yunni?"

Fenn smiled, but Asha's game face didn't waver.

"Okay, well, I'll be nearby."

Her expression softened a degree. "I know you will."

Outside, the humidity hovered between the warm asphalt and the misty orange dome. The area near the door was like the patio of any bar on a Friday night. People hung around with drinks, talking, smoking, toking, or necking. The two necking were both muscular guys in vests. Hardly surprising since the venue attracted few women. Fenn spotted Yunni chatting a short distance away with the big biker she'd high-five'd earlier.

He walked toward the back of the warehouse until he came to an industrial garbage bin. Good a place as any. The wet patch of asphalt on the far side implied he wasn't the first person to think so.

On the way back, he detoured to check on the Challenger. Each phalanx of choppers still had its designated sentry, and a few guys strolled around with beers in hand. Otherwise, the parking lot was quiet. He returned inside to see the two 'douche bags' fighting the Russian twins.

A prelude to Asha's match, the tag team format meant that one member of each pair would fight until they got tired and slapped the palm of their partner to swap. With the five second hit or block rule, this happened fairly quickly. The bout, however, had only one round. It would last until both members of one team were either too exhausted, or damaged, to continue. Pride made the women carry on longer than they should have. They were rapidly fading, but while they remained on their feet, the referee stood by, even when ribs were cracked or faces bloodied.

"It's a man's world!" crowed the MC, as the vanquished were assisted from the ring.

"Kiss my ass, you misogynist prick," said Yunni, cartwheeling over the ropes to stand beside him. She grabbed the microphone in what was obviously a staged scene. "Are you ready to see what real women can do?"

This garnered whistles and howls from the biker chicks.

"Absolutely. I especially liked the way you put my prick and your ass in the same sentence." The MC mugged as he took back the mike. Hands on hips, Yunni glared at him, then beckoned for Asha to join her.

"Alright. We all know you can take care of yourself, Yunni. So, who's this you're babysitting?"

Asha, shaking her head in mock disgust, gave the crowd a stage stare and said, "I'm your worst nightmare. Kneel before me, knave."

Playing along, the MC dropped to his knees with his face inches from her crotch.

"Is this where you want me?"

The crowd roared.

Asha raised a foot to his chest and pushed him over.

"Just start the match and stay out of my fucking way!"

It was evident that Asha hadn't seen their opponents. Her eyes widened when two linebackers from a semi-pro football team stretched apart the ropes and entered the ring. Fenn hoped she'd remember to fold her thumb into her palm when they shook hands, so they wouldn't crush her fingers.

When the mallet hit the bell, Yunni took the first shift. The guy she fought, while big, couldn't match her speed. Ever the showoff, she pranced or backflipped between her rapid jabs and flying kicks. Few of which seemed to have much effect. Her opponent seemed to tire more from trying to trap her in a corner. While the initial scoring favoured the women, the format was biased toward those who could take the most punishment. After three minutes, Yunni tapped out right after her opponent did.

Fenn had seen enough of Asha's sanctioned matches to know she liked to score early, and often. She was on the guy as soon as he cleared the ropes. He blocked with thick forearms, so she kicked at his thighs, trying to bruise the large, unprotected muscles. She had partial success. Her opponent began to limp but was no less determined to wrap an arm around her. Like Yunni, she was ready to tap out after three minutes, but when she maneuvered to their corner, her partner was nowhere to be seen.

Like the rest of the crowd, intent on the match, Fenn hadn't noticed Yunni slip away. Asha's opponent, also expecting Yunni to come in, quickly tapped out. Stunned, Asha looked around, wondering if she'd gone to the wrong corner. She turned just in time to deflect a blow that could have knocked her out. She staggered into the ropes and ducked a second roundhouse that had fractured jaw written all over it.

Fenn scanned the crowd for Yunni, then pushed through to the staging area.

"Where's Yunni?" he yelled. A couple of people pointed at the door, and he got there just in time to see Yunni clinging to the broad back of her biker friend as they roared out of the parking lot.

The double-crossing bitch!

The crowd inside also roared, and Fenn raced back in time to see Asha getting up from the mat, painfully. The linebacker, though limping, had his arms raised as if claiming victory. Sensing the kill, he tapped out to bring in his refreshed partner. When neither the referee nor the MC seemed inclined to intervene, Fenn realized they'd been set up.

He had to help Asha out of there, but getting past the bone busters patrolling the perimeter would be impossible by himself.

Unless he had a distraction.

Shoving folk aside, Fenn quickly made for the entrance door where the junction box was. He flung open the panel and yanked the main power lever down. The warehouse plunged into darkness. Temporarily night-blind, Fenn started back toward the ring, punching at anyone he bumped into. After five seconds, the emergency generator kicked in, though it only illuminated the exit signs and a few dim safety lights.

The disruption was a veritable spark in a tinderbox. The tension and bloodlust, primed by the action in the ring, exploded into an all-out brawl between the rival gangs. Determined to get to his fiancée Fenn shrugged off anyone who tried to engage him, and kept moving. Getting Asha out of there was his only thought. A chain swung by a biker missed its intended victim and caught him above the eye. Momentarily stunned, Fenn crouched to make himself a smaller target while he wiped the blood away with the hem of his t-shirt. On rising, he saw the bruisers moving to protect the bookies, but then he saw the action in the ring and charged forward. The referee long gone, the linebackers were now on either side of Asha with a single-minded purpose, and one had hold of Asha's arm.

The scorekeeper, not even watching the contest, stood by his table, unsure of where to go. Fenn shoved him aside, grabbed the mallet, and climbed into the ring. Asha was twisting furiously to prevent the one brute from getting his other hand on her, while kicking out at the partner who was circling. Fenn felled that fellow with a mallet blow to the skull, then landed a cracking thump on the ribcage of the brute. Now free, Asha planted her left foot and landed a kick to his solar plexus. The brute staggered back, tripped over his prone partner, and tumbled out of the ring.

Wiping more blood from his eye, Fenn took Asha's hand and raised it high. He pointed the mallet at the scorekeeper.

"Here's your winner, Dickweed," he snarled. "Mark it down!"

Whether or not the guy would, they really didn't care. The closest exit was through the staging area, which was now just a space surrounded by collapsed racks covered with crumpled curtains. They gave and took a few more blows on the way to the door. A shirtless guy with a scraggly beard swung at Asha. She deftly grabbed the arm and threw him over her hip. He landed with a grunt on his back.

The last obstacle was a fat dude who raised a metal pole. Fenn ducked under it and drove his shoulder into the flabby gut. The momentum carried them both through the door and onto the ground. Fenn hammered the side of his fist down on the guy's nose and felt a crunch.

Steering clear of bikers who swung at anyone nearby with knives, chains, and lengths of pipe, he and Asha ran down the side of the warehouse. Patrons not affiliated with either gang were hustling to their cars. The sound of squealing rubber was occasionally punctuated with a crunch of metal as bumpers backed into each other or fenders scraped door panels. Fenn knew it was only a matter of time before there'd be gunshots.

"Are you alright?" he asked as they reached the safety of the Challenger.

"I'll live," said Asha. She took in the gash above his eye and his blood-stained face and shirt.

"You?"

"Same."

She leaned forward with an arm across her ribs. Fenn could see the pain in her face.

"Anything broken? Should we find a doctor?"

She shook her head. "Just get us out of here."

CHAPTER 26

There wasn't a law that compelled businesses to maintain CCTV footage for any set number of days. At least not in Burlington. But, after visiting eight gas stations that erased their files after twenty-four hours, Detective Roy Flock had begun to wish there was. He didn't even need every minute of the past week, just the two hours on either side of eight a.m. on the day the Rollands were burglarized.

He'd worked in an expanding circle from the house on Lakeshore Road, along the streets the thieves could have used. He knew from the water plant footage they'd initially gone west. After that, there were a few routes through town they might have taken. Most of them eventually led to a freeway, and once on those thoroughfares, the chance of using Closed Circuit Television to identify the truck was near nil. While the nearby Highway 407 was a toll road, those cameras would only record the licence plate number. Which he didn't have.

The stifling heat notwithstanding, some of his late afternoon grumpiness was due to the lack of a decent lunch. Every gas station kiosk had a rack of snack bars by the counter and shelves of cigarettes behind. Trying to cut down on the ciggies, he'd consumed a Snickers, an O'Henry, a pack of Glosettes, and two pepperettes. Unwilling to admit defeat on the video front, he took out his mobile phone and called Sunil Naipaul.

"Sunil? Look, I'm stymied, here. None of the frikkin' fuel stops in town has any video older than my last shit. I need some suggestions?"

He heard Naipaul tap a few times on his keyboard after which he gave Flock the address of Kenny's Cable and Security Systems. It was on Lakeshore Road, near the base of Brant Street. Kenny's webpage featured live 24/7 CCTV coverage of the road and nearby Spencer Smith Park, as part of their advertising.

"Are you Kenny?" Flock showed his ID to a tall fifties-something male with a graying beard and hunched shoulders. The small shop was quiet. One side had a rack of cables, connectors, and other small parts in little plastic bags. The other side had displays of security cameras, wi-fi hubs, and other related pieces of surveillance equipment.

"What can I do for Halton's finest?" Kenny's smile was genuine. Probably grateful for the distraction, regardless of the unlikely sale.

"I'm looking for street footage from a few days ago," said Flock. "Apparently you have a camera feed on the web. Please tell me you keep the recordings longer than overnight."

"Let me show you something." Kenny opened a little gate to allow Flock behind the counter. Leading the way into the back room where pieces of computer and surveillance equipment lay partially dis-assembled on workbenches, he opened a door that revealed stairs to the basement.

"Watch your head," he said, starting down. Flock wasn't as tall, so the beam at the bottom only caused Kenny to duck.

Expecting a damp, dirt-covered space with moisture running down cinder block walls, Flock was surprised to find a well-lit, humidity-controlled environment with racks of network servers blinking a variety of coloured LEDs.

"Welcome to the heart of my evil empire," said Kenny with a grin. "I not only supply and install security equipment but offer monitoring services to my clients for a reasonable fee. I'd be giving poor service if I didn't store video files for at least a month."

Kenny sat on a stool and pulled a keyboard shelf toward him.

"What time frame would you like, sir?"

Flock told him, then watched the monitor as a day in the life of the street above was replayed in fast motion.

"There! Stop. Go back."

Kenny reversed the recording at half speed and replayed it in slow-motion.

"Freeze that, please." The detective leaned forward for a closer look. He clapped Kenny on the back. "Man! If I'd have come to you first, I could've had a proper lunch."

"Boss, I got it!"

Flock had been so amped at getting a clear picture of the tractor-trailer from the Rolland robbery, he'd called Lareault as soon as he got back into his car. Parked in the sun, it was hotter than a baker's oven.

"I've got the full number of the owner-operator's business registration, and a pretty good look at the guy in the passenger seat."

His fingers scrabbled over the armrest until they found the power window switch. It didn't work with the car turned off.

"Our suspects continued west, past Brant Street. My source also had access to a camera on North Shore Boulevard, which is just beyond the ramp for the QEW. The truck didn't pass by there, so I'm pretty sure they jumped on the freeway."

With sweat beading on his forehead, he worked a hand into his pants pocket for the key fob.

"Anyway, I'll get Sunil to give me the address attached to the registration. I hope it's not just a post-office box, but if it is, we'll track down the owner. *Ahh, fuck.* Sorry, Boss, just got my keys stuck in my pocket. Let me follow this up—I'll keep you posted."

He opened the door to get some airflow. The outside temp was still sweltering, but he knew why dogs and kids died when left in cars. His call finished, Flock stepped out so he could free his keys. The damp fabric of his shirt clung to his spine as he reached back in to start the car. He shut the door, then stood beside it while he speed-dialed Sunil Naipaul.

"Great tip on the cameras you gave me there, Suni-boy! Now we need to track these fuckers down."

He gave Naipaul the registration number and moved under a nearby shop awning for the shade. He could hear the tech tapping at his keyboard and softly muttering. A couple of young ladies approached the store and giggled when he held the door open for them. Glancing inside, Flock saw it stocked women's undergarments. Lettering on the window, below the brand logos, advertised that the establishment specialized in bra fittings. He decided the car had probably cooled down enough.

"Sorry, Sunil, I was just getting back in the car. What was that address?"

Not a post office box, it was a property on Concession 4 in Flamborough. While Naipaul worked on getting an actual person's name to link it to, Flock started driving toward the freeway. He'd take the QEW over to Highway 403 then jump off at Highway 6, which would take him up the escarpment into Flamborough. About a twenty-minute trip.

Naipaul called while Flock was stopped for the traffic lights at Clappison's Corners. He had a name. Marshall Stober. As stenciled on the truck's door, Stober was an owner/operator. Pretty much a one-man operation. His was the only name listed, so the accomplice was either an employee or some sort of unnamed partner.

He reached the concession and cruised slowly along, counting down the house numbers. The address belonged to a modest brick bungalow squatting on about an acre of sun-parched land. It had an overall impression of near abandonment. The lawn out front, a matted carpet of limp grass being choked out by equally wilted weeds, had seen neither a sprinkler nor mower in weeks. Flock figured the guy lived alone, and spent more time on the road in his truck than he did here.

A cracked cement driveway ran back along one side of the property to a garage large enough to house a Freightliner. Parked in front of the rusting door was a Nissan Pathfinder. It looked like the one in the CCTV footage of Sumra's workshop.

Bingo.

Flock pulled into the driveway, picked up his phone, and gave Naipaul the plate number of the Nissan.

"The place looks deserted. No white truck with black fenders, but I think we're onto something. I'm going to look around." Flock shut off the car and unclipped his seatbelt. "I'll call you back in a few. No need for backup—unless you don't hear from me in ten."

The Pathfinder was unlocked. Flock thought about doing a cursory search, but anything he found within the cab would be in-admissible without a search warrant. He walked over to the garage. This was locked, but there were windows on either side. Peering through the grime, he could see a couple of workbenches with a variety of tools, and a late-model Ford F-150 pickup truck.

The bungalow was also locked. He could have busted in and claimed he thought he'd heard sounds of distress. Better to wait for a warrant. From what he'd seen, he wasn't too concerned it might be the hub of a regional crime ring. Trampling down a large thistle, Flock looked in the living room window. The gap in the sun-faded drapes only provided a dim light. Enough to tell the furnishings were not from the Rollands' mansion. More like something found in the back of a thrift store.

The sound of a vehicle made him turn toward the road. A car sped past. These rural roads didn't get much traffic. He looked over at the garage again. Wherever they'd offloaded their stolen goods, it certainly wasn't here.

Flock reached into a pocket for his phone and found his cigarettes. What the hell. Nobody quit mid-pack. He lit one up, then called Naipaul.

"The owner of the Nissan is Devon Millcroft," said Sunil. "Age 27. Lives in Burlington at 1027 Prospect Street, unit 310. And it gets better. I thought his name seemed familiar—turns out it's linked to a call Devika Sumra made from her office phone. If you want to give the guy a ring, I can give you his number."

"Hang on to it for now, and start checking Millcroft's phone history. He's probably called Stober a time or two, so you can check his log as well. I'll swing by Prospect Street, though I doubt he's there if his Nissan is here. I'll also ask the inspector to put some eyes on both places."

He sucked in some nicotine and contemplated his tar-stained fingers. The sun was still fairly high. Only the breeze had dropped. Flock generally liked this time of year. He could sit on a patio with a drink and a smoke. None of his joints ached like they did in the winter, and he could rent a cottage by the beach where the women were all tanned and scantily clad.

Yup, summer was his favourite season—except for when he had to stand around a scraggy dust blown yard in a shirt, tie, and slacks.

Then it was just too damn hot.

CHAPTER 27

Considering it was less than a fortnight since they'd been cleaned out, the Rollands had done remarkably well getting their place refurnished. Even the artwork included original oils and watercolours, stuff mainly found in art galleries, as were the unique pieces of decorative pottery.

"I know the sofa doesn't quite match the armchairs," said Beth Rolland, as if the gentlemen sitting in them had noticed. "When we move, I'll probably get it recovered."

She cast an appraising eye over the rest of the room, still not sure she was satisfied with their acquisitions.

"Since the new place will have a contemporary design, we thought we should go with modern decor. And not that mid-century modern crap everyone seems to rave about. There's nothing nostalgic about orange stick furniture from the seventies." Her nose wrinkled at the repugnance of it.

"This room used to be mostly French Provincial. I guess you didn't see it. Nice pieces. Some Chippendale. Tiffany. That sort of thing."

She sat perched on the edge of her not quite right contemporary sofa, hands folded in her lap.

"Where are my manners? Would you like something to drink, Inspector? How about you, Sergeant?"

"We're fine, Mrs. Rolland," said Lareault. "Stopped for lunch before we came here."

Though Lareault had a few questions lined up, her comments had prompted another thought.

"Your realtor seems to be working hard to get this house sold, yet construction hasn't started on your other place. What will you do if someone makes an offer, here?"

Rolland sighed. "Yes, we discussed this with Catrina. They should have poured the foundation weeks ago. Once that was done, the builder assured us they would have the house built in two months—though I find that a bit optimistic. Anyway, we'd try to delay the closing as long as possible. Failing that, we'd have to rent somewhere to bridge the gap."

"And, what if we get your belongings back, what would you do with them?"

"Oh." She blinked. "Hadn't really thought about it. Do you think that's possible?"

Lareault gave a small shrug. "Something to be considered. We are in the business of solving crimes, and actually have a time or two."

"Of course."

"So, what would you do with your reclaimed goods?"

She looked around. "There was so much stuff. Some I would like to have back, and could find a place for. Most of the furniture, though, really wouldn't work in the new space. I'd either put it in storage, for when Mandy gets her own place, or put it on consignment in one of my family's antique shops."

"That's right, you have shops," said Lareault. "How many, again?"

"Just the two. One's in Hamilton, on Ottawa Street. The other is in Kingston."

"I always think there's an interesting chain of ownership, with antique shops, since nothing comes straight from a manufacturer. It's all second, third, maybe fourth hand."

Rolland nodded knowingly. "Every piece comes with its own little history."

"So, how do your stores acquire stock?"

Comfortable with the question, Rolland sat back and crossed her legs. On the suspended foot, her sandal dangled off toes with peach-coloured nails.

"Most of it comes from estate sales and auctions. Otherwise, people bring their items in—we'll purchase them if the asking price leaves some room for profit."

"And how do you know the legitimacy of those items?"

The leg she'd been casually swinging stopped moving. "We get pretty good at spotting fakes, though some do slip through."

"I meant how would you know the item belonged to the seller? That the art déco lamp isn't a stolen item?"

"Like my Lalique vase?" She smiled wryly. "Quite honestly, you have take it on faith they're the owner. Occasionally, they'll provide provenance: you know, have a picture of their grandmother sitting next to the lamp. But not often. And, yes, sometimes you get the feeling they're shady."

"What would you do then?"

"We'd take our time to look over what they'd brought in. Ask a few questions about it. If it still smelled funny, we'd politely say we haven't got the room, or the budget, or we're just not accepting stock, right now." She glanced over at Bloomfield who was jotting notes on a pad.

"Would you call the police?"

"That's not likely. We'd have no proof—unless we'd received a bulletin to be on the lookout for certain people or items. That happens from time to time."

"Having been in the business for so many years, you must know a lot of the dealers around."

"Quite a few, though more people are getting into it. Mostly hobbyists with a garage and a webpage."

"Have you put out the word to be on the lookout for your stolen items?"

Rolland shook her head. "It'd be like whistling in the wind. There's so many people in the trade. Be impossible to contact even half of them."

"The crew that cleaned out this place were organized. There've been other similar incidents this year. However, we now have a description of the truck because someone saw it in your driveway." Lareault paused as he felt a vibration from his phone. He saw the call was from Roy Flock.

"Excuse me a moment." He got up and made his way to the front door.

"Actually, perhaps I will have something to drink," said Bloomfield, to fill in the gap.

"Sure thing." Rolland seemed happy to get up and do something. "Coffee?"

"That would be nice, thanks."

Lareault returned a couple of moments before Beth Rolland came in with mugs, milk, sugar, and spoons on a tray. He had time to tell Bloomfield that Flock had a lead on the burglars, and that he'd requested stakeouts of their residences.

"I brought you a coffee, Inspector, in case you decided to join us."

"Very kind. Thank you."

Lareault waited until they'd all sipped at their mugs, then said, "We were talking about detecting frauds in the antique game. Have you ever heard of anyone making shady deals?"

Rolland met his eyes for a moment, then looked away. She shrugged.

"Folks in this business protect their sources, legit or otherwise. Mainly so others don't go fishing there. And it's all resale: there's no regulation, no limit, on how much something can be bought or sold, for."

"And mostly cash, too, I'll bet," Bloomfield chimed in.

That seemed to hit a nerve. "Yes, a fair bit of cash trades hands. Why not? Cash is still legal tender."

The big sergeant grinned. "Oh, I've seen some that wasn't. Even so, makes for a bit of leeway at tax time." Now it was his turn to hold Rolland's gaze.

"We always give receipts for everything."

"Receipts are good," acknowledged Bloomfield. "Speaking of which," he pulled a sheet from the leather satchel he'd brought, "you'll be pleased to know we've recovered your safe."

Rolland's expression of bewilderment morphed into a fabricated smile. "Oh, that's great! Who had it?"

"We'll get to that in a minute." Bloomfield slid the sheet across the coffee table to her. "Are these the safe's contents you claimed as stolen?"

Rolland picked up the page and gave it a cursory glance. "To the best of my recollection, this is what was in there." She made to hand it back.

Bloomfield waved it off. "You can keep that. It's a copy, though you might want to recheck everything. A few of the pricey items on your list weren't found in the safe."

"Well, um, maybe the thief had already passed them on or something."

"We don't think so. In fact, we're pretty sure they hadn't even opened the strongbox."

It was subtle, but her lips pursed slightly and her cheeks sucked in. "How do you know this?"

Bloomfield deferred to Lareault.

"We came upon the suspect before they got that far."

"In the nick of time, eh? Just like on TV."

Her weak smile faded when Lareault said, "Unfortunately, not in time for the suspect. They'd been murdered."

Her head dropped and made a little 'no' motion. When she looked back up, first at Lareault, then at Bloomfield, her eyes were becoming moist.

"What's going on here? First there's a body in my basement. Now the person who took my safe has been killed." She put a hand to her mouth. "Mandy? Are we going to be next?"

Lareault let that thought congeal for a few seconds.

"We can assign a car to sit outside. However, we would like to know where you were last Friday afternoon?"

Rolland made like she was searching her memory banks, but Lareault was sure she was assessing her situation.

"I was here, I think."

"You're not sure?"

"Yes, I was here."

"Can anyone verify that?"

Rolland slowly shook her head. "Julian was at work, and Mandy had gone shopping with her friend."

She watched Bloomfield make a note. "Is that when the other person was killed?"

"The other victim was called Devika Sumra." Bloomfield put aside his pad and pulled out a head shot of Sumra. "Have you heard of, or seen this person, before? We think she may have been to your home."

Rolland shook her head. "Our realtor may have shown them around."

"And the name Pamela Hovarth doesn't ring a bell?"

"Who?"

"That was the person in the rug. Is there anything else you can tell us about the burglary? Something you might have left out?"

"Nothing comes to mind. We were in Toronto a few days getting ready for the film festival. We got a call to come home and found the house emptied out. There was a body—this Hovarth person in our basement." A French-manicured finger wiped moisture from her eye.

She put her mug back on the tray and composed herself. Now sitting straight-backed on the edge of the cushion, she said, "Okay, so you've found someone with my safe. Anything else I should know?" Her tone matched her posture.

"We can tell you blonde hairs were on the rug wrapped around the corpse in your basement."

Lareault's stare left no mistake about the implication.

She looked away dismissively. "I already told you that wasn't our rug. And, if you must know," she lowered her voice, "mine's not natural. It's coloured."

"As were the hairs we found."

Either she didn't hear his comment or chose to ignore it.

"I go to Kim's Cuts. Only place in town that does a good colour job. Jennifer Heatherington gets her roots done, there."

Lareault didn't need reminding that his suspect was an old friend of his boss.

"So, we'd like to take some DNA samples…"

"From me?"

"…from you and your husband."

"Julian? Why?"

"Is your husband home, Mrs. Rolland?" Lareault didn't think so. Although it was a big house, he felt he could sense when other people were nearby.

"Er, no. He had to go to a script meeting."

"Not a problem. If we can get samples from his hairbrush, we won't have to bother him later."

"Um, I'm not sure about this. Should we be contacting our lawyer?"

"That is your right, if you feel the need to."

Beth Rolland got up from the sofa. "I think I should at least call my husband about this. Excuse me."

Casting a glance back as she reached the curving staircase, she ascended to the second floor.

The two policemen sat quietly but couldn't hear any of her conversation with Julian Rolland. When she came back down, she handed Lareault a hairbrush.

"Julian said to give you whatever you asked for."

Lareault handed the brush to his sergeant who placed it in an evidence bag from his satchel. Bloomfield then pulled on a pair of nitrile gloves and brought out a DNA sample kit.

"How often does your husband visit the building site at Rattlesnake Point?" Lareault asked.

Rolland waved a hand. "I dunno. Rarely. They have only staked the lot, so there's not much to see right now. Why is that important?"

"Because," said Lareault, watching her face. "We think he was meeting Hovarth there."

CHAPTER 28

Fenn had seen his fiancée battered and bruised before. You don't get to be a provincial martial arts champion without taking some knocks. This bout, however, had sent her home with fractured ribs. By the time they pulled into their driveway, the adrenaline had worn off and Asha winced in pain as Fenn helped her from the car.

She'd hunched under a hot shower, not wanting a bath in case she couldn't get out of it, then taken a couple of Tylenol 3's and gone to bed. Fenn also had a few tender spots, but only the gash above his eye stung when the water hit.

They'd slept until nearly noon. Fenn made brunch and was pleased to see Asha hadn't lost her appetite. He knew from personal experience there wasn't much one could do about rib fractures beyond applying ice packs and restricting movement.

His concern for Asha barely tempered his anger at Yunni for her betrayal.

"Do you think that conniving bitch even gave us a legitimate address?" Fenn looked at both sides of Nicolas Wray's business card.

"Let me see."

Fenn handed it to Asha. She was still in her flannel jammies. Her shoulder length hair was disheveled, and her eyes were slightly puffy from sleep. Fenn had to resist the urge to take her in his arms.

"Pretty sure a man wrote this. If not Wray, then maybe Dsuban." She handed it back.

The address was on Barton Street, a major thoroughfare which ran for miles through Hamilton

"I think this place is actually in Stoney Creek," he said.

"How can you tell?"

"Barton has three sections: Barton Street which is in Stoney Creek, Barton Street East, and Barton Street West."

"Okay. Assuming this really is where Benny hangs out, now what?"

Asha moved stiffly to an overstuffed armchair and put her feet on the ottoman. Fenn gave her a clinical once over. The only visible abrasion was a bruised cheekbone, yet he knew the discolouration beneath the towel-wrapped icepack held against her side would be much worse.

"I'm not sure, yet. Whatever it is, your part will be to stay right here."

"I'd be fine to sit in the car."

"And do what? All I want to do is check the place out, look for indications that Benny really is a fence. Maybe even talk to him. Wray was willing to listen. Who knows, this guy might be reasonable." He caught Asha's dubious look.

"Alright, there's a bit of risk involved. And, if things go south, you won't even be able to drive away. You can barely lift your arm."

"I could call the cops. Listen, I don't want you doing this alone."

"Maybe Demers can come with me."

Asha shook her head. "C'mon, Chas. Tony's getting married next weekend. He's got enough on his plate. Besides, if anything happened to him now, Kim would kill you right after I did."

She had a point.

"You're right, but we have a lead that should be followed, sooner rather than later. Let me think about this."

He turned on the radio. The noon news summary made no mention of the biker brawl the night before. He wondered if it had affected Wray's take. Maybe it had. Maybe not. Fifty bucks a head at the door should have covered the expenses—unless there were damages. He'd seen aluminum poles from the temporary barriers swung with malevolent intent, and a speaker tower for the PA system crash to the floor. Also, the night's premature end must have reduced profits from the bookies and the bar. Fenn hoped so, though that was poor compensation for Asha's injuries.

They spent most of the afternoon napping, Asha in the armchair and Fenn on the sofa with Mogg purring softly on his chest. Supper was pizza. Even after a lazy day, Asha's body still needed to heal and the Tylenol 3's made her dopey. She was back in bed and asleep by eight o'clock.

Fenn, on the other hand, had regained some energy. Itching to check out Benny's place, nothing on television held his attention. He'd watched enough crime shows to know a case goes cold after forty-eight hours, and it had been two and a half days since they'd talked to Nicolas Wray. The shelf life of tips from mobsters couldn't be much longer.

He looked over the business card again. He should at least drive by the place to see if the address was valid. An hour there and back, tops.

Fenn turned off the TV, went to the kitchen, and wrote Asha a note. Checked his pockets for wallet, phone, and car keys then laced up his Merrills.

"Guard the house, Mogg," he said on his way out the door.

Still on the sofa, Mogg twitched an ear and curled her tail over her nose.

Fenn cruised Barton Street until he homed in on the building that matched the address on the card. It was a one-storey square structure with a flat roof. The size of a mid-sized box store surrounded by a proportional parking lot, it adjoined a similar property on which, according to the signage, sat a manufacturer of hydraulic systems. No such signage existed for Benny's place. Fenn hadn't even seen a street number. He'd located it by the numbers on either side.

He drove the Challenger onto the deserted lot of the hydraulics factory and parked as far from Benny's place as he could. He shut the car down and for several minutes sat in semi-darkness, watching the traffic pass by on Barton. This stretch of road on the outskirts of Hamilton was no less busy than downtown at this hour. The only difference being fewer pedestrians.

With Asha declaring Tony out of bounds, he'd considered calling Joe Posada just to have someone nearby if needed. Joe, however, would be at one of Burlington's hot spots by now. Either with a date or chatting someone up.

Fenn got out of the car and surveyed the eaves of the hydraulics plant for surveillance cameras. Finding none, he moved close to the building. The wall facing Benny's place had a side entrance within an alcove. He stepped into the shadow of it and crouched in the corner to watch for signs of life. Across the way, the front entrance had a frosted glass door. A row of small windows ran along the top of the wall to allow natural light into the warehouse. Near the rear corner was a large overhead door. This would be the shipping and receiving entrance. The lack of a raised dock meant trucks would drive straight in to be unloaded, via ramp or forklift.

The brickwork on both buildings denoted construction in the fifties or sixties. As Fenn studied the exterior, he noticed a drainpipe running from the roof to the ground. It reminded him of a shoe factory behind which he'd played road hockey as a kid. At least once a day, their napless tennis ball would end up on the roof. Fenn would be the one to climb up and get it. He'd scale the drainpipe which was cast iron and fixed securely to the wall, unlike the thin aluminum guttering now used. These looked similar. It could be a way in. Climb onto the roof and see if there was a skylight, or access through one of the small windows.

Satisfied the place was deserted he stood up and stretched. About to leave, he froze when a bright light flashed across the alcove. He watched the bluish beam skate across the middle lot followed by a dark Mercedes that curled in to park near the frosted glass door. Fenn eased back into shadow. The sedan's interior lit up as the driver's door cracked open. Pushing it wide, a rotund man in dark slacks and suit jacket got out. He tapped at a keypad on the wall beside the front entrance and went inside.

Lights illuminated the frosted glass then the upper windows of the warehouse.

Fenn leaned against the alcove wall and folded his arms. That had to be Benny.

At least Yunni and Wray gave us that much, he told himself. *Now what?*

This evening was like the previous one. Warm with high humidity. Too much haze and sky glow to see stars. He couldn't remember the last time it had rained. Hopefully, it wouldn't for the wedding, which was going to be outdoors.

Alright, Fenn. Stay on task. What are you going to do?

He considered his options.

He could walk in the front door and pretend he needed directions to the highway. That might not get him much past the entrance.

He could tell Benny he knew about the fencing operation. Threaten to tell the cops unless he answered his questions. Very PI, that one, but he had no proof and Benny would likely tell him to fuck off. Or shoot him.

He looked at the drainpipe again. It might be good to get a peek inside the warehouse before he did anything else. That left two options on the table and would give him more time to think of a third. His mind made up, he moved away from the alcove. Then stepped back into it.

A tractor trailer was pulling into the parking lot. As it crawled past in low gear, Fenn saw the large overhead door start to rise. An expanding pool of light spread across the lot as it rolled up toward the roof. The truck moved toward it, slowing further as it turned to align with the entrance.

Once inside, the rig's air brakes hissed, and Fenn heard the clatter of a diesel engine shutting down. The door remained up near the roof.

Thinking it a safe bet Benny would be occupied with the truck, Fenn sprinted across to the Mercedes. Not one of the newer models and in need of a wash. He noted the plate number, then made his way across the front of the building and down along the far side. He figured he could circle the warehouse to come upon the rear door from the back. That way, he wouldn't be caught in the open if the truck suddenly backed out or Benny went to his car.

What he didn't expect was a similar bay door near the end of the other wall. It was closed but obviously the exit for large trucks. Along the back was a narrow lane. On the far side of the asphalt was an untidy row of shrubbery bordering a set of railway tracks. He hurried along to the next corner. Diesel fumes still hung in the air. Fenn could hear voices. One that he presumed was Benny's didn't sound too pleased.

He edged forward and risked a quick look. The truck was parked in the centre of three lanes marked on the stained cement. Benny was closing the trailer's back door. The heavy metal latch clanked into place.

"I ought to send this lot back with you. I don't mind paying back a favour, but, jeez, they should know better than to ship me stuff like this. Pass through or not. I mean, did you smell that in there? You must have had a friend at the Falls."

"Hey, man, I's jus' the driver, here. And I ain't goin' to try getting that back across the border. I only got the one friend. I either unhook right here, or drop it next door."

"You're lucky I ain't paying for this." Benny sighed audibly. "Alright. Drop it down. I'll have it gone in an hour, anyway."

Fenn squatted by the back wall and listened to the mechanical sounds of a trailer being detached from a tractor. Benny must have wandered away. His voice had a slight echo.

"Come to the office when you're done. There is something you can take back for me."

The tractor started up, ran briefly, then shut down. Probably moving away from the trailer. He risked a second look around the corner. The driver was walking toward the front of the warehouse. Once he drove away, the door would close and Fenn would be back to square one. On the outside.

He slipped past the door rails and quickly scaled the nearest storage rack until he could lie on the top shelf. Hidden from view. It was a fair bit warmer near the roof. He felt a lump in his pocket. His phone. He pulled it out and switched off the ringer. Another lesson he'd learned the hard way.

He could hear Benny and the driver talking in the office, though not what they were saying. The other bay door began to roll up and a light breeze stirred between the openings. It had little effect. Fenn felt sweat trickling down his side. The driver came back alone, carrying a large, padded envelope. He climbed into his truck and drove out into the night. The exit door came down, yet the entryway remained open. Perhaps Benny was letting the diesel fumes dissipate.

From his perch, Fenn peered down at the aisles of furniture, appliances, and crates of brand name merchandise. In a bay beside the door was a Bobcat forklift. His curiosity peaked by what might be in the trailer he descended stealthily and crept over to the back of it. The licence plate was a New York registration. Fenn didn't bother memorizing it in case he got confused with the plate number of the Mercedes.

Benny had turned on a radio. He was probably waiting for whoever was supposed to take the shipment away. His hand on the trailer's door latch, Fenn began to quietly raise it when he heard a polite cough behind him.

"About time you showed up. I thought you'd come to visit, last night."

Fenn lowered the lever back into place. Turning slowly, he gauged the distance to the door. If he could get outside, there was no way this pudgy fence could catch him. Then he saw the large gray pistol in Benny's hand. It was a German Luger. A World War II relic with a hefty hand grip and a long barrel. Quite accurate at close range.

"Nic said he'd heard a two-bit thief would drop by sometime soon to case the place. This your first job, or what? You didn't even check for a beam."

He pointed with the gun. The overhead lights made it impossible to see the thin laser beam, but Fenn now saw the modules, transmitter and receiver, on posts about knee high on either side of the entrance. Benny would have got a signal when Fenn tripped it. He'd turned on the radio, gone out the front door while the truck was leaving, then walked down the outside of the warehouse to get the drop on him.

Nicolas Wray had sold them out again.

"Look, I just wanted to—"

"Save it, Sunshine. Let's go to the office so I can call the cops."

Benny motioned with the pistol.

Fenn half raised his hands and made to walk up the aisle. He thought it was odd that a crook like Benny would offer to call the cops. But, before he could fathom why, a lightning bolt struck the base of his skull and his world went black.

CHAPTER 29

Benny looked at the guy lying on the cement, then at the Luger in his hand. These days it made a better club than a pistol, the previous owner having half-filled the barrel with molten lead. Benny didn't like guns, as a rule, but when you pointed a Luger at someone, you knew you had their attention.

He knelt beside the unconscious form of the intruder to make sure he was still breathing. The guy looked to be in his thirties and pretty fit, with broad shoulders and muscular arms. Benny was glad there hadn't been a scuffle. The last physical altercation he'd had was in grade six, and he'd mostly covered up until the bully lost interest. Never a fighter, and certainly not a killer, he now wondered what he was going to do with this guy. Out cold for the moment, he would eventually wake up.

"Fuckin' Wray," he muttered. Benny wouldn't be surprised if Nicolas Wray had sent the guy over, then ratted him out so Benny would owe Wray a favour. He had done little business with the mobster, and would rather not be in his debt.

"And yet here we are," he said to the body on the ground. Benny looked around until he found a roll of packing tape on a shelf. He pulled the guy's arms back and taped the wrists together, then brought over a wooden pallet with the Bobcat forklift. He left it beside the guy while he opened the trailer doors.

"Alright, settle down. I'm going to rearrange things a bit, and I don't want any nonsense from you lot." Several pairs of eyes stared back timidly except for one set that held pure malevolence. He raised the forks on the Bobcat and got to work. Normally, Benny would skim some of whatever came into the warehouse. This time, he was going to add something. It was as far as he'd go in making someone disappear. The Russians who received the load, however, would be much more thorough.

Knowing this, Benny didn't go through the guy's pockets before he rolled him onto the pallet. Better to not know anything about him, especially who he was. Plausible deniability. If the cops came by, he could honestly say he'd never heard of a guy with whatever name they gave. He wouldn't even tell Stober there was an extra passenger on the manifest.

He returned the forklift to its bay and took the Luger back to his office. Stober would be arriving any time now. From a small closet beside the bathroom, Benny pulled a fresh shirt off a hanger. The one he'd been wearing was damp from the exertion of rearranging the load on the trailer. It had also absorbed some of the stink.

He washed his face and slicked back his thinning hair. The image in the mirror wasn't flattering. Never had been, really, though lately he wondered if, after forty years, it was time he gave up this gig. He'd started with a pawnshop on King Street in Hamilton. Still somewhat profitable, it made a good front come tax time. He'd also been part-owner of an antique shop. When the other partner, a woman originally from Lithuania, died from lung cancer, Benny closed it down, not wanting to sit around and get old with the furniture. By then, he'd realized he could get better turnaround as a middleman.

There were always crews looking to offload their stolen goods. And also antique dealers or owners of used appliance shops, who weren't too fussy about where they got their stock. He was already fencing jewelry through the pawnshop, though just a few special pieces, discreetly, to stay off the radar.

The Barton Street warehouse had allowed him to branch out to new, still in the box, goods: stuff that fell off the back of trucks or, sometimes, even the whole load. It also took the pressure off the pawnshop, his semi-legitimate front. With the only such distribution centre in Ontario, the past decade had been profitable for Benny. Unfortunately, even in crime, demographics change. Competition from people like Nicolas Wray upped the ante, and there also seemed to be more violence attached to the heists. Hell, there was a dead body in the basement at Stober's last job.

And now, some fuckin' guy had come sneaking into the warehouse, looking to rip him off. There was no respect, no boundaries, anymore. Maybe he should do what his wife had always wanted: cash out and move to Florida while he still had some good years left.

That would be his first wife, Margot.

Margot had hung in there for sixteen anniversaries. He still wasn't sure why finding that motel receipt was her 'final straw' when there'd been nearly a dozen other straws over the years. His second wife, a gold-digger called Yulia, had been one of those straws. She'd kept dancing at the Velvet Glove for the whole three years, which he didn't mind since he was often in there. She'd made great tips, even after scaling back her lap dancing to just dancing on the laps.

Yulia had a great ass and a nose for coke. Though Benny wasn't into drugs he'd bankrolled her habit. Mainly because it made her horny. She'd go down deep enough to lick his balls. And, eventually, another guy's balls. Last he'd heard of Yulia she was living in Toronto with her dealer. Some stud who looked like a young Mike Tyson. She hadn't contested the divorce.

That was over ten years ago. He'd reconciled himself to living alone and, truth be told, didn't get the urge so much. If he wanted sex, he could go find a hooker. If he wanted loyalty and love, he could go find a dog. Simpler that way.

Lights flashed through the frosted glass, followed by the grumble of a diesel engine in low gear. Benny left his office with a sheet that had the trailer's destination address and a manifest. He watched Stober's Freightliner roll past the trailer. It pulled in front, then backed up ready to connect. Benny hit the button to open the exit door to let the fumes out. He was mildly surprised when Devon Millcroft hopped down from the passenger seat.

"Hey Benny! How's it hangin'?"

"What are you doing here, on a Saturday night? That's no way to keep your girlfriend happy."

The grin disappeared and Millcroft said, "Uh, well, that's over."

Stober came around the front of the truck. He put a hand on the black fender.

"Right, where we goin', and when do we have to be there?"

Benny handed him the paperwork.

"Windsor. Here's the address. It's what you might call time-sensitive, so the sooner you drop it off, the better. Just get a signature and come home."

Although both bay doors were open, an odour lingered that wasn't diesel related. Stober took a couple of sniffs.

"What's that smell?"

Benny handed him a packet. "Here's your twenty-five hundred. The longer you hang around, the worse the smell will get."

He started to walk away, then said, "I might have another load for you, Thursday or Friday. I'll let you know."

Back in his office, he pretended to be busy until he heard Stober's truck pulling out of the warehouse. It was nights like this that made him feel old. Too old to fight. Too old to fuck. Too old to give a damn.

Florida was looking better all the time.

CHAPTER 30

Stober liked driving late at night. Once they'd left the outskirts of Hamilton, the traffic thinned until only the odd vehicle cast light in the over-sized wing mirror. Bright, brighter, then dark until red taillights grabbed the eye and held it. Hypnotic points that got smaller and closer together until they disappeared completely on a curve or beyond the crest of a hill. Stober blinked and refocused. Sitting high in the Freightliner's cab, gauges glowing on the dash, he could watch the white lane markers flow past the truck's long hood for hours, the harmonic hum of road and engine a soothing white noise in which to think.

Extensive farmland bordered the highway between Ancaster and Brantford. In the pre-dawn darkness, the few dwellings were unlit, mostly invisible, adding to the sense of isolation. And truckers were solitary by nature. The journey always better than the eventual destination.

He looked over at Millcroft. Devon had been uncharacteristically quiet. Normally chatty, he'd mainly just stared out the window since they'd left Benny's place. Devika Sumra's death had been a shock, and the circumstances troubling. Stober understood. With the cops now investigating two possible homicides, and their burglary of the Rollands' place, someone would eventually connect the dots.

That had also occurred to Millcroft.

"I think we should take off, Marsh. Be somewhere else for a while?"

The same thought had crossed Stober's mind. Of course, that would be easy for Millcroft who had few attachments. Stober had a business to consider. Then again, he did work for himself. No employees, and the jobs were all freelance: a load here, a load there, and supplemented by the house clearing arrangements they had with the white witch and Benny. If he wanted to take off for a while, he was limited only by his savings, or ability to find work.

"Where would you want to go?"

"I've never been out west. Always wanted to see British Columbia."

"B.C. is nice. Rains a fair bit in parts."

"We ought to get out of Ontario, at least. Have you ever been to Quebec?"

"Parlez-vous Francais?"

"France? That's a bit far."

Stober grinned in the darkness.

"You know, Dev, if the shit really hits the fan and we have to take off, we may want to leave Canada altogether. It won't just be Ontario cops looking for us. It'll be the RCMP, nation-wide."

"So, down to the States."

"That'd be my choice. Lots of places where they're not particular about permits, and such. They're just happy if you'll haul their load for cash. Wouldn't be hard to get another set of plates. Should probably repaint the truck, too."

Millcroft turned back to stare out the window.

"We could head over now," he said, after a few moments. "Drop this load off and keep going. Cross the border into Detroit, and head south, or west. Wherever."

Stober mulled that over. And not for the first time. It only took a small misstep, or the right word in the wrong ear, for a criminal to become a fugitive. When he saw the body rolled up in the rug, he knew they should have abandoned the job. And would have if the trailer wasn't already full. They didn't know Beth Rolland had called in her own house, so figured there wouldn't be time to unload before the homeowners came back.

As it stood, Beth Rolland knew they were involved, Benny knew they were involved, Devika Sumra knew they were involved—and she was now dead. Who else?

"You might be right about bugging out, Dev. The cops are all over this, and if they get desperate to convict it won't matter we didn't kill anyone."

Millcroft slapped the dash.

"That's what I've been trying to tell you. I don't want to get strung up on circumcised evidence."

"Circumstantial."

"What is?"

"Never mind. You word is probably more accurate."

Millcroft removed his ball cap and ran fingers through his hair.

"So, are we going to go? Tonight?"

Stober became distracted by a warning light on the dash. It had come on earlier, then blinked out.

"Maybe. But I'd like to go home first. I've a stash of cash in my safe, and I wouldn't mind grabbing some more tools. Maybe a change of clothes. Is there anything you want from your place before we go?"

Millcroft shrugged. "Not really. I packed an extra pair of jeans when I came to your place."

"Passport?"

"In my bag, in case we got a cross-border run."

"Yeah: I keep mine in the—oh, I don't like the look of that."

Stober tilted his head so he could better see the brake indicator. It blinked off, then came back on. He looked up the road. The shoulder was wide and clear of debris if he had to pull over quickly. Then the buzzer started. It, too, was intermittent at first.

"We're losing pressure to the air brakes. We'll have to stop soon, but I'd rather stash the trailer somewhere, then find a garage. If we stop here and call for a mobile repair unit, we might attract a Ministry Inspector."

Millcroft understood. Ontario had a high standard for road safety regulations, and plenty of inspectors patrolling to enforce them. It was bad enough to get pulled over and issued a fine for a mechanical infraction. If they inspected the trailer, to make sure the load was secure and the contents properly stored, it would be game over. Showing the fake manifest Benny had supplied would be little more than a Hail Mary.

"What d'ya think is in the trailer, anyway?"

"Damned if I know. Sure smelled foul. Not sure I want to find out." Stober pointed ahead.

"Off-ramp. We're getting near Brantford." He signaled and downshifted. The buzzing sound continued, and the brake pedal felt soft.

From the ramp, they could see a small factory that overlooked the highway. Being Sunday morning, the place was deserted. As good a place as any to drop the trailer while they got the Freightliner's air brake system looked at. Stober drove to the back of the building where the loading bays were. It faced the highway, beyond which the horizon was brightening with the first hint of dawn.

Fenn gradually became aware of movement beneath him, yet didn't think he was moving. It was odd. Kind of like lying on a conveyor belt. You're not moving, but you are. Shifting slightly, he felt rough wood beneath his cheek. He realized his wrists were taped behind his back. He'd been packaged. Maybe he really was on a conveyor belt. Trussed up so his arms wouldn't flail and become damaged in transit. People hate getting damaged goods. Like that mixer Asha had to send back. Disappointing.

He vaguely wondered where he was being shipped to.

Maybe there was time for a nap.

A jolt brought Fenn back to consciousness. Still trussed and lying on wood, all seemed to be still though he could hear indistinct voices and some clanking. There was an engine idling nearby. It was also completely dark.

Open your eyes, Fenn.

That helped only a little. A very soft light reflected off a latticework of wire. Some sort of barrier or cage. The source was a square of clear plastic directly above. Fenn twisted his head for a better look and immediately regretted it. The dull ache at the base of his skull exploded into intense pain.

Let's go to the office so I can call the cops, Benny said.
Bullshit.

He lay still until the pain subsided. It chased away the last of the fog in his brain. Probably concussed. He moved his arms experimentally and concluded his wrists were bound with packing tape. There'd been a roll on a shelf in the warehouse. On the plus side, it would tear fairly easily if he could get it started. Gingerly, so as not to wrench his neck, he worked himself into a sitting position. The gaps in the slats beneath him were evenly spaced. He was on a wooden pallet.

But what was that fetid smell from?

He sensed a restlessness around him. And barely perceptible sounds. Not from the idling engine. That had stopped, or had driven away while he'd contended with the fireworks in his skull.

The restlessness seemed to be a response to his own movements.

He hitched himself fully upright. His back was definitely against the wire mesh of a cage. He stretched out his legs and his foot hit another cage. Instantly, there was a primeval wildcat scream and something powerful hit the mesh and slashed at his foot. Fenn tried to retract his leg but long claws snagged his laces and tugged angrily back while another large paw bashed at the mesh and tore into the leg of his jeans.

What. The. Fuck!

Fenn frantically kicked at the mesh with his free foot, two, three times. That only intensified the snarls and the beast's efforts to shred his leg. Sharp points scraped down his calf, tearing the skin and bringing blood until his fourth desperate kick unhooked his shoe. He quickly retracted both feet and sat panting from the exertion.

The short but violent clash had set off a cacophony of screeching, howling, and whimpering. None of it seemingly human. While he couldn't see what was in the cage near his feet, he could perceive the dangerous energy barely contained within the thin wires. Heart still pounding, he inhaled deeply and exhaled slowly.

Curled up on the pallet as far from the snarling beast as possible, Fenn looked around. He now had a good idea of the trailer's cargo, but had to get his wrists free before he could deal with it. The commotion gradually subsided while he felt around the wooden pallet for a sharp edge. His knuckles scraped over the head of a nail. It was raised maybe a quarter inch. Enough to start a tear in the packing tape and within minutes he was peeling the sticky plastic wrap from his skin.

He explored his pockets and was surprised to find not only his cellphone but his wallet. That Benny was certainly a strange bird. Hadn't called the cops, hadn't shot him, hadn't taken his belongings. Instead, he'd shut him in a trailer to be dealt with by whomever smuggled dangerous, and likely endangered, animals into the country.

The adrenaline rush diminished until it no longer masked the constant throbbing at the base of his skull. He reached up and gently probed the area. There was a small lump, but it didn't feel like the skin was broken.

So why was the shoulder of his shirt wet?

He switched on the phone and used the display light to look around.

Several pairs of eyes peered back. Small timid faces, white ovals trimmed with black fur.

Monkeys.

"Alright, which one of you little peckers pissed on me?"

Fenn sniffed his shoulder. Yup. Definitely pee.

He turned the phone toward the opposite cage. A pair of red eyes, hot like coals and unflinching, glared back. He could just make out the size and shape of the creature crouched in the back corner of its enclosure. Fenn guessed black leopard or maybe a puma.

"Well, shit," he said quietly.

CHAPTER 31

Lareault padded softly from the bedroom, down the short hall and into the living room with hands held out to each side in case he misjudged the wall. That didn't stop him from stumbling on the sandals Koki had left by the sofa. His recovery was inelegant but quiet, nonetheless.

The condo wasn't completely dark. There were a few bright diodes here and there. An amber one on his laptop computer, a red one on the coffeemaker, and the blue digits 4:17 on the microwave's clock. None reflected on the glass of the sliding balcony door, so it was an invisible barrier between the naked man, pale from head to toe from lack of sun, and the dark expanse of Lake Ontario, appearing like a black void from lack of a moon.

The lake had a few points of light to delineate its boundary. Mainly over to the right, toward Burlington Bay, where even at this early hour vehicles travelled the Skyway Bridge. Lareault wondered if the tractor-trailer that Roy Flock had been scouring video for had crossed it into East Hamilton or Stoney Creek or maybe down to Niagara Falls. While it was possible, the truck had gone the other way on the QEW, toward Toronto, the detective inspector felt it hadn't. Crime rates along the Niagara corridor had been rising steadily, and statistics suggested there was an arbitrary line between Burlington and Oakville that determined which way the goods flowed.

Perhaps because he wasn't quite awake, Lareault didn't startle when Koki's breath warmed his neck. She gently bit his ear and slid her silky arms around his waist. He covered them with his own and inhaled her subtle scent.

"I need to do a better job of wearing you out," she whispered.

"Sorry, I didn't mean to wake you."

She shuffled in closer, pressed her breasts against his back, hips against his buttocks, her feet sliding in beneath his ankles.

"Are you warm enough?"

"I am, now."

Lareault was momentarily lost in the embrace of someone he'd come to feel deeply for. Amazed even, that the affection he'd felt for his former wife had transferred so easily over to this woman, someone he'd first met while standing beside a partially burned corpse in a frozen farmer's field. Of course, she'd spoken his language: entry wound, contusion, fibrous material, blood splatter. As for shifting affections, his ex-wife had started that ball rolling when she'd signed up for art class and done more than sketch the live model.

"Want to talk about it?"

"The case?" he said, unwilling to let the past intrude on this new intimacy.

"I know we went over it, after supper, but sometimes you need to stand in the dark at, uh, half-past four in the morning whilst in the embrace of an exotic, completely naked, Kenyan queen to see things in a new light, so to speak."

Lareault chuckled. "Suddenly, I've completely lost my train of thought."

Koki loosened her grip and moved back a step. She slapped his butt.

"No, you haven't. Put the coffee on. I'll get our robes so you can concentrate on something other than me, and we can go over it again."

With the kitchen's under-mount lights as the main illumination, the condo was still relatively dark for the couple on the sofa waiting for their coffees to cool.

"Tell me again about Madam Rolland," prompted Koki.

"Well, you know about the hair samples she gave, and that we're waiting to see if they match those found on the rug."

"You only got them to me yesterday afternoon, and it is the weekend."

"And that's fine. Anyway, I also hinted to Beth that her husband may have been involved with Pamela Hovarth."

"Do you have proof of this?"

"Nope. I was fishing, but the way her mouth dropped open I could have snagged her with a salmon hook."

"Is he a viable suspect?"

"I mainly said it to shake her up—see if anything fell out—but it's another angle to consider. Beth said he'd been to the building site a few times, even though there wasn't much going on. Had he learned of the archaeologist's plan to hold up construction, it's possible he might have done something about it."

"How would he have found out?"

"He could have heard it from Jack Klaasen, the builder."

"But you don't think the builder killed her."

Lareault slurped at his coffee. "Fentanyl poisoning doesn't seem like Jack's style. That she got bashed in the head, with a rock from the site, means we can't rule him out completely, even if it happened post-mortem."

"If spiked coke wasn't Klaasen's style, what about Julian? He could have slipped her the tainted blow. Lots of it floating around the movie biz. And he'd have access to rocks at the site."

"True. And what if he and Hovarth really had an affair? He might have tried to end it, and so she threatened to tell his wife."

"That one's a classic." Motungi tucked her slender legs beneath her on the sofa and rearranged her silk robe to cover them. "Or perhaps Beth caught Julian with his trowel in Hovarth's trench, killed her, and dumped the body in the basement to scare the shit out of him."

Lareault chuckled at the metaphor.

"Be a ballsy move to drop a corpse in your own house. Beth also has an alibi, of sorts. She was in Toronto, as was her husband."

"Toronto is less than an hour's drive from Burlington. She could have nipped back to do the deed. So could her husband…or," Koki gave a little gasp. "Maybe they killed Hovarth, together, so she wouldn't hold up the build. People kill for less and, how convenient, they could alibi each other."

Lareault couldn't help but smile. He was drinking coffee in his robe, beside a gorgeous woman, trying to solve a homicide. Life didn't get much better.

"There is that. I'll make sure we verify their whereabouts for that timeframe."

"So, how does the rug fit into all of this?"

Lareault shrugged. "Someone moving a rug is less suspicious? Since it came from Klaasen's sales office, it becomes another link between our current suspects and the victim. The fact the office appeared to have been broken into doesn't mean it was, and only three people: Klaasen, his salesman, and the realtor, had a key."

"Is the salesman a suspect?"

"He's way down the list for the same reason that rules out his boss—neither had a key to the Rollands'. We're pretty sure the only people to enter the house, when the body could have been planted, were the burglars and the realtor."

"And you've ruled out the realtor?"

"No one's been ruled out. However, the realtor stood to lose a huge commission since she'd profit both ways: the sale, and the purchase of the new lot at Rattlesnake Point. But…" Energized by a new thought, Lareault stood up and went over to the sliding glass door. "…you roll up rugs when you want to move them. Quite the coincidence that all of Rollands' furniture actually got moved."

"Almost like the person who left the body knew 'movers' were coming to the house." Koki used her long fingers to make the air quotes.

"Yet, they took the furniture and left the rug. Someone was definitely sending a message."

"Exactly. We just don't know who was sending, or the intended recipient."

"Okay: who knew the movers were coming?"

"It's fairly obvious that Sumra would have known. And not a stretch to see a safecracker obtaining the keycode for the burglars."

"But she died from the same batch of coke and fentanyl that Hovarth did. Dumb mistake to make, don't you think?"

"That's what Heatherington said. And it's looking more like Sumra was killed to tie up a loose end."

"So, whomever killed Hovarth also killed Sumra."

"Quite likely. While we don't yet know who that is, on the plus side, Roy Flock may have identified the burglars. Sunil is combing their phone records, which already connect them to Sumra. We've also got eyes on their residences."

"Is it possible the burglars killed Sumra to cover their tracks?"

Lareault shrugged. "That would probably mean they also killed Hovarth and, apart from they were all in the Rollands' basement, we haven't found a connection between them."

"Well, perhaps the hair samples or the stakeouts will bear some fruit."

He rubbed his eyes. "Hopefully so, 'cause we need to find the piece we're missing. Something that will hold up in court."

Lareault turned to gaze at the gradual brightening over the lake. Koki left the sofa and, as before, wrapped her arms around him. A hand found its way inside his robe and slid slowly down his torso. His body responded to the gentle tug of her fingers.

"Hmm, I think I've just found the piece that *I* was missing. Shall we see if it will hold up in bed?"

She caught Lareault's glance at the microwave clock.

"It's Sunday, darling. You can take the morning off."

CHAPTER 32

When you're up to your ass in alligators, it's hard to remember that your initial task was to drain the swamp. A classmate had scribbled that in Fenn's high school yearbook. Surrounded, as he was, on three sides by monkeys and on the fourth by one of nature's most perfect killing machines, the quote fit though he couldn't remember the guy's name.

Phil?

Noel?

While the mini primates weren't exactly alligators, their cages did come up to his armpits. And despite the distraction of being scratched and pissed on, his initial task was to get the fuck out of the trailer, not to reminisce about old buddies. Standing in the center of the wooden pallet, he used the cellphone's weak display light to survey the interior.

Bagheera, as he'd called the black-furred assassin, watched his every move from the cage closest to the rear doors. The monkey's crates were stacked three high. Beyond them, the trailer was loaded side to side and a few feet short of the roof with large cartons of cigarettes. It was an odd combination. Smuggled smokes were usually the purview of Native-American crews. Fenn had once read that some tobacco companies actually encouraged this because of the high Canadian tax regulations. Exotic pets, on the other hand, didn't seem like something the First Nations would have an interest in.

Smaller details emerged as the two plexiglass skylights, each a foot square, got brighter with increased daylight. The temperature within was currently comfortable but, as the sun rose, the enclosed space would quickly become a sauna. His phone told him it was 5:20 a.m. Asha was probably still asleep and usually left her phone to charge in the kitchen.

Something he rarely remembered to do. He checked the power bar. Down to twenty percent.

Lots.

He thought about dialing 9-1-1, the emergency line, but figured if he didn't call his fiancée first he'd be just as dead even if he did get out.

She answered on the first ring.

"Chas! Thank goodness. Where are you?"

"Hi, Ash. Well, um, I'm stuck in a trailer."

"What do you mean, *stuck*?"

"Stuck, as in I can't get out. And I'm not entirely sure where I am."

"Jeez, I knew something was wrong when I woke up and you weren't there. I tried phoning you but it just went to voice mail. I was about to call the police—the hospitals..." Asha's voice broke with evident stress.

"Yeah, I'm sorry about that. I just thought I'd scope out Benny's place and, well, I'm going to need some help to get out of here."

"But you're not at Benny's?"

"Pretty sure he shipped me out. I've no idea which roads we took. I only know that our trailer has been dropped off."

"*Our* trailer? Is someone there with you?"

Fenn looked at the unhappy faces of his traveling companions.

"You could say that. Listen, we're wasting time and my battery is getting low. Call the cops. Ask for Bloomfield or Lareault. Have them call me back. Maybe they can trace my location. In the meantime, I'll see if I can figure something out."

"Okay, I'm on it. Be careful. Love you."

"Love you too. I'm hanging up."

Disconnecting he now saw there were three messages waiting. There was no way that would be the last time he'd hear her voice. He was going to get out of this damn box. And, when he did, Benny and Wray were going to pay.

Fenn tucked the phone into his pocket. Then, before the monkeys could react, he scrambled on top of their crates and over onto the cartons of Rothmans. He could walk across them hunched over, which meant if he lay on his back he could kick at the plexiglass in the skylight. The plastic flexed from his first few kicks. The next few cracked it. Catching his breath from the exertion, he noticed how shredded his shoe and pant leg were. Bagheera hadn't been messing around. Stretched out on the carton Fenn had to fight the urge to sleep. The couple hours he'd spent unconscious on the pallet didn't count as rest, and the encounter with the jungle cat had sapped what little energy he did have.

He summoned his strength and kicked again. His foot broke through. Removing the shoe, he put it on his hand and pushed the fragmented shards up and outward. Instantly, cool air flowed down through the opening. The primates perked up and started chittering excitedly. Even Bagheera sniffed with interest at the fresh scents diluting the stale funk in the trailer.

The skylight was too small for Fenn to climb through, but he could stick his head out. The first thing he saw was the brick wall of a large building. No windows on this side, so likely industrial. He turned carefully, so as not to slice his neck on a sharp edge. The trailer was in a deserted parking lot. A further turn revealed a highway, beyond which were fields of hay. The stalks rippled in languid waves as if being gently stroked by a giant hand. Beyond the fields, an unbroken horizon appeared to be giving birth to a pulsating ball of lava. Fenn watched the sun emerge, its colour rapidly changing from red to orange. Today was going to be another scorcher.

His phone rang, so Fenn eased himself down to his knees. The number wasn't Asha's.

"Chas here. Who's this?"

"*This* is Sergeant Bloomfield. Were you not told to stay out of my case?"

"I was."

"And now, you have a problem."

"You could say that. I got shanghaied by a fence called Benny."

"Serves you right."

Bloomfield said 'thanks' but not to Fenn. Then it sounded like he was sipping coffee.

"So, any idea where you are?"

"Apart from, in a trailer, I think I'm in an industrial parking lot beside a highway."

"Ms. Fabiani didn't think you were in physical distress. Are you?"

"Nothing major, though that could change. Even if the bad guys don't come back, it's going to get boiling hot in here."

"Understood. We're tracing this call as we speak. However, any details you can give will help."

"Well, from where the sun is, I know the highway runs east-west, and I'm on the north side. The only four-lane highway surrounded by such farmland, within the time I think we traveled from Stoney Creek, is the 403 heading toward Kitchener. The trailer is parked near a factory, and I saw an overpass, so I think I'm either near Brantford or somewhere close to Waterloo."

"The trace is centering on Brantford. Just stay on the line while we narrow it down."

That caused Fenn to look at his phone's display. A message was blinking.

LOW BATTERY

"Uh, Sergeant. My phone's about to die."

Fenn looked about the trailer for something he could signal with.

"Another few minutes and we should be able to pinpoint you within a couple of kilometers. Anything else that might help us to spot you?"

"Uh, yeah. Tell your guys to look for monkeys."

"Did you say, *monkeys*?"

"Some people send up flares," said Fenn, to the now useless piece of plastic in his hand. "I'm about to send up monkeys."

From their expressions, his audience didn't seem all that impressed.

"You do want to get out of here, right?"

Fenn crawled to the edge of the cartons and pulled the nearest cage up beside him. The enclosure's simple latch was on a metal plate wide enough to foil the little escape artists. He moved the crate to beneath the broken skylight and slowly tipped it until the access door was on top. Its occupant circled inside, as if a rolling cage was a natural thing, then sat holding the end of its tail with tiny hands. There was now a two-foot gap between the top of the cage and the opening in the trailer's roof.

"Before I open this, Marvin," he said, "understand that there's only one exit."

He pointed up but only got a blank look.

"Alright, little buddy. You can do this. Make me proud." With little confidence in his plan, Fenn opened the cage and sat back to watch.

At first Marvin seemed more concerned that his cage had been moved away from the others than about making a bid for freedom. He kept looking at his adopted troop and they, in turn, were watching him. Some, though, looked hopefully at the open vent in the roof. Fenn noted which ones were cognizant of the opening. They'd be the next 'volunteers' in his mission to freedom.

He scarcely registered the movement when Marvin leapt on top of his cage. The little primate looked briefly at Fenn, then at the open skylight. Fenn wished he could have seen, in slow motion, the way Marvin reached up as his hind legs catapulted him through the small square hole in the roof. He disappeared from sight, and Fenn quickly pulled the crate away so he could poke his head out. He found Marvin sitting on his haunches, about halfway to the rear of the trailer, looking around.

"Wait there, Marvin," said Fenn. "I'll get you some company."

He brought up the cage of a monkey that had shown interest in the skylight. This one was not so timid as Marvin. He seemed to thrust out his little chest.

"Okay, Chester. Are you ready? Three—two—one!"

Fenn opened the crate, and there was no hesitation. In two fluid motions, Chester was out of the cage and out of the trailer.

"Atta boy!"

Fenn periscope'd again. Chester had gone the other way, toward the front of the trailer, but Marvin was still pretty much in the same place. This was good. The idea was to have movement all over the trailer, to attract attention. He elected to send up one more—Humphrey—for good measure, then keep the rest in reserve in case the first squad wandered off for a beer.

Having done all he could, and hoping Bloomfield's efforts to find him soon paid off, he lay back on the cartons once again. Cooler air continued to flow gently down, though, having had some of the fresh stuff while looking outside, he noticed once more the putrid pong from the caged animals. He wondered if it would affect the tobacco products he was lying on. He hoped so. Smoking was a disgusting habit.

And it was with that thought that he realized the animals weren't the only ones who had to pee while in captivity.

CHAPTER 33

Fenn, cross-legged on the cartons, was telling his fellow captives about Dieter and Carole Lundsen when the first sign of rescue came.

"I'm sure if you met Dieter you'd see he was a pompous ass. And Carole, well, butter wouldn't melt if she had hot coffee in her mouth. If it wasn't for Asha working there, I'd have been gone long ago. I must admit, though, not many can pull off the sixties and seventies fashion style like those two. You really do need long legs to do bellbottoms justice. And where does one buy orange and brown crocheted vests and velour pants? And those suede leather headbands. I don't see Carole hitting the thrift shops, but maybe she—oh, hey. Did you hear that?"

At least two sets of sirens were getting louder. Fenn stuck his head out through the broken skylight. Marvin was still on the roof, looking around like he'd been dropped off by aliens. Chester and Humphrey must have found their way down. Fenn couldn't see where they'd got to.

The sirens ceased when a patrol car, followed by an ambulance, came around the side of the building and stopped near the trailer. They must have startled the monkeys on the ground because they ran from under the trailer and toward a fence at the edge of the property. The cops got out of their car. One officer hesitantly followed the little fugitives. The other said something into his shoulder mic, then peered up at the trailer.

"Good morning," said Fenn to get his attention.

"Chas Fenn?" The cop was looking warily at Marvin.

"No, he's Marvin. I'm Chas." The joke sailed into the ether.

"Okay, sir, we'll have you out shortly. Are you in need of medical attention?"

"Well, since you brought medics, we should give them something to do." Fenn knew there'd be rabies shots at some point, courtesy of Bagheera. That his shirt reeked of monkey piss bothered him more than the cat scratches or the throbbing lump at the base of his skull.

"Uh, sir? Regarding the monkeys. Anything I should know before we open the trailer?"

"Yeah, there's nine more in here. But they're all caged. Oh, and a black leopard."

"Did you say, *leopard*?"

"Might be a puma. I'm not sure. She's a little cranky."

"In a cage, yes?"

"Affirmative."

"Right. Good. We've contacted the MNR and they're sending someone out. Shouldn't be more than ten minutes. Is it okay if we wait for them?"

Even if the cop opened the trailer, Fenn would rather not squeeze past Bagheera's crate. There were other parts he didn't want clawed. Better to let the Ministry of Natural Resources deal with her.

"That's probably wise."

The officer nodded, glanced again at Marvin, then went to help his partner shepherd the strays away from the fence, beyond which was the highway.

Fenn went back to sitting on the cartons. Ten minutes stretched to a half-hour before he heard a couple of raps on the trailer wall.

"Mr. Fenn. Chas? We're going to unlatch the door. Are the animals secure in their cages?"

"Their bags are packed. Let's go, already."

Fenn felt like shit, looked like shit, and smelled like shit. He just wanted out of there. And he wasn't the only one. There was almost a collective sigh of relief when the large trailer doors swung open. Fresh air flooded in with the sunlight. En-masse, the monkeys moved to the exit side of their cages and stood on hind legs, their fingers hooked through the mesh like inmates hoping for release. Opposite, the humans stepped back as the rank smell wafted out.

A man and woman in MNR uniforms stood beside the cops. They'd come prepared with thick-leather gauntlets. The woman held an air pistol loaded with a tranquilizer dart. She approached slowly. Bagheera, however, had been darted before and moved as far from the pistol as the cage would allow.

"It's best if this goes in the hip, Mr. Fenn. It would help if you could get the cat to face you. Do you think you could distract her?"

Fenn rubbed a palm across his brow. "Why not. We've become old friends."

He eased down from the cartons where he'd removed monkey crates and tapped his foot on the wooden pallet until the puma looked at him.

"Ready for round two, sweetheart? I've still one good shoe." He stepped incrementally closer. With ears flattened and whiskers back, Bagheera moved each paw, as if stalking, until she had turned toward him. A second later, the cat wailed shrilly and spun around. Fenn could see the dart with its hairy red stabilizer stuck in the black fur. Bagheera began to limp in a small circle.

"It's alright," he said, soothingly. "You're just going to have a little nap. I'd like to have one myself. That's it. Just relax."

The cocktail of medetomidine and ketamine worked fairly quickly. Within minutes, the cat was sprawled in her crate. The MNR pair moved in to maneuver the cage off the trailer, and get health monitors attached.

"Okay, Mr. Fenn. Your turn."

He put his hands up. "I'll come quietly. Don't dart me."

The paramedics led him toward the ambulance with the two cops in tow. He now saw the MNR had sent four officers: the two dealing with the caged animals, and another pair working to corral Chester and Humphrey.

With all that going on, no one immediately noticed the white Freightliner with black fenders rolling into the parking lot. The engine clatter and air brake hiss from the driver's sudden stop got their attention. While its significance was clear, Fenn knew more and yelled, "Stop that truck!"

The cops drew their guns, but the truck was already into a U-turn. Thick black smoke erupted from the chrome pipes as the driver ran through the low gears. Doors slammed on the patrol car and its lights and sound were on before it hit the street. The truck wouldn't get far. Fenn could see a black and white on the overpass speeding up to intercept.

A hand landed on his shoulder.

"I'm not sure if I should arrest you or give you a badge."

Fenn turned and saw a familiar face beneath the MNR cap. He'd last seen Officer Andrew Bryce during a raid of an illicit gambling night run by Nicolas Wray. Deer poachers were indirectly involved. As was Fenn.

"Officer Bryce. We really have to stop meeting like this."

"I was called out here. What's your excuse?"

"Fell asleep, and woke up in that trailer." It was close to the truth.

Bryce pursed his lips and gave him a once over.

"If you must know, I was looking into a murder. Got shanghaied and given a one-way ticket to wherever the hell this is."

"You're a private eye, now?"

"You know, you're the second person to ask that."

"Who was the first?"

Fenn tapped the side of his nose. "That's confidential."

"At least tell me where this trailer came from."

"You'll have to wait your turn, officer. He's ours right now." This from one of the paramedics, who again took Fenn's elbow and ushered him toward the ambulance.

The medic cleaned and dressed the scratches on his leg, advised him to get rabies shots, then went through a protocol in case he was concussed from the Luger blow to the skull.

"What's your full name, sir?"

"Charleton Fenn."

"What month is this?"

"August."

"And the year?"

"2000."

"Do you have a headache?"

"Yes"

"Ears ringing?"

"No."

"How many fingers?"

"Eleven."

"Any memory loss?"

"How *would* I know?"

The paramedic gave Officer Bryce a weary smile. "He's all yours."

Bryce and Fenn moved away so the EMS guy could close the back doors to the ambulance.

"I think the trailer came up from the States. Crossed over the Rainbow Bridge at Niagara Falls. Driver said he had a 'friend' there. He dropped it off at a warehouse in Stoney Creek. It's owned by a fence named Maurice Goodman. Goes by Benny."

Fenn paused, and they both watched the puma's crate being loaded into the MNR truck.

"Livestock isn't Benny's thing. That Freightliner was to take the trailer to its destination. I don't think this is it."

"Have you any idea where it was supposed to go?"

"You'll have to ask those guys when you catch up with them. However, you might get bumped by Lareault and Bloomfield. They're also connected to a suspicious death."

Bryce looked skyward with a sigh. "It's never just one thing when you're involved, is it?"

Fenn shrugged. "That's just how I roll."

"Well, you really should watch where you roll. Some poor guy still has to drive you home."

CHAPTER 34

Sergeant Bloomfield checked his watch and decided to wait a few more minutes before calling his boss. It was Sunday morning, after all, and even detectives should get the occasional sleep-in. He was also aware of Lareault's budding relationship with Koki Motungi, and if that didn't require a bit more rest, then they really were taking it slow.

Bloomfield was always the point man when Lareault had a case. He'd get the call from dispatch, and would pass the details on to Lareault, or designate a response as he saw fit. The eleven to seven switchboard shift always apologized for calling when his phone would be on the bedside table. Luckily, Arlene was used to it and went back to sleep once he'd padded from the room.

The message he'd got at six was that a Charlton Fenn had been stowed in a trailer and shipped off somewhere. Basically kidnapped. The victim's name rang an all too familiar bell. Fenn had a nose for trouble, and often found it, though he never got charged with a crime. The sergeant knew some snitches like that, yet Fenn was different. The guy also had a knack for breaking logjams in a case, so if Fenn was in a fix the chances were good he'd stirred something up. And movement was always good for an investigation.

Bloomfield had dressed, then dialed the number given by the switchboard for Asha Fabiani. Bloomfield recalled she was a capable young woman who knew how to take care of herself. Although she had sounded stressed, she'd told him calmly what she could of Fenn's situation. She'd also provided his cell number. Since Fenn didn't know where he was, the best option was to try for a signal trace. For that, Bloomfield went to the office and woke someone else up.

The trace got them close but it was reports from drivers on a nearby highway, of monkeys on a trailer, that ended the search. *Monkeys on a trailer.* That had Fenn written all over it. Still, Bloomfield had to give the guy credit: the Freightliner Roy Flock had busted his ass after was seen near the trailer, and local law was in pursuit.

His phone rang. It was the Brantford Police Service. The Freightliner had been stopped, and the suspects apprehended. It was the call he'd been waiting for. He arranged for the detainees' transport to Halton, then dialed Lareault's number.

He glanced at his watch while listening to the rings. It was just after nine.

"Hi Frank."

"Morning, Evan. Sleep well?"

He could almost hear Lareault smile at the innuendo. "You know. On and off. What's up?"

"The Brantford Police have just arrested Marshall Stober and Devon Millcroft."

"Really? How'd that happen?"

"Charlton Fenn, if I'm being honest."

The pause was brief. "Go on. Tell me."

"I don't know the full story yet. He's on his way back from Brantford, as are the suspects. We've got time for breakfast if you like."

Bloomfield's receiver took on that silence of a palm clamped over the other-end's mouthpiece.

"Let's meet at the Harvest Table in half an hour."

The Harvest Table was Lareault's go-to Sunday morning brunch place. Always busy, but if you could find a place to park, then you could find a table. He spotted Bloomfield in a booth, looking over the menu.

"The number two, full-English breakfast, is good."

Bloomfield looked up. "I've ordered coffees to start."

A waitress with a full urn stopped at their table and filled their cups. "Ready to order?"

When she left, Lareault said, "I hate to ask, but tell me about Charlton Fenn."

"Oh, you'll love this story. It has monkeys."

It was too early on a Sunday for the seasoned detective to do more than raise an eyebrow as he emptied a packet of sugar into his cup.

"I'll go to his house, from here, to do the interview. He wanted to get cleaned up first—sounded like he had a rough time. Somehow, through the course of teaching Mandy Rolland to drive, he overheard Beth Rolland discuss the body in her basement with a trucker. She mentioned a fence called Benny. I don't yet know how, but he found Benny's base of operations and went to talk to him."

"Why not come to us?"

"On day one, I told him to stay out of our case. But I will ask him that. Anyway, Benny wasn't the chatting kind and he stuffed Fenn into a trailer full of monkeys."

"I like Benny, already."

Bloomfield chuckled, then said, "The trailer had to make an unscheduled stop. Fenn was able to contact his fiancée, who called us." He paused for a sip of coffee.

"Here's where it gets good. While the Brantford cops and the MNR were getting Fenn out of the trailer, Roy Flock's Freightliner shows up."

Lareault's smile grew. The trifecta of Beth Rolland, the burglars, and Benny the fence made a compelling chain of possession for the Rollands' stolen goods. If the burglars were in the Freightliner, the dominoes would fall in order.

"I'll cancel the stakeouts at Millcroft's and Stober's," he said as their waitress placed a full plate of breakfast special number two before each of them. "Then I'll update Jen Heatherington. See if the super wants to observe the interviews."

Until he invited Sergeant Frank Bloomfield inside, Fenn hadn't thought the basement flat he shared with Asha was that small. Even Mogg looked up wide eyed, before taking her tail somewhere those size thirteen boots were unlikely to go.

"Let's sit in the living room. Would you like a coffee, Sergeant?"

A long hot shower, a change of clothes, and a nap had revived Fenn just enough to be hospitable. He knew he should be grateful for the assistance in getting out of the trailer, but just didn't have the energy to show much emotion. He offered Bloomfield the recliner while he and Asha slouched on the couch. Asha grimaced a little as she shifted position.

"We must look a right pair," Fenn said with half a smile.

Bloomfield's look was sympathetic. "Let me put it this way. Whatever you two get into, you do it together and you don't hold back. It's all-in or nothing. And I really admire that."

Asha nodded and put her hand on Fenn's knee.

"Thanks for getting him out of there."

"You're welcome. Now, you can both pay me back by telling me all you know. You talk, I'll listen, and we'll go from there."

Fenn made an attempt to sit straighter and began.

"You know I'm teaching Mandy Rolland to drive. And I suppose you know her dad is in the movie biz. Well, Mandy arranged for Asha and me to be extras on a film shoot in Hamilton. While we were there, I overheard Mandy's mom talking to a trucker about leaving a body in her basement."

Bloomfield held up a finger. "What did she say, exactly?"

"Exactly?"

"Close as you can remember."

"Okay. I don't think Mr. Rolland knew Mrs. Rolland was at the shoot. She was just in the truck corral, actually. She wanted money from the trucker and wasn't pleased by his response."

"Which was?"

"I didn't hear, but I think the gist was it wasn't what she expected. The trucker said it had something to do with the body in her basement. And she said, 'why did you leave it there?' Then he said something like, 'what should I do with a dead chick in a rug?' I don't know if that meant he was supposed to take it. Did she put it there?"

"That's something we'd also like to know."

"So, she's a suspect?" said Asha.

Bloomfield was non-committal. "We haven't crossed anyone off just yet. So, how did you find out about Benny the fence?"

"Because Mrs. Rolland asked the trucker, 'how did Benny find out?' I guess that had something to do with the money she expected." Fenn tenderly probed the back of his head. The lump had subsided somewhat, but he wouldn't be sleeping on his back tonight.

Bloomfield looked up from his notepad. "There's got to be more to this. How did you find out where Benny's place was, or even think about tracking him down?"

He watched them exchange a glance.

Asha cleared her throat. "I have to say that we might not have gone as far as we did if you hadn't suspected Jack Klaasen."

"Jack Klaasen?"

"He's my best friend's father, and she's getting married next weekend."

"We just brought Mr. Klaasen in for questioning. He wasn't arrested."

"Be that as it may, we felt we had to do something."

"I'll accept that. So, what did you do?"

There was another glance between the couple on the sofa.

"We organized a stakeout," said Fenn.

"Of what?"

"The Rollands' mansion."

Bloomfield jotted that down. "Did you see anything?"

"One of our team followed Mrs. Rolland to a spa and heard her mention 'a fence called Benny'. Tried to make like it was a joke. We didn't buy it," said Fenn.

"Okay. And what did she say about this Benny?"

"Nothing, really. She just mentioned being burglarized."

"And did she mention Benny's address?"

"No."

"So, how did you get it?"

Fenn pressed his lips together, then said, "A friend of a friend?"

Bloomfield tilted his head. "You're not going to tell me."

"Promised we wouldn't."

"Does it have anything to do with Ms. Fabiani also being a little worse for wear?"

"This was from a martial arts bout," said Asha, pointing to the yellowed bruise on her cheekbone. "No pain, no gain."

"Alright, we'll leave that little detail for now. How about you tell me where we can find this Benny?"

Fenn took Nicolas Wray's business card from his pocket and read the address written on the back.

"Can I see that card? Make sure I've got it down right."

"Sorry. But I will read it again." Fenn did and put the card back in his pocket.

"What does Benny look like?"

"About average height, like me," said Fenn. "Late fifties. Slicked back thinning hair. Heavyset, bordering on obese. Drives a dark-coloured Mercedes." Fenn gave the plate number. "Oh, by the way, Benny's real name is Maurice Goodman."

Bloomfield took out his phone. "Let me just make a call."

From what they heard, Bloomfield requested a stakeout of Benny's warehouse, and an APB for one Maurice Goodman. That done, he flipped to a fresh page in his notebook.

"So, you went to see Benny. Then what?"

"A tractor-trailer pulled into the warehouse. Benny wasn't pleased by what was in it. When that driver left, I went into the building. Benny found me and, before I had a proper chance to talk to him, bonked me on the head. The rest you know."

"Did you see what was in the warehouse?"

"Yeah. It looked like a big consignment shop. Lots of furniture and appliances. Used but in good condition. And some stuff still in their original crates."

Bloomfield jotted that down, then said, "Benny Goodman. Ever listen to his stuff?"

"I have, though I prefer Benny and the Jets."

"Anything else you can think of?"

"Only that Beth Rolland's family own shops that sell antique furniture, and she deals with Benny the fence. Does it mean she put the body in the basement? If she's bent, who knows what her limit is."

Bloomfield just nodded and began to fill out a more official-looking document, referring occasionally to his notepad. When he finished, he let Fenn read it.

"This is a statement form. Is this an accurate account of what you've just told me?"

Fenn scanned it, nodded, and handed it to Asha. She looked it over and gave it back to the sergeant.

"Just print your full name and sign at the bottom, please."

Fenn did, and Bloomfield filed the sheet in his portfolio.

"Alright," he said, rising from the armchair. "I've helped you, and you've helped me. Now, will you leave this matter to the professionals?"

"We will," said Asha, also rising to take the sergeant to the door.

"Good. In the meantime, don't leave town. We'll want you to identify Maurice Goodman when we bring him in. He'll be charged with several offenses, including assault, and forcible confinement. You just went to talk, right, Chas? You weren't trespassing."

"I didn't break in to Benny's place, if that's what you mean."

"That's all I need to hear. We'll let the lawyers deal with the technicalities."

With the policeman out the door, Asha returned to sit beside Fenn.

"I think we've done all we can. I'm still not happy you got into that mess, but it sounds like we've given the cops some good leads. Hopefully, it's enough to turn suspicion away from Kim's dad." She leaned against him and put her head on his shoulder.

"The wedding's next weekend, isn't it?"

"It is. So can we concentrate on that, and forget about the Rollands, and Benny, and Nicolas Wray?"

Fenn turned and kissed her forehead.

"Concentrate on the wedding? Absolutely. Forget what Nicolas Wray and Benny did to us? Not a chance."

CHAPTER 35

Roy Flock took little running steps to catch up to Bloomfield and Lareault. He put a hand on a shoulder of each, a smile of delight on his face.

"Cheer, cheer, the gang's all here."

They were walking down the hallway toward the boardroom for a strategy meeting before interviewing the two alleged burglars of the Rollands' house. The prisoner transport vehicle had delivered Marshall Stober and Devon Millcroft to the Halton headquarters about an hour ago. They'd been put into separate interview rooms, and both had requested lawyers. It was going to be a busy Sunday.

Already seated and chatting were Detective Sharin Adabi and the support tech, Sunil Naipaul. Superintendent Heatherington was attending a confirmation, and had requested Lareault delay the interviews until she arrived. That was fine. It never hurt to let suspects ferment for a while on hard-backed chairs. Especially when they'd already been up all night. The inspector left instructions not to let them nap.

On entering the boardroom, he went straight to the whiteboards and put up the booking photographs of the two detainees. Then he added a driver's licence picture of Maurice Goodman.

"I always enjoy putting a name to a face," he said, capping the marker he'd just used. "This new player in the arena, Maurice Goodman, goes by the nickname of Benny."

"Benny Goodman," mused Flock. "Now there's some musical royalty."

Bloomfield nodded agreement while Naipaul and Adabi gave each other a 'whatever' look.

"Alright, let's get caught up," said Lareault. "Sunil, I'll let you start."

"Thank you, Sir. The phone records were quite interesting. I've uploaded a list you can access, but here's a summary of the notables. There are calls logged between Millcroft and Stober: Stober and Maurice Goodman. Sumra had called Millcroft, and the realtor Pailin. Beth Rolland had called Stober, her husband, Pailin, and Goodman. I also dug into Maurice Goodman. From his car's plate registration, I found his home address, and that he owns a pawnshop in Hamilton. Addresses of both are in my report."

"Thanks, Sunil," said Lareault. "Superintendent Heatherington signed off on approaching a judge for a search warrant. It's just for the warehouse, though we should expand that to take in his other locations. As of now, there is an active BOLO for Mr. Goodman."

He turned his attention to Adabi. "Your turn, Sharin."

"As you know, I've been looking into the stolen jewelry found at Devika Sumra's house. I was told by a detective in the Break, Enter, and Robbery Unit that there have been similar house clearings in Greater Toronto and Hamilton, and a few where only jewelry was taken. On that note, two of Ms. Sumra's cousins have priors for trafficking stolen property. Mostly small items that are easily passed through a pawn shop—you know, anything with gemstones or made of gold or silver. However, they never went through Maurice Goodman, and that makes me think the murders and the burglary are more coincidental than connected."

The inspector perched on the edge of a table. "How so?"

"Let's say Stober and Millcroft and Beth Rolland and Goodman were working together. Since Goodman is a fence, he could easily move jewelry through his own shop. Why would they give the trinkets to Sumra? While Sumra appears to have been a safecracker, Beth Rolland could have told Goodman the combination to the strongbox, just like she could have given the garage combination to Stober and Millcroft. Sumra seems like one of those bits left over, like when you fix your mantle clock and there's an extra screw on the table. Same with Hovarth, the archaeologist. Apart from being rolled up in a rug and left in the basement, she doesn't fit the burglary. Especially since she was left behind."

"I'm inclined to agree," said Lareault. "We'll have to see if the interviews bolster that theory. Now, the arrest of Millcroft and Stober comes courtesy of Roy Flock's legwork—well done, Roy—and also through some intervening by Charleton Fenn."

"Is he one of ours?" said Flock.

"Fenn is a private citizen that has assisted us in the past," said Bloomfield. "Though, his *intervening* is more like *interfering*. Anyway, Fenn learned that Beth Rolland and Goodman had a relationship. He found the location of Goodman's warehouse and went for a chat. It didn't go well, and Fenn got shipped off in a trailer that was picked up by Stober and Millcroft. The trailer contained smuggled cigarettes and exotic animals. The MNR, RCMP, and Canada Border Services are investigating. However, according to Fenn, Goodman didn't want to touch the load."

"So, he shipped Fenn off with the rest. Two birds with one stone," said Adabi. "Some other folks would've killed Fenn for sticking his nose in, yet Goodman didn't."

"Good point," said Lareault. "From what Fenn told Frank, our Benny doesn't seem the killing type." He looked at the door as Superintendent Heatherington stepped into the room. She took a chair beside Sharin Adabi.

"We're just wrapping up," Lareault told her. "And I think it's time we hear what our burglars have to say. Frank and I will start with Stober. Roy and Sharin can talk to Millcroft. Sunil, you're welcome to watch the monitors with the Superintendent, if you like."

"Actually, Sunil," said Flock, "before I interview Millcroft, I need a couple of stills off the CCTV clips."

On their way out, Heatherington stopped Lareault for a word.

"I have to leave shortly, but anticipate you'll want to bring in Beth Rolland at some point. When you do, I want to sit in on that interview."

"Understood," said Lareault. "I'll let you know."

Interview rooms don't have windows or clocks and Millcroft had been relieved of his watch and phone. He'd been waiting for over two hours, which felt like five, when his public defender showed up. The lawyer took a folder and notepad from his briefcase.

"Cooperation will work in your favour," he said. "Having said that, don't feel you need to speak unless they ask you something. When they do, keep your answers brief. If you're not comfortable with a question, then we can confer."

"Don't you want to know what they have charged me with?" PDs were for those who can't afford their own defense counsel, and Millcroft was wondering if you got what you paid for.

"The initial charges are just so they can detain you. Depending on the supporting evidence, those could be dropped, or additional charges laid. Let's see what they present, and go from there."

Not exactly reassuring since Millcroft knew the load they'd been hauling wasn't kosher. Like many other jobs they'd done.

The door opened and in came two detectives. A man and a woman. The man put a tape in a recording machine.

"The time is 1:28 p.m. Attending this interview is Detective Roy Flock, Detective Sharin Adabi, and the detainee—state your name, sir."

Millcroft cleared his throat. "Devon Millcroft."

"Mr. Millcroft has the counsel of a public defender."

Flock took a seat beside Adabi. From a folder, he retrieved a couple of photographs: printouts of stills taken from CCTV video.

He motioned to the lawyer. "You might want to write this down. We're considering charges of break, enter, and theft over five-thousand dollars: transporting stolen goods: tampering with a corpse: trafficking endangered species: forcible confinement: human trafficking: smuggling: and two counts of murder. How are we doing so far?"

Millcroft tensed and the lawyer put a hand on his arm. "My client has no response until we hear what evidence you have to support these frivolous charges."

"Save it for the courtroom, Perry. We've got plenty." He slid a picture toward Millcroft.

"I'm sure you're familiar with this rig." It was a side view of the Freightliner hauling the trailer used at the Rollands' house. Millcroft looked at the picture without comment. Flock slid a second picture across. This one was somewhat grainy, having been enlarged to capture features of a person that was some distance from the camera.

"This guy looks a lot like you. Even has a ball cap just like yours. And that Nissan, on the left, could be same one that's parked at Stober's house."

Again, Millcroft kept his silence though Flock saw his jaw muscles flex.

"Look closer, Devon. Recognize that building? You do know why the fire trucks and ambulance are there, right?"

Millcroft looked up. "They were already there. The picture shows that. I didn't do anything." Nonetheless, he cast a somewhat worried look at his lawyer.

"Alright, if you weren't there earlier, to start the fire, then why are you in this picture?"

The lawyer leaned over and whispered in Millcroft's ear, who shook his head and replied, "Nah, man, it's not on. She was my girlfriend."

Millcroft looked across the table at Flock and Adabi, who stared back with passive expressions.

"Whatever you've got, that you think will stick, will probably stick. Yeah, I've stolen stuff, but that's it. Stober and me only moved goods from place to place. We've never hurt nobody. But you try to lay a murder on me, that ain't gonna fly."

"Alright," said Flock. "I'll table that for now. However, you still haven't answered my question."

Millcroft exhaled. "To be honest, I'm kinda glad we're having this conversation. We got freaked out when we found that girl in the basement. Then Devika got killed. I mean, what the hell's going on?"

"So, we're talking about the Rollands' basement, right? Who else was with you?"

"Nobody. It was just me and Marsh."

"We found the Rollands' safe in Devika Sumra's workshop. How'd it get there?"

"We gave it to her. I took it to her shop the night before the fire."

"Some sort of payment?"

"It was her cut for getting us the combination to the garage keypad."

Flock looked over at Adabi. "This making any sense to you?"

Adabi shrugged.

"Mr. Millcroft," she said, "how many, um, illegal house clearings have you and Marshall Stober done?"

Millcroft thought for a moment. "Five or six."

"And how do you choose which houses to hit?"

"The white witch tells us."

"The who?"

"Sorry. We call Beth Rolland the white witch on account of her blonde hair and snarky attitude."

"Didn't it strike you as odd that Devika Sumra gave you the garage combo for Beth Rolland's house? Rolland could have done that. Hell, she could have left the door open for you."

"We didn't find out 'til later it was her house. Like, what up with that—why all the centrifuge?"

The lawyer gave a polite cough. "I think he means subterfuge."

"We get it." Flock leaned back and crossed his arms. "So, how many are involved in your little operation?"

"There's always just been the four of us. Me, Marsh, Beth Rolland, and Benny. He's a fence."

"What about Devika Sumra?"

"She was only on the last job. I met her in a bar and we just clicked. A week later, she gives me the combo to do this house. See, Marsh and I were thinking of branching out. We knew Benny would take our stuff. Wouldn't need to give the witch her cut. It was only later we found out it was Rolland's place. Said she'd been auditioning Devika for future jobs."

Flock held up a finger. "If Beth Rolland brought Devika Sumra into the job, then you meeting her at the bar was not really by chance. Rolland and Sumra set you up. And I'll tell you what I think. You realized you'd been played, got pissed off, and killed Sumra."

"No way!" Millcroft half-rose from his chair.

"Sit down."

"Look, yeah, once we found out that Beth had called the shots, then sure, I wondered. That's why you see me in this picture. I was going to ask Devika about it. I mean, we'd really connected."

"Do you do drugs, Devon?" This was from Adabi.

Millcroft shrugged. "I toke. Sometimes pills, a snort of coke now and then."

"What about fentanyl?"

"Nah. That stuff's dangerous. I just want to get high, not die."

Flock took a third photo from his folder. It was the coroner's head shot of Pamela Hovarth.

"Do you recognize this person?"

Millcroft shook his head. "Is that the person from the basement?"

"You didn't see her?"

"Not her face. Just her arm. We don't mess with no bodies."

Flock gathered up the photos and stood. Adabi also rose.

"Sit tight. We'll be back in a while."

"Do you think I could use the washroom?"

"Someone will take you over. And let them know if you need coffee. The MNR, RCMP, and Border Services might also want to chat."

Millcroft didn't want a coffee. He wanted to go home. To be anywhere but here. Somewhere he could sleep. He put his head on his arms and closed his eyes. He heard the detectives leave the room, and ignored his lawyer who simply said that he was also leaving, but would return soon.

We should have just crossed the border and not looked back, he thought.

Fuck.

CHAPTER 36

Marshall Stober's mug shot was an accurate depiction of the man who sat opposite Detective Inspector Lareault in the interview room. That of a rather gaunt, unshaven man in his fifties. Fifty-two years, eight months, and fourteen days, according to the birth date on the admittance form. The brown eyes were a little more bloodshot, the stubble a little darker, the hair unkempt from fingers being run through, but the mug shot was about as real as it got.

Sitting across from Sergeant Bloomfield was a young woman in a navy-blue pantsuit. Stober's appointed public defender. Asian features. Bloomfield guessed Korean heritage.

Lareault started the tape, recorded the intro, then sat back with arms folded to study the detainee. Stober stared back, his arms resting on the table, nicotine-stained fingers twitching.

"We have a No Smoking policy in the building," said Lareault. "But I'll have you taken outside for a few minutes once you've answered a few questions."

"I thought you guys already knew everything. Isn't that why I'm here?"

His PD wrote something short on her notepad and showed it to him.

Stober sighed. "Alright." He looked back at Lareault. "What do you want to know?"

"Let's start at the end, for a change, and work backwards," said Lareault. "Tell us about the load you were hauling when you were arrested."

"My client wasn't actually hauling anything. He just happened to pull into the area where you found the trailer."

Lareault's smile was dismissive. "You should save your ammo, Miss. The charges only get worse as we go. The traffic violations incurred while Mr. Stober was failing to pull over for our officers are small potatoes."

To Stober he said, "It's a simple equation. The more you tell us, the less time you serve."

Stober's fingers now tapped lightly on the table. "How about you tell me what you've got, and I'll fill in the blanks."

Lareault glanced at Bloomfield, who said, "It doesn't work that way but, hey, if you want more time to think, the boss and I'll go for a coffee and come back in an hour or three."

Stober closed his eyes for a couple of seconds.

"We picked up the trailer in Stoney Creek. We were to drop it at a warehouse near Windsor. The manifest said it was canned goods. We never looked inside."

"That's too bad, because *inside* there were contraband cigarettes, live monkeys, a puma, and a person who is lucky to still be alive," said Lareault.

"What? Jeez, no." Stober sat back.

"And for that, you'll be charged with smuggling, transporting stolen goods, forcible confinement, and human trafficking. You might also get plugged with cruelty to animals, but that's up to the MNR."

"Hey. No. We didn't know about any of that shit."

"Oh, c'mon. You picked up the load from someone you knew was a fence. Didn't the smell tip you off?"

"Sometimes a trailer smells. Depends on what they'd hauled last."

Lareault looked again at Bloomfield. "You know, I actually wouldn't mind a latte. There's a new Starbucks on Trafalgar Road that we could try."

Stober turned his hand palm up. "Alright, yeah. We're paid just to haul and not ask questions. Nature of the business. Is that person okay?"

"They're recovering. What do you know about Maurice Goodman?"

"Benny? He's such a fuck. Didn't tell us nothing about that. No wonder he was in such a hurry to get the trailer gone."

"Tell us about Benny's business."

"You're making note I'm cooperating, right?"

Lareault nodded. "We'll award points depending on what you tell us. So, about Benny…"

"He's got a large warehouse where he receives hot goods from several sources. Depending on what he's got in stock, he ships the stuff out to various buyers."

"Like who?"

"Could be store owners looking to reduce their bottom line. Could be connected individuals who want furnishings for rental properties. We delivered one load to a triplex in Markham. Was being set up as a brothel. Lots of beds. Sometimes he'll fill a shipping container and send it off to Eastern Europe."

"Do you know any of his contacts?"

Stober shook his head. "Benny holds his cards close."

"He dealt with Beth Rolland, didn't he?"

"Hmphh. That one I know. Real piece of work. She approached me about a year ago. I sometimes haul for her husband's production company. We got to talking about her stores. She asked if I'd be interested in doing some house clearings, you know, while the homeowners were away."

"How'd she know you'd be a candidate for that sort of proposition?"

"Once or twice I brought undeclared items over the border for Julian, and also found him some, ah, highly discounted equipment."

Lareault waited while Bloomfield jotted that down. Tapes were fine, but handwritten notes were easier to review.

"So, what was the arrangement with Beth Rolland?"

"It was pretty simple. She'd give us an address, and a time to go there. Dev and I would break in and empty the place. We'd all dealt with Benny before, so everything just came together."

"How many homes did you hit for Beth Rolland?"

"I dunno. Maybe one every couple of months."

Bloomfield clicked his pen a couple of times. "We need more than that. Think for a minute. Where and when. Help us close some cases."

Stober beckoned. "Give me your pen and pad. I'll see what I can remember."

He scribbled a few lines, thought a bit, scribbled a couple more, then he put the pen on the pad and slid it back to Bloomfield.

"I don't recall some specific addresses, and some dates might be off. We only went to these places once."

"This is fine, for now," said Lareault. "The B and E team will work with you on that. How did you get inside? Did you have a key?"

"No. The places Beth picked didn't have alarm systems. Devon would usually go around back and break a window, or jimmy a door."

"And when you'd loaded up, what then?"

"We'd take the stuff to Benny. He'd pay what he thought the load was worth—pawn shop prices, of course. I'd subtract the cost for running the truck, then we'd split the rest three ways."

"You, Devon Millcroft, and Beth Rolland."

"Yeah."

Lareault leaned over to look at Bloomfield's notepad.

"I see the Rollands' place is the last on your list. What did you think when Beth told you to clear her own home?"

Stober gave a little snort. "Still can't believe she'd pull that stunt. Dev and I thought nothing of it because she didn't say it was her house. We'd never been there."

"Is that why you left her a little present in a Persian rug?"

"Hey! Whoa! We didn't know nothing about that. And we only found out later whose house it was."

"You didn't find it odd that you were there to move stuff, and there was a rug all rolled up and ready to go?"

"Yeah, we thought it was weird. And we left it right where we'd found it. Whatever strange shit was going on, we wanted no part of it."

Bloomfield looked up from his notepad. "Did you think about calling it in, you know, an anonymous tip? Would have been the morally responsible thing to do."

"We figured the cops would be there soon enough, once the homeowners returned."

"You said Rolland always picked homes without alarms. Hers had one, and you were given the code to a keypad," said Lareault.

"This one was different. Dev hooked up with a cat burglar who gave us the address and code. We figured we didn't always have to work with Rolland. Only found out later that Rolland had set the whole thing up. That hit Dev hard."

"Millcroft's contact was Devika Sumra?"

"You know about her, huh?"

"We know she's dead. And we think Millcroft may have killed her."

"Oh, c'mon! We take stuff. We sell stuff. We don't kill people."

"So, tell us. Who should we look at?"

"I ain't saying she did, 'cause we don't know, but I'd be looking at the white witch."

"And who is the white witch?"

"Beth Rolland."

Lareault, Bloomfield, Roy Flock, Sharin Adabi, and Sunil Naipaul had crowded into the inspector's small office. The sun beaming through the south-facing window made the room even stuffier. Adabi stayed by the door, lightly fanning herself with a file folder.

"It sounds like our burglars have their stories straight," said Lareault, from behind his desk. "They confirmed much of what we surmised, so I'm inclined to believe their account."

"Do we scratch them off as murder suspects?" said Adabi.

"Most likely, yes. While pointing a finger at Beth Rolland, Stober also implicated Julian in other potential crimes. Though, any proof at this point might be hard to find."

He handed Flock the list Stober had provided.

"Roy, let's have you review this list of break-ins with the robbery squad. And you may as well give them the search warrant for Goodman's properties. I doubt he's connected to the homicides, and we should concentrate on those."

"Sharin, I'd like you to verify that the Rollands were in Toronto for the whole time they said they were. Check hotel registrations, their meal charges, event attendance. Sunil, go through their credit and bank card transactions for those days. Let's see if we can find any gaps where one or both could have left and killed Pamela Hovarth. Frank, let's you and I go collect our prime suspect."

They filed from Lareault's office in a first-in-last-out procession. Bloomfield hung back until Lareault said, "I'll meet you downstairs, Frank. I just want to tell Heatherington we're about to arrest her old friend."

CHAPTER 37

Bloomfield put the car into PARK and looked through the windshield at the Rollands' Mediterranean-style mansion.

"What would you like to charge her with? Conspiracy? Accomplice to burglary? Trafficking stolen goods? We could even go for RICO."

Lareault smiled. The last time they'd enacted RICO, the Racketeer Influenced and Corrupt Organizations Act, it was against Nicolas Wray. The mobster had wriggled away, that time, but RICO threw quite a blanket and could be used against Rolland.

"I thought we'd start with something simple like insurance fraud."

He opened his door and a hot breeze pushed its way in.

"Is your tie straight? This be a high-class place."

Bloomfield grinned. "I polished my 'cuffs just this morning. Think she'll notice?"

Their light mood was tempered when the door was answered by Mandy Rolland. Arresting parents in front of their kids always had some emotion attached.

"Hi Mandy. Inspector Lareault and Sergeant Bloomfield. We were here, before."

"Yes. I remember," she said. "Have you caught the burglars?"

"We have. And we'd like to talk to your mom. Is she home?"

"Yeah. She's out by the pool. Come on through."

As they walked across the polished floor, Lareault said, "Is your dad with her?"

"I think he's in his office." She yelled up the stairs. "Dad. The detectives are here."

Mandy pulled on one of a pair of sliding glass doors and led them onto an expansive patio. The water in the kidney-shaped pool glimmered a lighter shade of blue than the lake, which sparkled beyond the edge of the property. Beth Rolland, in a white tube top and peach-coloured shorts, was on a chaise lounge reading a magazine.

"Mom," said Mandy with some excitement, "they've caught the guys that took our stuff."

Mrs. Rolland looked up and saw the two policemen standing with her daughter. It was hard to gauge her expression behind the oversized sunglasses. She sat forward and turned sideways so as to put her feet on the ground. She didn't get up, just put the magazine beside her on the chaise.

"Sorry to intrude on your Sunday, Mrs. Rolland. Are you familiar with Marshall Stober and Devon Millcroft?"

"Is that who broke in here?"

"It is. Do you know them?"

"I, er, oh Julian," she said to her husband, who had come onto the patio. "Didn't Marshall Stober do some driving for you?"

"Oh, I'd have to check with the logistics department. Why?"

"We have arrested Stober and his partner for the burglary, here," said Lareault.

He turned back to Beth Rolland. "What do you know about Maurice Goodman?"

While the sunglasses mainly hid her reaction to the question, her cheeks sucked in slightly.

"Nothing. I don't know who that is."

Julian Rolland stepped forward. "Are you implying something, Inspector?"

Bloomfield saw that Mandy's smile had faded, her brow now furrowed.

"Mandy, could you get me a glass of water, please? With ice, if you don't mind."

"Uh, sure. Would you like one, too, Inspector?"

Lareault gave an almost imperceptible nod to Bloomfield and said, "Thank you. That would be nice."

She looked at her parents. "You guys want anything?" Neither one did.

Once Mandy was out of earshot, Lareault turned to Beth Rolland.

"Stober and Millcroft have implicated you as the leader of a burglary ring. To start, we are arresting you for insurance fraud. Further charges may follow. You have the right to remain silent. Anything you say can and will be used against you in a court of law. You have the right to an attorney. If you cannot afford an attorney, one will be provided for you. Do you understand the rights I have just read to you? With these rights in mind, do you wish to speak to me?"

"What's going on? We're the victims, here." Julian moved to get in front of them. Bloomfield stopped him by placing a large hand on his chest.

"If you'll come quietly, Mrs. Rolland, we won't handcuff you in front of your daughter. We'll take you to the station and your husband can gently let her know what is happening."

Beth looked up at her husband who stared back in disbelief. She nodded just as Mandy came back with two cut-crystal tumblers of ice water, condensation already forming on the sides.

"What's going on?"

"We need your mom to come with us to identify the suspects." Lareault drank half the glass of water. Bloomfield drained his and handed back the tumbler.

Beth Rolland rose and gave her daughter a hug.

"Julian, call Richard and get him down here."

"He's probably at his cottage—"

"Get. Him. Down. Here."

"Yes. Of course. I was just saying."

As they walked through the house, she said, "Can I get my purse?"

Lareault stopped. "Are you taking any prescription medicine?"

"Just birth control."

"Best leave everything here for now. We'll make sure you get what you need."

"You do know your superintendent is a good friend of mine."

"I do. She's expecting you."

Jennifer Heatherington preferred not to wear the starched white shirt with the black epaulets, or the black slacks with blue pinstripe, on a Sunday. Especially in the summertime. Today, however, she would use the uniform as a statement of separation. She would not be Jen, the spicy-food loving roommate from Uni. For any interaction with Beth Rolland, she would have to be Superintendent Heatherington, staunch upholder of the law.

She reminded herself of the many years since Beth had been her drinking and dancing buddy at the university pub. Among other things. That was then, and this is now. She inhaled deeply and exhaled slowly to relax. It had already been a busy day. Her niece had been confirmed at church that morning, then her sister had hosted a celebration luncheon that she'd been late for. When the migraine hit, she'd made apologies and gone home, leaving her husband and daughter to enjoy the party.

Anticipating Lareault to call, she'd taken a Maxalt and lay on the bed with the drapes closed. The pill always made her dopey, and she was just dozing off when her phone chimed. Lareault had Beth Rolland in custody.

There was a tap on the office door. She opened her eyes, and the inspector walked in. She couldn't remember driving back to work. The Maxalt dulled the pain and everything else. She'd get through it.

"How'd it go, Evan?"

"She claimed not to know Stober, Millcroft, or Goodman. Came along quietly, though made it clear she wouldn't talk without her lawyer present. He's coming down from somewhere in Muskoka. Depending on Sunday evening traffic, he probably won't get here before nine tonight."

"So where'd you put her?"

"Since there won't be a bail hearing until tomorrow morning, I gave her a choice. She could wait for her lawyer in an interview room for four or five hours, or go to the holding cell where she'll likely spend the night. At least, there, she'd have a bunk. She chose the bunk."

"How'd Julian and Mandy react?"

"I feel sorry for the kid. As for Julian, he's got secrets of his own but was still caught off guard."

Her eyes felt a little glassy. She wondered if the inspector had noticed.

"I'll go see her in a few minutes. Perhaps she'll talk to me."

The holding cell duty officer opened the door for Heatherington and locked it behind her when she stepped inside. Beth Rolland was on her bunk, back against the wall, her arms wrapped around her knees. When she saw her visitor, she immediately got to her feet, a look of relief taking over her features.

"Jen! I didn't want to ask for you, it being Sunday, but I'm so glad to see you."

She stepped forward with her arms spread, and Heatherington allowed a brief hug.

The superintendent glanced around, knowing she'd find a clean, though spartan cell. These were temporary containment areas.

"Shame we had to meet up like this. Are you warm enough?"

"I'm okay for now. Does it get cool here at night?"

"I'll have someone bring you an extra blanket."

"No chance you can let me go home, I guess."

"Afraid not. You're in the system." Heatherington had them both sit on the bunk. "Tell me about Mandy. She must be quite the young woman now."

"Yes, she's learning to drive," Rolland gave a funny little grimace. "Not sure how I feel about that, though it'll be nice when she can take herself to her various activities."

"And how's Julian?"

"Oh, he's Julian. Still works too much but he's head of his own department. How about you? It's Claire, isn't it, your daughter?"

"Claire's doing well. She just started ballet, so we'll see how long that lasts. You know how they are. Brad's still running his construction company. He's got six guys working for him now, so I know what you mean about long hours. Though, I'm guilty of that, too. Like today. I was supposed to be at my niece's confirmation party."

"And you're here because of me. I'm sorry, Jen. What a mess."

"Do you fully understand what you're being charged with? The allegations are pretty serious, and Detective Inspector Lareault has some compelling evidence against you."

"But I've got you in my corner, right?" Beth patted Jen's thigh.

"What do you mean?"

"Well, you'll tell the Inspector to go easy on me. I'm not sure what he can prove, anyway. And I've got an exceptional lawyer."

"I don't interfere in my detective's investigations, Beth. Not even for old friends. I have faith in the system. I'm sure your lawyer will do everything he can."

"What if I get convicted? Will I have to go to jail?"

"That all depends on what they convict you of."

"And you won't help me."

Heatherington rose from the bunk. "I can make sure you're treated fairly, but that's it. Anyway, I have to go. Other matters to attend to." She walked to the cell door and knocked on it.

Rolland's expression became sour. "You can't just cast me off, Heatherington. I know things about you. We were more than friends. What if I told your husband, and everyone here, that prim little Jennifer has a very talented tongue? Some nights, I still dream about it."

Heatherington nodded, dismayed but not surprised. "You do realize this is a police station? Everyone here has heard or seen it all before. Hell, the vice squad deals with stuff every day that would curl your toes—and not in a good way. As for Brad, I actually think he liked those stories."

The cell door opened. The duty officer stood outside.

"I'll see you get that blanket. Enjoy your evening."

CHAPTER 38

Little needle-like points, the tips of Mogg's rear claws, penetrated the thin sheet and pricked Fenn's lower back while her big front paws kneaded the muscles between his shoulder blades. With her weight, the kneading bit was somewhat therapeutic and Fenn let her until she started nuzzling his ear with her moist nose.

He groaned and with some effort rolled her off him. She probably wanted her supper or breakfast or whatever meal she ate at this time.

What time was it?

Shit!

"Asha. We've slept in." He gave Asha a gentle nudge, then a bit of push.

"What? It's Sunday."

"It was, now it's not. C'mon, you shower and I'll call...oh, never mind, that's probably Carole, now."

Fenn walked quickly from the bed to the kitchen, with Mogg trotting hopefully behind. He picked up the phone.

"Hi Carole."

"Chas? Uh, hi. It's Mandy."

"Oh, hi, Mandy. I'm running a little behind, but I should be on time for your lesson."

"Yeah, uh, that's why I'm calling. I have to cancel. I tried to phone your office, but there was no answer."

That was interesting. Although Asha generally opened up fifteen minutes early, Carole was usually in by nine. It was now nine-twenty.

"Are you not well?"

"No, I mean yes. I mean I'm fine. It's just that my mom got arrested yesterday, and I don't know if we'll have to go to court today."

"I see. Listen, I understand, but from what I know of these situations, if she goes to court today it'll just be for an arraignment where evidence gets presented and a judge decides if there should even be a trial. If so, then a bail will be set, one I'm sure your dad will honour. So, I'm sorry to hear you're going through this, but I think your mom will likely come home today."

"Okay. Thanks for telling me that. My dad's been a bit of a mess since the detectives took her."

Asha came into the kitchen, dressed but with wet hair. She opened a cupboard and pulled out a cereal bar. She looked questioningly at Fenn. He mouthed 'Mandy'.

"I'm sure that's stressful, Mandy. But if you still want to have your lesson, we can."

After all, no lesson, no pay.

"Here's an idea," said Fenn. "I'll come to your house, and if you have to go to the court, then fine. If not, we go for a drive. If word comes through that you have to go, I'll have my phone and we can come straight back to your house."

"Okay. My dad could call me, too. I've got my own cell phone."

Of course you do, thought Fenn. It's only dinosaurs like me that relied on two tin cans and a piece of string, as a kid.

"Great. I'll pick you up at ten."

Fenn folded his flip phone just as their land line rang.

"That'll be for me," said Asha.

Carole was her usually snarky self. "Coming in today? I've been run off my feet since I got here."

"Sorry about that," said Asha, rolling her eyes. "I'm just leaving."

She pulled her hair into a scrunchy and went to the door. "Apparently, things are really busy this morning," she said, slipping into her shoes.

"Take that with a grain of salt," said Fenn. "Mandy just told me she got no answer at the office."

"Good to know." She grabbed her purse and car keys and gave Fenn a quick kiss.

"See ya."

Asha didn't always wear makeup, particularly when she had a summer tan, and this morning there wasn't time for that sort of thing. It was only when she looked in the rearview mirror that she realized she should have at least covered the bruise on her cheekbone. Her ribs were still sore, but as long as she didn't raise her left arm too high, it was manageable.

Naturally, Carole noticed the yellow and purple tinge below her eye, right away.

"Don't tell me you lovebirds had a little spat. That looks nasty. You know, if Chas did that to you, you should report him."

"Chas didn't do this. He would never."

Carole didn't seem convinced.

"Regardless, whatever problems you're having is no excuse for being late. The phones have been crazy this morning."

"That's not what I heard," retorted Asha.

"Oh. And what did you hear? From whom?"

"Good morning, you two." Dieter Lundsen strode into the office. He was wearing one of his signature satin shirts with the long collars, and tan polyester flared pants over brown suede boots. It all sort of matched Carole's suede miniskirt and yellow cotton scoop-necked t-shirt. Her double-stranded necklace had the same coloured beads as adorned her sandals.

"What happened there, my dear?" He pointed at Asha's cheekbone.

"She's denying that Chas hit her. Maybe you should talk to him, Diets."

"I was in a competition. It wasn't Chas."

Asha's protest fell on deaf ears as both Lundsens went to their respective offices. A moment later, Dieter came back to the reception desk.

"Speaking of Chas," he said. "The chappy hasn't updated me lately on the Rolland affair." He said *Rolland affair* as if it was a docket for MI6. It wasn't just fashion that turned Dieter on about the Swinging Sixties. It was anything British from that period. Asha sometimes wondered why he drove a Lexus and not a little MG.

"Has he said anything to you? He would have, wouldn't he?"

"Actually, Dieter, Mandy called him this morning and said her mom had been arrested."

"Her mother. Really? Well, isn't that something." He tapped a couple of fingers on the countertop and returned to his office.

It was the first cloudy morning Fenn could remember in weeks. And not just cloudy. The air was heavy with humidity, moisture that was long overdue. The few glimpses he'd had of the lake were of whitecaps curling on gray water. When the wind blew from the east, it was usually a harbinger of rain.

He watched Mandy come down the front steps of her house. She glanced at the sky, yet her steps lacked their usual spring, and when she got in the car, he noticed a little puffiness below her eyes.

She held up her phone.

"Can I put this in the cupholder in case my dad calls?"

"Sure. Any news about your mom?"

"Not yet. We're just waiting to see what the lawyer says."

"Well, from experience, I know that can sometimes be a slow process. Let's buckle up and go for a drive. Think about something else for a while."

Fenn got her quickly into traffic, hoping it would distract from other thoughts. And it did, but only for ten minutes. As the first drops of rain hit the windshield, he heard Mandy sniff, then saw her finger a small tear from under an eye. They were on Brant Street, a main road. Fenn had her turn onto a side street and pull over. Not a bad time to do so, for the skies chose that moment to open up.

As the downpour blanketed the car, he said, "Want to talk about it?"

"I'm sorry." She sniffed again. Fenn retrieved a box of tissues from the back seat. She took one, wiped her eyes and blew her nose.

"I'm scared she'll have to go to jail. My dad said she got involved with some people because the antique stores weren't doing well. Then they put that poor dead woman in our basement. It didn't bother me much at the time but, now, I don't want to go down there. I just want to move, and our other place isn't even built, and what if we have to sell everything to keep mom out of jail…"

She grabbed another tissue from the box and cried into it.

Fenn watched the water stream down the windows while Mandy let the stress out of her system. In the years he'd been on the job, tears came for various reasons and he always did his best to find the appropriate response.

"We always imagine the worst when we don't know what's going to happen," he said. "And it rarely turns out to be that bad. Some things won't be pleasant, and not always fair, but when life throws you a curve ball, the best thing to do is keep your chin up, and try to knock that damn thing out of the park."

Mandy must have liked the analogy, for she gave a little laugh and nodded. She blew her nose again and took one more tissue to dry her eyes and cheeks. The rain also appeared to be letting up.

"Want to drive some more, or have you had enough?"

Mandy put her hands back on the wheel. "I'm okay. How much time have we got left?"

"About twenty minutes. You decide where we go. I'll just sit here and enjoy the ride."

After dealing with the usual Monday morning calls from people booking or canceling lessons, and Asha passing the information on to the instructors, the DriveCheck office became quiet enough that Dieter departed on some undisclosed errand.

Carole had stayed in her office with the door shut, and at one point had spoken on the phone in such a low tone that Asha could barely hear her. Not that she wanted to listen in. It was just unusual because Carole had a commanding voice, and liked to use it.

It was about eleven, and Asha was wondering what to do for lunch when two middle-aged women, one taller, one chubbier, came up to the front counter. She gave them her usual inquiring smile.

"Welcome to DriveCheck. Looking to book some lessons?"

Both women noticed her bruised cheekbone and gave Asha looks of concern.

"Are you Asha? We received a call from Carole Lundsen. Is she in?"

"I'm here," said Carole, emerging from her office. "Perhaps we should go into the classroom where we can all sit. Asha, these two ladies would like to speak with you." Her smile was like that of a mother whose child suddenly needed expensive dental work.

Asha had a feeling she knew where this was going but decided to comply until she found out more.

"I'm Beryl Freemore and my partner is Barbara Rochette," said the taller of the two.

"You can call me Barb," said the other.

"We normally like to keep calls to us anonymous, but Ms. Lundsen wanted to be present for support." Beryl looked over at Carole, who nodded.

"Support of what?" Asha also looked at Carole, whose expression of concern struggled to fit her face.

"Are you being abused, dear?" Beryl leaned forward. "I see you have a nasty bruise, and I couldn't help but notice you were a little stiff sitting down."

Asha's eyes flashed angrily at her boss. She took a deep breath so she wouldn't blast the wrong person.

"No. I am not being abused. I thought I'd made that clear to Ms. Lundsen this morning."

"Barb here is a nurse. Could she have a look at your side?"

Asha glared again at Carole, but figured it couldn't hurt to have a medical opinion.

"I will show you, but you need to understand that I compete in martial arts. That's where I get all my bruises."

She stood and raised the hem of her top to reveal the discoloured skin over her ribcage.

"Oh, Asha." Barb gently ran her fingers over the area, checking the position of the ribs. "Nothing appears to be broken, though a couple may be fractured and out of alignment."

Barb probed a bit more. "Does it hurt?"

"Only when I laugh." Asha's attempt at humour fell flat.

"And when did he do this to you?" Beryl now had a notepad on her lap.

"*He* did it on Friday night. But *he* was another competitor. I hurt him just as badly, if not worse."

"I've seen Chas come into the office with grazed knuckles, on more than one occasion," said Carole. "Does he get drunk, violent, maybe hit walls?"

Asha stepped away from Barb and dropped her shirt.

"Really, Carole? How long have you known Chas? Nine, ten, years? You know damn well he's a rock climber. Those scrapes are from jamming his knuckles into crevices. When these ladies leave, you and I are going to have a word."

"I'm just trying to help."

"Help to do what? Split us up? Get Chas charged with assault?"

Barb and Beryl glanced at each other. This reaction was not new to them. There was often denial from the abused partner.

"Now that we're here," said Beryl, who seemed to be the administrator, "we need to just check a few facts. You said you got these injuries in a competition. Aren't they usually posted on the Internet? You know, announcing the event, and the winners, and such. Perhaps we can confirm…"

"You won't find this one," said Asha. "It was unsanctioned. Very loosely organized."

"Okay. Well, is there another event that shows your attendance? Then we can show due diligence—that we checked as best we could."

"Yeah. There certainly is. Let's go to my computer."

Asha led them to the reception area and sat at the keyboard to her workstation.

A few keystrokes and mouse clicks brought up the WKC Canada page for the Ontario Provincial Martial Arts Championships. She clicked through to a link that showed past winners, then scrolled down a list and clicked on another link. She turned the monitor for all to see.

"Right there. My name. My bruised face, the other cheek that time. My fucking trophy. Can we put this to bed now? You do see that if my fiancé, yes, we're getting married, tried to hurt me, I could kick the shit out of him."

Barb gave a flat smile. "It doesn't always work that way. Just because a woman could leave an abusive relationship, doesn't mean she will. Could we at least talk with your fiancé?"

"Absolutely not. He'd walk barefoot on hot coals and would, actually almost did, take a bullet for me. Something like this would upset him no end. For the last time. I'm not in an abusive relationship. Thank you for your concern, but I'd like you all to leave now, so I can type up my letter of resignation."

CHAPTER 39

Before bail can be set, there has to be an arraignment. Before there is an arraignment, suspects and their lawyers have to be informed of the charges. And, somewhere in there are the interviews. A much nicer word than interrogations, which would probably happen if the lawyers weren't present.

A homicide case grows cold quickly, and Lareault was prepared to hit Beth Rolland, metaphorically speaking, as hard as he could. Suspects out on bail were always less cooperative than those who weren't. Knowing the inspector's time was limited, Heatherington stayed in the observation room so Beth couldn't discompose the meeting by dredging up their past.

The monitor showed the accused and her lawyer sitting opposite Lareault and Bloomfield. The superintendent recognized the legal counsel. It was Richard T. Reed, of the respected law firm Carpenter, Reed, and Zdriluk. Dressed to impress, Reed was highly competent and his expertise wasn't cheap. Either the Rollands' had deep pockets or Julian was hoping to write this off through his business.

Unfazed by the counsel's credentials, the inspector got straight to the point.

"Mrs. Rolland, we have testimony from Marshall Stober and Devon Millcroft that you organized burglaries of several homes, including your own, between October 1999 and August 2000. They also attest you arranged to have the goods offloaded with a fence, name of Maurice Goodman, sometimes known as Benny."

He held up a hand as both Rolland and her lawyer leaned forward to speak.

"Object or deny all you want, but I'm going to ask my questions and you can decide whether to answer. At this point, we have enough to convict on several charges. You know what you've done—we're still trying to decide who gets hit with the worst of it. Not to belabour the point, but the more you tell us, the more favourable your sentencing. And, please, no more bullshit or we'll add obstruction of a police enquiry to your shopping cart."

The lawyer sat back in mock surprise.

"Must I advise my client to take the fifth, on account of her accuser's combative attitude?"

"Just talking the truth," replied Lareault. "And so will your client if she wants to avoid a murder rap. Actually, two counts, as I'm sure you know. Even reduced to manslaughter, she could get up to twenty years, and that's with time off. How old will your daughter be by then, Beth?"

Hands in her lap, Rolland glanced around the room like a sullen student in detention. Though Heatherington wasn't surprised at Beth's stony facade, she knew Lareault's words had struck home.

"Just leave my daughter out of this," she said. "I haven't killed anyone."

"And yet, two women with connections to you are now dead. Stober and Millcroft said they weren't the killers, and either couldn't or wouldn't vouch for you. You don't have an alibi for one, and we're checking your whereabouts for the other."

Lareault glanced at Bloomfield to check he had his notepad ready.

"While you think about that, let's do some housekeeping. Score some points and tell us about the burglaries. Here's a list Stober provided."

He handed it to the lawyer who looked it over, then nodded.

"Yeah, okay," she said. "There's not a lot to it. I told Stober which homes to hit. He and Millcroft would do the job. As for Benny, I first met him at an auction about eighteen months ago. We were competing on a Lalique sculpture. I was feeling competitive that day and overpaid just to beat the guy. But we got to talking and found we could help each other out, so to speak."

"In what way?"

"I had to increase the antique stores' profits. Even with estate sales and up-cycling, we still were just scraping by. Too much competition from the Internet. I think I told you that. Anyway, Benny wanted to expand and had seen the need for a one stop, off-market, clearinghouse for those who don't question the provenance of their purchases."

"So, Benny agreed to accept the goods you sent to him, knowing they were stolen."

"Hell, of course he knew they were stolen. Benny wouldn't buy anything through proper channels."

"And what did you get out of it?" Lareault glanced at the lawyer, who made the odd note but remained silent.

"Benny would pay Stober for the load, who would subtract his transport costs, then we'd split the profit."

"*We* being Stober, Millcroft and yourself."

"Yes."

"And how did this help the bottom line at the antique stores?"

"First off, with the cash from Benny, we could purchase stock from legitimate sellers. Then the stores would also buy select pieces from him, at rock-bottom prices."

"Why didn't you just take the stuff you wanted off the truck before it got to Benny?"

"Two reasons. First, there just isn't time to pick and choose when clearing a house. And, second, Stober and Millcroft can't even tell leather from pleather never mind actual wood from pressboard."

The comment made Bloomfield chuckle.

Rolland gave a bitter little laugh.

Lareault gave her a quizzical look. "Something funny?"

"Benny actually ended up with the Lalique I outbid him on. And the slimeball wouldn't sell it back to me."

Lareault gave a wry smile. *Karma's a bitch*, he thought.

"Let's talk about the places you hit. How did you choose which were prime targets?"

"I didn't."

Lareault and Bloomfield exchanged a glance.

"Who did?"

"Catrina Pailin."

"Your realtor."

"Yes."

"Why would Stober or Millcroft not mention her?"

"They didn't know. Catrina said she wanted a buffer, and that was me. Said it wouldn't be good to have a realtor linked to break-ins. I mean, she had a point."

Lareault wondered why the Break, Enter, and Robbery Unit hadn't picked up on the pattern.

"Were these all homes listed for sale, like yours was?"

"Maybe a couple, but usually not. Catrina's familiar with a lot of neighbourhoods. She's at open houses all the time, and notices when nearby homeowners are on vacation. She'd give me an address and I'd send the boys over."

"You said you'd split Benny's payout three ways. You, Stober, and Millcroft. What was in it for Pailin?"

"I'd split my take with her, knowing I'd make it back when the stores sold whatever we bought from Benny."

"So, how did it work for the last job? You didn't need Pailin to choose your own house. Was she out of the equation?"

Rolland opened her mouth, then hesitated. She leaned over and whispered something to her lawyer. He nodded.

"My client wants assurance that, in helping you to close some cases, her cooperation will be considered favourably at the appropriate time."

Of course, Rolland wanted a deal. Everyone in her position did.

It was like a card game and, while none were to get out of jail, Rolland still had a couple to play. Lareault, on the other hand, knew he had a mitt full: conspiracy to burglary, trafficking stolen goods, money laundering, insurance fraud, obstruction in a couple of flavours, aiding and abetting, tax evasion. Alleged, if not proven, he could also pull two counts of murder, and indignities to a corpse from the deck. A useful draw should the suspect stonewall.

Lareault looked up at the camera mounted in one corner. It fed the monitor in the observation room, where he knew Heatherington was watching.

"My boss likes to say that it's all in the value of the return. But, yes, we will take everything into consideration. In fact, to show goodwill, we'll drop the charges for obstruction and for insurance fraud."

Rolland looked at her lawyer. He nodded though raised an eyebrow at Lareault. Both men knew Rolland's insurance company might lay their own charge of fraud. But that would be another fight for another day.

"I'm a firm believer that you should quit while you're ahead," Rolland said. "I wanted out, and since we were moving it seemed like a good time to cash in. We'd get money from Benny and from the insurance company, as well as dispose of our old furniture, which the antique shops could then pick up for a song. All good quality stuff. I saw it as a win-win-win."

"How did the rest of your group feel about that?"

"Stober and Millcroft didn't know. I didn't think they'd be too concerned anyway, since they were looking to do their own thing—that is, until they found out Devika was a setup."

"And Pailin?"

"I tried to ease her into the idea by telling her she wasn't needed for the last job."

"But you didn't cut her out."

"No. She said it was my turn to get a buffer. Since we were doing my place, it was a little close to home—pardon the pun. She said she'd met someone we could use as a go-between."

"And who was that?" Lareault suspected he knew, but wanted Rolland to say it for the tape.

Rolland lowered her eyes. "Devika Sumra."

"When we spoke at your house, you denied knowing her."

"Can you blame me?"

"What was the arrangement?"

"It was mostly down to Cat. She decided to have Devika slip the information to Devon Millcroft. I guess she didn't expect them to hit it off."

Bloomfield said, "Did they really hit it off, or was Sumra pressured into it?"

"Cat and Sumra had their own thing going. Though, I wouldn't put it past Cat to use blackmail, if she had something on her."

"This *thing*," said Lareault. "What was it? Burglaries?"

"Nooo," said Rolland with a small smile. "It was of a more intimate nature."

"Ahh. Devika Sumra was dating both Catrina Pailin *and* Devon Millcroft."

"Call it dating if you like, Inspector."

Lareault watched Bloomfield draw a little three-pointed arrow between the names on his pad.

"If you wanted Sumra as a buffer, didn't it defeat the purpose when you told Stober and Millcroft you'd arranged it?"

"That was my bad. I let it slip when talking to Stober."

"And Sumra's payment for her part in the scheme was the contents of your wall safe, was it not?"

"It was. As you now know, my best jewelry was not in the safe. I'd left just enough for her compensation."

"Did you kill her to stop her asking for more, or to keep her quiet?"

Rolland must have been expecting that, for she tapped Richard Reed on the arm.

"Earn your money."

"My client's cooperation hinges on questions of which she has knowledge. She has been open and frank, and will not be a scapegoat for your unsolved crimes."

"Unsolved, yes," replied Lareault. "Unfortunately for your client, she doesn't have an alibi for the time of Devika Sumra's death."

"And Millcroft does?"

"Millcroft is not the focus of this interview."

Lareault turned his attention back to Rolland. "It also suited you to have Pamela Hovarth out of the way. Was it because she delayed the build, or because your husband was involved with her?"

Rolland shook her head in denial.

"Neither of you admitted knowing Hovarth, but you knew there was an archaeologist on the site. Your husband must have seen her, and surely the old skull was a hint."

There was a tap on the door. Lareault ignored it.

"Who did you conspire with to kill Hovarth and Sumra?"

Reed sat forward, about to interject, when the door opened, and Heatherington leaned inside. She ignored Rolland and held out a paper for Lareault.

"This just came in. Thought you should see it." She handed him a forensic report and went back to the monitor room. Lareault scanned it and silently cursed. The analysis of the blonde hairs found on the rug were of a female whose natural shade was brunette turning to gray. It was not a match for the samples provided by Beth Rolland.

Nonetheless, he smiled and handed the sheet to Bloomfield.

"Looks like we have the proof we were looking for." He said it to the sergeant, but loud enough for the accused and her counsel to hear.

He then looked directly at Rolland. "Remember the hair samples you gave us? That forensics report has compared them to the strands we found on the rug. It's not looking good, so I'll ask you again, who murdered Pamela Hovarth—you or your husband?"

Rolland's head lowered. Her voice little more than a whisper. "She said she'd do something to Mandy if I ever said anything. My beautiful girl."

Lareault felt Bloomfield tense beside him.

"Who did?"

"Catrina."

CHAPTER 40

Lareault strode quickly down the hall with the sound of Bloomfield's thick-soled shoes close on his heels. Ahead of them, Roy Flock and Superintendent Heatherington were exiting the observation room. They, too, had caught the significance of Beth Rolland's statement and knew what had to happen next.

"I'll phone Julian," Heatherington called over her shoulder as she took the stairs to get to her office. Flock slowed to let the others catch up.

"Where do you want me, Boss?"

"We need a BOLO issued for Catrina Pailin. Get her picture out to the patrols, description of vehicle—you know what to do. If Sharin's still around, have her come see me."

Flock veered off to his own cubicle. He saw Naipaul talking to an officer.

"Suni! With me. I need a reg check."

As they reached his office, Lareault said, "You saw that report, Frank. Since the blonde hairs weren't Rolland's, and we now know Pailin has something to hide, it fits that the carpet was from the real estate sales office. I'll need you to get a warrant for Pailin's home, or homes. She's a realtor, so might have more than one. Let me know when you have it, and I'll get forensics over there."

Bloomfield left, and Lareault picked up his phone.

Koki Motungi answered with "Hey," and he could hear the smile in her voice. She must have seen his number on her display screen.

"Hey, yourself. Busy?"

"Busy enough. You got my report, right? I sent it over marked for immediate attention."

"I got it, thanks. It provided the break we needed. Our lead suspect is now one Catrina Pailin."

"Really. What changed?"

"As you know, the hairs on the rug weren't Rolland's. However, Beth has been telling us some interesting tales. So, just a heads up that you'll be going to Pailin's place once we have a warrant."

Lareault noticed Sharin Adabi was standing in his doorway. He beckoned her in.

"I guess I should sleep at mine tonight," said Koki.

"Probably best until we see how this pans out. I'll call you as soon as Frank gets the knock and enter." He grinned as a kissy sound snuck into his ear.

"You look happy," observed Adabi. "Roy told me we have a new suspect."

"Catrina Pailin," said Lareault. "I know you looked at her briefly, but I need you to go back over everything. Take pictures of Rolland, Pailin, Sumra, and Hovarth over to anywhere they may have gone socially—bars, restaurants, motels, hotels. Find someone who'll attest to seeing any of them together. Video footage would be good. You can probably narrow it down if Sunil gets access to Pailin's credit card statements."

Adabi waited just long enough to ensure the Inspector had nothing further. She already knew of two places she'd like to hit first.

Lareault sat back and went through a mental checklist. Satisfied he'd covered all the bases, he dialed Heatherington's extension. It was busy. Rather than wait at his desk for a return call, he went back to the interview room where he'd left Beth Rolland and her lawyer. He could understand how Pailin's threat had kept Rolland silent, but once the realtor realized Beth had been arrested, all bets would be off. Rolland wouldn't take a murder rap for her, or anyone else, and Pailin likely knew that.

The Inspector pressed the RECORD button on the tape machine and took his seat across from Rolland.

"We've put out a BOLO for Catrina Pailin, and dispatched a patrol car to sit in your driveway in case she shows up there," he told her. "For now, it's still your word against hers, but this is your chance to stack the deck. Let's start with Pailin's threat to Mandy. Was that intended to keep you quiet about her involvement, or because you wanted to stop the entire operation?"

"Either. Both. Does it matter?"

Lareault looked at the lawyer. "Let's ask the expert."

If Reed was surprised at the invitation, he didn't show it.

"On the surface, it tells us whether or not she'd accepted your decision to end your illegal side-venture. If she made the threat just to ensure your silence, that would carry a charge of uttering threats but would show she was ready to move on—at least without your involvement. If her threat was to ensure you stayed in the group, then it's coercion. While both can be coupled with blackmail, the first instance is somewhat passive—you do nothing, and neither will I. Whereas the second instance is aggressive—if you don't do something, then I will. That's a far more dangerous mindset, and one that could compel Pailin to act upon her threat."

Lareault was impressed.

"Thank you, Mr. Reed. So, which is it, Beth?"

Rolland closed her eyes and rubbed her forehead slowly.

"Catrina didn't want to stop and didn't want the dynamic to change. She was getting a sweet little kickback, all under the table, for doing nothing more than providing the occasional address. Low risk, nice reward."

"Is that when she made the threat?"

Rolland nodded. "Totally caught me off-guard. Until then, we'd never had a disagreement. I mean, I know realtors have to be nice to their clients, but we'd have her over for parties and barbeques, then she and I started our little scheme together."

Rolland paused and studied the hands in her lap for a moment.

"Things changed when she started going out with Devika. She became, what's the word—manipulative."

"Do you think Catrina Pailin also killed Pamela Hovarth and put her in your basement?"

Rolland looked to the ceiling, her eyes a little moist.

"Yes."

Lareault saw Reed writing on his pad.

"Let me rephrase that. Did you *know* Pailin killed Hovarth and put her in your basement?"

"When we first found out about it, we weren't sure what to think. Julian had recognized Hovarth, and when he told me later, then the skull made sense. Pailin called that evening and told me it was a warning. That I'd better keep my mouth shut, and do as I was told, or Mandy would be next."

"*Mandy would be next.* Were those her exact words?"

"She said, 'wouldn't it be terrible if that happened to Mandy'. Her tone sent a chill through me."

"Did you mention this to your husband?"

"Well, no. Catrina said to tell no one. She frightened me, so I took her literally."

There was a knock on the door. Heatherington stepped in. This time she looked at Rolland briefly, then said to Lareault, "A word, please, Inspector."

Out in the hall, Heatherington made sure the interview room door was closed before she quietly said, "Mandy is with Pailin, and we don't know where."

Lareault's hands went to his hips, and he stared down the hallway, his lips a tight, thin line. After a moment, he looked back at the interview room door and motioned they should move further along the hall.

"How'd that happen so quickly?"

"I called Julian to tell him his realtor was our prime suspect, and that he should keep Mandy in the house. I barely got that out when he shouted we weren't doing our jobs and that he would sue us for falsely arresting Beth, or if anything happened to his daughter. I told him we'd sent a patrol car to sit by their house, and that's when he yelled we were too bloody late. Pailin had already been there and picked up Mandy."

"Were you able to get anything else out of him?"

"Once I'd got him calmed down, he said Catrina had called to check-in and let them know the build was delayed due to the police investigation. That's when he told her Beth had been arrested. She acted surprised and suggested that Mandy might like a distraction. She could use some help to stage an open house. Mandy had just got back from a driving lesson, so Pailin said she'd be right over."

"How late were we?"

"Pailin picked Mandy up five minutes before I called Julian. I had him try calling Mandy—the kid's got her own cellphone—but her driving instructor answered. She'd apparently left it in his car."

"Do we know what Pailin's driving?"

"Yes, a pearl white Escalade. There's probably a dozen or more in town, but it's better than looking for a red Toyota. Anyway, the word's out. Hopefully, she's still in the area."

"Did Julian know where the open house was?"

"No. But that may have been a ruse. We could call her, though if she's as smart as I think she is, her phone will be off."

"It's worth a try. I'll get Sunil to look up her listings. We have to start somewhere, and can't be late again."

He took a step towards his office. "Do me a favour: inform Beth Rolland and her lawyer about the development. Might be awhile before we resume the interviews."

"I will. And you have my authorization for a wiretap. Sooner or later, Pailin will want to talk."

Striding away, Lareault raised a hand in acknowledgment. Kidnappers and hostage-takers invariably call their victim's family with threats or demands, so installing a listening post at the Rolland house was the first logical step.

CHAPTER 41

Hess Village, known for its restaurants and bars, was a trendy spot after sunset. The light of day, however, showed it to be more shabby than chic with its peeling paint, missing mortar, and cracked cement. Like an old madam, she looked her best in the gentle glow of patio lanterns and fairy lights. Adabi found a spot to park just a couple of doors down from Cranny's Nook and sat quietly to get a feel for the neighbourhood.

Wedged between a vintage clothing shop and an interior design studio, The Nook had a small space out front sporting a quartet of table sets within its wrought iron border. The main entrance featured a large, ornate wooden door. It opened and an employee came out with a bar towel. She set to work, wiping the top of each table and the seat of each chair. As Adabi approached, she looked up and smiled.

"Sorry, we're not open just yet. Can you come back at five?"

The detective smiled back and held up her ID.

"I could, but I'm pressed for time. Are you the owner?"

"Server. The owner's inside." The employee unlatched the filigreed gate and pointed to the bar's entrance. "Her name's Marta."

"Perhaps you can still help me," said Adabi. She brought out four glossy photos and placed them on a table. "Do you recognize any of these women?"

The server looked at them carefully, slowly shaking her head. "I've only been here a few weeks. Still getting to know the regulars." She put a finger tentatively on the picture of Hovarth. "I might have seen her once or twice."

"What about the others? Take your time."

"Those two could almost be sisters or cousins." She pointed to the headshots of Rolland and Pailin. Both blonde, they had somewhat similar features.

"Either one come to the bar?"

"Maybe her." She pointed to Pailin. "Marta would know better than I." She moved to an adjacent table and resumed wiping.

Adabi took out her notepad. "Can I get your name, please?"

"Trish. Trish Fraser."

"Thanks, Trish."

Adabi entered the dimly lit bar and removed her Ray Bans. As narrow as the exterior suggested, there was a serving counter along one wall, a row of tables along the other, and a small dance floor at the far end. The decor was more wine bar than tavern, and the chalkboard menu items more upscale than burgers and fries. Or they just had fancier names.

Adabi heard a rattle. From a room near the dance floor, a woman wearing a short-sleeved top and dark slacks entered with a rack of glasses. She took it behind the counter without noticing the detective. Adabi gauged her to be in her forties. Thin, with ropey muscles, her was hair shaved close to the skull on one side and combed straight down on the other. She had a few piercings in the usual places and an assortment of tattoos on her arms and neck.

"Are you Marta?"

The woman gave a little start. "Oh!" She took a breath. "Didn't see you there, darlin'. Good job you're pretty or you'd have scared the shit out of me."

"Sorry. Didn't mean to." Adabi showed her identification. "Detective Adabi. Halton Regional Police Service. I'm hoping you can help me."

"If I can. Would you like a glass of something? I haven't put the coffee on yet."

"Perhaps another time." Adabi spread the pictures out on the bar.

"Do any of these people look familiar to you?"

Marta leaned in and pulled the shot of Hovarth closer.

"That's not Pam, is it?" Her expression was one of sadness. A coroner's picture left no doubts. "What happened to her?"

"We're investigating Ms. Hovarth's death. How well did you know her?"

"She came in at least once a week, sometimes twice. We chatted over the bar, as you do."

"Did she come with anyone?"

"Usually came stag. Often found a friend to leave with."

"So, she was cruising?"

"Aren't we all, in one way or another?"

"Recognize any of these others."

"Don't know her name, but she's been in." Marta fingered the bottom of Pailin's photograph. "If I recall, she and Pam got cozy at that corner table. Can't say I've seen either of them since."

She gave Adabi a meaningful look. "I hope what I'm thinking didn't happen. I want this place to be a sanctuary, not a stalking ground."

Adabi nodded, but pressed on. "What about the other two? Ever see them in here?"

"I'm pretty good with faces. Don't recall those." She put a hand on Adabi's wrist. "Sure you won't have a drink? After this, I think I need one."

"I can't. The clock's ticking. I'll come back, though." She gathered her pictures, gave Marta her card, and got one in return.

As she left Cranny's Nook, she checked her watch. It was getting to be rush hour. Luckily, she'd be driving from Hamilton, toward Toronto, rather than getting jammed up with everyone trying to leave 'the big smoke'.

Sunil Naipaul had given Adabi a printout of Pailin's recent credit card charges for anything under Meals and Entertainment, or Accommodation.

There were quite a few. Realtors could not only afford to eat out a lot, but they also often took clients to lunch or dinner. Why not when most of it could be expensed.

There were charges for Cranny's Nook on two separate dates. The other purchases the detective wanted to follow up were from the Fairmont Royal York, one of Toronto's landmark hotels. She'd read in Koki Motungi's report on Hovarth's residence that there'd been a bathrobe embroidered with the Royal York's logo. It was a lead she'd meant to follow up sooner, but other events had taken priority. The thought of Pailin's meal charges now made her hungry. Perhaps she'd grab a bite in the hotel's famous Library Bar. That was where she'd go to seduce someone. They even did a really nice tea service.

The front desk manager and clerks on the reception desk were all shown her photos. She got a couple of maybe's for all four of the pictures. Expected, if not too helpful. She requested to see security footage and was taken to a room in the basement.

"Taj will give you whatever you need," the manager said. Taj Tomba looked like he could have played for the Toronto Raptors. A good attribute for a security guard.

Adabi knew from the credit card statements when Pailin had been to the hotel. She requested video of the reception area, the one place she would have certainly been, if only to check in or out. The Royal York was a busy hotel with lots of activity at the desk. Luckily, things like check-ins were time stamped. It helped to narrow down the hours of footage available.

Their first hit came on the earliest date in the month. Pailin was clearly seen at the desk getting her key card. Hanging back as if next in line was Pamela Hovarth. Hovarth wandered out of the shot before Pailin finished registering, but another feed showed them walking toward the elevators together.

"That's what I'm looking for," said Adabi. "But a decent lawyer might still claim it as coincidental. They don't hold hands, and Hovarth isn't listed on the registration."

"We have video from a couple other lobby cams. We can screen them for the two days your suspect was registered. Might take a while to go through so, if you haven't had supper, I'll get the kitchen to send us something."

Encouraged to order whatever she wanted from the room service menu, Adabi started with a French onion soup with lots of gooey cheese. That was followed by a chicken pot pie and topped off with a baked lemon posset. All served with polished silverware and a linen napkin. At Tomba's insistence, she washed it down with a buttery Chardonnay.

It was a video review to remember, even though it only garnered a brief clip of Pailin and Hovarth, hand in hand, in the atrium. And, the view was from behind, therefore not conclusive enough for court.

However, the footage from the next date that Pailin had checked in was more interesting. This time the realtor was leaning against the desk, laughing, with her arm around Devika Sumra. Their body language was intimate and loose, as if they'd enjoyed some libation, or other stimulant, prior to check-in. As before, Pailin's was the only name on the registration, but the detective now had the connection she was looking for.

Tomba tempted Adabi once more, this time with the offer of a complimentary suite for the night. He made it clear it was a sign of respect for her job, and not a come on. It was hard to turn down, but she thanked him for the hospitality and headed back to Halton with her copies of the video clips.

Some days really were better than others.

CHAPTER 42

Tyandaga Towers was a pair of sixteen-storey apartment blocks halfway up the escarpment on Brant Street. It was a fairly new, upscale, condo development that boasted spectacular views of Burlington. Especially for those with penthouse units. Whatever Catrina Pailin had paid, it was worth every penny thought Koki Motungi.

She stood by the floor to ceiling windows taking in the panorama. Lareault's place might overlook the lake, but that was nothing compared to this. She slid aside a glass panel and went onto the terrace. The outdoor space circled the unit so you could either chase the sun or hide from it on one of the many lounge chairs and outdoor sofas or wicker chairs that were arranged in sociable seating groups. These were all draped with see-through weatherproof covers, as was the industrial-sized natural-gas barbecue.

In one corner there was a wet bar, and in another a hot tub. Motungi lifted the spa's insulated cover and read the display. 103F. Perfect.

"Thinking of moving in, Boss?"

Her assistant, Trevor, had joined her to take in the vista.

"Not sure I'd want to lug groceries all the way up here, but I could maybe make it work."

"It's all about compromise. That's what they say on them shows." Trevor took one more look around and went back inside.

Inside was white. White walls. White furniture. White tiled floor. There was a splash of colour here and there, from the rugs, pillows, pictures, and objets d'art, but mainly in pale blues and light grays. If Pailin had killed Hovarth here, she sure as hell hadn't stabbed her. Hiding blood stains in this environment would be damn near impossible.

For all that, the place wasn't what Motungi would call tidy. At least not by her standards. Slippers had been sloughed off by the door, newspapers and magazines had been dropped haphazardly on coffee and end tables, along with real estate brochures. A blanket had been loosely tossed onto the back of one of the two leather sectional sofas in the expansive living room.

And it was dusty.

White hides dust pretty well but it doesn't repel it, and it had been a while since this place had a good cleaning. Motungi ran her fingers along the top of the dining table, then wiped them on her coveralls.

Trevor had nearly finished his digital record with the camera, so Motungi had him do a sample luminol check on the likely spots where blood, or perhaps bleach, might be found. While he did that, she went over the kitchen surfaces with her portable HEPA-filtered vacuum.

Since Pailin didn't employ a cleaning service, Motungi thought she'd appreciate having all the crumbs swept up. Not that any cleaner would be as thorough as a forensics team, as there wasn't a crack, seam, or sink lip left untouched by the fine bristles of the brush. That step complete, she went over the counters, cutting boards, and tabletops with a new product called DrugWipes. It was a gauze patch that was swiped over any surface a drug user might have used.

She also pulled the plastic bag out of the waste bin under the counter and tied the top closed. This wouldn't be going to the trash chute, though.

"If you can start with the main bathroom, Trev, I'll check out the bedrooms."

The master suite was nearly as big as the living room, the king-sized bed absolutely necessary if only for scale. This room was also tastefully furnished, that is if one's taste also ran to life-sized oil paintings of female nudes with an abundance of hair in all the places that women often shaved.

The sun was getting low and Motungi could see in the dust where Trevor, in his protective booties, had walked around to take pictures. She could also see partial footprints, presumably Pailin's, alongside the bed. The prints, mostly over-trodden by others, went around to the other side. Motungi assumed that was from Pailin making it, as everything there was neat, and the pillows stacked decorously.

The en-suite bathroom had Italian marble, a jacuzzi tub, and a chandelier. The expansive walk-in shower had more jets than a drive-through car wash, and the switches on the wall also controlled pot lights in the ceiling, the make-up lights around the mirror, and heat lamps. The towel bar was heated, and Motungi guessed the floor was, too. She checked the medicine cabinet and the vanity. Only the expected items were found. Pailin didn't appear to need prescription drugs.

There was a huge walk-in closet with a who's who in fashion labels, shoe racks of stylish sandals and pumps of every colour, and a treadmill in case Pailin didn't have the energy to go down to the condo's gym. She checked the drawers, finding nothing more interesting than some female-oriented sex toys, and a few joints in a baggie. A baggie. In this place. Now that was a surprise.

The only place she hadn't checked was under the bed. She pulled a small Mag-Lite from her pocket, lay down on the floor, and peered beneath the bed skirt. The bright little flashlight lit up the dust like the sun had previously, exposing a few wispy clumps of hair, a champagne cork, and the part of the footprints that were normally hidden by the skirt. Motungi almost missed the significance.

But she didn't.

"Trevor," she called. "Bring your camera in here."

Catrina Pailin swung her Escalade into the parking lot and parked near the entrance to a hardware store.

"I just need to get a couple of things, Sweetie," she said to Mandy.

She returned a few minutes later and handed a plastic bag to her passenger.

"Just hang on to that for me."

Mandy peered inside and saw that Pailin had bought a box cutter and a roll of duct tape.

"I've got to pack up a few things at the client's house. I've got some flat-pack boxes in the back."

Mandy nodded. That would explain the casual attire: shorts instead of skirt, running shoes instead of heels.

"So, where we going?"

"A new place, not even listed yet, up near Dundas Street."

Pailin started the Cadillac and got back onto Walker's Line, heading north.

"Quite a surprise, that—your mom getting arrested. Do you know why?"

"Dad said she'd made a mistake and got involved with the wrong people. She was trying to save the antique shops."

"Did she get charged for the body in your basement?"

"I don't think so." Mandy began to look worried. "Why would she?"

Pailin reached over to touch Mandy's shoulder. "No reason. Just wondering."

She changed lanes, then said, "Has your dad mentioned anything else?"

"Like what?"

"Like who might have put the body there?"

"He doesn't know, but thinks the guys who stole our stuff might have."

So intent was she on Mandy's response that she didn't see the LandRover that had just passed her the other way, suddenly dive into a gas station and quickly turn around. Walker's Line, however, was a busy thoroughfare, and the LandRover had to wait for a long stream of traffic before it could get back into a driving lane.

Pailin sailed through an amber light, leaving the LandRover to contend with a red. She turned at the next side street then, almost immediately, into a townhouse complex.

"This is a bit like where my grandma lives," observed Mandy.

Ever the realtor, Pailin said, "Is your grandma thinking of moving?"

Mandy laughed. "I don't think so. She really likes where she is."

The Escalade stopped in a parking spot opposite a middle unit in a row of identical looking townhomes.

Pailin plucked a set of keys from the console. She gave them to Mandy.

"Right there. Number eighteen. If you can take that bag with you and open up, I'll bring in the boxes."

The interior was also similar to Mandy's grandma's house, even down to the clutter. One difference was the musty smell. Pailin dropped her armful of flattened boxes and slid open the patio doors. A light breeze soon flowed from the front door to the back.

"If I'm to get a decent price for the place, we have to move a lot of this stuff. And by move, I mean put into storage. So, we need to carefully pack most everything on the tables and counters, and whatever else makes this place looked too lived in."

Impatient for the light to change, the LandRover's driver hit the gas and swerved between the vehicles still crossing the intersection. The cacophony of honks and squealing tires, as the sudden application of brakes nearly caused a fender bender, was not missed by the patrol car slowing for the opposing red.

The officer at the wheel flicked on his light bar and did a U-turn but didn't hit the siren switch. He thought he'd let the guy add speeding to his list of infractions.

The LandRover took the first street on the right and accelerated hard. Its brake lights flashed as it passed the driveway to a townhouse complex.

It then sped into the next street, which was a cul-de-sac. The officer had seen enough and positioned his patrol car to block the LandRover's exit. Undeterred, the SUV drove straight at the black and white's passenger door but at the last moment jumped the curb, went across a lawn, and turned back onto the street it was just on.

Julian Rolland stopped his LandRover behind Pailin's Escalade and, with the motor still running, jumped out. He saw the door to number eighteen was open and went right in.

"Mandy," he yelled. "Mandy, you in here?"

"Dad? I'm in the living—"

"Stop right there, Julian. We need to talk, you and I."

Julian Rolland froze at the entrance to the living room. Catrina Pailin had an arm firmly across his daughter's chest and was holding the blade of a box cutter close to her throat.

"I guess Beth didn't heed my warning," she said

"It wasn't Beth," said Julian. "The cops have a warrant out for your arrest. What happened with you?"

He took a step into the living room. Pailin tightened her grip on Mandy.

"Stay where you are, or this little twat gets cut!"

Julian raised his hands in supplication. "Just let her go, Cat. Hurting Mandy won't help you, now."

"That's right, Miss," said a voice from the hallway.

A police officer was holding his service revolver in a two-handed grip and moving up purposefully behind Julian.

"Step aside, please, sir. I'll handle this."

The hallway was narrow. As the two men were momentarily engaged in changing places, Pailin thrust Mandy away and bolted through the open patio doors into the backyard.

The backyard wasn't much to speak of. Just a small grassy area with a rusting barbeque, outdoor dining set, and the officer's partner. He was panting from having run around and climbing the wooden privacy fence. They'd recognized the Escalade from the BOLO and called for backup. Sirens could be heard approaching.

With nowhere to go, Pailin swung desperately with the box knife and found her wrist clamped in a vice-like grip. Her arm was twisted, painfully, and she found herself face-down on the ground. She still struggled, but all her gym-time was no match for the officer. With a knee on her back, he handcuffed her wrists.

"I'll tell them, Julian," she yelled, raising her chin from the dirt. "I'll tell them. Do you hear me?"

CHAPTER 43

Lareault absently tapped a marker against his thigh while he perused the gallery on the whiteboards. This was perhaps the first time since getting the case he hadn't tacked up a new face. He hoped that was a good sign. When he turned to face the room, the gang really was all here. Flock, Naipaul, Heatherington, Bloomfield, and Adabi. They ceased their chatter when the Inspector cleared his throat.

"Thanks to everyone's hard work, and a fortunate break or two, I'm confident we're on the cusp of breaking this case wide open."

Lareault paused to take in the moment. It wasn't often that this group of people had cause to smile at the same time.

"Hopefully," he crossed his fingers, "Catrina Pailin will see fit to admit to the charges, although she has requested her lawyer be present and may still clam up. However, the arresting officers heard her make accusatory remarks about Julian Rolland, so we'll also have to see where that goes. Julian is currently in one of our guest suites, on traffic violations."

Lareault drew a line to connect their pictures.

"If there is a link between them, we may be able to leverage Julian to further implicate Pailin. Couple that with his wife's allegations, plus the evidence we've gathered, and we should have a strong case to convict."

"Yes, but convict her for what, exactly?" The Superintendent had a good question. Having options was all fine and dandy, but multiple charges often ended with some getting tossed out in court. It was important to focus on those that would guarantee the best result. Or at least have the best odds of.

"We're holding her on charges of uttering threats, reckless endangerment, assault with a weapon, assaulting an officer, conspiracy to burglary, conspiracy to trafficking stolen goods, coercion, suspicion of murder, indignities to a corpse, and arson—that's from the Fire Marshall's verdict that the fire at Sumra's workshop was no accident."

Lareault drew a few more lines from Pailin's picture to those of Beth Rolland, Devika Sumra, and Pamela Hovarth.

"Alright, Evan, let's group those. For the first counts, we have credible witnesses—police officers. Done deal. The conspiracy charges are based on statements from witnesses we have in custody. I'm hopeful we can find more to support their claims. However, to pin murder on her, we're going to need hard evidence. What have you got?"

Lareault was glad she'd brought this up now, because standing before a judge was not the time to realize there were holes in your boat.

"For starters, we know Pailin had a relationship with the first victim. Detective Adabi found a witness who'd seen them canoodling at a bar, and she also has video footage of them together at the Royal York Hotel. The best evidence of their relationship, though, was uncovered by CSI Motungi. She spotted a partial footprint under Pailin's bed that belonged to Hovarth."

"Enough for a match?"

"All six toes. Dennis Collier, down at the morgue, confirmed it this morning." Lareault looked at the report. "Forensics also found hair samples in Pailin's shower-drain and hot-tub filters that match both Hovarth and Sumra."

"I really need to get me a penthouse," said Flock with a chuckle. He looked around and got the usual reaction to his jokes.

"Anything else?" said Heatherington, her focus still on Lareault.

"Couple more things. Koki, er, CSI Motungi matched the hair strands found on the Persian rug to samples she took from Pailin's hairbrush. She also found traces of cocaine and fentanyl in the condo."

Heatherington nodded. "All good links. They prove there was an intimate relationship between Pailin and the two victims. And that drugs were likely involved—the discovery of fentanyl helps since that appears to be what the vic's OD'd on. But it won't be enough. Despite the fact we know both women overdosed, the connection to Pailin is still tenuous: Sumra died at her workshop, and there's nothing to suggest that Hovarth met her end at the condo. Pailin can afford good representation. If we don't find something more substantial, she could end up walking."

It was a hard truth that had been lurking at the back of everyone's mind.

"Not on my fucking watch," muttered Flock.

"We'll keep looking," said Lareault. "It makes a difference when you know who to concentrate on."

This time, the room seemed unanimous with dubious smiles. Except for Bloomfield.

"She strikes me as a narcissist," he said. "Having allegedly killed two people, along with being involved in several other crimes, she still stuck around. Went about her business as if she'd never get caught. She's got the sexy pad, flashy car, flashy jewelry, flush bank account. Her credit card statements show she treats herself very well. She threatened the Rolland family when it looked they might disrupt her plans, and likely murdered for the same reason."

Lareault agreed. Pailin fit the mold. "I think we should play on her arrogance when we question her," he said. "See if we can strike a nerve."

"Still might boil down to Beth Rolland and Pailin pointing fingers at each other," said Flock. "A classic case of *she said, she said*."

"I might be able to help negate that, at least for Hovarth's death," said Adabi. "Sunil and I checked Rolland's alibi. As far as we can tell, she was with her husband in Toronto, attending functions related to Julian's work, during the time they stated. Not an exact science, I'll admit, but if it lends credence to Rolland's alibi, it will weaken any assertion by Pailin that Beth could have killed Hovarth."

"Or that Julian did, for that matter," said Flock. "By the way, what's happening with their daughter if both parents are banged up here?"

"Mandy's staying with her grandmother for now," said Heatherington. "Nice kid. I feel sorry for her."

"Shame how the kids always suffer for their parents' misdeeds."

Richard T. Reed was already representing Beth Rolland, so one of his partners, Helen Carpenter, had been brought in to hold Julian Rolland's hand.

Lareault knew that to minimize a lawyer's influence, during an interview, he had to convince the suspect it was in their best interest to be forthcoming. In other words, get them to answer the bloody questions.

Climb over that hump and it was usually clear sailing.

Unless the suspect lied. Which was possible.

Or clammed up.

Sigh.

"One of our officers heard Catrina Pailin say that she would tell us about you," said Lareault. "What was she going to tell us?"

Julian Rolland pressed his lips together for a moment, then said, "I've no idea."

Not over the hump, yet, thought Lareault.

"Your wife has been connected to a burglary ring. A corpse was found in your basement—someone that *you* knew. And a second murder victim was found with your safe in her possession. Pailin has her sights on you, and I'll bet the house she'll shovel a shitload of trouble your way. Your wife understands what's at stake here, so she's talking to us. You, sir, are in a mess, so don't make this harder for your daughter than it needs to be. Prison visits are no fun for kids."

His lawyer raised an eyebrow, but Lareault didn't care.

He'd sat across from many career criminals who'd maintained a stony silence and either gazed distractedly at the ceiling, or made like they wanted a nap. Rolland wasn't in that category. He fidgeted, shifted in his seat, and tried to maintain a neutral expression, though Lareault could detect the internal struggle. Finally, he glanced at his lawyer. Like Reed, she appeared to be a person of style and substance. Money might talk, but she only gave Rolland the briefest of nods.

He inhaled deeply and rested his hands on the table.

"I don't know what Catrina has said, or is planning to tell you, but the only thing she can accuse me of is getting her some blow."

"By *blow*, you mean cocaine."

"Yes."

"Anything else?"

"Sometimes a few pills."

"Okay. What about fentanyl?"

Rolland shook his head emphatically.

"Nope. She wanted some, but I wasn't about to go near it. Mis-handle that stuff and it's game over."

"How'd she respond to that?"

"She thought about it for a minute, then told me to get her some oxy."

"Oxycontin?"

"Yes."

"And did you?"

"I did."

"And when was this?" Lareault glanced over to make sure he wasn't going too fast for Bloomfield who was making notes to back up the tape.

"I dunno. A few weeks ago."

"Where do you get your supply from?"

Rolland hesitated only briefly. "One of our set designers."

"Name?"

"Thelma Bevan."

Lareault nodded. Another lead for the drug squad.

"Did you know about your wife's venture with Pailin, Stober, and Millcroft?"

"No. Not until the shit hit the fan and you guys showed up."

Lareault sat back and crossed his arms.

"Let's talk about Pamela Hovarth. You recognized her when we were in your basement, correct?"

Rolland nodded.

"Respond verbally for the tape, please."

"Yes. I recognized her. I saw her scraping away at the dirt on the build site. She told me about the archaeological significance of the area. Hinted that it might delay construction."

"Did she say anything about a bribe to have her go away?"

"Not to me."

"So, what did you do?"

"I went to talk to Jack Klaasen, our builder. Told him to get rid of her."

"And?"

"And Jack said he would."

"How?"

"I've really no idea. Next thing I know, she's in a body bag, and you lot were there. Is Klaasen a suspect in her death?"

Lareault unfolded his arms and rose from the chair. He turned to Helen Carpenter.

"Besides Mr. Rolland's traffic violations, we will also charge him with obstructing a police investigation, trafficking a controlled substance, and two counts of accessory to murder: don't draw a line under it, once we speak to Pailin there may be more to come."

Carpenter paused her notetaking and gave Lareault a hard look.

"On what are you basing your accessory charges?"

Lareault moved over to the tape machine.

"We believe your client supplied the drugs that contributed to the death of the victims."

Carpenter simply gave a curt nod.

Lareault terminated the interview and stopped the tape.

"You'll get a full deposition in due time," he said, as he and Bloomfield made for the door.

CHAPTER 44

If Asha wanted to avoid ringing phones, she'd have done better to stay at the DriveCheck office. She'd just got in the door and put her shopping on the kitchen counter when the first call came.

"Hi, it's Asha," she said, tucking the receiver between her shoulder and chin while she unpacked the bags.

"Hey, girlfriend," said Brenda Woodhill. "I just heard. Is this for real, or are you just taking Carole down a notch?"

"As real as the two bottles of champagne I'm holding," Asha said, actually having a bottle of Prosecco in each hand. She carried them to the fridge.

"Well, good for you. The place is going to struggle without you, but it was quite satisfying to see Carole in such a state."

"You were at the office?"

"Dropped in with my timesheets. Been a while since I've seen such crocodile tears. She couldn't decide whether to tell me she was swamped, or that she was perfectly fine without you."

They both laughed, then Asha said, "So, do you want to know what happened?"

"Why do you think I called, sweet cheeks? I'm as nosy as the next broad. Gimme the dirt."

"Yeah, dirt." Asha sighed. Anger takes energy, and it was an emotion she rarely had. Now it had subsided she felt listless, like she'd been beached by an outgoing tide.

"She tried to suggest that Chas beat me."

"You're kidding! Boy, she sure got the wrong end of that stick—is it okay to say *stick*, dear? It won't traumatize you or anything?"

"Don't worry about that. I'm about to start self-medicating. Anyway, that was just the final straw. She's been taking digs at Chas for ages, and only tolerates me because I'd be hard to replace."

"You got that right. I am going to miss you."

Asha phfsssh'd. "I don't see why. You know where I live. You're welcome here, anytime. Well, until I find something else for during the day."

"I know, but you're such fun when I call in. Talking to Carole is like sucking lemons. Anyway, I've got a lesson, but keep me posted."

Mogg wandered in as Brenda hung up. She stretched her front paws way out in front, chest down, tail up, then sat primly looking up at Asha.

"Yes, I'm home early. And, no, I won't feed you."

She searched the cupboards for something decent to drink champagne from. Her choice was a low-ball glass, a beer tumbler, or a yellow coffee mug. She chose the mug, thinking the handle might be useful later on.

The phone interrupted her struggle with the cork.

It was Joe Posada.

"Hey, Asha, Brenda just told me. So, are you guys going to start your own driving school?"

"Um, hi Joe. What?"

"Your own school. Chas said you were thinking about it. Is that why you quit? Kind of sudden notice, though can't say I blame you."

"Um, maybe, no, and yes."

"What?"

"Chas and I have talked about starting our own school, but it's not that simple. Anyway, that's not why I quit. Carole just pissed me off one too many times."

"Did you karate chop her?"

"No, I didn't karate chop her."

"Too bad. I'd like to have seen that."

"That's not very nice, Joe."

"I know—just kidding. What does Chas think about all this?"

"I don't know. I haven't had a chance to tell him." She checked her watch. "He should be home soon, anyway."

"Okay. Well, I'll let you go. Remember me when you look to hire for the new school."

"You have my word."

Mogg had wandered off, which was just as well because it gave Asha more room to gyrate around the kitchen with the champagne bottle between her knees, wrestling with the cork. Her bruised ribs protested as she twisted the uncooperative stopper.

The phone rang again.

Fuck!

"What?"

Silence.

She put the bottle on the counter, inhaled deeply, and said, "Hello?"

"Asha, it's Dieter. Do you have a minute to talk?"

"Hi Dieter. I don't think there's much to talk about."

"I've spoken to Carole. She was only trying to help. Just looking out for your best interests."

"Did she tell you she called people in and suggested that Chas beat me?"

"She was concerned."

"That Chas beat me? How long has he worked for you?"

"I don't know—five or six years."

"Almost ten, Dieter. The best and most reliable instructor you'll ever have, yet you try to pass him all the shit assignments. I'm standing by my resignation. The person you should talk to is Chas."

"I tried, but his phone is off, or dead, or something."

"I'll tell him you called."

Asha hung up, feeling the heat return to her cheeks. Guess she wasn't completely drained of anger, after all. Where'd she put that damn bottle?

Fenn parked in the driveway, surprised to see Asha's car there. He checked his watch. 3:34. He didn't call out once inside, in case she'd come home with a migraine and was sleeping. Mogg met him at the door and rubbed her cheek against his hand as he undid his laces.

"In the kitchen," Asha called.

Fenn walked in to find her at the table, perusing the classified ads section of the local rag, yellow coffee mug in hand. On the counter was a half-empty champagne bottle and a pair of vise-grips.

"Grab a mug, or swig from the bottle. Doesn't matter, there's another in the fridge."

Bemused, Fenn took the first thing to hand, a low-ball glass, and poured a generous helping of bubbly.

"And what are we celebrating?" He leaned over and saw she'd circled a couple of things in the help-wanted column.

"Freedom from tyranny. The start of the beginning of the first day of the—how's that go again? Whatever, I quit and I'm glad." She tipped her head back and drained her drink.

Fenn took a slug of his own. "Well, good. Too long in coming. Want to tell me how it happened?"

Asha held out her mug. "Refill me, and I'll relate the whole sordid tale."

"Sordid. The best kind."

Two hours later, after the celebratory drink, and the celebratory pizza, Fenn and Asha were slouched on the couch, her head on his shoulder as they watched TV. When Fenn put it on mute for the commercials, their thoughts went to the job they had just left.

"I've a couple of students going to test this week," he said. "I'd rather not leave them in the lurch."

Asha understood. If they were just ordinary lessons, he could have re-booked them at another time with either Joe or Brenda. Driving tests, however, were booked weeks in advance. Joe and Brenda may not have those time slots free.

"Other than that, we're out of work."

"We've got some savings," said Asha. "And we haven't taken vacation this year. We should go up north: rent a cottage on a lake for a week or two. Once we start new jobs, it'll be another twelve long months before we get any significant time off."

"So, we go on holiday, then what?"

"Joe thinks we should start our own driving school."

"Joe just wants to do what we're doing."

"Could we start our own school, though?"

Fenn put his head back and gazed across the room.

"Be expensive. We'd have to register a business, then rent a location for an office and a classroom. We'd need equipment: computers, phones, desks, chairs, stationary. There'll be utility bills, and let's not forget advertising—can't get students unless they know we exist."

Asha gave him a gentle slap on the thigh. "Well, aren't you just a wet rag. We'd have a successful business because we're good at what we do. The income would more than pay for the expenses."

"Oh, I'm not worried about profitability. It's getting to that stage that'll be tricky. We'll need a start-up fund. Money to pay for the first few months until we get up to speed. It takes time to build a sustainable customer base. DriveCheck is a good franchise with an excellent reputation. Hard to compete with."

"Yeah, but their courses are pricey. We could do it for less. Maybe we could get a business loan, or I could ask my parents to help us out. They're fairly well off."

Fenn fell silent for a moment.

"I've never had much in the way of help, Asha. Always been pretty self-sufficient. I'd feel funny about asking them—like we can't stand on our own feet."

"We could pay them back with interest. Would that be better?" She raised her head to meet his eyes.

"We'll figure something out. We could take on a second job until the school got busy. We're good at other stuff."

"We could do that," said Asha, her attention back on the TV. "Only takes half-an-hour to renovate a house."

Then she gave Fenn a mischievous grin.

"I bet you'd look great in a toolbelt."

CHAPTER 45

The diamond draped fashionista that had given a statement two weeks ago was a far cry from the Catrina Pailin that now sat in the interview room.

Her casual attire was rumpled and grass-stained, the jewelry she'd worn when arrested had been bagged, and her self-confident smile had been replaced by a sullen smirk that validated Bloomfield's assessment of her.

So far, she hadn't said a word since the interview started. Neither had Lareault. He'd just sat patiently, watching her scan the walls of the room like a bored child in detention. Her lawyer, while not from the same company as Reed and Carpenter, was nonetheless cut from the same cloth. Montblanc pen held lightly in a hand that rested on a notepad, he, too, sat quietly waiting for the first move as if watching a chess match.

The inspector had already kept them in the room for an hour, not only to get under Pailin's skin but to give his team as much time as possible to gather more evidence. His current silence was an extension of that, but it was a ploy the lawyer had seen before.

"Is there a question forthcoming for my client?"

"Sorry," said Lareault, as if coming out of a reverie. "I was just wondering how anyone could hold a box knife to the throat of a young girl—the daughter of people who considered your client a friend. I mean, what sort of pathetic coward does that?"

His dig had the desired result. Pailin turned to face him, though she had enough self-control to consider her response.

"I wouldn't have hurt her. Julian surprised me. I was just trying to buy some time."

"With a razor's edge against the jugular vein of Mandy Rolland? That could have gone sideways in a heartbeat."

"I'd retracted the blade. Julian didn't notice."

"The same way the arresting officer didn't notice you'd sliced through his tunic?"

"I was scared, alright? I panicked."

"Scared of what?"

"Well, duh. Going to jail. I'm sure Beth's been telling you some lovely stories about me."

"Are they true, then?"

"Depends on what she told you." Pailin peered at some dirt under her nails, as if that were more important.

"She spoke of your involvement in the burglary ring. She told us you admitted to killing Pamela Hovarth. She said you'd threatened Mandy."

"Her word against mine. What if I said that she'd killed Hovarth?"

"We know she didn't. She has an alibi. Do you?"

Pailin shrugged. "I'm sure I can come up with something."

"Now would be a good time."

"When did she die, again?"

"C'mon, Catrina. You know you killed her a few hours before you called us in."

The lawyer tapped his pen like a little gavel. "That's an unsubstantiated claim."

Lareault gave him a flat smile. "Don't worry. It won't be for long."

Turning back to Pailin, he said, "We know that you and Ms. Hovarth had a relationship. We have pictures of you together. While I've never stayed at the Royal York myself, I hear that it's very nice. So is your condo, apparently, though someone said the decor was a bit tacky."

That got her attention. "In my business you have to know how to stage. Your 'someone' obviously has no taste. Yes, she and I dated a couple of times. Pamela thought my place was great."

"Was she stoned? Julian told us he supplied you with drugs."

Pailin started to respond then closed her mouth. Lareault didn't have to look at Bloomfield to know his sergeant was holding back a smile. Lareault's pre-emptive strike about Julian Rolland had trumped one of her high cards.

To her credit, she recovered quickly. "You guys know Pam was looking for artifacts on the Rollands' building site. Well, Julian supplied her as well."

"Julian said he got you some cocaine, and that you'd asked for fentanyl."

"What of it?"

"Why fentanyl? Not the safest of drugs to be playing with."

"Just curious. All drugs are dangerous if you don't know what you're doing."

"He said he got you oxycontin instead."

"That's right, he did. Are you going to charge him with dealing?"

"But the oxy you got wasn't the genuine article, was it? You knew that most of the so-called oxy on the street is counterfeit. And by that, I don't mean generic. Those fake pills are a way to move fentanyl around. While Julian thought he was getting you oxy, you were pretty sure it would be fentanyl."

Before Pailin could respond, her lawyer placed his hand on her arm.

"I'm hearing a lot of conjecture, and possible hearsay. How about some substance?"

"Forensics found traces of cocaine and fentanyl in Ms. Pailin's kitchen. The samples suggest that the oxy pills were crushed to get powdered fentanyl, then mixed with the cocaine. Since powdered drugs like this are taken in lines, and often shared, we find it odd when one person dies of a severe overdose while the other does not."

"Hardly proof that my client provided the fatal batch of drugs that allegedly killed Ms. Hovarth. You'll have to do better than that, Inspector."

"We also found empty oyster tins, a box of crackers, and other assorted food remnants in your client's condo that match the stomach contents of the victim. Her last meal, so to speak. Oyster juice and cracker crumbs were also found on the rug the deceased was wrapped in."

The lawyer didn't respond. He was busy jotting notes on his pad. Lareault waited until he finished, then said, "While you're at it, write this down."

From a folder, he slid some pictures in front of Pailin.

"Either you saw Hovarth at the site, or Jack Klaasen told you about her. After all, you had a buyer for one of his lots. Either way, if the build was held up, and the Rollands bailed on the deal, you'd lose out on commission for both their house sale and the lot purchase. That might be a hundred and fifty thousand dollars, out the door. Pretty good motive for making a little blackmailer disappear.

"So, you struck up a relationship with Hovarth, got cozy at Cranny's Nook and the Royal York, then one night you invited her for a spaghetti supper. Some red wine, perhaps a line or two of untainted cocaine. She'd brought one of her artifacts to show you—a skull. Since you didn't want her to OD in your condo, where you might be seen disposing of the body, you suggested a midnight snack up at the dig. She could show you where she found the skull. What fun!

"So, off you go. Hovarth, the skull, crackers, oysters, another bottle of wine, and a bag of deadly powder in your purse. It's all very romantic. You have a key to the sales office up at Rattlesnake Point. You sit on the rug and have your picnic, and then perhaps while looking at one of her trenches, you slip her the tainted coke. *Here, dear, you go ahead—I have to drive.* Is that what you said?"

Pailin stared at him, passively, but was so motionless that both Lareault and Bloomfield could tell a nerve had been struck.

The lawyer felt this would be a good time to earn some of his coin. "Fascinating story, Inspector," he began, but Lareault cut him off.

"Then you'll want to hear the rest. The part where Hovarth expires. Your client briefly considers burying her in one of her own trenches. After all, the lots were almost ready for the first pour. Get the foundations in and she'd never be found. Then she has a better idea. Beth Rolland wants to quit the burglaries. This would be a good warning to her—the old carrot and stick, where the carrot is the build no longer be delayed, and the stick is the threat of Mandy ending up in a rug."

Pailin was now a little more animated, looking anywhere except at the policemen opposite her. Lareault wasn't about to let her evade.

"Catrina. Look at me and tell me how I'm doing."

Pailin tilted her head to meet his eyes, then clapped her hands slowly.

"A story worthy of the Giller Prize. Who's going to play me in the movie?"

"I'm not sure," said Lareault, "but she'd have to be fit, like you, to roll Hovarth in the rug, then get the bundle into the back of your Escalade. And I'm sure you could have because Hovarth only weighed fifty-three kilograms. Our female officers handle more than that when they use a fireman's carry in training. Plus, once you got her to the Rollands', it was all downhill, so to speak, to the basement."

Pailin flexed a bicep with a smile. "I am pretty buff, aren't I?"

CHAPTER 46

Lareault, Bloomfield, Heatherington, Flock and Adabi were in the hallway, outside the observation room. They had arranged that Heatherington would call Lareault's cellphone to allow him to pause the interview. When it buzzed in his pocket, the inspector had thought it just another stall tactic.

For once, he was glad to be wrong.

"We've got her," said Flock. "Both counts."

The Superintendent handed over a forensics report. Koki Motungi had found fibres from the Persian rug in the back of Pailin's Escalade.

In the case of Hovarth's death, it was a slam dunk.

Flock, just as determined that Pailin wouldn't walk, had also gone back through his video files.

"Come with me, Boss. I've something you should see."

Lareault restarted the tape and the interview. The lawyer paused his doodling on the corner of the notepad and listened.

"Would you like to know the flaw in your scheme to murder Pam Hovarth?"

Pailin looked mildly interested.

"You should have rented a vehicle to move her and the rug from the sales office to the Rollands'. We found matching fibres in the back of your Escalade."

She didn't even blink.

"Of course you did. I bought that rug for the sales office."

"Nope. Jack Klaasen confirmed his wife bought that rug."

"I took it to get cleaned."

"Nope."

Lareault handed her counsel a copy of the forensics report. The lawyer scanned it, then leaned over and whispered to his client. Pailin gave Lareault another hard look, then found another spot on the wall to contemplate. Lareault gave her all the time she needed.

"She was a blackmailing little skank, you know."

"Was my summary of events, correct?"

"You want me to applaud again?"

"Anything you'd like to add?"

"She asked for it. I offered her ten grand to fill in her trench, but she was confident Jack would give her a lot more."

"Jack Klaasen?"

"Yes."

"Is that why you hit her with the rock after she OD'd? Make us think Klaasen had got mad and killed her?"

"That, and to make sure she was dead."

"What did you do with the rock after?"

"Tossed it behind the office."

Lareault glanced at the camera that was sending video of the interview to the observation room. Heatherington would be dispatching a search party up to Rattlesnake Point.

"Did she OD in the office or outside?"

"We were in the office. She was snorting off the display table. When the drug hit, she staggered out onto the little porch and puked over the railing. Then she collapsed. I left her there while I packed up the picnic and put it in the car."

"Why take the rug?"

"Ever tried to get a dead body into the back of a Cadillac? Arms, legs, head, body, all floppy. Don't know why they call 'em stiffs. A rolled-up rug is much easier to handle, even with a body inside. And, yeah, it was a struggle, but my gym membership paid for itself that night. That gave me the idea to smash the window and make it look like kids had partied in there. Be a little suspicious if I'd taken the rug and locked up, don't you think?"

"And the skull?"

"What else was I going to do with it? Besides, she always did like a little head."

Bloomfield raised his eyebrows, whereas Lareault allowed a dry smile to keep her talking.

But that seemed to be all she had to say.

Lareault looked at the lawyer. The lawyer looked back, poker-faced as ever.

"Time to start a fresh page," Lareault told him. "With the header: Devika Sumra."

He went back to Pailin. "Well, Catrina?"

This time, Pailin leaned over to her counsel and whispered something. The lawyer nodded.

"My client admits to knowing Ms. Sumra. They had a couple of dates, that's all."

Lareault sighed theatrically.

"Alright, let's start there. How'd you guys meet?"

"We had adjoining barstools at *Pourquoi*, a lounge for like-minded ladies in Mississauga. Got to admiring each other's tennis bracelets. One thing led to another, and another, and eventually to her confiding that she acquired cut-rate jewelry."

"Beth Rolland told us about your plan to use Devika Sumra as a buffer. Why did you give us her name when we asked for a list of open-house attendees?"

"Come now, Inspector. Surely you know a red herring when you see one. I wanted to give you another suspect for Pam's demise. I figured it was a done deal when you found the Rollands' safe in her workshop."

Her comment made Bloomfield look up from his notepad.

"I never mentioned Sumra's workshop, or the safe," said Lareault.

Pailin barely missed a beat. "You didn't have to. Devika told me about it."

"So, you set her up to be found with evidence you hoped would tie her to Hovarth's body. Rather convenient that Ms. Sumra overdosed on the same lethal combination of drugs as Pamela Hovarth."

Pailin was back to studying her nails. "Lots of people die from that. Call it an unfortunate coincidence."

"We also have video of your vehicle leaving the workshop parking lot shortly before the fire in Sumra's unit was discovered."

This was what Roy Flock had found upon his review of the video. For most of that time period, a delivery truck had blocked the camera's view. But it had moved away just as the Escalade had exited the lot. He hadn't twigged at the time because Pailin hadn't been a suspect, nor had Flock known what she drove.

"Another coincidence." She turned to her lawyer, irritation on her face. "Do I have to say all your lines?"

"And is it coincidence that the fire was started by a welding torch igniting a tipped over a can of paint thinner traces of which our forensics team found on sneakers in your closet?"

"Sometimes I have to touch up the paint in the properties I sell. I use thinner to clean up with."

"So, if we go back to your place, and check out your storage locker, we'll find paint, and brushes, and drop cloths, and thinner. Maybe a ladder and coveralls…"

No response.

"We've also catalogued your jewelry, both what you were wearing on admission, and at your home. Some pieces had been reported as stolen."

Lareault turned to the lawyer again. "I forget, did we have her down for possession? If not, add it to your list."

Then back to Pailin. "Your counsel isn't saying much because he knows it's a done deal."

Lareault noticed the lawyer shake his head.

"Oh, no doubt he'll put up a great defense, but you've already admitted to the murder of Pamela Hovarth. With all the other evidence, any jury will come to the obvious conclusion about Sumra's death. Your best bet to get out of jail before your old age pension kicks in is to make a clean breast of it."

At that, Pailin looked down at her grass-stained top and closed her eyes resignedly.

The lawyer gave it one last shot.

"We've a good argument for involuntary manslaughter. That my client was unaware of the quantity of fentanyl, and that the victims would consume such—"

The inspector shook his head.

"Save your breath. For that, your client would have to prove she partook of the same batch. To do that, she'd need a blood test. Her problem, there, is the blood test would show no evidence of fentanyl in her system. Isn't that right, Catrina?"

Lareault spoke the truth, sort of. While any fentanyl in her system would have been flushed out in urine within a couple of days, he doubted Pailin or her lawyer would know that. He wanted her to feel cornered, yet defiance was as close to admitting defeat as her ego would allow.

"Screw you and your blood test, Lareault. Let's see how smart you are in court."

CHAPTER 47

One thing about being unemployed the week before Kim and Tony were to be married, was that Asha could help the bride-to-be and her sister, Eileen, finalize the arrangements, and Fenn had time to buy a new suit for the occasion. He also picked up a new pair of Merrill cross trainers to replace those shredded by Bagheera.

The Saturday afternoon nuptials would be unusually intimate by Klaasen standards. Only a hundred guests. The venue was the Royal Botanical Gardens on the outskirts of Burlington. The ceremony would be in the famous Rose Garden, and the reception in a large marquis nearby. On the remote chance of inclement weather, the RBG's indoor banquet hall had also been reserved.

As father-of-the-bride, Jack Klaasen would spare no expense for his youngest daughter's big day. While not directly involved in the planning, he'd told Kim that she had a blank cheque to work with. One that her mother, Jack's ex-wife, was determined to take full advantage of. Kim had reined her in, somewhat, though it would take three people to assemble the six-layer cake.

Thursday was the obligatory stag and doe night. The does, led by Kim's mother, went to a Chippendales male stripper review at a club in Hamilton. The stags, just Tony and Chas because Tony wasn't really into the bar scene, went to the barn in Kilbride. That was their perfect venue. They had a few beers and changed the spark plugs on *The Black Mariah*, Tony's '67 GTO.

"Scrub those fingers well," said Fenn, when they were done. "Wouldn't do to have Kim see grease under those nails when she slips the ring on."

"Hey, this is the best grease money can buy."

"I know that, and you know that," Fenn said, uncapping a couple more beers. "But we can't expect your future wife to know that."

"Almost had her convinced we should drive this old beast on our honeymoon."

"Almost?"

"She said her dad had rented a limo to take us somewhere. How often do you get to ride in a limo?"

Friday night was the rehearsal.

Asha suggested she and Fenn just have a light snack for supper, since Kim's mom would likely put on a spread for the rehearsal party.

Just before they left, Asha checked the mail. She came back waving an envelope. At first, Fenn thought it might be his final paycheque from DriveCheck. When he'd gone to the office to drop off his car roof sign and last paysheet, Carole had pretended to be on the phone. She'd kept up her animated conversation with a supposed new customer while he dropped his stuff at the reception desk. Dieter was nowhere to be seen. So, after a ten-year relationship, none of them had said goodbye.

The envelope didn't contain his paycheque. It had a UBC logo and return address. Asha's cousin worked at the University of British Columbia. The letter inside referred to something that they had almost forgotten about.

Not quite a year ago, Fenn had come into possession of a compact disc containing the formula for a new, yet illicit, drug. Not knowing at the time what was on the disc, Asha had sent it to her relative who was a software engineer at UBC. He, in turn, had sent it to the University's medical research facility where it was determined the drug formula had properties that could be used in treatments for several neurological diseases. On her cousin's advice, Asha and Fenn had taken out a patent on the undocumented formula, its original creator being deceased.

"It says here that preliminary trials have shown great promise, and we should expect an initial royalty cheque from the Canadian division of Bristol-Myers Squibb for—get this—ten-thousand dollars!"

Asha threw her arms around Fenn's neck, and he swung her off her feet.

They kissed deeply, then looked again at the letter. The cheque had been approved and would be issued on the fifteenth of the next month. Additional cheques to be issued quarterly as long as the patent was in use.

Asha glanced at the clock.

"Damn, we don't have time to jump into bed."

Fenn grinned. "You might want to bottle that for tomorrow. Traditionally, the best man, me, is supposed to bonk the maid of honour. However, since Eileen's sister is the maid of honour, and she's married, then the bridesmaid, you, will have to step up and take one or more for the team."

Asha kissed him on the cheek and danced away. "Well, we can't buck tradition now, can we?"

The bride's walk down the aisle was to be at three p.m. Fenn had arranged to be at Tony's house an hour before. Actually, Kim had arranged that, threatening parts of Fenn's anatomy if he and Tony were late arriving at the RBG.

"Kim's a hell of a catch," Fenn said. "But if you're having second thoughts, just say the word and I'll get you on a flight to Venezuela."

"Thanks, but you can save your Air Miles. I've never been more certain about anything."

"Fair enough. I'd just be remiss in my duties as best dude if I didn't provide an escape plan."

"Here's your most important duty," said Tony, handing Fenn Kim's wedding ring.

For safekeeping, Fenn wrapped it in a linen handkerchief he'd brought especially for that purpose, and put it in his pocket.

"Are you ready?"

"As ready as I ever will be."

Fenn in his smart new suit and Tony in his tux, still had forty-five minutes to kill. Fenn suggested they go for a cruise around town in the Challenger.

Historically, the weather during the last weekend of August was perfect for camping, barbeques, picnics, and weddings. This one stayed within the trend, a little hotter perhaps, so the guys removed their jackets and buckled their seatbelts. Fenn cruised around Burlington, always mindful of how long it would take to get from where they were to the Royal Botanical Gardens. As they drove along Fairview Street, approaching Guelph Line, Fenn suddenly pulled into a car dealership and turned around. Tony saw him stare intently down the road.

"What's up?"

"See that Mercedes, the one up ahead in the right lane? That's Benny."

"Benny the fence?"

"Yup."

Fenn sped up to draw near the dark sedan, then followed a few car lengths back.

"Are you sure it's him? Lots of those old Mercs around."

"Pretty sure, but I'll get closer."

Fenn gradually maneuvered through the traffic until he was in the adjoining lane and able to read the licence plate.

"Hmm."

"Hmm, what?"

Fenn moved into the other car's blind spot, then slowly crept up beside it until he could see the driver in profile. Then he backed off.

"He's changed the plates on the car, but that's definitely Benny."

"Do you think the cops let him go?"

"I think they're still looking for him. That's why he's changed the plates."

Fenn glanced at the dash clock.

"We have to break this off—it's time I got you to the RBG." He drifted toward the right lane.

Tony checked his watch. "If we jump on the highway to get across town, we'll still have a few minutes to spare. Let's see where he's going."

"You sure?"

"Five minutes."

With the Saturday afternoon bustle, and Burlington's plethora of traffic lights, five minutes wasn't a lot of travel time. They were now following Benny on a service road that ran parallel to the highway.

"We've got to give it up, man," said Fenn. "I won't have you late today of all days."

"There's not much along here so we must be near to where he's going," said Tony. "Besides, we can access the highway at the end of this road."

Tony was right. Benny turned into the parking lot of a motel. Fenn pulled into the adjacent lot of an upholstery shop.

The motel had been there for decades and looked it. Independently owned, its fortunes had waned dramatically with the influx of Super 8s, Days Inns, and other franchised rooms now in town. In fact, apart from an old red Mazda outside the office, Benny's was the only car in the lot.

The two guys watched Benny heave his portly frame from the driver's seat and take a bag of groceries into his unit.

"What do you think?" said Tony.

"I think he's hiding out, and that he'll keep for now." Fenn hit the gas and left a trail of rubber from the parking lot out onto the service road.

"Are you going to call the cops and tell them where he is?"

Fenn thought about that before answering.

"I will. But not just yet."

He signaled for the on-ramp and sped up to merge with traffic. His phone pinged. He gave it to Tony. It was a text from Asha.

"She wants to know where we are," said Tony. "Shall I tell her we had car trouble?"

Fenn shook his head. "Just reply that we're nearly there."

He threaded through a loose congregation of cars onto an open stretch of road, then pushed the speedometer past 120mph. The off-ramp came up quickly and Tony held on to the armrest as the Challenger's stiff shocks allowed Fenn to take the curve at a good speed.

"You know how the bride is supposed to keep the groom waiting at the altar," Fenn said, as he downshifted to turn into the RBG's entrance. "Well, maybe we've just turned that around. A new trend."

"Wow," said Tony. "Have you ever seen a limousine like that?"

Fenn hadn't. The white wedding carriage with dark tinted windows seemed to stretch forever. A back door opened and Asha emerged. She walked quickly to where Fenn had parked the Challenger.

"What were you guys doing? You're late."

"No, we're not." Fenn held up his watch. "Look, one minute to three. We're right on time."

"Well, get on down there. Everyone is waiting." She pointed to a manicured path bordered by blooming plants. "You look very handsome, by the way, Tony."

Fenn just got an I'll-deal-with-you-later look.

"And you look lovely yourself," said Tony. And she did, though Fenn would have used the word sexy.

Her glossy dark hair had been put up, artfully, with a couple of tendrils left to curl beside her ears, and her gown was a shimmery, burnt-orange, off-the-shoulder number with matching heels. Eileen, the maid of honour, wore a similar hair style and colour, though her dress had a different cut to it.

The bride, of course, was absolutely stunning in her white Vera Wang gown. A hush fell over the Rose Garden as she appeared on the arm of her father.

With Kim being Catholic, and Tony an atheist, they had found a priest sensitive to both views who conducted a beautiful service that satisfied both bride and groom, along with the various religious leanings of their guests.

Naturally, the catered meal was to die for, and then came the speeches. Fenn didn't think his roast of Tony was quite that funny, but the champagne had been flowing for a couple of hours, so he'd had a pretty loose audience to work with. A laughing Asha had squeezed his thigh and kissed his cheek when he sat down.

When the newlyweds cut the cake, they did so with care. With similar dimensions to the Eiffel Tower on a smaller scale, they were nervous that the elegant confectionery might collapse. There must have been a subtle theme there, because Jack announced that since the happy couple already had a house—they were going to live in Kim's cottage on the escarpment plateau—and were quite happy with their vehicles, his wedding present was a month-long Mediterranean cruise for their honeymoon.

Fenn gave Asha a nudge.

"With all the money we're getting from Bristol-Meyers, we could maybe join them."

"They don't want us tagging along on their honeymoon."

"Tony wouldn't mind."

"Forget it. Is there any champagne in that bottle?"

The five-piece band, three men and two women, was great. They played everything from Elvis to The Beatles, and from Shania Twain to Matchbox 20. They danced until the band took a break at eleven, which was when Kim and Tony departed for the airport. Some sneaky maneuvering on Eileen's part found Asha standing alone the moment the bride threw her bouquet. Clutching the flowers, Asha looked at Fenn with a rueful smile. He nodded with a grin, and everyone cheered.

CHAPTER 48

The wedding reception went until one in the morning. The best man and the bridesmaid, new suit and slinky gown cast onto a chair, fell asleep just after three. When Fenn got up at seven, to go to the bathroom, Mogg attempted to trip him with a paw, so he scooped some tuna more or less into her bowl and went back to bed.

It was a little past noon when they finally rose and had showers. Still feeling tired, they went to a nearby restaurant for brunch. Then, back at home, Asha called Eileen to chat about the wedding while Fenn watched a soccer game. To top off their lazy afternoon, they had a nap until it was time for supper.

Fenn set the table while Asha used a wooden spoon to stir the contents of a sizzling wok. She was doing a little shuffle and singing.

"*Hands up, baby, hands up, doo-doo-dooo-dooo…*"

"I see you've got your energy back," he said, feeling somewhat revived himself.

"That was such fun last night, wasn't it? What a beautiful wedding, and the band was great."

Fenn glanced at the clock. "I imagine Kim and Tony will be somewhere over the Atlantic by now, heading for their cruise."

"Where shall we go for our honeymoon?"

"I guess it depends on what our bank account looks like. We'll have to see how nice those royalty cheques are going to be. Don't forget, we still have to figure out how we'll make a steady income now we're no longer at DriveCheck."

He opened the cupboard and reached for a mug.

"What would you like to drink? I'm having coffee."

Asha spooned the stir-fry into a serving bowl.

"It's not like you to have coffee in the evening."

That was true. Fenn rarely drank coffee, anytime, since caffeine seemed to give him voltage he hardly needed.

"Yeah, about that. I didn't want to say anything yesterday, to spoil the happy mood, but the reason Tony and I were almost late—"

"You were late."

"*Almost*—anyway, we found Benny."

Asha paused, then put the steaming bowl on the table. She returned to the stove and put the wok in the sink. Then she leaned back against the counter.

"Okay. Where was he?"

"We saw him driving around and followed him to a shitbox motel on the service road. I think that's his bolt hole."

"Did you call the cops?"

"Nope."

"Why not? You've got to tell them where he is, Chas,"

"I know, and I will. But first, he and I have some unfinished business."

Asha recognized the hard look on Fenn's face and knew there was only one thing she could say.

"I guess I'm also having coffee, then."

With the windows down, a rush of warm night air swirled into the car along with the throaty growl from the powerful engine as they flew along the country road toward Kilbride. This close to midnight, with scarcely any traffic, Fenn chased the high beams through the curves like a rally driver. There were a few things he wanted to get from the barn before they went to find Benny.

He'd worn a dark hoodie, jeans, and his new Merrill cross-trainers. Asha, her bare legs shining in the moonlight, had worn denim shorts, a dark tube top, and navy-blue sneakers. She had brushed out her hairdo from the day before and sported a ponytail.

He was less than five minutes inside the barn. He padlocked it and handed Asha a cloth bag containing his supplies. The drive back to downtown Burlington was just as exhilarating, and once they hit the lower speed of the city streets their adrenaline was flowing. They cruised past the motel slowly. Only Benny's car was in the lot. The staff obviously didn't stay on site overnight. Fenn pulled into the adjacent lot again and shut off the motor.

It was now after midnight, and even the nearby highway had little traffic. The night was quiet enough for them to hear the occasional tick as the Challenger's exhaust pipes cooled. Fenn took the bag from Asha, and they walked toward the motel, scanning for security cameras along the way. Seeing none, Fenn stopped by the door of the unit next to Benny's and had Asha stand against the wall behind him.

"Stay there until he comes out."

He pulled a pair of snug mechanic's gloves from the bag and put them on, then reached in again and brought out a rubber mallet. He glanced around once more, then strode purposefully to Benny's Mercedes and swung the mallet hard against the driver's door. The resulting *thump* put a good-sized dent in the sheet metal and set off the car's alarm.

Fenn stepped quickly to the wall and flattened himself beside the entrance to Benny's unit. The horn pulsed loudly for about thirty seconds before the curtains twitched, and the alarm suddenly stopped.

Fenn turned to Asha.

"That's no good," he whispered to her. "The weasel used his key fob to stop the alarm."

Asha peered past his shoulder.

"Give me a sec. I've got an idea."

She jogged back to the Challenger and came back wearing Fenn's dark sunglasses. She pulled the scrunchy from her ponytail and shook out her hair. Making sure that Benny's lights were off, and curtains closed, she hopped on the hood of the Mercedes, crossed her legs, and pulled her top down to her navel.

"Hit it again," she hissed to Fenn.

Silently mouthing, *Ookay...,* he put a huge dent in the roof.

It was a good thing the other units were empty. The German sedan had a healthy horn. This time, only ten seconds passed before the curtains twitched, and the horn was silenced. Then the curtains parted further and Benny's bewildered face appeared between them.

Asha gave him a bright smile and waved. The curtains drifted back together and moments later the door opened, and Benny peered out. He'd thrown on some pants but otherwise was barefoot and shirtless, his belly flab hanging over the waist of his slacks.

Asha smiled again. "Nicolas Wray sends his compliments," she purred.

"What?"

Asha licked her lips slowly and beckoned to him. Fenn, doing his best to merge with the wall, held in a laugh. He raised the mallet and waited. Taking the bait, Benny came out of the unit and took a couple of steps toward Asha.

As he did, she slid off the hood and pulled her top back up.

"I said Nicolas Wray sends his compliments."

Fenn brought the mallet down on Benny's skull, hoping the wide rubberized surface would only stun the man. There was a satisfying *thap* and Benny staggered for another a step. He went down to his knees, then fell forward with his arms beneath him.

Fenn knelt beside him and quickly dumped the other contents from the bag: a roll of duct tape and a can of black spray paint. Benny groaned but otherwise lay still while Fenn tore off a strip of tape and put it over the fat man's mouth. He then put the bag over Benny's head, and after a bit of tugging on the flabby arms got the wrists taped together behind his back.

Fenn stood up and scanned the ground nearby.

"Looking for these?" Asha held up Benny's car keys, which he'd dropped when he fell.

"Open up the trunk," said Fenn. He checked Benny's pockets, but they were empty. "Oh, and put that can of spray paint on the passenger seat. I'll be right back."

Asha put her hands on her hips and stood with her head to one side.

"And what's the magic word?"

"*Please.*"

He went into the motel room and switched on a light. A wallet was on the bedside table. It contained a couple hundred dollars, which Fenn put in his pocket. He then opened the small closet and rifled through the coat and jacket. He found an address book with several names and phone numbers, and a billfold with about three grand in large bills. There was also a passport with Benny's picture next to the name *Joel Steiner*. On the closet floor was a briefcase and a satchel holding a laptop computer. He opened the briefcase on the bed. It was full of jewelry.

By all appearances, Benny was ready to take off. Disappear. Fenn wondered if he'd stuck around, waiting for the forged passport, so he could cross the border as Joel Steiner. He tossed the computer, passport, and address book on the bed, tucked the cash-laden billfold in his waistband, and left with the briefcase. He locked the door on his way out.

Asha was standing by the car.

"Anything interesting in the trunk?"

"Nope. There's plenty of room, even for his fat ass," she said.

The problem would be to get him in there. Fenn poked him in the ribs with his foot.

"Hey! Wake up."

Fenn poked again.

Benny stirred and half-rolled onto his side. Fenn crouched beside him.

"Nicolas Wray has axed for your presence," he growled, trying to disguise his voice. "He said I could kneecap you if I need to. Do I need to?"

Fenn tapped Benny's head with the handle of the mallet. Through the hood, Benny wouldn't know it wasn't a gun barrel.

The hood moved side to side.

"Good. Let's get you up."

Fenn got his captive into a sitting position, then stood in front and put his hands beneath the pudgy arms just below the shoulders. He lifted and Benny got his legs positioned to stand and take his weight. Just as he came upright, the fat man suddenly lunged forward, his legs pile-driving like a defensive tackle trying to sack a quarterback. They careened off the back door of the Mercedes. Fenn stumbled and fell backwards with Benny landing on top of him.

He could hear the man snorting beneath the hood, trying to answer a sudden demand for oxygen through only his nose. Fenn, also winded, struggled to get the suffocating weight off his chest. Benny had his knees on the pavement and Fenn's thrust helped him to regain his feet. Panicked, he began to run blindly across the parking lot. Fenn rose just in time to see Asha sweep her foot around and cause Benny to trip. It looked like he'd taken a flying leap. With hands taped behind his back he hit the ground hard, first with his chest and then with his chin.

Both Asha and Fenn grimaced at the sight.

Benny lay on the ground, huffing and moaning in pain. All fight knocked out of him. Fenn figured this was as pliable as the guy was going to get.

"Let's get this done," he said.

With Asha's help, he pulled Benny to his feet once more, and frog-marched him to the back of the car. A gut punch doubled Benny over the lip of the trunk. Fenn pushed him forward and swung his legs in. Benny offered little resistance when Fenn folded his knees to get his feet inside.

Asha slammed the trunk closed and sat on it.

"So, did that go how you thought it would?"

Fenn used the sleeve of his hoodie to wipe the door handle, hood, and trunk, where Asha might have left prints.

"Well, um, the end result was the same."

"Okay. Good to know. Now what?"

He traded her the billfold for the sunglasses, then swapped the keys to the Challenger for the Mercedes set.

"Now we go for a drive. Follow me."

CHAPTER 49

They drove for forty minutes on the highway. When they exited, Fenn was pretty sure that Asha knew where they were headed. He stopped on a side street by a closed convenience store. There was a payphone beside it. Asha pulled up behind him.

Fenn walked back and she rolled down her window.

"Wait here. If I'm not back in ten minutes, call the cops and split," he said.

"Cops—yes. Split—forget it."

He leaned in the window and gave her a kiss.

"I'll be right back."

He steered the Mercedes over to the next street, but stopped a block from his destination. Getting out, he pulled the hoodie up to cover his head and donned the sunglasses. With the can of spray paint in the hoodie's pouch, he walked purposefully through the plaza where Nicolas Wray had his office. Staying close to the units, he uncapped the paint can. He slowed down just long enough to coat Wray's surveillance camera with the black paint.

Unable to leave it at that, he turned around and spray painted a smiley face on the sidewalk by the door.

Right. Now to drop Benny off.

He thumped on the trunk of the Mercedes before he got in.

"Alright, Benny?"

There was a muffled response. Fenn smiled and started the car.

He cruised along the road until midway past the plaza, then slowed and cranked the wheel as if to make a U-turn. When he stopped the car across the lanes, it was aimed directly at Wray's unit.

Tony's gonna be pissed he missed this, he thought, and pushed back into the seat to snug up the belt. He put the selector into the lowest gear and gripped the wheel tightly. His left foot on the brake, he depressed the accelerator with his right.

Unlike the Challenger, which would have spun the rear wheels in what is known as a brake torque, the German six-cylinder motor could only strain against the brake pads. However, that loaded up the transmission, and when Fenn released the brakes, the car lurched forward with some power. It bounced up over the curb, crossed a small grassy verge, and hit the parking lot with increasing speed. Fenn now had the gas pedal floored.

Reflecting the sedan's headlights, the mirrored glass of Wray's front window seemed to rush toward him. From the driver's seat, it looked like an imminent head-on collision. Fenn felt the front wheels hit the storefront sidewalk and instinctively closed his eyes.

The low cinder-block wall and glass pane were no match for the three-thousand-pound battering ram. With the motor roaring, it blasted through the hollow concrete sill, smashed the tempered pane, and demolished Wray's Scandinavian boardroom table and chairs. Fenn had let off the gas when the airbag hit his face, but the car plowed on, busting through wallboard into the back office where it crushed Wray's mahogany desk and leather chair against the rear wall.

The motor stalled.

The airbag deflated, leaving Fenn coughing, and his face covered with talcum. Considering the impact, the Mercedes wasn't quite a write-off. The front end was crumpled, the windshield cracked, and the exhaust likely mangled, but Fenn thought the car could still start and limp away. But that wasn't his intention.

He wiped off his sunglasses, unclipped the seatbelt, then pulled the key. He'd wanted Benny to suffer but didn't want to kill the guy if an electrical short set the car on fire. The briefcase full of jewels had fallen off the seat into the passenger footwell. He reached over for it and forced the door open. His feet landed in steaming water. The Mercedes also had a punctured radiator.

The place was in shambles. Dust filled the air and the odd tile fell from the ceiling. Fenn used his gloves and a sleeve to wipe Benny's prints from the briefcase. He opened it on the trunk and put Nicolas Wray's business card, with Benny's address on the back, inside. Climbing onto the car's roof, he pushed the case into the drop ceiling where a tile had fallen out. He made sure to leave a good part of it visible.

Fenn hopped down and banged on the trunk again.

"I just did you a favour, Benny. Hope you appreciate it."

He thought he heard a low moan. Good enough.

As he stepped over the crumbled wallboard and shattered glass, the coffee station caught his eye. His blood still hot, he wrenched a leg off a broken chair and used it to beat the hell out of Wray's fancy espresso machine. Then, with a home-run swing, swept the little china cups off the counter and clear across the room. His bat-flip would have made any major-league slugger proud.

The doorway was a mangled mess of bent aluminum and shattered glass, so he clambered over the broken blocks of the windowsill into the silence of night. Lights had come on in a couple of houses across the road. Hood up, sunglasses on, he walked calmly from the scene. If someone hadn't already called the cops, he would do so at the payphone.

Fuck you, Benny.

Fuck you, Nicolas Wray.

Lareault sat across the desk from Superintendent Heatherington, suit jacket undone, one leg crossed casually over the other. He picked a small bit of something off his slacks, because that's what you did to avoid eye contact when being given a compliment. As far as he was concerned, the murders of two women had been solved, a burglary ring had been busted, a fugitive caught, and a mob boss taken into custody.

While the next phase would be in the hands of judges, juries, and lawyers, the detective inspector was proud of his team. Together, they had done what they'd been tasked to do.

Her praise quietly acknowledged, he briefed his boss on what Sergeant Bloomfield had told him earlier. How an anonymous call had led to the arrests of both Maurice 'Benny' Goodman and Nicolas Wray.

"Goodman was bound and gagged in the trunk of his own Mercedes, which had crashed into an office unit leased by Nicolas Wray. The Niagara Police showed up after the tip was called in. Wray was on site, having also received a call. He played the victim until an officer noticed a briefcase full of contraband stashed in the drop ceiling. Wray's now in custody trying to explain that one away—an uphill climb since Benny wasn't inclined to claim it. The local blues cordoned off the unit as a crime scene, which also gave them probable cause to confiscate the desktop computer that was on site. Not sure if Wray would leave sensitive information on it, but our techs will break it down—see what's on there."

"When did all this happen?"

"The first tip came just after one this morning. A second call came a few minutes later to our Halton switchboard. Both from a payphone near Wray's office. The tipster also wanted to inform us where Maurice Goodman had rented a motel room. We checked it out and found a laptop computer, a forged passport, and an address book. Considering they all belonged to a known fence, we expect they also have potential to solve other crimes."

"Do we have any idea who this tipster was?"

"Goodman was led to believe Nicolas Wray sent someone to abduct him. However, Wray denies this, and the fact his office got destroyed lends credence to that."

Heatherington gave a contemplative nod.

"Sounds like someone had a grudge against both Goodman and Wray. Someone who saw an opportunity to kill two birds with one stone."

"Most likely the tipster."

"Any idea who that might be?"

"I've someone in mind, but for now I'm happy with what we have—which is enough paperwork for the next month, if not more."

Heatherington's lips took on a knowing grin.

"In that case, we shouldn't look a gift horse in the mouth, Evan."

"You know," said Lareault. "Those were Sergeant Bloomfield's exact words."

THE END

ACKNOWLEDGEMENTS

While searching for an opening quote, I came across this one, also from Samuel Johnson: *The greatest part of a writer's time is spent in reading, in order to write: an author will turn over half a library to make one book.* Although my stories are based on topics familiar to me, I feel that verifying details keeps a writer honest and the readers happy. Luckily, the Internet simplifies this process and, besides using Google, I have found certain Facebook groups valuable for finding experts in particular fields. To name a couple: Cops and Writers, and Trauma Fiction have both helped me to crayon within the lines.

Once the manuscript was complete, I was fortunate to have Tedd Reed, my former English teacher, read it with a critical eye and offer his insights. As always, his suggestions made the work better and I appreciate his support and continued encouragement.

I must also acknowledge all the readers and bloggers that post reviews. Reviews are the high-octane fuel of an author's world, so one way to get them to write more books is to post a review: don't be shy - a few words will do.

ABOUT THE AUTHOR

Glenn Muller was born in New Jersey, USA, then spent his early years in England before immigrating to Canada where he would attain Canadian citizenship.

After high school he enrolled in various community college courses for hotel administration, driver education, computer applications, and bookkeeping. These all led to related occupations, the variety of which Glenn feels has been an asset to his writing.

His Fenn & Lareault series was first inspired by the twelve years he spent as a driving instructor, and influenced by the social group of muscle car owners and racers he knew at that time. While the darker characters and situations in the books are pure products of imagination, some of the police procedurals were culled from Glenn's experience as a witness for a murder trial.

Other writing credits include book reviews for Astronomy Magazine, a specialized sports-column for a local newspaper, and articles and presentations for amateur astronomy clubs and conventions.

For more information, please visit the author's website:

www.glennmuller.ca

BOOKS BY GLENN MULLER

TORQUE
(Fenn & Lareault)
JACKLIGHTER COPSE
(Fenn & Lareault)
RUGGAGE
(Fenn & Lareault)

BOOMERANG

Short Story

THE LETTERHEAD AFFAIR

Manufactured by Amazon.ca
Bolton, ON

39402102R00187